Cruel Truth

Rachel Lynch is a million-copy bestselling author of crime fiction, best known for her gripping DI Kelly Porter series as well as several standalones and the Major Helen Scott military police thrillers. Born and raised in Cumbria, the haunting beauty of the Lake District seeps into every story she tells. After teaching history in London and living across the globe as an army wife, Rachel eventually returned to her greatest passion: writing. Travel and the shared human experience comprise the fabric of her work. She explores the darkest corners of humanity with empathy and edge, weaving gritty realism with unforgettable characters. Alongside multiple standalone novels, she now brings her stories to life in a whole new way, through her podcast *The Killer Storyteller: A Podcast with Rachel Lynch*, where she unpacks every twist and turn, book by book.

Also by Rachel Lynch

The Rich
The Famous

Helen Scott Royal Military Police Thrillers

The Rift
The Line

Detective Kelly Porter

First Act (prequel)
Dark Game
Deep Fear
Dead End
Bitter Edge
Bold Lies
Blood Rites
Little Doubt
Lost Cause
Lying Ways
Sudden Death
Silent Bones
Shared Remains
Cruel Truth

RACHEL LYNCH

CRUEL TRUTH

First published in the United Kingdom in 2026 by

Canelo Crime, an imprint of
Canelo Digital Publishing Limited,
20 Vauxhall Bridge Road,
London SW1V 2SA
United Kingdom

A Penguin Random House Company
The authorised representative in the EEA is Dorling Kindersley Verlag GmbH. Arnulfstr. 124, 80636 Munich, Germany

Copyright © Rachel Lynch 2026

The moral right of Rachel Lynch to be identified as the creator of this work has been asserted in accordance with the Copyright, Designs and Patents Act, 1988.
All rights reserved. No part of this publication may be reproduced or transmitted in any form or by any means, electronic or mechanical, including photocopy, recording, or any information storage and retrieval system, without permission in writing from the publisher.
No part of this book may be used or reproduced in any manner for the purpose of training artificial intelligence technologies or systems. In accordance with Article 4(3) of the DSM Directive 2019/790, Canelo expressly reserves this work from the text and data mining exception.

A CIP catalogue record for this book is available from the British Library.

ISBN 9 781 83598 122 1

This book is a work of fiction. Names, characters, businesses, organizations, places and events are either the product of the author's imagination or are used fictitiously. Any resemblance to actual persons, living or dead, events or locales is entirely coincidental.

Cover design by Jet Purdie

Cover images © Shutterstock, Unsplash

Printed and bound in Great Britain by Clays Ltd, Elcograf S.p.A.

Look for more great books at
www.canelo.co | www.dk.com

I'd like to dedicate this book to the incredible cancer nurses at Elstree Cancer Centre, UK, for looking after me during the most challenging period of my life. When I was writing this book, I never imagined the subjects within would become such intimate parts of my own life and I'm profoundly awed by the work of scientists all over the world who continue to strive for ways to treat triple negative breast cancer.

Chapter 1

Sometimes the surface of the lake appeared more like glass than the finest tumbler of crystalware. Today was one of those days. It was so still that a summer pond-skater plonking its fat feet on the miniscule veneer could be spotted from metres away.

A waddling duck searched for discarded bread crusts from the tourists who'd sat all day at the nearby Faeryland café.

Surrounding the little inlet were undulations of fells, brown and purple from different heather species, as well as from the glaring rays of the burning sun, giving the impression that all moisture had been sucked from the land.

A ripple of movement sent swells towards a colourfully painted rowing boat which was face down at the water's edge, in the reeds, solitary in its misery.

The boats for rent were painted in bright hues of red, orange and green and they gleamed and boasted from the water's edge, all in a little row like Christmas decorations in a box. They were given names. *Theodosia*, *Romany*, *Sprite*.

This one was called *Water Nymph*.

The hills in the distance cocooned Grasmere inside its own suspended time and space. Stone walls and pathways looked like little scribbles across the fields, drawn by the hand of a child. The nearby café was closing for the day.

A grey squirrel darted from behind the *Water Nymph* suddenly but he hesitated. There was something unusual about the smell. The rodent sniffed and looked about warily. The aroma didn't belong near his favourite café, where the staff gave him bits of leftover cake and provided bowls of water. This was his patch. He charmed the tourists as he nibbled the seeds he found on the ground after people had dropped local artisan bread covered in them. Sometimes he got too close, and he took treats straight out of the hand of a visitor.

He knew who to trust.

But whatever was under the *Water Nymph* wasn't part of the ordinary construct of a summer afternoon at the Faeryland café.

The day had been another scorcher. Grasmere had hosted crowds of people sharing picnics and frolicking in the water. A place Wordsworth called 'the loveliest spot that man hath ever found'. Rydal Water, next door, and the smaller sibling of the pair of lakes, was connected by a grassy vale ridge with a bridge and a forest, and was less busy, but then she was better at hiding.

The squirrel wasn't concerned with the weather, though, or the lay of the land. Despite having better shelter under the canopy of the Rydal woods, he preferred scavenging here. His main concern was just which intruder had disturbed his patch.

Until he found out, he decided to sit next to the *Water Nymph*, on guard because his innate sense of danger warned him that a predator had wandered into his territory.

A few flies landed on his face, just next to his nose. He twitched it to get rid of them, but they kept coming back. More numerous with each passing minute.

He moved away and realised that they were less interested in him and any spare crumbs he found for supper, courtesy of the day's customers, and far more interested in whatever was underneath the rowing boat.

Chapter 2

Kelly was about to add sugar to her espresso when news of a dead woman in Grasmere stirred Eden House to action. The red-stone four-storey house had once been a Victorian lodge for a well-to-do family, courtesy of Cumbrian slate. From the outside, the imposing address appeared regal and at ease, which was more than could be said for the top floor where Detective Inspector Kelly Porter ran the serious crime unit for North Lakes. Cumbria might be one of the largest counties in England but it didn't boast the most crime. The cities were welcome to their grim stats.

Dead bodies weren't welcome here.

However, they appeared nonetheless.

Details were sketchy. *Definitely* a homicide. 'Definitely' being a euphemism for a grisly scene. Young victim, no ID, underneath a boat at the Faeryland café, which was a shame because they'd all enjoyed coffee and cake there at one time or another, beside the lake, watching the ducks waddling ahead of their young, the reeds blowing in the wind, the lovely rowing boats bobbing up and down and causing ripples on the water, and the sun shining over Loughrigg beyond.

Back at the office, DS Dan Houghton screwed up his face, because the location jarred with the occasion. DC Emma Hide excused herself and Kelly thought she'd never seen her queasy before at the mention of a dead body. Her second-in-command, DS Kate Umshaw, said 'bugger me' and their newbie, DS Fin Maguire, pretended not to hear.

A corpse tossed aside in the reedy underbelly of one of the most beautiful lakes in the national park wasn't the early Monday evening they were hoping for. Kelly had imagined a jacket potato covered in oozy cheese, and an earthy glass of malbec to wash it down with. Perhaps a chat with her father and some special time with her daughter, who'd soon turn two years old. Lizzie was vocal and Kelly had encouraged it. She wanted to raise a girl who asked questions. Sometimes she reckoned the toddling tot would turn out to be a detective herself, though Kelly wouldn't recommend it. Cuts and budgets prevented satisfactory resolution for victims' families and it pained her to her core. She wanted more for her daughter.

It was difficult to believe Kelly had been the detective inspector for North Lakes for almost seven years now. She reflected on how much had happened in those short but long years back in her native Cumbria, and each time she did, her disbelief grew. Where had the time gone? She was a mother and a daughter. Bereaved. Responsible.

But was she enough?

After she finished stirring sugar into her coffee, she slugged it back too quickly, then gathered her things and prepared for a drive over to Grasmere.

Kate agreed to go with her.

Which reminded her that Lizzie was in good hands because her nanny, Millie, was Kate's daughter, and Kate was who she inherited her natural mother's intuition from. Kate Umshaw was Kelly's dependable right-hand woman. A solid pair of hands. If she mothered Millie like she investigated cases, then Lizzie's future was assured.

The others seemed relieved and went back to what they were doing. Days out with the boss were like a free go on a petrifying fairground ride; they could be fun but mostly they were unpleasant. But Kelly and Kate were similar in that they could shut off from the mayhem and use the opportunity to chat in the car to catch up on work and other things. After the death of her mother, Wendy, Kelly had missed the input of a wiser, older influence. And her worries plagued her. Low-level anxiety seemed to sit constantly between her shoulders. It was as if everything she'd worked for was coming to an end. Could she work like she wasn't a parent? Could she parent like she didn't work? The constant tearing apart and cleaving of her parts took its toll. When she was at work she fretted over her daughter, and when she was at home, she thought she could be doing more to catch bastards.

She sighed, and the sound irritated her. She was never a whinger but lately she'd grown tired of bad people. Her stamina was waning, or was it more that she was getting bored of the same old tricks? People thought they could get away with heinous crimes and not be caught out. But they always were.

Criminals were idiots, she thought, and it buoyed her. She felt momentary gratification that with her father's help, they usually caught their perp. He was the chief coroner for the northwest of England and he carried his experience on practised shoulders.

Nobody was above the law.

But the feeling of confidence was fleeting as the realisation that an innocent woman had been killed sobered her senses and she remembered where she was going.

Apparently, the body had lain in the reed bed all day. The gorgeous little café at the water's edge had operated throughout the morning and afternoon as normal. Boats had been rowed; bathers had frolicked, and people came and went.

Nobody knew that a body had accompanied them there.

It was the smell that alerted them in the end.

Carrion.

It stung the nostrils and signalled to all animals that something rotten was amongst the living and didn't belong.

A few tourists had gotten a whiff of the effluvium and complained. A waitress had gone to investigate and got the shock of her life.

Maybe it was a deer? Or even a dog?

The poor sod who'd followed the pungency with her nose had found out the true terror of discovering a dead body. It wasn't pretty, or clinical, or matter of fact.

It was repulsive.

—

The sun was still high in the sky when they pulled out of Eden House staff carpark to head to Grasmere. They'd stop in Glenridding for a couple of coffees and head over Kirkstone Pass. In the tiny hiking hamlet of Glenridding, walkers were coming home from the fells and Kelly gazed across at the Ullswater Way. It stretched all the way along the south coast of the majestic lake, and one could start at either end. Kelly's favourite was to start at Pooley Bridge and end up in Patterdale. Another mile along the lake and Glenridding pier marked the end of a very long walk. Plenty of visitors underestimated the puff needed to make it from one end to the other free from sunburn, blisters and fatigue.

She smiled at Kate, who walked back to the car with the drinks and got in. They'd discussed the dead woman all the way from Penrith.

'I almost bought some cigarettes. Did you know they were over twenty pounds a packet?'

Kelly smiled. 'You're doing well. Don't give in now. I remember how hard it is to give up. Just think of all the money you're saving.'

'And not giving the government in tax,' Kate added.

'Exactly.'

Kelly pulled away after Kate had steadied the hot drinks in the holders.

The road to Kirkstone Pass was predictably busy for mid-July but it was such a pleasant drive that Kelly didn't mind.

'Did you return Johnny's call?' Kate asked.

They'd been chatting about Kelly's ex, and Lizzie's dad.

'No. I'll leave it a couple of days. I think he's climbing in Scotland. I need to get my head around it all,' Kelly said.

Break-ups were always painful but this one seemed to have scarred Kelly deeply. She knew Kate missed him almost as much as she did. But the worst part was that it had been her decision.

Kate stared out of the window.

'What's your instinct telling you?' Kate asked.

Kelly might have told anyone else to fuck off and mind their own business, but not Kate. They'd been through too much together.

Johnny had texted her out of the blue to tell her about his settlement with his ex-wife. They'd finally divorced and had divided their capital fairly. Johnny had been left with more cash than he thought, but he was still in debt.

He was sorry.

He was always sorry.

'What about Fin?' Kate asked.

Kelly gripped the wheel.

'Jesus, Kate, I should have brought somebody else. I'm not in the mood to examine the men in my life. Your turn, any action recently?'

Kate smiled and sipped her coffee. 'Not likely.' She'd split with a long-term partner recently too. They were both single and pretending to be independent warriors in no need of a bloke. 'I know you too well, Kelly Porter. Come on. What's on your mind?'

Kelly stared out of the front windscreen and pretended to concentrate on the road. Then she gave in.

'I've thought about moving Fin on, you know, getting him out of the office. I told him it's over, I just can't work with somebody I'm sleeping with, it's distracting, and I haven't got time.'

'Or, you could just be honest and admit he was just a plaything all along. You needed to get over Johnny, and now you've had some space, and another bloke to keep you entertained, it's time to think about what you really want.'

Kelly nodded to herself, but Kate saw it too.

'It's been fun,' Kelly said.

Fin Maguire had moved to their team last year. Just as she was breaking up with Johnny. The timing sucked and it had been messy but now it was time to move on.

Again.

'He doesn't like Lizzie.'

'What?' Kate was indignant.

'I don't mean he actively dislikes her; I can just tell he's not that into babies. I get it. It's a drag. He's too young. He finds her boring, I can tell.'

'Fuck him, then,' Kate said.

Kelly laughed. She could almost see Kate dusting her hands without a side glance for proof.

'Johnny's still single,' Kate added.

'And how would you know?'

'Millie told me.'

–

When they pulled into Grasmere, the roads were busy with travellers seeking food for the evening or returning from walks around the surrounding fells. They parked along the road and already they could see a small group had gathered outside the Faeryland café and the uniformed coppers were trying to maintain some kind of order.

A journalist snapped pictures of Kelly and Kate as they approached the entrance. Kelly put up her hand to hide her face. She hated attention, especially from the press.

Word had got out fast.

A dead body on the side of a lake was big news in Cumbria. Something about the beauty of the place being sullied with death encouraged armchair analysis from all corners of the villages in the park. Unsolicited theories were highly unwelcome by Kelly most of the time, but particularly right at the beginning of an investigation.

They dipped under the police tape and approached the witness.

The unfortunate waitress looked deathly pale. She was a small slip of a thing, as her mother Wendy would have said. Fragile. Breakable. Unreliable.

She'd been given strong coffee and the owner of the café sat with her. He was introduced to Kelly by a uniform, and she thanked him. She could see a SOCO had already begun her work. Scenes of crime officers were specialists in the layout of a moment in time, left forever behind as a reminder of what had gone before. Reading a scene was a science. It was mechanical, cold and clinical. Every aspect of expiry that could not be explained was dealt with in a dispassionate flurry of words and diagrams until they had all their information neatly expressed in a report. It was Kelly's job to bring the human touch to the inquiry. Interpretation was for the lead detective. Gathering information, submitting samples to labs, measuring blood spatter, taking fibres and putting them in plastic tubes, all of that was subsidiary to Kelly's central duty. She enjoyed doing all those things, and it satisfied her scientific brain, but the real work was in reading the hints and the character of a scene.

So, she stopped short of the witness and studied her for a split second.

The girl was probably in her twenties, and she looked terrified. People thought dead bodies were simply inanimate objects, devoid of all life, but they weren't; they were reminders of life itself and what had been lost. Kelly could tell just by looking at her that it would take her a long time to recover from what she'd witnessed here today.

Kelly smiled at her warmly and introduced herself to the owner.

She heard cameras clicking in the background and the waft of tarpaulin as a SOCO erected a barrier over the upturned rowing boat called the *Water Nymph*.

Kelly could tell Eric, the owner, was protective over his staff. He sat like a concerned parent and Kelly reassured him.

'She's been held here for two hours now,' he said.

'Andrea?' Kelly said the girl's name and she looked up. 'You've had a terrible shock. I know you've been here a long time, and you can go soon. I just wanted to go over the statement you gave to the first responders,' Kelly said. She sat down and waited for the girl to acknowledge her. Kelly smiled gently. She found situations like this a challenge. Dealing with the fallout of trauma wasn't the same as getting justice for it. It required a different skill set.

'Do you know her?' Kelly asked.

Andrea shook her head.

'Were you here all day?'

A nod.

'And did you see any suspicious activity around the boats?'

A shake of the head.

Kelly read her statement through.

'Did you notice anyone else over there today?'

Another shake.

Kelly changed tack and asked the waitress about her time working at the Faeryland café. It was a summer job. The girl was from Yorkshire and was saving money to go travelling with her friends before starting at university next year. Kelly knew this event would change the girl's outlook forever. It was her bet she'd cancel her plans and face months of therapy, thanks to a chance encounter with a woman she didn't even know.

Kelly thanked her and told her she could leave.

Then she made her way over to the SOCO.

Chapter 3

Ted Wallis parked his car and went to find Kelly. As well as being chief coroner he was also Kelly's local pathologist working from two north Cumbria hospitals. It was a happy coincidence and neither wished for it to change.

He saw her and waved.

Her face showed signs of concern, and well it might, given the circumstances, but as soon as she saw her father, it relaxed her a little. They stopped short of embracing and kept their distance when in professional environments, but it was good to see him.

He was due to visit her house tonight to spend some time with his granddaughter, but, like her, he'd been called away.

It wasn't Ted's job to attend murder scenes, but Kelly was thankful for his intervention when the circumstances were puzzling like this one. And he didn't need much persuading when the body of a young woman turned up with no ID in mysterious circumstances. Having him see the body in situ was always a helpful exercise if he had the time, which he did.

'Oh dear,' Ted said. 'Poor young woman. What do we know so far?' he asked his daughter.

'Not a lot,' Kelly replied.

Ted tutted. He was old school and made noises instead of committing to statements. His quiet certainty reassured his daughter and they pulled on gloves and approached the newly erected tent around the cadaver. It gave the victim privacy, as well as preserving any evidence they could gather, which in this case was vital because they had no idea who she was.

Cumbria's tourist industry provided a transitory population that was sometimes untraceable. Occasionally, murders remained unsolved because they failed to trace the ID of the victim. A solitary decapitated head found in Wastwater ten years ago was the most famous example.

Kelly hoped this wouldn't be the case here. But this was police work. Bodies didn't behave and they certainly didn't get in line. A chill suddenly made her shiver and she wished she'd brought a jumper to put over her thin polo top. Her lanyard provided little coverage, and she rubbed her arms.

The burden of investigation was on her. It was down to her team to decipher what had gone on here to result in this unfortunate woman's death. Ted could only point the way.

Inside the tent was stuffy but at least it provided a little warmth. Stepping inside was like moving between worlds, one that was pretty and photogenic and the other that was ghastly and deviant.

She'd enjoyed coffee and cake at the Faeryland café many times and she recalled how pretty and serene the location was then. Today was something quite different. Now the punters had gone home for the day and the café was closed, which was a small mercy.

The Faeryland boat landing was northwest out of the village of Grasmere, on the way to the circular lake path that was rammed with visitors at all times of the year. Kelly had spotted the famous rowing boats that were painted beautiful colours, shored up by the lake after a busy day. The café had made a distinctive brand from creating a theme of fairies in a magical land, with cute artwork on teacups and boats. Also, their cakes were legendary.

The view of the lake from the café was stunning.

But inside the tent, they quickly forgot all that.

They were greeted by a SOCO covered in white plastic standing with her hands on her hips, gazing down at the victim and pointing. The noise of the synthetic suit wrinkling jarred

Kelly's nerves. The upturned rowing boat was just to the side, at the water's edge. The girl was half in the water, head partly submerged. She looked to be in her mid-twenties, like the witness who'd discovered her. These girls were two-a-penny in the Lakes. They came from all over the world, looking for jobs and staying anywhere that was cheap. It was easy to disappear.

'What have we got?' Ted asked, kneeling.

He was in his seventies, but it was his work that kept him vital, as well as bouncing Lizzie on his knee. Kelly couldn't imagine him doing anything else.

'Her clothes seem undisturbed,' Kelly said. 'Indicating either a lack of sexual assault, or a killer who took the time to redress her.'

'She's in rigor, so my guess is she's been here only since this morning or last night. But we've managed to turn her head and she's been beaten pretty badly, by an object, I think,' the SOCO said.

'Did you find any ID?' Kelly asked.

The SOCO shook her head.

'Cause of death?'

Kelly watched Ted, who examined the girl closely without touching anything. She knew that he liked to take his time searching the scene for clues as to what happened to the victim before they expired. That quiet moment as the body gave up and preserved the victim in perpetuity. There was a wealth of indicators to be found around the area, not just on the cadaver.

'My guess would be drowning, given the location, but the beating and the lack of blood makes me think she was brought here after death. Because she's partially submerged, I made the decision not to move her. When we do, then we might find more evidence of how she died.'

As the SOCO spoke, she watched Ted. Kelly observed how a lot of professionals did that. It wasn't just a matter of respect, but curiosity too. Ted's reputation was impressive. All the time the SOCO talked, Ted examined the scene.

Kelly thanked the SOCO and walked across to the boat which was next to the body. The *Water Nymph*. She felt a wave of depression come over her that her day had come to this. Normal people enjoyed swimming and ate picnics on hot days like this in the Lakes. They didn't examine dead bodies.

The young woman, who appeared no older than twenty-five, looked asleep. If it hadn't been under the current circumstances, she might call the scene peaceful, it was so quiet, compared to some she saw. The girl's skin was ghost white with a tinge of blue. The smell of wet fish reached Kelly's throat, and she swallowed. Insect activity had begun in earnest. She could kick herself for not rubbing perfume under her nose.

She watched as her father examined the bruising patterns on the girl's neck and head. The poor thing was petite and a heavy-handed assailant with intent had caused terrible damage. Kelly felt hot anger bubble up inside her but tried to remain non-judgemental for now.

'I wonder what he wanted,' she whispered.

Ted turned his head.

'Or she,' he said.

Kelly nodded. Occasionally, and they'd seen it themselves right here in the Lakes, women killed, and everyone remembered. They couldn't rule out female killers until they had solid proof otherwise, but the stats said that it was likely to be a male. And there was a high probability the victim knew her killer.

'Did anyone touch the body?' Ted asked.

'Yes, the owner tested for a pulse and signs of life.'

The general British public rallied in a crisis, but equally, most of them were nosy and offered advice when it wasn't required. Their 'help' was often counterproductive. In Cumbria, Kelly had the added problem that lots of witnesses were often tourists, who were scattered to the four corners of the globe when they left the scene.

'What do you think?' she asked her father.

'Homicide for sure. No ID, purse, phone, or a coat. The beating is terrible, and I agree with the SOCO that the killer likely used an object but I won't know for sure until I get her on my table.'

'Of course.'

Kelly looked around. It was a nightmare scene for an investigator, she thought. Open air, elements, animal activity and remoteness, this scene had it all. Countless people had trampled through here, and witnesses could originate from anywhere. As if agreeing with her sense of depression, a grey squirrel lay motionless next to the upturned boat. She hadn't spotted him before. He looked as though he was asleep but when she peered closer, he wasn't moving at all. The little fellow had popped his clogs right there beside the unfortunate woman.

A flash of bright colour caught her eye, and she bent over, reaching out with her gloved hand. Underneath the dead animal was a colourful plastic sachet with the name *YouthBlast* emblazoned on it.

'Can someone bag this squirrel?' she asked.

The SOCO stared at the poor dead animal and then at Kelly.

'Yeah, I'm not going mad,' she said. 'I want that sachet kept too.'

Chapter 4

Jamie couldn't get through to his sister.

This was it. This was their chance to make a new life away from the corporate rat race, away from their past, away from the incessant clashes between people pulling them away from their dreams.

He'd vowed to take care of her but recently it had been the other way around.

He'd left her at the hotel and told her not to leave her phone and now he was cut off from her. He went through all the scenarios in his head regarding what could have gone wrong. Low charge. That was it. Her phone was on low battery, so she'd plugged it in somewhere and forgotten about it. Or she could have gone to the toilet, she could be in the shower, she might have nipped downstairs at the guesthouse to order food, or she might have been exposed.

What was it that Sandy had said to him? *'She's in love, Jamie. A woman in love is a woman distracted.'* Had she been too distracted to see danger? He hoped not.

Only one of the explanations made any sense to him, and a creeping feeling of regret and fear settled in his gut, and he couldn't shake it.

He tried her number again.

Nothing.

The conference was going well. Today was Tuesday, only the second day of the convention, so why did he feel sick to his stomach? All he had to do was see it through. He was lead chair of the annual innovation convention of Hampton-Dent

Pharmaceuticals. This year, the setting had been suggested by him. As a relatively junior CEO of one of their premier health enterprises, FairGro, touting everything from green juices to supplements for the gym, he was a rising star and they listened to him. The old guard at the centre of the empire was on its way out and Jamie was their new blood.

He'd chosen the UNESCO World Heritage Site of the Lake District, and it was a masterstroke. It was remote, familiar and suitably impressive. The conference was about wellbeing after all, and gurus, bloggers, podcasters and scientists from all over the world had been invited to take part in the four-day event at the exclusive Heron Hall Hotel on the shores of Rydal Water.

It sounded idyllic.

He tried his sister's number again.

'You look as though you're calling the police to report a dead body,' a voice said behind him.

He swivelled around and saw Paul, his partner, standing in the hall outside the main conference room. Compared to Jamie's beguiling charm, which he'd honed from years of grafting in sales, Paul looked more comfortable at the bar sporting a pint of lager and a pork pie. Jamie was the embodiment of the firm's ethos, smart and stylish; Paul was the sturdy foundation, hard-wearing and brawny.

'No, I just can't get hold of Angie,' he said.

Paul frowned. Jamie knew that his long-standing partner had a thing for his sister, and had done since they were starting out, in the bedsit they'd rented in London after working on the chemical components of a compound they believed could transform the health industry. Paul's concern was touching but Jamie suspected it was more to do with the eight million dollars they each stood to make from their headline product. If everything went to plan. If Angie picked up her goddamn phone.

They were what was commonly referred to as flying. They were living their best lives. They were on the up.

And shouldn't you always quit when you're ahead?

'You worry too much,' Paul said, right on cue, suddenly confident again. He was the level head to Jamie's nervous energy.

Jamie smiled, but it wasn't one of his light-up-the-room usuals; it was reserved and hesitant. Paul slapped him on the back and Jamie flashed a wide, veneer-enhanced grin.

'I spoke to the lab this morning,' Paul said, as if that would help.

Jamie raised his eyebrows.

'The results are in, and the new batch is completely safe.'

Jamie stopped and stared at Paul. They were both in their late twenties, with the world at their feet. They were intelligent, financially wealthy, and their product sought after, but Paul couldn't half be a stupid fucker.

'Mate, "safe" and "FairGro" shouldn't be said in the same sentence,' Jamie said.

'Shut up! Jesus, here of all places. Christ, keep your voice down,' Paul warned.

Jamie laughed. 'Since when were you scared of them? You know what's going on at Dow Bank House, as well as I do, and Angie knows it too.'

Paul glared at him.

'And once this thing gets out, it's all over. Boom.' Jamie threw his hands apart as if simulating a nuclear explosion of biblical proportions. Paul looked terrified, but Jamie was losing patience with him, with Sandy, with the lot of them. They'd sold their souls for money and it was starting to show.

They stood in the doorway of a small side room off the main conference suite and Paul closed the door. The large windows allowed shafts of light to flash across the floor. They could see the tiny lake from here.

'Come on, Sandy is speaking in ten minutes. Angie will call back,' Paul assured him. 'And nobody misses Sandy's presentations.'

Sandy Cooper was a fifty-year-old woman who wore her history on her face. Both men were scared of her. Like all good scientists, Sandy didn't practise what she preached but she added legitimacy to their product. Sandy's word meant something in the industry.

After all, the guarantee of efficacy was more important than delivery. People just had to believe it.

Sponsorship was flying in and the main shareholders in the holdings of Hampton-Dent Corporation would be getting very good news indeed come next Monday when the value of the deal was realised by the markets in New York.

Everybody was happy.

Except Jamie.

He was at saturation point and Sandy Cooper knew it.

The true numbers of litigation cases against Hampton-Dent for personal injury and even death simply disappeared, and Sandy smoothed the way.

The supplement business was as dirty as the arms trade.

Product was brokered, sold, and then signed off. Fallout was considered collateral damage. The promise of profit was everything. Competitors clamoured over one another to sell their chemicals to hide inside the colourful packets of powders, potions and sachets of poison they convinced health freaks to consume, and billionaires like the owners of Hampton-Dent got richer. Paul left.

Jamie bit his lip.

Something was wrong; he could smell it. He thought about driving to the guesthouse but it was a good half hour away along winding roads. That had been the whole point; she was hidden.

He went over in his mind who knew Angie was here in the Lakes. He'd taken her to a remote hotel, one with a bone-chilling legend that made Angie laugh. Jamie didn't believe a word of it, but Angie said she wanted to paint the pretty bridge there.

His sister was a fine artist, and her talent blew his mind.

He'd paid off the guesthouse owner, triple locked the door, left her with strict contact instructions, hidden the suitcase and given her a secure phone. They'd been to the caves, and she'd showed him a watertight hiding place for the file.

He'd thought of everything.

He left the hotel and wandered down to the lake on his own.

A few media types hovered around him but soon got the message that he was trying to make an important phone call and disappeared. He had the lakeside to himself. Sandy's keynote speech would be starting soon and sycophants took their places early.

The hotel was set in stunning surroundings. Which was the whole point. Nobody would suspect that deep in the heart of the Lake District National Park, a salesman was plotting the downfall of one of the most lucrative and successful Big Pharma global corporations which turned over more than fifty billion a year.

He had enough to bring them to their knees.

He wasn't a hero. And he wasn't a stoic. He hadn't suffered a crisis of conscience after suddenly discovering that the shit they sold was killing people. He didn't suffer from guilt. Nor did he seek revenge.

He saw Sandy come out of the hotel and saunter confidently down to the lake. She liked to cut things fine and wouldn't have made notes.

He heard frolics from across the water and saw people in the distance enjoying their summer. The days when he'd been carefree like that were long gone now. He couldn't imagine enjoying himself like that ever again.

Sandy was the type of woman who gave somebody one chance to speak and if they bored her then she switched off and turned away. Losing Sandy Cooper's attention could cost a career. Gaining it could cost a life. Jamie smiled broadly and flirted with his eyes. Sandy reciprocated and lit a cigarette.

'They'll kill you one day. You should know better,' he said.

'Fuck off, Jamie. Don't lecture me. We of all people know that everything we get told is bad for us is actually the opposite. I'm never giving up my nicotine. It cures cancer.' She winked and he laughed.

It was their favourite pastime, to discuss conspiracy theories and how with their insider knowledge they could probably prove 99 per cent of them true. Cancer was just one example. Jamie believed he could prove that Big Pharma had been sitting on the cure for sixty years but to admit it would lose them money, and what business wanted that? Same with diabetes, atherosclerosis and Alzheimer's. The cures were simple. The ancients knew it. The scientists knew it. Spiritualists knew it. Big money knew it.

Hampton-Dent wanted customers not cures.

Jamie threw his arm around Sandy's shoulders. He could perform when necessary. All good salesmen did.

'It's going well,' he said.

It wasn't an invite to agree, more a holding testimony. He was buying time.

Now they had *YouthBlast* and the chemical compound called Neurohydroxy-14 that made it unique, his days were numbered. He was expendable, and so was Angie.

And that's why he'd hidden his money and was ready to run.

But only if Angie was safe.

'You seem jumpy,' Sandy said, catching him off guard.

'I can't get hold of Angie,' he told her.

'Ach, she'll be busy painting, no doubt, or finding out more local legends of ghosts and witches.' Sandy winked.

And that's when he knew.

They knew.

Chapter 5

Jamie finally decided to drive over to the Old Man Guesthouse, where he'd left Angie, but conference commitments kept getting in the way. He felt pulled this way and that and couldn't make a decision. For a well-paid executive he felt like an amateur adrift more recently, and he knew Sandy saw it.

She'd delivered her keynote address at 3 p.m. and it had been blisteringly good. The woman spoke like a 1930s dictator before everyone discovered their real intentions and Jamie reckoned Sandy's weren't too far off the nefarious ambitions of Mussolini or Stalin either. She rallied the troops like obedient soldiers desperate for their futures to start. She inspired them with her promises of greatness. She didn't use notes. She used her hands like missiles and her smile melted the ice in the free cocktails.

The content wasn't so much the important theme, more the passion, and she had conference attendees eating out of her hand and trying *YouthBlast* in their complimentary water bottles, emblazoned with the FairGro logo of course. The company insignia was a clever design of four leaves intertwined with the outline of a child. It was simple and effective: innocence and health all rolled into one. Their marketing of *YouthBlast* was equally genius with the use of bright colours and the promise of everlasting health.

But the promise of immortality was a far cry from the truth.

Enter Sandy Cooper, stage left, who hypnotised the hardest audiences with her wizardry and scientific legitimacy. She had the law behind her, and enough documents to sink the *Titanic* again, many times. Afterwards in the bar, they'd laughed.

The story of the *Titanic* was the greatest psy-op that Jamie loved to talk about. The fact that it had been scuttled by J. P. Morgan to get rid of his competitors to make way for the Federal Reserve and dominate banking for the next hundred years, making him the world's first billionaire, was a common story of heroism and genius in financial circles. The opposing fact that the mainstream media called the theory a conspiracy and stuck with the old iceberg fairytale proved the very point that it was important what the public believed, not what really happened.

He'd looked at his watch repeatedly and Sandy eyed him suspiciously.

Her energy on stage was fuelled by something Jamie had got too close to, and it had knocked the wind out of him. Morally ethical, versus morally bankrupt. Good always won out in the end, he knew deep down. He'd always known, he'd just been blinded by the money. Greed coloured everything and changed people from ordinary and creative to evil and empty.

Sandy was not a good person and he'd been a sucker to trust her.

Now, he sensed danger. He'd been a fool dragging Angie in, he thought, as he went to his room to grab his keys. Maybe he should have let Joe in after all. His sister's boyfriend deserved to know where she was, but Jamie had deemed it too much of a risk and even Joe was distanced from her. Jamie had isolated Angie, and he was terrified he'd made a mistake.

Joe wasn't answering Jamie's calls either.

Jamie went to close his phone and pop it into his briefcase, but he closed the tabs first and came across the YouTube channel that he'd been following. The Clem Allins podcast had climbed the charts to become one of the most influential and most listened to in the health and fitness world. It was a significant achievement given the competition, but something about the guru was mesmerising. Jamie had been using the podcast to meditate and focus on his inner strength. It helped him move away from material wealth and discover inner riches infinitely more powerful. Or at least that was the bullshit spin.

Even Clem Allins couldn't help him now. Hampton and Dent would hunt him forever.

A creeping feeling of dread invaded his stomach, and it wasn't the thought of *YouthBlast* gurgling in the innards of the conference attendees; it was pure terror that his sister's life was in danger.

He heard a sound and swung around to see his suite door opening.

A few things crossed his mind as he watched the handle flick down. His key card should be the only one to work. Nobody else should have one, except perhaps the cleaner? But it was an odd time of the day for housekeeping. Another momentary thought was that it might be Sandy, wanting to down a whisky or two to celebrate her speech, but they'd already done that. The other thought was that he hoped it wasn't Tilda Dent.

The woman was sexy as hell, but she wasn't his type.

And she was already sleeping with Paul.

Before he could sort out his head, the door opened fully, and Jamie thought it could have been a mistake. Keycards weren't rocket science, or manipulative chemical compounds even.

A face popped around the door and Jamie sighed.

It was Paul.

'Hey, mate, are you OK? Tilda wanted me to come and check on you,' his partner said.

'I'm good, mate. I was just going to take a drive.'

'A drive? We're celebrating downstairs. Tilda has her eye on you.'

'Oh, stop it, mate, she's not my type.'

'Not your type? Jesus, are you a eunuch? What the fuck is wrong with you?' Paul was drunk and it was one of the reasons he wasn't let loose on real customers.

'Come on, mate, she's vacuous, and mind-numbingly spoilt. And already taken. The days of you and me sharing are long gone.'

'Since when did that stop you?' Paul asked.

Hampton-Dent had sent the big guns to the conference. Tilda Dent and Hank Hampton were both in attendance, and it demonstrated the importance of *YouthBlast* for the firm: to make it marketable and mainstream.

'How did you get a card to my room?' Jamie asked, suddenly wary.

A cloud of irritation fell over Paul's face and Jamie moved awkwardly, fiddling with his car keys.

'Going somewhere?'

'Like I said, I'm going to get some air.'

'In your car?'

'What's this all about?' Jamie asked. 'Since when do you get to tell me what to do? And you still haven't told me why you have a key to my room.'

Paul ignored him and simply stared. Jamie saw he was sweating, and his face was swollen and high coloured. His eyes were like saucers.

'What have you taken?'

Paul held up a FairGro water bottle.

'You drank *YouthBlast*? You idiot. It'll devastate your kidneys if you drink too much.'

'You preaching to me now, too?'

Jamie knew that in some cases, Neurohydroxy-14 could turn test animals into vicious predators. He also knew that their human trials had been shut down. It was just another reason to be nervous. He didn't recognise his friend standing in front of him. They were using him.

For some reason he found himself nostalgic about the good old days. The day a Texan called Hank Hampton walked into their lives and offered them more money than they'd ever dreamt of.

That's how it had started.

A light knocking on the door distracted Jamie and he peered behind Paul, but he couldn't see who was tapping. He laughed nervously. Perhaps it was Paul messing about. Jamie couldn't see his right hand, which was still behind the door. Maybe he was toying with him because he was high or drunk, and soon he'd be deliriously inebriated and incapable of adding any value at all.

It was embarrassing.

But the door opened a little wider and Jamie knew that it wasn't just Paul who'd come to see him.

Chapter 6

Kelly met Ted at the Penrith and Lakes hospital, where the body of their unknown woman waited on a cold steel slab. Kelly had spent a restless night tossing and turning, but it wasn't unusual when a big case crossed her desk.

She assumed all people dreamt about their jobs; it was just hers involved murder and brutality.

The body lay under a sheet, waiting to communicate her final secrets. Ted was already in scrubs and testing his mic. He looked up at her and she slid onto a steel stool. She'd already slathered her top lip with Vicks. Gentle classics played in the background and Kelly absorbed Ted's calmness. Late afternoon in Ted's mortuary was a glaring paradox. Death and life in one breath. She felt more alive in here sometimes than she did sat at her desk at Eden House.

It was a moment of serene calm, and one in which she forgot time. Her team at Eden House was busy creating a victim profile for the woman in the hope they'd identify her soon. For now, she was called Water Nymph. The woman had no personal belongings and so the usual social media and phone checks weren't an option. The unfortunate woman was merely a lump in a heavy-duty bag with a loud zipper that reminded Kelly of an old 50cc motorbike she used to ride in London past the Museum of Childhood.

They'd released an artist's sketch to the local media hoping someone might identify her.

The postmortem operation began. Seeing a dead body after refrigeration, stripped and bolstered by wedges, ready for autopsy, took away the last vestiges of humanity for Kelly.

'Contusions consistent with blunt trauma across left mastoid, travelling along sternocleidomastoid muscle. It looks like she was overwhelmed from this side,' he said, looking up at Kelly. 'These muscles are torn and badly bruised,' he added. He pointed to where he observed the worst injuries to the woman's neck and Kelly got off her stool to get closer.

'Evidence of some kind of strap used?' she asked.

'Not that I can see from the surface wounds. I've seen it before when something has been put over the victim's head, like a jacket or coat. The force of it has damaged her ability to support her own neck.'

'So, she was surprised,' Kelly said.

She took in the vision of the woman naked. Ted's technicians did much of the work of examining the body externally before the coroner got down to the internal state of the victim. Her clothes had been cut off and sent for testing. All they needed was one small drop of DNA to match with a suspect. Her skin was discoloured from rot and bloating. Underneath the rowing boat had provided a cocoon-like oven for the multiplication of pathogens and insect larvae in abundance. It left her skin looking like a modern painting of clouds forming across the sky. The bruising had turned green and purple against a background of a body devoid of lifeblood. It would be poetic if it wasn't so repulsive.

Her skull was bloody and damaged extensively and Kelly thought about what might have caused it. Kelly didn't want to imagine the poor girl's last moments, but she forced herself to for the sake of the life she'd fought so hard to hold on to.

'Scraping underneath the fingernails,' Ted said. He worked methodically and it was almost soothing knowing where he'd go next. She knew his routine so well that she felt looked after by him in this space, as much as he looked after the poor souls he was trying to put to rest. Eternity was something she couldn't understand, but Ted made it a little easier. Nobody was more thorough, and if there was anything to find on the body – or inside her – that might aid them further, Ted was the man to find it.

'This is quite a wound here on her hand.'

Kelly looked at it.

There was a dent in her palm that was deep and appeared like a real hole. In death, the skin hadn't popped back and healed like it would have if the woman had survived and so it was forever imprinted on her flesh.

'She fought hard. She's got several broken fingers too.'

Kelly winced, imagining this small woman fighting her aggressor, knowing she was losing the battle.

'Her fingers appear stained with something like charcoal,' he added.

Kelly peered at the digits. 'Mud?'

'No, that would have washed off; this is engrained in her ridges and looks like it's from a habit like handling ink or paint.'

Ted moved lower down the body and Kelly felt her heart pump a little harder. This was where Ted would tell her if he thought the woman had been sexually assaulted and the horror might get even worse.

She had.

'Sorry,' Ted said. 'It's conclusive, even after her being in the water for a night. The contusions are uniform and consistent with violence.'

'God, this is so tough. It gets harder,' Kelly said.

She wouldn't have said it to anyone but her father because she knew he agreed.

'I know,' he said. 'Why don't you sit this one out?'

'No, I need to be here. I'm OK. I promise. Please continue.'

Kelly wiped her eyes on her cardigan sleeve and focused.

'Wait,' Ted said.

She looked at him.

He palpated the woman's abdomen as he took swabs.

'I think she's pregnant.'

'Oh no,' Kelly said. 'Are you sure? Is that a stupid question?' The tragedy hit them both like a warhead. She saw her father wrinkle his brow and she got off her stool and they peered at the woman. Kelly placed her gloved hand over Water Nymph's brow and thought of Lizzie and how excited she'd been when she carried her inside her body.

'I'm pretty sure. I'll tell you definitely in a few minutes, but I can feel changes in the uterus, cervix and surrounding tissues consistent with gravid.'

Kelly had heard the official term before but today it sounded as sterile as the walls, and just as inhuman. Two murders had occurred on the shore of Grasmere. Whoever killed this poor girl killed her baby as well.

When Ted cut into the body, Kelly forced herself to be present because it was the least she could do for this poor woman who'd suffered so much.

'Oh dear, that is unexpected,' he said.

She saw what he meant straight away. There was muddy water in the woman's lungs. He cut further and pulled out a soggy mass of gunk. The organs gurgled and fizzed with air and water and Kelly watched as the brown gunge ran across the woman's chest.

'If she was dead when she was placed under the boat, she wouldn't have inhaled any water from the lake. There's only one way to be sure, and that's to test the water. Bath and shower water is very different under the microscope,' he said. He took a small sample and peered at it under his microscope, then he glanced back at Kelly. 'Mites and organisms consistent with fresh open water in my view,' he said gloomily.

'Jesus, poor woman. She was still alive when he left her.'

Kelly looked up at the sterile ceiling and anger burnt her chest.

Chapter 7

What to feed a group of health and fitness influencers was a headache Lee Lovett took seriously. So far, everything had gone smoothly. Canapes from the 1970s playbook were out of the question. Avocado mousse, mini sausages wrapped in bacon, cute bite-sized pies and vol-au-vents were firmly off the menu. In their place, Lee had overseen the genius construction of protein powder shots, banana blinis, yogurt sorbets and lettuce wraps. He was pleased with himself.

These healthy types had to eat too, but they were the sort to turn their nose up at food they deemed to be too predictably full of enemy calories. Lee reckoned he'd cracked it with the variety of dishes on offer and he'd even tried some of them. He wasn't one for health and fitness, and he barely had time to do anything other than earn a wage, but his new job was important to him.

His promotion to head of conference and banqueting at the Heron Hall Hotel on the shore of Rydal Water had gone to his head, and he waltzed around the final event of the afternoon checking the guests were happy with their low-sugar ginger champagne cocktails. He was consummately friendly and professional.

It was only day two of the four-day conference and everyone was on a high after the speech by the woman who sneaked away for a clandestine cigarette whenever she could. Her mutiny amused him.

Lee had worked silently in the background as speakers lectured about pills and potions that could reduce your waistline, stop depression, lower cholesterol and promote longevity. They were lofty promises, and he was cynical about their efficacy, but it wasn't his place to question the claims of science, and there were plenty of experts here. They knew better than he did. His weekly shop consisted of whatever he found in the supermarket, and he wondered who had time, or the money, to shop for the concoctions being promoted by the guest speakers.

He was tired of hearing slender women in their twenties promising diet shakes that really worked and testosterone-fuelled gym bunnies proclaiming a miracle new protein bar delivering every nutrient required to achieve their rippling physiques. They were liars and charlatans. He'd seen them in the hotel gym when he topped up the water cooler, and he recognised the telltale signs of starvation and medical injections: that gaunt skeletal look that was so in vogue now.

There was nothing wrong with steak and butter in Lee's book, but he kept his views to himself and pocketed the generous tips and smiled sweetly. The attendees of the conference were mostly young, ignorant and very wealthy. As well as sales and marketing reps, they also had podcasters, YouTubers and Instagram stars who made money from followers and clickbait. It was a symposium of beautiful people who knew everything but understood very little. They lived in a bubble and for the duration of the forum, Lee indulged their whims. It was a well-orchestrated sales event, that was all.

But the woman called Sandy stood out. She was an older woman and not like the others. She smoked heavily – he'd seen her down by the lake when he nipped out for his own nicotine fix – and she looked exotically wizened, as if she'd existed on common sense her whole life.

Lee couldn't help thinking that they were all a bunch of lunatic Dr Frankensteins playing with the human body, but it wasn't the woman's speech he'd been interested in; it was the mischief in her smile. He could tell she'd once been a good-time girl and Lee had been working in the hotel industry long enough to spot when a woman was lonely. He'd watched her from the back of the hall, between giving out orders for clean napkins. She was an expert speaker, bringing just the right balance of emotion and professionalism to her presentation. She'd received a standing ovation for her delivery, and he could tell she was respected in her field. She'd talked of metabolism, disease management and clinical experiments and had received rapturous applause, but Lee wasn't interested in any of that.

A couple of days ago, before the conference got going, they'd shared a cigarette during one of his breaks down at the lake. She'd joined him on the jetty, overlooking the tiny body of water, and he'd asked her how she was able to smoke cigarettes and preach about fitness at the same time. She'd laughed and told him that her job had nothing to do with her personal life. Her lips had tripped over the words in a way that made him feel intrigued and had assured Lee that she was flirting with him. The age gap didn't bother him. A beautiful woman stayed beautiful no matter her age. She wore no ring on her wedding finger and her eyes twinkled like stars when she lingered a little too long on what she wanted from the bar. She'd insisted it was brought to her room and that's when he'd enjoyed her company for a couple of hours, learning not for the first time that older women not only knew exactly what they wanted, but also how to get it.

Now, his eyes found her as she appeared beyond the entrance outside, through the highly polished glass doors. She didn't see him at first but then she nodded over her shoulder at him. He guessed she'd been out for a cigarette, enjoying the glorious sunshine of the late afternoon. She looked distracted. The hotel buzzed with energy and the hum of conversation filled the seating areas near the foyer.

He put down the tray of nibbles, which nobody was interested in anyway, and headed to the double doors, his body tense with anticipation of a repeat of this afternoon when they'd spent an hour in her suite.

He got halfway across the entrance, which sat underneath a dramatic atrium, before a loud bellow, followed by a crunching noise, made everyone duck.

The sound of chatter ceased immediately, and people looked at one another, unsure what had occurred, until a delegate screamed, and Lee covered his ears.

He lost sight of Sandy through the glass doors, and his lust deserted him as he tried to make sense of the chaos ensuing rapidly around him.

Then he saw the blood.

The crunch had been a body breaking on the tile floor as it dropped from the atrium above the main entrance.

People screamed, some darted away, others reached for their phones. The VIPs' bodyguards from the US, who hung around the organisers, drew their weapons and people only screamed louder and panicked even more. He saw a podcaster recording on her phone.

Lee realised his legs had turned to jelly but he knew he must take charge. He walked quietly to the scene, aware that he felt terribly sick, and he knew that his body had gone into the first stages of shock. He breathed deeply, not wanting to look, but not being able to glance away either.

The man's body was skewed awkwardly, twisted and crumpled. Blood seeped from beneath him. A woman behind him gasped and another cried.

'He jumped!' someone shouted.

Lee looked up to the atrium and saw no one up there.

Then the man moved.

Lee shot back, along with those standing around him.

The poor bastard was still alive.

The sense of the surreal which had taken hold now eased and noise and life rushed back at Lee and he heard more screaming, running and phone conversations. Somebody shouted that they'd called an ambulance.

Two floors encircled the atrium, and the top one was thirty feet above their heads. The guy had hit the ground like a sack of rocks, headfirst, but he had definitely moved.

Then a gurgle left his lips, and his head shifted, just an inch, but enough for Lee to holler at everyone present to stand back.

His staff scuttled around, some being helpful, others less so. Some cried; others ran away. Humans behaved curiously in a crisis…

The bodyguards put away their weapons and stern words were given by the large Texan VIP in the cream suit. The hawk-like woman with him, the one called Tilda Dent, covered her mouth.

Lee went to grab a tablecloth to cover the man but stopped, questioning if he was contaminating the scene of a suicide. Or something else… His brain whirred and his managerial head made him indecisive. Instead, he held up the sheet to block the view of the body and as he did so, his heel backed into the man's blood. He slipped backwards and fell over, dragging the sheet on top of him and ending up across the man's broken body.

The man groaned and Lee desperately scrambled to his feet. But now he struggled to gain traction to get himself up because his hands were in the blood and his knees were soaked in it. It was slippery and Lee was surprised by its warmth. It felt as though the blood itself was more alive than the man.

He saw that the podcaster with the phone was still filming the whole thing and Lee tried his hardest to stand up, holding out his hands to prevent the camera closing in on his face. She continued recording even though he screamed at her to stop. The dreadfulness of the moment seemed like a slow-motion horror show and he saw faces staring at him in bewilderment.

Another member of staff threw serviettes over the blood and helped Lee up. He turned back to assess the mess. There was smeared blood all over the floor of the atrium and the lights of the water feature in the middle illuminated the sheen on the tacky red liquid draining from the man. Behind him, people continued to shout and scream and sob. But nobody did anything.

The man on the floor groaned once more, and Lee went to him.

'Hang in there, man, an ambulance is on its way,' he whispered to him. Lee knelt alongside him and humanity, from somewhere deep inside of him, made him hold the guy's hand. He thought he saw him move his mouth and he leant close to see if he could make out what he was telling him.

As he got closer, the guy whispered something, though it could have been a gurgle of blood as he fought hard for breath. Lee was unsure, but he could have sworn he said something.

He looked up and into the eyes of the two VIPs with whom he'd been liaising for the duration of the conference, and months before that. One was the Texan; the other was the hard-balled woman from New York. Hank Hampton and Tilda Dent. Their bodyguards stood around them protecting them rather than checking if there was an existential danger of anyone else getting hurt. They stood over him as if demanding answers, as if it was his fault.

Funnily enough, he did feel guilty.

Their suits were clean and their cheeks rosy from the champagne cocktails. Their smug faces were framed by the lights above their heads and Lee felt as though he was being judged, as if he was part of the tragedy on the floor. They looked at him as if he was leaching blood too. As if he was a lab rat being experimented on by mad doctors. They seemed more concerned with the mess than with the suffering of the poor sod who'd fallen.

Still, nobody helped him.

Then the man's hand slipped out of his and Lee realised he'd stopped moving altogether.

Instinct kicked in and he fingered the man's neck. There was no pulse at all, and the guy's face was turning grey and his lips blue. His eyes remained wide open, and Lee reached out to close them.

He looked at the man's name badge pinned to his yellow T-shirt, now covered in thick, oozing blood, though Lee already knew who he was. The man who'd plunged from the atrium was Jamie Robbins.

And Sandy had disappeared.

Chapter 8

Melvin Stone heard the commotion from outside the hotel, where he'd been walking the dog, and stood still, staring at the entrance, trying to decide what to do about it. Around Rydal Water, whose shores housed a cluster of homes rather than a village to speak of, blood-curdling screams of the sort more at home in a horror film were unheard of. But tonight, across the water from the ancient caves of Rydal, panic reverberated around the tiny lake which was just over a mile long and three hundred feet across. It sounded like somebody had been murdered.

Melvin stood just outside the entrance to the grand hotel, peering in through the glass doors. Acorn was tied to a bench near the pebble beach and she looked over at him patiently, wondering when she could join him. He'd left her for quite some time.

The screaming could be heard across the lake, and it bounced off the water as if they were inside some kind of modern recording studio, famous for its acoustics. Rydal was one of the most picturesque lakes in the whole of the national park. Most of the shore was National Trust property and undeveloped, which was why Melvin liked it. It was remote and untouched by human drama. Here, he could exist without fuss and investigation into his past. The still waters were not accustomed to dramatic events unfolding on her shores, apart from the odd dog barking at a floating stick, or a toddler splashing noisily in the shallow water, perhaps dropping their Marmite sandwich as they did so. But today, it would seem, was different.

It had been a blistering day, and the temperature was still heady; Melvin wore scruffy shorts and a thin shirt. He pushed his hand against the large glass door and went in, straightening his attire as he did because he was unused to such scenes of grandeur and looked out of place.

Inside, people darted this way and that. They appeared panicked.

Then he heard sirens.

Instinct made him look at his watch. It was five-fifteen in the afternoon. Years of being alert to danger had honed his skills and they were unshakeable. One never quite left the services. His days of volunteering in disaster zones were over. But now he must see if anyone needed his help. One heard all sorts of rumours now about mass stabbings – and worse – even in sleepy backwaters like theirs.

His brain was on high alert by the time he saw what was on the floor of the grand atrium. One fella was on the floor, trying his damnedest to save the poor sod. Others stood by and watched, as was human nature. Heroes were rare in this world. Melvin looked around and took in information from the scene. His chest felt calm, and he was glad he'd left the dog outside. Big, burly fellas who looked like guards kept an eye on two people who stood out from the rest. Melvin was too old to take them on these days, and anyway he wasn't here to cause a spectacle. He was here to contain it. He nodded to them, and they acknowledged him.

People stared and he couldn't help thinking how undignified a scene it was. The lobby was busy and getting fuller, as more people squeezed into the space to get a look at the mess on the floor.

A woman, a good-looking smart one with impressive jewellery hanging off her, stared at him and he almost greeted her like an old friend but thought better of it. She backed away and the moment was cut short by the noise behind him.

Paramedics stormed in, as if on drill for a war zone, and their boots on the lobby floor reminded him of soldiers. He glanced at his own muddy boots and tutted as he realised he was leaving tread marks.

He was pushed back by the ambulance staff carrying emergency equipment. Somebody administered CPR to the victim on the floor, who was surrounded by a pool of blood, which looked as though it had been wiped up hastily, while groups of people sobbed, held each other, and whispered about what might have happened.

Apparently, it was a suicide. Others said the bloke fell.

Melvin looked around and noticed the bodyguards had disappeared, along with the woman with the jewellery and the big guy in the cream suit.

Melvin looked at the body, then peered up at the atrium above and recalled another incident many years ago which never left him, and he thought how unlikely it was that a man would jump off the lip of a banister like that for drama, in front of as many witnesses as were here tonight, and for foul play not to be involved. But the victim might be an exhibitionist. He'd see it before. His head hurt suddenly, and it occurred to him that he might have been here just at the right moment. All around him, people were losing their heads, and Melvin's heartrate didn't go over ninety. He'd be valuable to the police when they arrived here eventually, as he knew they would. Until then, he'd take a seat and try to help as best he could.

He felt a tap on his arm and Melvin peered at the man who'd stopped him. He read his name badge. *Lee Lovett, Conference and Banqueting Manager.*

'What are you looking at?'

Melvin looked around.

'Did you see it happen?' he asked Lee from banqueting.

The man nodded.

'I'm sorry, it must have been awful.'

'Who are you?'

'Melvin Stone.' He held out his hand but retracted it when he saw that Lee's was covered in blood.

'You tried to help?' Melvin asked.

Lee nodded.

'I was walking my dog. I heard a commotion.'

Lee Lovett nodded. Melvin could tell he was in shock, but he was holding it together well under the circumstances. Civilians didn't normally have to deal with trauma on this scale. Melvin, on the other hand, was used to it.

'There's not much going on around here, is there? The noise travels.'

Lee nodded again.

'You know him?' Melvin asked.

They both peered towards where the man lay as the medics stopped CPR and called it. He was proclaimed deceased and they stood up, deflated they'd lost a soul. A woman screamed and Melvin saw that Lee looked at her oddly. It was the same woman he'd seen outside only moments ago. The woman whose name badge said "Sandy".

The body language of Lee from conference and banqueting indicated that he cared about her and was affected by her pain. She fell dramatically to her knees and threw herself onto the dead guy. Melvin thought the behaviour rather over the top but understandable if the pair were a couple, which on further examination was highly unlikely because the woman was more Melvin's age than the victim's. The whole performance was rather uncomfortable. It was as if she was his mother.

Melvin watched Lee, who went to her and put his arms around her. The woman looked around and recognised the manager, then sank her head into his shoulder. As she did so, her eyes met Melvin's, and he looked away. Perhaps it was embarrassment that Melvin read the signals between the older woman and the much younger manager, or maybe it was something else.

They stood there, over the corpse, embracing, suspended in some bizarre ménage à trois, until a paramedic asked them politely to move.

He waited for an opportune moment to inform one of the young, uniformed coppers that they might want to get a detective down here because there was no way that was a suicide, and if the fella had suffered an accident, then that would need to be investigated too.

'And what makes you say that?' the copper asked quietly, suddenly taking an interest in him.

'Look at his phone,' Melvin said.

The scene's integrity had been secured, and the dead guy's phone was about two feet away from his body. It was intact but the screen had frozen. The damage it had suffered from the drop had caused some kind of malfunction, but the light was still on the handset. Whatever the man had been watching had been locked and was there to see plain as day.

'That's a Clem Allins podcast,' Melvin said. The copper didn't have a clue.

Melvin tutted. 'He's a wellness guru. Why would somebody watch a positivity podcast that focuses on being your finest self and living your best life if they were planning on killing himself?'

Chapter 9

Kelly's team at Eden House prepared for the evening shift.

The news about Water Nymph being pregnant subdued the mood. Young Emma Hide lost her sparkle, distinctly unchirpy about a local fell race she'd missed. Dan fussed over her and Kelly felt almost voyeuristic when she caught them whispering in the brew room. Fin spun on his chair and the sound of it clicking got on Kelly's nerves.

It was an afternoon for staying in her office but Kate plonked herself in a chair opposite her and raised her eyebrows.

'What?' Kelly asked.

'You've forgotten how it feels?' Kate said.

'What?' Kelly grew weary of the riddles.

'Didn't you see Emma's face when you said Water Nymph was pregnant?'

Kelly closed her eyes. Of course. Emma had been off coffee and cake – not that she ate much of it – and she was miserable because she was missing fell races, and Dan had been flapping around her like a mother hen.

Emma was pregnant. It was obvious now.

'Oh, bloody hell, I hope I wasn't insensitive. How far along do you think she is?'

'Second trimester,' Kate guessed.

A call from downstairs interrupted them.

Kate stared at her, knowing something important had come up. Kelly grimaced.

'I'll get over there now,' Kelly said. Then she hung up.

'Trouble?' Kate said.

'Suspected suicide over at Heron Hall, on Rydal Water. The uniform on site has flagged up some unusual details apparently. First responders are on the scene.'

'Unusual details?'

'Something about a podcast. Things not adding up. Nervy witnesses. The conference and banqueting manager suspects something off.'

'Knee-jerk reaction?' Kate said.

Kelly nodded. 'Probably.' It was true that shock caused strange behaviour in otherwise level-headed witnesses. Rydal Water was nestled just across the weir from Grasmere and Kelly was well aware that she should be sending her team home for the evening, not asking one of them to accompany her over there again. The two lakes were separated by a forest and a bridge, and it crossed her mind that it was only five minutes away from where Water Nymph's body had been found.

'Did they say why the manager suspects something is off?' Kate asked.

'Something about it being out of character,' Kelly said.

'Isn't that what everyone thinks of suicide?' Kate asked.

Kelly acknowledged the common opinion that suicide victims were somehow different to everyone else.

Kelly read the email from her desktop computer to Kate.

'Apparently it's a health conference and they're all wealthy influencers,' Kelly said.

'Influencers? Good God, that's all we need. It'll be all over the sodding internet,' Kate said.

'That's the problem, it's been recorded.'

'Oh, please, social media is vile. I can't convince any of my daughters it's not real, it's just clickbait,' Kate said.

The whole concept depressed Kelly, who had a two-year-old. What would the world be like when Lizzie turned fifteen? She worried about it constantly. A need to check on Emma took hold of her and she went to the incident room to make sure she was OK.

She approached Dan first and told him about the incident at Heron Hall. Then she hugged Emma, who stiffened then relaxed.

Fin glanced over, none the wiser, confirming how lacking in awareness he was. In that moment, Kelly was disappointed she'd slept with someone so shallow and suddenly wanted Johnny. Thinking of Johnny made her finger the ruby ring on her right hand. The stones sparkled happily. It had been his grandmother's. Wearing it had become something of a lucky charm for her.

She coughed and pulled back, then briefed her small team, distancing herself from unwanted thoughts.

'The scene is secure, but they have numerous traumatised witnesses to handle.'

The uniforms on site weren't trained to deal with mass shock. 'Some of the guests have already left,' Kelly said. 'We need to nail down the witnesses; this has come from Carleton Hall because – get this – the conference was a gathering of important health influencers hosted by a big American company.'

Dan whistled and Fin spun around on his chair.

'Feck, it sounds more like murder to me,' Fin said.

More and more, Kelly witnessed the business class seeking private hideaways in the Lake District to conduct their deals and conceal inconvenient truths. When one of their kind got into trouble – especially so young – she often smelt a rat. Jamie Robbins had been twenty-nine years old. Caution was required with all suspected suicides, but Fin had a point. Her hackles were raised already and she wasn't even there yet.

Two deaths in as many days wasn't something she'd expected when she'd begun the week.

'It's a messy scene. Emma and Dan, I want you to sit this one out. Kate will come to Rydal with me tonight.'

Kate nodded.

'First responders have made a start on statements. It was very public.'

Under British law, the police couldn't coerce anyone into helping their inquiries but luckily there were plenty willing to do so. Two senior members of the company were present at the conference and had convinced the attendees to hang around.

'Tilda Dent and Hank Hampton,' Kelly said.

The names were met with expected sniggers.

'Now, now,' Kelly warned them.

'They sound rich,' Dan said.

'They're the big cheeses.'

'What are they doing here?' Emma asked.

'What is so important to bring in *les grands fromages*?' Dan added.

'I didn't know you spoke French,' Kelly ribbed him.

'Mange tout,' Fin added.

'It's a good question, though,' Kelly said.

Kelly's mobile phone buzzed and she saw it was a call from Millie. As any mother knows, having a phone available around the clock in reach is a double-edged sword. Millie wouldn't call for something trivial. She hoped Lizzie was OK. She answered it quickly. At almost two years old, Lizzie was a handful and sometimes Kelly didn't stop to take a breath until her head hit her pillow at gone midnight. Lizzie had picked up a cold over the weekend and Kelly constantly checked her dress for signs of snot she'd forgotten to wipe up. She did it now, absentmindedly, her hand batting off imaginary pathogens from her clothes.

'Millie?'

'Hi, Kelly, just to say Lizzie is struggling to go down after her bath; she's hot.'

Kelly heard her daughter wailing in the background and her heart was split in two. The detective in her wanted to walk away and let Millie do her job. The mother in her wanted to rush back to make an emergency appointment with the doctor.

'How hot?'

'I can't find a thermometer.'

'Oh. How hot do you think?'

'Very. She's red and squealing.'

'I can hear her. Calpol?'

'Yep, done. I've got a cold flannel on her head. I rang the doctor and I'm due a call back.'

'Right, let me know, my phone is on loud. I'm heading to Rydal so it'll take me a while to get back if you need me.'

They hung up.

Millie was a sensible young woman and wasn't one to flap.

Neither was Johnny. He was down to earth and a godsend in emergency situations. That was part of the problem. They were no longer together because he was so laid back and she wanted more. Or at least she thought she did.

She felt torn between giving the Rydal job to Kate, and driving home to nurse her daughter. It was Kate who reassured her. 'Mums work. That's life. She's probably teething,' Kate said. 'Was Millie worried?'

'No, it was more of a letting-you-know type call.'

'Good, let's go then.'

—

Rydal Water was serene. They arrived at Heron Hall around 7 p.m. Kelly had never stayed there but she'd heard plenty about it. There was something particularly quaint about this part of the national park, and Kelly sniffed the clean air. It smelt of leaves, blue sky and deep lakes. It was cool, as if the sun didn't reach beyond the hills surrounding the rolling fells skirting the two lakes. Wordsworth's favourite home, Rydal Mount, nestled just off the road, overlooking the tiny lake, and its impeccable gardens gave the impression that he still lived there and might emerge from the grand entrance in a top hat, reciting poetry.

Heron Hall wasn't a typical Lakeland retreat. It was small, unique and special. Its clientele was in the luxury bracket. The cars parked in the generous spaces outside were Mercedes, Audis, BMWs, the odd Aston Martin and one Bentley. Off to the side, behind a row of bushes, was what she assumed was the staff carpark and there she saw Fiats, Seats, VWs and Minis. The gravel crunched as she rolled hers to a stop and they got out. Ted had been heading over to hers but insisted on accompanying them. He was already waiting for them in the carpark. He got out of his car to greet them and Kelly instantly felt more whole. Kate felt it too.

'I'm adopting him,' Kate said.

Kelly wore thin cotton trousers, with a belt, a simple polo top and white pumps today, not knowing she'd be out so late. She'd popped some extra gloves in her pockets, taken from the SOCO at the Faeryland café, unaware she'd need them so soon. She searched for a cardigan in the back seat of her car and threw it around her shoulders. The sun had gone down across the lake and there was a chill in the air. She tied her auburn hair back with a scrunchie and peered up at the accommodation and wondered how a suite cost five hundred pounds per night. Where did all that money go? What type of service did they offer? She and Johnny had stayed in little boutique hotels, getting away for the night on a date, or just for a change of scenery, and they paid ninety pounds, tops. But it was the way of plenty of elite hotels across the national park, and that's how they made their money. Tourism was worth something in the region of three billion pounds to Cumbria annually, but Kelly knew that just underneath the surface another economy thrived too. Only last week a hotel had closed in Ambleside, not far from here, because it was trafficking illegal migrant workers.

Ted hugged his two favourite ladies, excepting his granddaughters, of course. They set their game faces and spread out. Kelly assessed the approach to the entrance and looked around. Kate chatted to a uniformed officer who ID'd Jamie Robbins' top-of-the-range BMW M4 in the carpark for them. Ted stared at the lake. The location was shrouded in trees and shrubs. It was well hidden. This afternoon, the shores of Grasmere and Rydal would have been busy with summer visitors wanting to cool off, and plenty of folks had heard the commotion. But the lakeside here at Heron Hall was private and it was only one local dog walker who'd poked his nose in, who Kelly was keen to speak to. There were no other hotels around the lake.

Kelly studied the outside of the hotel and walked around the back. The staff accommodation was a neat little row of white cottages. Great real estate these days, she thought. It was one of the staff members, the conference and banqueting manager, who was their main witness. Lee Lovett had seen the whole thing, from the moment the bloke hit the floor to the aftermath. He'd also dealt with the logistics of stemming the rising agitation of the other guests. By all accounts, his actions were just what they needed in a terrible situation. Kelly had seen plenty of broken bodies, but the uninitiated could easily panic when faced with blood and gore. Sometimes the people unaffected by it were the ones she looked at closest for that very reason.

From the staff carpark, she could make out the roof lanterns of the atrium. It was a huge tent-like structure that rose up in the middle of the hotel like a wigwam, and it was brightly lit. Suicides were usually private, but that didn't mean Jamie Robbins hadn't done himself in. Last flurries of exhibitionism weren't unheard of. Equally, it could have been an accident, but initial inquiries into whether the man had been drinking, or if the floor above was recently made wet by cleaning for example, had returned negative.

Satisfied with her cursory examination of the layout of the building, she went to the main entrance and greeted the uniform guarding the door. The place was a potential crime scene, and Ted had called a forensic team to attend just in case. You never knew when you might need those details further down the line. She spotted him talking to somebody at the reception desk. Those members of staff who were still about were either sitting on sofas waiting their turn to be interviewed or were getting on with perfunctory tasks. All of them looked pale and shocked. Kelly had dealt with trauma victims before, many times. It was going to be a very long and taxing evening.

The copper told her that no one had heard a fight, and nobody was unaccounted for, suggesting that the man had been alone upstairs before he jumped. No witnesses reported seeing or hearing a scuffle. It was an isolated scene, and they had that fact on their side.

However, Kelly was immediately suspicious when the uniform told her there were items of clothing (a ladies' purple scarf), and a smashed glass inside the man's room upstairs, which did indicate a struggle.

Inside, Kelly was greeted by the sight of a blue forensic structure at the foot of the stairs and knew that a body lay under there. It was a stark realisation of why she was here. She'd get around to him in good time, but first, she spoke to her father.

Ted nodded in the direction of the restaurant and Kelly followed her nose. She smelt food and supposed even the traumatised had to eat. The hotel was doing a good job of looking after a group of very worried guests. Of course, by now everybody would have been on their phones, if not social media, sharing their story with the world. Some people were sick in the head. Some handsets had already been requested for evidence. The first responders had requested that names not be posted, to respect the families.

'Do you know who Melvin Stone is?' she asked Ted when they reunited inside the lobby. The uniform outside had mentioned several key witnesses, and the old dog walker was one of them.

'He's the one with the dog,' Ted said, pointing to a man in the restaurant who stood out, not just because he had a beautiful golden lab next to him, but he didn't fit in with the corporate types.

'The dog?'

'He couldn't take it all the way back home, he was in the middle of a five-mile walk, so he kept it here.'

'Do we know his story?'

'He lives locally. Ex-military. Astute. Talkative. Full of unsolicited theories. He has a disabled wife at home who he takes care of.'

'That's very thorough,' Kelly said, not completely surprised her father had learnt so much in such a short time.

'He's a talker; he told his story to the guy on the door.'

'Has he checked on her?'

Ted shrugged.

'That's all I need.'

'A spousal check?'

'No, another military expert in my life.'

Ted smiled at her. Her ex, Johnny, was an army man.

'He's very particular about what he saw,' Ted said.

'I want to talk to the woman who recorded it,' Kelly said.

'Dear me,' Ted said.

'I know, I'd love to have been from yours and Mum's generation,' she said.

The mention of Wendy made her father wistful and she touched his hand.

'Is that what you think is on his phone?' Ted asked.

She'd tried to fill him in on some of the details.

'No, that's something else. Apparently, the deceased was watching a podcaster called Clem Allins when he fell; apparently he's a big deal to these people.'

'That's odd. Do you buy it?'

'Well, I certainly think it's an unusual choice just before you jump to your death.'

'Well, if there's one thing medical science agrees upon, it's that no one knows what goes through the mind of somebody intent on that behaviour. It's a mystery.'

'Worth checking out though.'

Ted agreed.

'Have you been up there?' she asked.

'I had a wander. It would be pretty hard to accidentally fall over the edge. Take a look for yourself.'

Kelly headed to the staircase and walked around the blue dome. She peeked inside and found the man alone, as he'd died, twisted and bloodied. Only experience allowed her to decipher where his body parts were in relation to his terrible wounds. It had been a violent and sudden fall. Police tape still sealed off the area where he'd landed. She went back to her father.

'Can we get him out of here soon? It's terribly traumatic for the guests,' she said.

He nodded. 'I know. The van is on its way.'

'Sorry to keep you up, Dad; you can go whenever you're ready. Lizzie is a bit poorly but I think she's teething.'

'I don't have to stay tonight,' he said.

'No, please do, I could do with the company. I'll meet you at home.'

—

The hotel staircase was wide and grand, and swept around the circular atrium dramatically. In the centre was a fountain, which twinkled pretty reflections on the lantern glass and the walls. As she walked up the stairs, she realised that it was a miracle Jamie Robbins had missed the fountain. She paused on the first floor and saw that corridors led off to suites, then she carried on to the top. The banister was highly polished and smooth. As she reached the top and went to the location where witnesses had indicated Jamie fell from, she realised for herself that it would have taken a freakish accident to mistakenly step off the lip of the banister. It was waist height. She walked back and then towards the lip, bumping into it on purpose. She assumed that a body would bend over the edge and try to right itself, but Jamie had stayed here for a couple of nights before the conference; he would be used to the layout of the hallways and stairs. She peered over the edge and looked at the blue dome. It was a long way down, and she shuddered at the thought of slamming flesh and bone into hard tile at speed. She could see there were smears still left on the floor around the dome. Somebody had mopped but hadn't done a very good job. She guessed nobody wanted to be responsible for removing the last signs of a body. After Jamie had been moved and the remaining delegates left, the owner would hire a professional to do it. Somebody who didn't know what had happened here, or at least hadn't witnessed it.

The whole scene reminded her of a young witness who'd jumped off a carpark in London to evade the police, almost twenty years ago. That's where she'd started out as a young detective, then moved to murder squad, before coming back to Cumbria about seven years ago. Each year, the increasing crime wave in the wildernesses of Cumbria reminded her she'd escaped London for nothing.

Falling into thin air went against every human instinct there was. To do it on purpose took some next level kind of crazy determination, or lunacy. And by all accounts, Jamie Robbins was a highflyer with everything to live for.

Chapter 10

Kelly peeked her head around the door to Jamie's room and called the SOCO over. Back in the day, ordinary coppers did everything. They secured the scene, reported it, interviewed witnesses, gathered evidence and conducted the investigation. Now everything was specialised. The SOCOs she worked with had studied their craft at university and gave time to the scene she couldn't possibly. This one had been at the Faeryland café yesterday.

'Spatter on the lower floor is consistent with the height of the atrium. He fell two floors for sure. I've sent you the scene in CAD by email. Our biggest problem is the public nature of the site. With delegates and staff trampling all over this place, it's almost impossible to isolate Mr Robbins' movements.'

'Forensics?'

'In here. They want to talk to you.'

Jamie Robbins' life was being slowly erased as scientists and experts pored over what was left of it. His last chance to speak would be at the postmortem.

Kelly had dealt with all manner of falls before and they were all horrific. Survivability depended on lots of things, though, not just height. She went inside to find a forensic officer and looked around. Bodies in plastic placed evidence in bags to label and number. There was a box which was almost full of items. They discussed the possibility of a scuffle both inside and outside Jamie's room, given the discarded items. The information had been kept under wraps for now.

'Did you identify the scarf?' the forensic officer asked.

Kelly shook her head. 'Sadly, I can't subpoena everyone's suitcases, or my life would be so much easier, and we'd all be home by now, wouldn't we?' She grinned. 'Any of the women here could be missing a scarf,' she added.

'When we first arrived, what struck us all was the room was pretty tidy for a bloke, I have to say. He might have been the fastidious type; that's for you to find out. This is the most interesting thing.'

The forensic officer pointed to a laptop.

'It was easy to unlock; we've had a browse and there are three or four emails you might want to look at. It'll go to forensic tech for a full review but I'm giving you the heads up, he was being pursued by several lawyers about a case of corporate manslaughter. A woman in the USA is suing him for damages because she's saying that one of his products caused her all sorts of medical conditions.'

Kelly took in the information. 'Anything else?'

'A large collection of porn.'

'Really?'

'See for yourself.'

She showed her several bags of USBs and photos. Kelly flicked through the images and it struck her that the grubby nature of the haul didn't really fit the profile of the deceased in her mind. The picture she'd been building up of Jamie Robbins was of a thrusting young company director, on the up, making his fortune, and balancing work and life. There was no suggestion of deviance in his past. She'd read a little bit about FairGro and they paid popstar wages – not that rich people weren't perverts – it just added another more complex layer to her investigation. Jamie Robbins, it seemed, lived a double life.

'Do you know what's on these?' she asked, pointing to the USBs.

'More of the same.'

'That's depressing.'

'It always is.'

'Where did you find them?'

'In a suitcase in the wardrobe.'

'Prints?'

'Done. We'll send them all for digital testing too.'

'Excellent.'

'Did you get the attachment from the phone with the footage on it?'

'I'm just about to look at it now.'

She left the room and found a bench along the second-floor corridor to sit on her own to watch the video taken by the podcaster of the aftermath of when Jamie fell to his death. It was a curious thing to do, to take out your phone when faced with a dying man, covered in his own brains, to film him. It showed a deep lack of humanity that sat badly with Kelly. It smacked of a lack of empathy that was fast becoming prevalent in modern crime. They saw it all the time. Violence was becoming commonplace. Force was used excessively, and perps seemed to enjoy inflicting suffering, as if the crime itself wasn't enough. People had become desperate for kicks found in the worst places.

The young woman who'd filmed the scene had been questioned at length and she'd been threatened with arrest if she'd used the footage online before the police seized it.

She'd assured them she hadn't, but a search of her X account told them otherwise. She'd been taken to Penrith for questioning. She'd broken data protection laws if nothing else. She'd interfered with an ongoing investigation and solicited clickbait. But that wasn't Kelly's concern. She'd be dealt with by the CPS.

It was peaceful up here, she thought. The corridor was brightly lit and decorated pleasantly. The huge window at the end overlooked the lake and threw in light.

She opened the attachment and found the footage. She pressed play.

People screamed and some ran, while others stood stock still. The footage was shaky but clear. The woman filming walked closer to the person lying on the floor and Kelly saw the amount of blood spreading quickly beneath him. He didn't stand a chance.

Nobody helped him.

Until Lee Lovett took charge and tried to block the filming with a sheet or tablecloth. But then he slipped and fell on Jamie. It was desperate and extremely distressing.

Jamie was still alive. Even she could see that from the footage.

Then she saw the woman identified as Doctor Sandy Cooper screaming, which was a little excessive for a colleague but Kelly knew that people reacted to shock in different ways. She watched Lee struggle to get up and raise a bloody hand to the camera, and Sandy throw herself over the body.

Then she watched it again with full sound.

She rewound it over and over again, stopping and starting.

Two things stood out.

One was somebody behind the camera talking with an American accent. The other was the bodyguards with drawn weapons.

Chapter 11

'Have you heard of FairGro.com?' Kelly asked Ted when she returned to the ground floor. They stood near the stairwell. The feature was impressive and stunningly beautiful.

'Yes, in fact I have. I get promotions on drugs all the time, like all doctors. They want to sell me their stuff constantly. I ignore most of it, but this company is huge. They're responsible for most of the anti-cholesterol drugs being pushed by GPs at the moment.'

'So, they're not just health and wellness then?'

'No, it's owned by a pharmaceutical company.'

'So, pharmaceuticals are into food supplements now?' she asked.

He peered at her down his nose and raised his eyebrows in his unique way. It said to Kelly that she was either being very naïve or foolish. She grinned.

'The clue is in the word "supplement",' he said.

'Like Johnson and Johnson, Pfizer, Roche, AstraZeneca?'

'Yep, as well as Hampton-Dent, Merck…'

'Never heard of them.'

'There are ones who don't have such a high profile,' Ted said. 'And those are the ones which are the richest, generally.'

'You say that with a hint of menace, Dad.'

She took out her phone and googled FairGro.com and got her answer. She read out loud.

'Hampton-Dent owns them. Holy crap, they turn over fifty billion a year.'

'That's about right,' Ted said. 'Told you.'

'I'm in the wrong business. Does anyone ever ask if what they push on us is actually good for us or just good for their pockets?'

Ted laughed. 'You're just questioning that now? Call me a cynic but I don't think the curative drug industry is there to make us well. They're manufacturers of chemicals, and they have been since the Second World War. Did you know that chemotherapy drugs were developed from mustard gas.'

'Dad, I'm shocked. You're a part of that industry.'

'Not really. The medical profession is like the front line. We put out the fire with what we're given. That's why I prefer to stay away from the industrial side of pathology. It's become too commercial.'

They often had conversations about what made people ill. A detective saw death differently to perhaps a pathologist. Both found themselves thrust into the middle of it, but for different reasons. Whichever way they looked at it, Kelly couldn't understand why nasty diseases were so prevalent when the world was so full of clever people. Ted liked to point out that man was put on the moon in 1969 but we still can't cure obesity.

'Are you suggesting their huge profits are gained dishonourably?' Kelly asked.

'Now who's the cynic?' Ted asked.

'I can't wait to talk to the VIPs. That's seriously how they were passed on to me, as VIPs,' Kelly said. Her father chuckled.

'They take themselves very seriously. Being an expert is very expensive,' he quipped. 'You have to know the right people.'

'Have you met them?' Kelly asked.

'No. I don't tend to get involved with witnesses; they muddy the waters for me. But I did spot them from afar. The well-dressed ones with bodyguards?'

'I haven't time to interview them all properly tonight. It's getting late and we have initial statements. A bigger worry is the close protection you mention are carrying weapons. The US Embassy was involved apparently, after I reported it – it's above my pay grade but I don't like it. Any advice on speaking to drug pushers, then?'

He raised his eyebrows. 'That's a good way of describing them, although I doubt they'd appreciate it.'

'From what you've told me in the past, these people who bully you into buying their miracle drugs are worse than Colombian cartels.'

'Just as deadly, but these types are the sellers – they're glamourous, smooth and manipulative. Did you see the cars parked outside? This is the slick end of the operation.'

They loved a good conspiracy theory, and Kelly could listen to her father's insight into the world of Big Pharma endlessly. She winked at him and the thought of corruption lingered in Kelly's mind as she left him to seek out the uniformed officer who'd tried to organise her witnesses. He'd done a good job of compiling a list, including the bodyguards, who, she'd been informed, had full licences from the US Embassy to be carrying weapons. Kelly sniffed. They still shouldn't be brandishing them in public, no matter who they were.

The copper pointed her in the direction of a conference room, and she found it and went in. She found two VIPs huddled together speaking quietly, who stopped chatting when she closed the door. Both had American accents. One man and one woman. Plus three huge bodyguards. The largest of the three stood out to her because Johnny would have a fit if he saw his attire. Close protection recruits were supposed to fit in. To melt into the background. The big one wore a Mercedes baseball cap. Noticeable. Recognisable.

Stupid.

She eyed their trousers and there were no bulges apart from egos and she wondered where their weapons were. They got her back up and Mercedes man stared at her.

The Americans looked ruffled, but suitably professional, as Ted had warned her. They did not appear to be bereaved or bewildered, more flustered, but the gentleman in a wildly inappropriate but charming cream suit recovered quickly. She introduced herself and pulled out a chair.

She understood that under such circumstances, an inconvenient and potentially embarrassing death could cause a scandal for the company Jamie Robbins worked for. Here, hidden away on the edges of Rydal Water, it was easy to be seduced into thinking news wouldn't travel fast, but in the age of social media, anything involving a global brand must be managed. Their American office had already been on to Eden House to request tactful handling of the story via the press department, and together with Carleton Hall's input, it unsettled her. Kelly felt trouble brewing and didn't like anybody else's hands on her investigations.

She ignored the bodyguards.

'I appreciate how shocking this must be for you and all the attendees. I'm happy that we've got statements from you both and we'll be returning tomorrow once we've had time to review them. I'd like to assure you that we'll get to the bottom of what happened as soon as we can.'

Kelly eyed the paperwork and noticed that the surnames of the two VIPs waiting for her next move were Hampton and Dent. They really had sent the big guns.

'Of course,' the woman said with a sophisticated American accent that spoke of good education. 'Tilda Dent,' she added, holding out her hand. Kelly wasn't well versed in American dialects, but she knew it was Eastern Seaboard. It wasn't quite NYPD, but equally it didn't sound old South either. More New England. Kelly took her hand and they shook. A waft of expensive perfume drifted towards Kelly's nostrils and a silky-smooth handshake indicated a luxurious beauty regime. Tilda's handshake was what Kelly expected from a successful predatory female in business. Her suit was impeccably tailored, her hair shone like honey, and her jawline was tapered away from her face a little too smoothly. Tilda was the type of woman to wear a beautiful scarf, but not a common type like the one found in Jamie's room. Kelly couldn't work out her age, but it was irrelevant, as if these people were ageless and androgynous, all some kind of automatons working for a money-god in the sky. Kelly recalled meeting people in the city of London with a similar kind of atmospheric fog around them.

The elite.

Millionaires were so *last year*. These were the billionaire jet-set who were untouchable. The knowledge sent a teeny tingling sensation down her spine.

The other VIP, in the cream suit, was introduced as Hank Hampton. She was aware that she was likely sitting opposite more money than she could ever imagine but she reminded herself that they were just people, and part of her investigation.

Despite their status, they must breathe the same air and worry and smile and cry like everybody else.

But there was something about Tilda Dent that indicated to Kelly that she was the trickier character of the two. It was in the way she sat, and hogged the conversation, speaking over the man, who was more relaxed. He possessed old-fashioned Texan manners. A gentle giant in a cream suit and white beard, with big hands, who called her ma'am. Hank smiled broadly and Kelly was reminded of an old movie actor, like one her mother used to rave about, before her time. Charlton Heston or Gregory Peck. His voice took up space and she recognised it from the video footage.

'What do you think of the Lake District?' she asked him.

'It's beautiful, ma'am. Small, but pretty.'

She had her ID of the man speaking in the video. Hank Hampton's voice was unmistakable.

'What brought you all the way over here?'

'Jamie was an important part of the future; he'll be sorely missed.'

They locked eyes. He hadn't answered her question.

'We've got a place near here called Dow Bank House. We have interests in the Lake District, but this is the first time I've been.'

Kelly assumed it was something to do with making big money that kept a poker face intact. Regardless of the reason behind it, it was impressive. She couldn't read him. She knew that Dow Bank House was near Grasmere and was more like a castle than a meeting venue.

'Jamie was a happy guy. Everything at his feet,' Hank added.

'Everything to live for?' Kelly asked.

Hank nodded. Tilda smiled. It was forced.

These were successful people, and Jamie was one of the star players. It went some way to explaining why the heavies were here but neither showed real emotion; perhaps they were incapable of it. She glanced over at the largest of the bodyguards to find him staring at her again. Mercedes man looked away first.

A picture of Jamie as a highly driven and well-liked individual was presenting itself to her and she was inclined to agree with Ted that the case needed more investigation. But it also indicated what was at stake here. These people had travelled across an ocean, to a backwater in the middle of the Lake District, for what? Only one thing brought so many hustlers together, and that was money.

'He was running a health conference,' Hank said.

'What were you selling?'

It was crass and she knew it, but she must put witnesses under pressure to see into their realities. Hank smiled. It was wide, charming and very white.

'Our product is chemicals.'

Hank reiterated what most other witnesses had said. *The conference had gone well, nobody noticed Jamie missing for a long period of time, nobody else was missing, there were no obvious squabbles, and it all happened so quickly.* She thought of the smashed glass and the purple scarf and suspected differently.

'Chemicals at a health conference?'

'I'm not a scientist,' Hank said.

'Are you?' Kelly asked Tilda Dent, who snorted.

'I think I heard him holler,' Hank added.

'Jamie?'

'The atrium was busy; we were in between speeches and dinner. The noise was like a cry, a warning, an appeal.'

Hank used his hands to articulate himself. There was emotion in his eyes that took Kelly by surprise. It was a chink in the corporate armour.

'What's your role in the company, Hank?' she asked. 'You don't mind me calling you Hank?'

'No, sure, go ahead, ma'am,' he said. 'I'm based out of Dallas. I run the executive arm of Hampton-Dent, like a chief operating officer.'

'You get things done?' Kelly asked.

He smiled. 'Sure, that's what I do.'

'And the company has your name.'

'It's in my family.'

His Texan drawl was infectious, and Kelly noticed his easy unpicking of complex issues. He was matter of fact but warm with it, the polar opposite of Tilda.

'I'm Hank the third. The original founded Hampton-Whalley corporation, of Silicon Valley fame, and then merged with Dent-Whalley.'

'And what happened to Whalley?' She felt a little foolish for asking.

'Bought out by my granddaddy.'

'Where did Jamie fit into the hierarchy?' she asked.

Hank looked uncomfortable for the first time. 'Well, ma'am, that's the thing. Jamie was a rising star. He was the future really. It's wholly devastating, it sure is.'

Kelly noticed his discomfort. 'I won't keep you much longer.'

'I know he had his issues.'

'Issues?' Kelly asked.

'I don't like to speak ill of the dead, ma'am, but I am led to believe he had a few drug-addiction matters that he was trying to sort out. That just came to my attention this weekend gone. Now, the company doesn't tolerate such behaviour. It's a delicate but deliberate policy we have, and so I was aware that he might be moving on.'

Kelly looked between the two VIPs but it was difficult to read them. A drug company taking issue with an addict wasn't an irony one got to witness every day.

'Your rising star? Did you ever witness any evidence that he might be a substance abuser?'

'No, I did not.'

'And who told you he was?'

'Well, I don't think I should…'

'If it's for an investigation under the UK legal system than I must insist, Mr Hampton.'

'Right, well, it was Tilda here who told me.'

Kelly looked at Tilda Dent.

'Paul, his partner at FairGro, told me,' she said, rather too quickly. Kelly made a note.

'And you represent *the* Dents?' Kelly asked her. Her Google search had produced more than their annual turnover.

Tilda's very manicured eyebrows raised a little.

'Isn't FairGro owned by Hampton-Dent?' Kelly asked.

'My great-grandfather was Waldo Dent,' Tilda said.

Kelly nodded. She had no clue who Waldo Dent was, but she knew that the minute she left this place she'd look him up and get her team working out the hierarchy of the company. A suspicious death was a fly in the ointment to any successful firm whose reputation was important. They'd no doubt want the matter dealt with quickly.

Tilda Dent was the more tight-lipped of the two, giving the impression of coldness, which might be unfair. The woman was built for business, that much was obvious. Her voice was staccato and factual as she saw it, but that could be shock.

'Did you know Jamie well?' Kelly asked.

'Yes. Jamie was an excellent colleague.'

'So, you're in a good position to note his recent mood? What was his behaviour like? Did you witness his substance abuse first hand?'

'No. Jamie was a charmer. He was always fun and happy, a little too casual perhaps.'

'And recently?'

'No change.'

There was a slight hesitation and Kelly picked up on it.

'Nothing at all? Stress? Bad news? Erratic behaviour, something out of character?'

'Nothing.'

'Apart from his alleged drug addiction?' Kelly asked.

Neither answered directly.

'Did he have enemies?'

'I thought he jumped,' Tilda said.

'The coroner won't rule that until after a thorough investigation.'

'But we all saw him fall.'

'Tell me, are you familiar with Clem Allins?'

'*The* Clem Allins?' Tilda looked excited, as if she'd just mentioned a girlhood celebrity crush. It showed Kelly a more vulnerable side to the woman. It was curious that this softer side hadn't naturally emerged after the death of a colleague; Tilda kept her true self concealed well.

'The podcaster?' Kelly said, sounding like she knew their world.

'Yes, of course I do! I've met him. He's incredible.'

'I'm new to the party but I guess it's people who are looking to be the best version of themselves who listen to him?'

'Of course, that's our whole ethos. Clem has done work for us. He's the ideal advocate for wellness.'

'Profitable, hey?' she said.

Tilda's mask slipped again, and Kelly saw a scowl.

'So, did you see Jamie at all, before he fell?'

'He gave the most incredibly affirming speech, in here, about three hours before he…'

Kelly looked around. The stage was set up for a presentation and she imagined a keen audience of fifty people packing in here to listen to a man tell them how to live their best life when he was planning on taking his own. She looked back to Tilda, who was wiping her eye.

'Here,' Kelly said. She'd picked up some tissues before coming in. Tilda took one and wiped her eyes, but Kelly noticed the tissue wasn't wet. Hank stared at her with a puzzled look on his face.

'What was the speech about?' Kelly asked, hoping the answer wouldn't be a sales pitch.

'How his innovation could help millions of people rediscover their health.'

'Really?' Kelly asked. 'That's quite a claim. Which product is that? I think I need some.'

Tilda got up and walked to a white flip chart, which faced the wall. She turned it around; there was a large orange and green poster clipped to it. Kelly read aloud from it.

'Increased muscle mass, bone density, energy, performance, less brain fog.' Kelly looked back to Tilda, who was beaming like a proud parent. Kelly carried on. 'Boosts youth… crikey… all-natural product, no dyes or chemicals, proven to invigorate mood to pre-depression levels and holy shit, weight loss too.'

Kelly examined the poster. The colours were formidable and clean but welcoming too. The colours of sunshine and grass were warm and comforting, the scene natural and alluring, the wording placed just right, and the promises seductive. Marketing on steroids. Bold claims. 'Easy to administer… just stir into your favourite smoothie…'

Kelly kept a straight face.

It couldn't be a coincidence. She didn't believe in them. The sachet of *YouthBlast* she'd found by the body at the Faeryland café jumped into her head.

How had it got there? Was it a popular supplement that she simply didn't know about? Was everyone drinking it? Had somebody left a packet at the café, and it blew on the wind under the same boat as a dead body and a squirrel?

The small hairs on her arms stood up and she felt as though she wanted to shiver. 'Is *YouthBlast* trademarked by Hampton-Dent?'

'Yes. Jamie was so proud of it.'

'So why kill himself?' Kelly asked.

Tilda stared at her for a second, and then looked back to the poster. Hank was the one who answered.

'We'll wait for the inquiry, ma'am. I wouldn't have said Jamie was the type to do that, but I've lived a long time and seen people do surprising things.'

'Does it work?' Kelly asked.

'What?'

'The smoothie powder, does it work?'

'I have no idea; that's not the point. He had the perfect product to sell.'

'But you have no idea if it works?'

'We sell hope, Detective. That's what people want, and Jamie understood that. He's a huge loss to us. It wasn't yet on the market; there were a few tweaks required, licensing, marketing, final ticks in boxes, that sort of thing.'

'Ah, so this conference was about promoting a new product? Attendees were given samples, then?'

Tilda nodded.

Kelly's gut turned over. If *YouthBlast* wasn't on the market that meant that somebody at the conference was also at Faeryland café, and it couldn't be a coincidence.

'Can I ask you to look at this for me – do you recognise her?'

She showed them the sketch of the girl under the boat.

They shook their heads.

'Why?' Tilda asked.

'Unconnected,' Kelly said. She nodded to the marketing poster for *YouthBlast*. 'And this is what people want? A magical smoothie?'

'Exactly. Magic. People need to feel as though they're doing the right thing and the easier we can make that for them the better,' Hank said. It was as if Tilda had lost her tongue.

Kelly felt queasy suddenly. Being brought up on fresh air, cold water and real food, Kelly didn't trust chemicals to do the work for you. These people were aliens to her.

'It's the job of the scientists to pass these products for efficacy and safety, our job is to market them and make people think they can't live without them,' Tilda said proudly.

Kelly stared at her. Tilda Dent had just been brutally honest with her about the history of marketing on human beings, but it left her uncomfortable. Weren't salespeople just a bunch of professional liars?

'Was the conference going well?'

Tilda looked back at the flip chart. 'Jamie secured important backing for us. It'll be difficult calming the market after this.'

Tilda spoke wistfully, as though talking about Apollo 13 almost being lost forever, and not the contents of a smoothie.

'You'll go ahead with the product, then?' Kelly asked.

'Yes, ma'am,' Hank said. 'A legacy, if you will.'

Kelly didn't know what to say. The perversion struck her across the face.

'Did you know if Jamie had any personal problems, aside from the recreational drug taking? It's clear his working life was excellent.' She thought about the porn in his room.

'It wouldn't surprise me, Detective. Jamie had restless feet. He had everything he wanted, fast cars, women, holidays, foreign properties, celebrity friends. It wasn't ever good enough. He sought something he could never have.'

'And what was that?'

'Peace.'

'And you can't make that into a smoothie?'

Tilda looked at her acidly, but Kelly smiled pleasantly.

'Are you planning to head off in the next couple of days?'

'We actually have a few more meetings here in the area. We'll be staying at Dow Bank; where is it, Hank?' Tilda asked her colleague. 'I can drop you a pin, Detective.'

Kelly knew where Dow Bank was.

'Excellent. Here's my number.' She handed Hank a card. 'You're free to go.'

She eyed the bodyguards.

'One more thing, did Jamie have close protection?' She nodded to the guards.

Hank looked at Tilda.

'No, he didn't. Our paid security is for CEOs only,' she said.

'Shame. If one of them was watching, we might not be here.' Kelly paused. 'Right, all being well, I'll see you both again tomorrow. I won't say have a restful night, that would be crass, but if you can think of anything that might be helpful to us, I'd appreciate your input.'

Tilda nodded and dabbed her eyes again. Kelly saw that the tissue was still bone dry.

She reckoned what Tilda Dent meant to say was that Jamie Robbins' untimely death was a huge loss to their profits. Somehow, she didn't believe that Jamie's life was worth as much as his innovation.

Chapter 12

'So, what is that stuff?'

Melvin Stone joined a group of young-looking professionals at a table outside the Heron Hall Hotel. They fussed over his dog and petted her. Acorn was a docile Labrador who loved attention so everybody was happy.

One of the people he sat with poured a sachet of powder into a glass of water and gulped it. Melvin read the sachet.

'*YouthBlast*? You don't need that! A Cumbrian steak and a glass of stout will see you right. Why do you young'uns trust these powders and potions?'

The young man threw Melvin a look of disdain and he might as well have said, *'Old guy, you know nothing!'*

'What's in it?' Melvin asked.

'Everything!' a woman enthused. She lectured him about enzymes and elements and his eyes glazed over.

'Seems too good to be true. You'd think by now we could have worked out how to keep humans healthy. If I were a cynic I'd say they're trying to keep us sick,' Melvin said with a smirk.

'Who?'

'The faceless blob in power. It doesn't matter, they're all the same. My point is that I think we all know what's good for us but there's no money in it. Look at me, fresh air, exercise, good local Cumbrian food and laughter. That's all I need to stay healthy and happy. Nowadays, am I supposed to believe that I need a sachet of powder made in a factory to be happy?'

The group chortled collectively but still Melvin wasn't put off. They had no clue, this lot, he thought.

'I reckon Acorn knows what's good for her,' he said, stroking his dog. Acorn looked up at him and smiled, panting in excitement that her master was paying her attention.

'Why does it have to be so complicated?'

The youngsters were growing bored of him, he felt. They moved off one by one. He looked at the hotel entrance and noticed the heavies were still there, like hawks, watching the kids who were here to further their own careers. Melvin was reminded of close protection in the army. They weren't here to babysit or watch folks paddling in the shallow water for their own safety. Somebody here was important, and Melvin had a feeling they were twitchy now some fella had died.

'Was it something I said?' Melvin asked the empty seats.

One young man remained seated at the table with him – the one drinking the powder. Melvin thought he'd seen him somewhere before.

'I agree with you,' he said. 'But maybe just not on the night my friend died. I think everyone's a little shocked and upset.'

'Your friend?'

'Jamie. The man who died.'

'Oh I do apologise. I was insensitive. I'm a little forgetful,' Melvin said.

Melvin noticed that the young man's hands shook. It was almost invisible, but Melvin knew it was there because he'd witnessed men the lad's age falling apart during war. It was a nervous condition – what was called shell shock in the Great War – and it was involuntary, meaning the sufferer was unlikely to know he was doing it.

'So you sell this stuff too, then?' Melvin asked.

The young man nodded.

Melvin held out his hand and the younger man took it. 'I'm Melvin. I live over there,' he said, pointing to a bunch of trees at the end of the lake. 'I'm in trouble with my wife for being late, but I had to come in and help. I was in the wrong place at the wrong time and now I've been told by the police to hang around. And this is Acorn.'

'Paul Burlington,' the man said in return. He stroked Acorn. 'Have you spoken to the detective yet, Paul?' he asked.

Paul shook his head.

'Do you seriously drink this stuff?' Melvin asked, watching Paul stir his drink with a fork taken from the restaurant. 'You'd be better off poking that fork into a fat sausage.'

Paul laughed and glugged his juice.

'It works,' Paul said.

'You're a fit lad now, but that's because you're young. If you keep supplementing real food and exercise with this crap, you'll be sorry when you're my age.'

Paul sniffed, but it was good natured.

'I was raised on eggs, butter, fish and home cooking. You lot eat rabbit food,' Melvin said.

'If we're going to save the planet, we need to be less selfish with our own desires and learn to share what we've got,' Paul said.

'And that's what the factories tell you to say? They don't seem to run out of ingredients to make pies, cakes and cereal, do they? Plenty of that about. They don't seem to be short on the energy or the water they need either, or the land.'

Melvin got up and walked to the lake edge. He bent over and picked up a stick, throwing it for Acorn. She bounded into the still water and swam to retrieve the stick. After a couple of times, Melvin made his way back to the bench.

Paul watched him and he smiled generously at the lad.

He held out his hand and introduced himself. 'Melvin Stone, and you are?'

The bloke looked at him curiously, and he felt a sinking feeling in his guts.

He'd done it again. He'd lost huge chunks of his memory and had wandered across the wrong side of the lake.

'Have you seen my dog?' Melvin asked the man, who pointed to his side, where he saw the lab panting for her stick.

'Nice to meet you, I'm Melvin,' he said, holding out his hand.

The chap pulled back and looked over his shoulder. Melvin had seen the look before; he was repeating himself again.

'Did you know the chap who died?' Melvin asked.

'He was my partner, Melvin. But you already knew that.'

'Did I?'

'Yes. We just talked about it, sitting here together.' The young chap was terribly polite.

'I do apologise, it's my condition, you see, I forget things.'

'Ah, I see, I'm sorry.'

'No need. It happens at my age. I take lots of medicine.'

Paul smiled at him sympathetically and Melvin wondered why the man looked so worried. He then excused himself and Melvin watched him return to the hotel looking back a few times, as if he'd forgotten something. Come to think of it, he did recall seeing him before, but he didn't know where.

Melvin stared at the hotel and knew he'd been here before. The people inside must be wealthy, he thought, but he couldn't quite put his finger on it.

A chap had died.

Yes, that was it. That must be why the big lads were here. They looked like bodyguards. One in particular – the largest one – looked ex-military. Nasty. Mean. Hard.

He bent over and picked up a sachet off the floor and lifted it to his nose and smelt it. It was a colourful package, like they were when they were full of promise and lies. He licked his finger and poked it into the residue powder and tasted some. It didn't taste bad at all.

And very familiar.

Chapter 13

In the restaurant, Sandy Cooper placed crustless quiche slices onto her plate. She was ravenous but she was never bowled over by the healthy crap on offer at these events. Juices of all colours were laid out lovingly and laden with supplements (all plant based of course). Real sustainable local food full of nutrition and adorned with labels suggesting pairings were on offer too. Glasses of superfood shots and all kinds of shakes boasted longer life and vitality but she ignored them and moved on, trying to not think about the police who were standing around the smeared stain in the foyer and huddled together trying to decide if Jamie jumped or was pushed. And now a detective had arrived.

Her phone vibrated in her pocket, and she took it out to look at it with one hand while she balanced her plate with the other. She eyed the caller ID and looked around. Then she ignored it and put it back in her jeans pocket. Some people said – especially other women – that women of a certain age shouldn't wear jeans, but Sandy thought they could go and fuck themselves. It was nobody's business but hers, and the conference and banqueting manager didn't seem to mind.

Sure, she was getting a little soft and flabby around the edges. Her body wasn't what it used to be. The menopause had hit with a vengeance and no matter how many creams, pills and potions she consumed, nothing seemed to pep her up.

But this weekend had been shaping up nicely in that department until Jamie fell off a stairwell.

She found a seat in the dining room and noticed Lee hovering at the buffet, panicking that his guests would tell the world what had happened here.

In time, the hotel would benefit from a high-profile suicide, she was sure of it, but now wasn't the time to tell him. She must be gentle with him. The death had been spectacular. Typical Jamie. Consummately dramatic.

Jamie had been a creative type. Paul was the brain behind the supplement subsidiary they'd invested in with Hampton-Dent money. Jamie had been the artist. The visionary.

What a shame it was all over.

She was hungry.

The dining room was quiet, and most people had skipped the delicious array of food laid on by the hotel, free of charge of course, as if that would erase the memory of what had happened here. They'd lost their appetites. She had a table to herself and devoured her food.

The vision of Jamie's broken body was still fresh in her mind. If he was planning on ending it all, then he could have done it privately at least. Her decision to cast judgement on his selfishness helped with the guilt. Could they have done more? Could they have seen it coming? Addictive personalities were beyond help. She should know. She'd studied them for long enough.

Her work with Hampton-Dent had afforded her the luxury of reading the most up-to-date literature on human behavioural science years before the rest of the world became aware of it. The drugs that followed were fed to mass populations via various routes like medicines, food and supplements and it was all perfectly legal. Hampton-Dent had been part funded by the World Economic Forum since 1971 – the year of its inception – but they didn't boast about it.

She was an advocate of preventative medicine. Prevent the public from knowing.

She chuckled, but soon became serious again.

The atmosphere of excitement surrounding the products on offer had gone from life affirming to life ending, with one wrong step. Sandy reckoned Jamie must have been drunk, deranged or murdered. She never saw him drink more than one glass of champagne and she'd certainly never witnessed him lose his cool. To her, he wasn't the jumping type, but neither was he a saint. This was all part of chewing over what she would tell the detective when they got round to interviewing her.

She looked up to find Lee staring at her like a forlorn puppy. She gave him an *'if only I could talk to you about this'* type of glance and went back to her food.

She felt his gaze on her body as she went back to the buffet for dessert. Puddings were thin on the ground, as they always were at these damn conferences, but she loaded her plate with air-light flan covered in fruit, as well as pouring a strong coffee.

She was in the mood to get inebriated on booze but that wouldn't help anyone.

'Sandy?'

She looked up into the perfectly taut face of Tilda Dent grinning at her. Her heavies stood behind her. Fat lot of good they'd done.

Suddenly, she lost her appetite.

She felt sympathy for Lee, who'd put so much labour into the catering only for it to end like this. The smell of cooking meat filled the atrium, and she couldn't help thinking about Jamie's flesh, smashed apart on the floor. The smell made her consider fleetingly that they were serving up the memory of Jamie already, and he was barely cold. Life went on. Bodies functioned, people needed to eat and to sleep and to talk. But at the same time, the smear of blood and the blue tent reminded them what happened only hours ago, which perhaps explained why Tilda wasn't eating at all.

She smiled insipidly at Tilda, who seemed maudlin but that was her normal state; it had nothing to do with Jamie's death. But the panic in her eyes was real. The conference had ended in disaster. Sandy asked her to sit, which she did, and Tilda fiddled with the skin around her nails. Tilda had spent thousands, if not hundreds of thousands, of dollars on tightening her skin, rejuvenating her body and replacing what God had given her with what men wanted in magazines. To Sandy, it wasn't worth it. If you got a man – or woman – in your bed, the last thing they wanted was plastic, except if it ran on batteries.

She studied the CEO of Hampton-Dent.

They'd first met years ago when Tilda had become the new hotshot of Daddy's company, after she graduated from college and took over the family business in New York. Sandy's opinion of her hadn't changed much since then.

'Don't worry, everything will work out. Are you thinking about our stock?' Sandy asked.

Tilda looked at her as though she'd stubbed a cigarette out on her hand. 'No! I was actually thinking about Jamie's family.'

'He hasn't got any, remember?' Sandy said.

'His sister?'

Sandy raised her eyebrows. 'More importantly, what are you going to tell that detective? The one with legs up to her armpits and skin that smacks of long runs in the countryside?' Sandy enjoyed winding Tilda up.

Tilda eyed her. Their youth was behind both of them. Tilda was forty but showing signs of loss of skin elasticity that Sandy recalled vaguely from her distant past. The detective on the other hand was one of those old-school types who breathed real air. She was not the target audience for pharmaceuticals.

'I've just been speaking to her. She's clever.'

Sandy smiled. 'Look, after a short period of loss, due to the shock, the company will rally and we'll continue as normal. Jamie's value will remain. This is business, remember.'

Tilda nodded.

They were very different women. Sandy spent ten minutes getting ready each morning, forgoing expensive moisturiser she knew didn't work, and instead downing a few waffles and a double espresso. She had worked too hard to surrender her cynicism now. Everybody died some day and nips, tucks, Botox, fillers, whatever the hell else Tilda was full of, didn't make one damn bit of difference.

She could see the younger woman was struggling with how to handle the fallout of such a shocking event, but this was what she was here for. To manage expectations and steer the ship. She'd been doing it for long enough.

'What do you think?' Tilda asked.

'What do I think about what?' Sandy asked, finishing a mouthful of lemon-tasting fluff, her appetite returned.

'You know, Jamie. This awful thing.'

Sandy eyed her. 'There's money on the table. The very smell of it makes lunatics out of ordinarily sane people. Whoever did this is inside this hotel right now, perhaps eating, or chatting to people. He might even have given a statement to the police already.'

'It wasn't me!' Tilda said defensively.

Sandy laughed. 'I know it wasn't you. Besides, aren't the police saying it was suicide?'

'You're making me nervous,' Tilda said. Sandy stared at her.

'Everything makes you nervous, Tilda. Why did you even come? You can't go anywhere without those gorillas on your tail. You belong in your ivory tower in New York. The English countryside is an inhospitable wilderness.' She laughed, but Tilda didn't find it funny. 'We'll get to the bottom of this eventually. It's probably a jealous competitor. It could be Paul for all I know.' Sandy became serious again.

'You think he was pushed?' Tilda said, her voice low.

Sandy smiled. 'I have no idea.'

'What jurisdiction does that detective have?' Tilda asked.

Sandy looked to the door. A few people had come and gone, taking food with them and not saying much.

'It's different here. The US has a treaty with the UK to share witnesses etc, but I've spoken to head office and we'll be heading to New York shortly. Don't worry. Just act normal. But perhaps ask your gorillas to not cock their weapons around here. You know someone was filming? That shit is illegal in the UK, even if you are rich.'

Sandy looked the CEO up and down and stood her ground. Tilda Dent had no idea what normal was, and frankly, at the moment, neither did Sandy. The fact that it was left to her to contact New York and come up with a damage limitation strategy said everything.

The skin around Tilda's neck turned pink and Sandy saw fear grip her. 'I've told the detective that we'll stay here overnight and be available for statements in the morning.'

'More statements?'

Tilda shrugged. 'I didn't speak to legal before I agreed.'

'Calm down, Tilda. We'll give our statements and then head to Dow Bank House. When we're done, we'll head home. Investigations like this take months in the UK. They have no money, and their legal system is broken like an old Ford engine. Tell them what you know, and we'll hear from them in a year when they close the inquiry, if there is one. Did you see that old guy who is the coroner? He looks as though he's going to fall asleep any minute.'

Tilda laughed. It was a rare moment and Sandy thought Tilda quite attractive when she chilled the fuck out.

'Tell me honestly, Sandy, do you think he was pushed? Do you think it was deliberate? If it's a competitor, they might not stop at Jamie. What we have is worth killing for, isn't it?'

Sandy went to take a sip of juice from one of the colourful glasses but thought twice about it and sniffed it instead, for signs of interference. The best poisons were odourless, but that didn't mean there wouldn't be telltale traces, such as dyes, or a weird texture. She examined the liquid carefully and stared into the glass.

'I think the less you know the better,' Sandy said.

It did the trick. Tilda stood up and backed away and bumped into Lee on her way out.

Sandy forced a weak smile.

'Am I disturbing you?' he asked her.

Sandy assessed if she had time to play.

She did not.

She looked around but couldn't think of an excuse to get rid of Lee and decided to stay and watch the show. The global empire of Hampton-Dent had been brought to its knees in the middle of the English Lake District and suddenly, Sandy felt like laughing. The story of Jamie Robbins' death had reached the other side of the pond and a scandal was brewing.

'Everybody is in shock,' Lee said, looking around.

She saw he wore fresh, clean clothes. The remnants of Jamie's lifeblood had gone. She'd done the same. The police had allowed her to take a shower but they'd asked for her clothes to test them. As a scientist herself she knew it was to screen them for fibres and trace material to check that no third party was involved. She and Lee were both the closest to the area on the floor where Jamie had landed. She supposed both she and Lee would be covered in splatter and just as blood-pattern experts traced the trajectory of bodily fluids up walls and across carpets and tiles, so they could do it on other items.

'They let you change,' she said.

Lee smiled and nodded. 'You too?'

She nodded.

'I made a fool of myself,' she said.

'No, you were in shock,' he reassured her.

'I'm a scientist; I should know not to do things like that,' she said. Which was exactly why she'd done it, to get as much contact with Jamie's body as possible.

Lee reached out his hand and laid it gently on hers.

'I contaminated the scene,' she added.

'No, you didn't, you comforted him at the… end.'

The door opened and they caught sight of movement in the foyer.

'The big guns have arrived.' Sandy nodded over to the entrance where the female detective in plain clothes and a lanyard around her neck chatted to a forensic officer. 'Have you given a statement yet?' she asked.

'I've been told that I'll give a lengthy one in due course. They know who I am. I'm going nowhere. You?'

'I didn't see anything; I'm no use to them,' she said.

'Had you been for a smoke? I saw you come in from outside, you know, just after Jamie fell.'

Sandy shook her head. 'No, you must have been mistaken,' she said. She brushed his hand with hers and he smiled.

'I suppose they'll want to know his movements over the last couple of days though, won't they?' Lee said.

'I really need to get back to New York,' she said.

'Under different circumstances I was going to invite you to stay here a bit longer,' he said. He peered at her longingly and Sandy realised just how much she'd encouraged him over the last couple of days. The looks, the flicker of her eyelids, and the shared cigarettes, the conversations, the innuendos. The sexual fumbles when she took charge and guided the young manager to be more confident and assured with his prowess. He wasn't bad.

He was a nice bloke, but he was one thing to her.

An alibi.

'I'm sorry I misled you,' she said. 'It's not your fault, Lee,' she said softly, taking his hand.

The female detective and the old coroner glanced in her direction from beyond the doorway and she looked away, but not before the detective locked eyes with her.

She dropped Lee's hand and left the table. There was a queue for the lift so she took the corridor behind the reception to the back stairs. She'd become adept at using the network of hidden routes to navigate her way around the hotel when Jamie was alive. It was a secret maze of corridors and doors that reminded her of children's novels and spies.

She and Jamie had discussed future strategies, and she'd kept an eye on him, all the while knowing what he was up to, and now he was gone. She'd miss him. He could sell water to a fish. Jamie Robbins could convince you to hand over your grandma. He was the most charismatic and charming salesman she'd ever met. But more than that, Jamie was clever and streets ahead of his audience.

That's why she knew he didn't kill himself.

Chapter 14

Kelly agreed that they'd done all they could for the evening. She'd been in liaison with the uniforms in Grasmere working on the Water Nymph case. A search of the surrounding area had turned up nothing about the dead woman. House-to-house visits had drawn a blank. Nobody saw how she ended up under the *Water Nymph* and it was as if she'd been deposited there by aliens.

The guests at Heron Hall were frazzled, and Kelly knew she must push lightly to get the best out of them. The witnesses were beginning to leave but she'd agreed with Tilda Dent and Hank Hampton that some of them would be available for statements in the morning.

Everybody needed a good night's sleep, though she didn't imagine they'd get one after what had happened.

Lee Lovett had confirmed, after liaising with the general manager who was based in their sister spa hotel in Manchester, that the hotel was closed to the public for the time being and the current guests could stay another night without charge. Kelly had noticed his hands locked with the scientist's when she'd seen them together in the dining room earlier. Their hands had touched, and not by accident. Sandy Cooper spotted her looking too. It provided another element to her case, though it could be nothing. People jumped in and out of each other's beds at these functions all the time. It was none of her business if a hotel manager fucked a guest old enough to be his mother.

Good on Doctor Cooper, she thought.

She dropped Kate off at home at gone 10 p.m. and met Ted back at her place. Ted took Millie home and Kelly cooked a very simple light supper. Lizzie had been awake but the sight of her grandfather at least distracted her from her teeth for a while and she watched as they sang and played.

Later, around eleven, Kelly washed the pots and listened to Ted reading a story to Lizzie. Occasionally, the two-year-old would butt in and finish a word or a sentence. Her chatter was non-stop, and Ted had the patience of a saint. Lizzie was bathed and ready for bed and Kelly saw her eyes closing as her grandfather read to her about fire engines and unicorns. Finally, her daughter's muttering grew less and less until Ted stopped reading, and Kelly saw that Lizzie was asleep in his arms. They took her upstairs and settled her into her cot and closed the door to her room gently.

Back downstairs, Ted finished off the pots from their supper. At first, after Johnny left, Kelly noticed his absence keenly whenever they might have shared time together late at night after Lizzie went to bed. It had been one of the only times of the day when they'd been able to be a couple again. Now, she faced the loneliness of not having a partner to chat to at the end of a hard day, but she also had a new type of freedom which released her from some of the unwelcome boundaries that had crept into their romance.

Secrecy.

His unusual behaviour towards the end of their relationship, mainly over his wife, Carrie, had begun to seep into her psyche and make her feel uncomfortable at home. It was as if there was no place for her to be herself. It had never been like that with him. Now, when she missed the practical stuff, like him helping to bathe their daughter, fixing broken cupboards, doing the shopping, or collecting wood for the fire, she caught herself falling into the habit of pining for what once was, just in time to remind herself that they'd been heading for inevitable disaster.

He'd lied to her, plain and simple, and no matter how comfortable she was in his arms, she couldn't allow herself to continue to lie to herself. Accepting Carrie was still his wife would have been a betrayal of everything they'd built their trust on.

But she missed him.

She'd spent time with Fin, in hotels, here in her house, walking in the national park, getting to know one another, and she'd felt herself wanting to like him more. It was as if she'd forced herself to make another relationship work. But it was too soon. She wanted to experience life selfishly, without picking up the pieces for somebody else. After Fin, she'd promised herself that.

Besides, Fin Maguire didn't like kids. Lizzie irritated him.

It had been awkward at first when she'd suggested they call it a day. Her mother would have called their relationship 'flogging a dead horse'. He took it better than she thought he might, and their working relationship never suffered, and only Kate Umshaw knew the truth.

'I have no idea why anyone would want to hurt a child,' she said to Ted out of the blue. They dried pots together in the kitchen.

'What brought that on?' he asked her.

'I have no idea,' she said, smiling. 'I'm suddenly philosophical.'

'Be careful, a philosophical copper is an unhappy one.'

'Why? Because we never make a difference?'

'Something like that. If you stop too long to ponder all the pain out there, you'd never be able to do your job.'

'I get that. I see it all the time. Do you think people go through stages?'

'In their careers?' he asked.

She nodded.

He took a sip of red wine. They finished drying up and went into the lounge. There was no fire needed between May and

August. Her terrace doors were flung open, even though it was terribly late, and the light of the moon flooded through onto the wooden floor. Shadows of purple and silver changed the walls into a kaleidoscope of mystery.

They sat down.

'I think some cases always come along that affect you more than others.'

'Does it get to you too?'

'Of course. I'm not immune. I look at each one of the people on my slab and see the life they lived. It's an ending to one life and a gateway to the next. That's the way I see it.'

'Like religion?'

'Not necessarily, I just don't buy it that the end of our biological existence is the end of us. We are more than just our organisms. I see signs of people with superhuman strength fighting back in the face of unspeakable danger, and I just believe there's something else to us. A force that lives inside us that can't be destroyed.'

'Gosh, I like that,' Kelly said. She sighed. 'This country is so small. You would think there's nowhere to hide. Yet thousands of people simply vanish into thin air. They get erased from the face of the earth.'

'Is it a good time to suggest finishing that Netflix show?' he half-joked.

'The true crime one?'

He nodded.

They'd got into a show about serial killers in the USA and they critiqued it from the standpoint of their respective experiences. It was almost like a game for them, each bringing something different to the investigation in question. This was their Risk, their Monopoly.

'You know what they say about people who watch true crime in their leisure time?' she joked.

'Psychopaths? Yes, I've heard that. Well, I won't tell if you don't.' He winked at her. She yawned.

'Is it too late?' he asked.

She got up and flicked on the TV in answer and searched for the correct link. They were on part three of a seven-part series.

'Do you often wonder why these things are so popular?' she asked him.

He thought for a bit and then sipped some more wine. 'I think people love the brutality and the drama. Netflix is our circus.'

'Our circus?' she asked.

'You know, give the masses bread and circuses... It keeps them in check and all that. The Romans... People attribute it to Cicero, but I think it was Juvenal.'

'Who?'

'A satirist.'

'Hmm,' Kelly pondered.

'What are you thinking about?' he asked her.

She finished her drink and started the credits of the third episode. 'Conspiracy theorists.'

'Oh dear.'

'Aren't they the modern-day social commentators, a bit like your Juvenal? Social media rebels who challenge the establishment? After all, plenty of them talk about placating the masses.'

He stared at her, and she laughed.

'I know, right? This case has got to me. I did a bit of research on Hampton-Dent, and guess what I found?'

Ted waited. Kelly paused the TV.

'There's one podcaster in particular who is a thorn in the side of these big pharmaceutical companies. He has millions of followers; he's called the DiggerMan because he won't stop digging until he gets to the truth,' Kelly said with a grin.

'I like him already,' Ted said.

'I know, right? Well, he goes for Hampton-Dent regularly and they hate him. There have been a few lawsuits but he has money behind him and they haven't been able to silence him yet.'

'Silence him for what?'

'Accusing them of corporate manslaughter, illegal clinical trials, dodgy patents, it's all conspiracy stuff which can't really be proved.'

'So he's playing with fire.'

'Yes, but don't you find it interesting? I searched Jamie Robbins' name and he came up a few times; Joe Folly appealed to him publicly to be a guest on his podcast. Coincidence?'

Ted raised his tired eyebrows. 'I think it's time for my bed.'

'It's potential motive, Dad. Do you think there are people out there powerful enough to kill people who get in their way?'

'I think you're getting ahead of yourself. You don't seem to have a break from work nowadays.'

'Is this your way of telling me I'm turning into a sad loner who watches too much Netflix?'

He laughed. 'Perhaps.'

'Remember Colin Day?'

She referred to a local case – her first in Cumbria – when a man who controlled the narrative in local government and media turned out to be a money-laundering, people-trafficking murderer.

'Big Pharma is a thousand times more powerful than him. And they have way more money,' she said.

Kelly had seen the amounts of cash flowing through Colin Day's bank accounts and she shuddered to think of how a multi-billion-pound corporation could skew a narrative across media platforms. A seed had been planted in her mind, and she couldn't ignore it.

'Have you got any evidence?' he asked her.

She shook her head.

'I guess we'll know more once I perform the postmortem tomorrow.'

Kelly nodded.

She resumed the documentary.

'Let's finish this episode,' Ted said.

They fell silent as the murderer on screen closed in on his victim from a reconstruction. In hindsight, it was always so easy to warn a woman in danger to avoid certain hazards, particular pitfalls and lapses of judgement, but the whole point of programmes like this was to strike fear into women, not make society stop killing them. In Kelly's head, it wasn't the woman who walked alone, or took a risk, or failed to predict danger in her life who was at fault; it was those around her who failed to do anything about it.

Chapter 15

At 2 a.m. Kelly couldn't sleep. She'd shared almost a bottle of malbec with Ted and the true crime programme whirred in her mind as if she was on some kind of macabre roller coaster heading straight for doom. She'd ridden on plenty of funfair rides in her youth, and some more recently with Johnny at the fair in Kendal when they'd taken Lizzie. They'd shot pellets to win a fluffy penguin, they'd hooked plastic ducks to win a goldfish, which still swam in its bowl in the kitchen. And they'd taken Lizzie on the teacups, a ride so slow and tame that Kelly and Johnny had laughed at the absurdity. The throw-your-head-back laughs that people allow themselves when they exist in a moment of time and forget their worries.

She'd tried to turn over her pillow to the cool side. She'd sipped water and been to the loo. Nothing worked. The images of dead people remained steadfastly inside her brain. Stubborn like a nasty stain.

Eventually she gave up and her wide eyes stared at the curtains, where a tiny crack allowed the moon to taunt her further. She threw the covers off and reached for her phone. The blue light hurt her eyes so she switched to dark mode.

The information (little of it trustworthy or verified) that could be raked up in an internet search was chillingly bewildering to a police officer like Kelly. In the short years spanning her career, since starting out in Bethnal Green nick in 2006, she'd seen a beast emerge that was now uncontainable.

But it had its advantages.

She googled Jamie Robbins and settled in for the read.

Like so many people who underestimated the horrors of global connections, Jamie Robbins' life was easy to find.

Jamie's professional profile at Hampton-Dent had been updated to acknowledge his passing, but there was nothing about his cause of death. Nothing about suicide or accident, or homicide. *Died 15 July, 2025.* It was final and brutal. If Wiki said it then there was no going back.

Jamie Robbins had been raised in UK care homes. His was a rags-to-riches story. One of those feel-good memoirs to teach the younger generation not to scrounge. 'If he can do it, anyone can!' Jamie was the young Richard Branson of wellbeing. His game was supplements. His name was attached to some of the most famous food substitutes on the market and his personal wealth was valued at seventeen million pounds. Not bad for a twenty-nine-year-old orphan from the wrong side of the tracks. As she dug further, she got sidetracked with peripheral data. Paul Burlington, his partner, for example, was twenty-eight years old, and had a similar upbringing. The two young hotshots had been taken on by Hampton-Dent via their internship for kids from underprivileged backgrounds. Kelly raised a weary and cynical eye at the forced philanthropy of these big companies. Instead, she wondered what the company received in return, what control they held over these gifted kids who came from nothing.

The answer was always money.

Profit, growth, control.

Powerful people could get anything they wanted.

Her wider search of Hampton-Dent threw up more fascination for Kelly as somebody who never mixed in such circles. She'd only seen it, like most people, from afar, when they announced a scientific breakthrough, or a huge philanthropic vaccine programme for some developing country.

Hampton-Dent had been founded after the Wall Street Crash by two savvy New Yorkers who'd bet on the crash and made a killing. Waldo Dent inherited from his father and so a billionaire was born. The current CEO was his great-granddaughter, Tilda Dent, and Kelly examined her photo. It reminded her of those niche graduation books where the subject sat slightly to the side and attempted their best smile. Except if they turned out to be serial killers, then their college profile pictures turned out to be unusual, moody, or disagreeable in some way. Tilda's was an image of a classic homecoming queen, as Kelly imagined one. Big smile, excellent skin, and blonde shiny hair. She looked the picture of American wealth and status.

She found Hank Hampton's bio elsewhere on the website. The Hamptons had bought out Whalley Holdings in 1958 and they'd merged with the Dents in 1971. The company owned 10 per cent of the world's food suppliers and 15 per cent of farmland in the USA, as well as 12 per cent of the pharmaceutical industry.

Jamie Robbins had some power behind him and it begged the question why such a huge corporation would choose a small Lake District setting like Rydal Water for a conference attended by two of their most senior executives.

Then Kelly googled *YouthBlast* and a brightly coloured image of a plastic sachet filled her screen; above it was the FairGro logo. It was clever marketing. It looked fresh, vibrant and youthful. She wondered how much the design and marketing team had been paid for coming up with it. As a brand it gained permission to trade last year. The FDA in the USA and the Food Standards Agency in the UK passed the supplement for general consumption eight months ago. But she couldn't find any testing in the public domain previous to 2023.

There was an article on the benefits of the supplement written by Doctor Sandy Cooper. There were few links beyond that.

The ingredients list included the usual words which Kelly couldn't pronounce: synthetic vitamins, colours, 'natural flavourings', as well as some compounds which were trademarked. Deciding she was already down a rabbit hole, she googled them and found vague references to diuretics, hormones and organic plants grown in Peru. A tiny asterisk accompanied one of the chemicals and she squinted her eyes to search for the note. It took a while. She found it at the very bottom of the page, tucked away inside a minute footer with the Ts and Cs.

Neurohydroxy-14 performance compound. It came with a warning attached but for that you had to download an app.

She was none the wiser and got up to make a cup of tea.

Chapter 16

Melvin couldn't sleep either.

All the lights were off in his modest cottage at the edge of Rydal Water. He navigated his way in the dark, used to the touch of the furniture and the walls, and familiar with wandering round in the middle of the night when the memories were the most upsetting. He went from room to room searching for Ursula. Acorn stayed close to his side, and he looked down at her, realising she needed to eat.

'I'm sorry, old girl,' he said, bending down to stroke her.

He forgot what he was doing and flicked on some lights, finding himself in the kitchen. Then he searched for a packet of food for Acorn and filled her water bowl.

'Now, where was I?' he asked himself out loud. His disease was progressive, irreversible and untreatable, or so he'd been told.

It was at night, when it was silent like it was now, that he was at his most lucid and he remembered where he was. He recalled the conversation by the lake with Paul, and he recalled the female detective marching in like she owned the place. It made him chuckle because Ursula had been like that once. Bossy, powerful. Beautiful.

He walked into the sunroom, which was Ursula's favourite, and gazed out of the large window, overlooking where he knew the lake to be. It was in complete darkness now and all he saw was shadows but it wasn't unusual for him to steal moments like this when he was alone to assess his deterioration. They'd spent their life savings on the place. It had been a hovel. Doing it up had been a dream. Their project. They'd imagined a refuge away from the madness of the world and when they found it they thought the rest of their lives were sorted out. Until Ursula began to forget things. She'd sleep late. She burnt herself on pans. She forgot his birthday.

He'd paused the renovations while she got better.

But she never did.

This half of the house, facing the lake, had been completed, and he lived in here with her. He had a bed moved into the lounge and they spent their days in the sunroom if it was summer or winter. It was the view. It was mesmerising.

The fuss over at Heron Hall had been a welcome distraction in the least salacious way. It wasn't the death, the brutality or potential journalistic interest. It was simply that it gave him something to do other than look after Ursula. He overestimated how much she needed him. She did just fine on her own, but her silence made him feel guilty that he'd spent so much time away from her.

He remembered he'd made a cup of tea and he found it on the side, switched off the light once more, and took it to the window and gazed out at the blackness for a few minutes. Then he pulled a chair up to an occasional table and removed the potted plant off it. He sat his MacBook Pro on top of it and opened it and sat down.

'You look like you're looking for a conspiracy, Melvin Stone.'

He looked up, thinking he'd heard his wife. Her voice was smooth like the caress of wearing a cashmere scarf for the first time.

'I am, my love. You know me. I was there, Ursula. I saw him. He was only twenty-nine.'

When Melvin was twenty-nine, he'd been serving in Bosnia. Jamie Robbins was dead on a slab somewhere and he had no chance to grow old. It made Melvin melancholy suddenly and he reached for Ursula's hand.

He loved her more than the first day he met her, three decades ago. He grinned at himself, recalling some half-baked memory of them in Cyprus together. They were posted close to the green line in Nicosia. The war with Turkey had finished but hatred remained, like in all war zones, and the great city was a gateway between right and wrong. But nobody knew which was which. It was the same with his illness. His mind felt like a broken city, sliced in two. One minute he was Melvin Stone, veteran, husband of Ursula and retired, living his best life on the shore of Rydal Water, like Wordsworth. Every spring he took Ursula to see the daffodils across the lake and remind her how to live.

'I've got so much to tell you,' he whispered to her. 'I'm almost there,' he said. An imaginary shaft of sunlight warmed his face and he closed his eyes and sat down in his favourite seat close to the window.

He imagined Ursula standing before him, willing him to live, or die, but to at least make a decision and he grinned. He was terrible for procrastination. Bourbons or custard creams, he could never decide.

'I really need you now, Ursula my love,' he whispered again.

Going back to the MacBook, he settled down to write finally, adding notes to a Word document that was already fifteen pages long.

An alarm sounded on his phone, and he went to the kitchen to prepare Ursula's potions for the morning. A bird sang outside and a new day was creeping across the lake above the trees. It was this time of day that the coffin bearers carried the dead to Grasmere for burial a hundred and fifty years ago because the ground at Rydal was rocky and unsuitable. He imagined strapping lads, about the age of Jamie Robbins, with coffins digging into their shoulders, perhaps with a pony for company, making their way come rain or shine, across the rugged terrain to respect those who passed on. He walked Acorn along it most days looking up at Nab Scar and Loughrigg keeping a watchful eye on those below as they had done for centuries.

Ursula used to come too.

He looked down at the bottles and packets in the emerging light and felt an urge to read the labels of all the drugs she was prescribed but he got himself into such a muddle and dropped a few of the packets. Then he turned to the chair Ursula always sat in and realised that she wasn't there. It was too early for her and she spent most of her time in bed now.

He saw that some pills had scattered across the floor and got down on his hands and knees to pick them up. Dust and cobwebs clung to his fingers and he worried about his knees. A spell of dizziness gripped him and he sat down for a rest.

What had he been thinking about?

Paul Burlington. Jamie Robbins. The young man's face, full of youth and ambition.

Why did he feel he knew him? Perhaps Ursula would know.

Thinking of her now, guilt piled onto the emotions he already felt and he sat quietly contemplating what they'd sacrificed.

He'd been told that the drugs prolonged her life, but for what? So she could gaze across the water and see what she couldn't achieve for the rest of her life? He couldn't really tell if she was happy. But she'd trusted him like a small child trusts a parent. They'd come here together happy and fit. They'd taken the money, built a life, thinking their futures made.

Had Jamie Robbins made the same mistake? Who had he trusted? Did that faith kill him like it killed his wife?

The realisation hit Melvin like a rocket and his cognition collided with reality. He looked at one of the bottles on the floor and saw that the use-by date had expired years ago.

Ursula was no longer with him. There was no bed. No favourite chair and no walks along the coffin trail.

He slammed his hand into a cupboard and red-hot pain cut into it and he cried out because he now remembered with vivid clarity that Ursula was dead. She'd passed a long time ago. His habit of forgetting was a side effect of the treatment but the lapses in and out of certainty took their toll on him and he lowered his head into his hands. The one he'd injured throbbed in agony but at least it reminded him of the truth. Now the long loneliness hit him and he realised he'd rather forget. He'd prefer to be somewhere else most of the time. Even though Paul had looked at him curiously as if he were a mad man and he repeated and embarrassed himself.

Which was better? Presence and incurable torture, or blackout and perpetual confusion? They'd taken her away and she left an abyss in their home. This space was different but the same and it would be forever hers. As the light crept across the floor and illuminated the small kitchen, he cried and wished she was here with him.

Nothing was the same.

Chapter 17

Kelly's team assembled at 11 a.m. on Wednesday. Kelly walked to her seat at the head of the table and put her coffee mug down on a coaster with a slogan on it. It said, *I'm a police mum, like a regular mum with back-up*. Millie had bought it for her for Christmas. It reminded her why she caught bad people, to protect the good ones at home. People shuffled papers and the mood was sombre. They waited for her to take the lead. They had little to go on with the Water Nymph case but Kelly was more hopeful they'd get to the bottom of what had happened at Heron Hall. She'd caught perhaps two hours' sleep eventually in the dawn light and by the time she woke up she wanted more.

They were a small unit in the North Lakes and they were tight as a result. Familiarity sat comfortably alongside their inquiries and the atmosphere was hushed but serious. This wasn't the Met, where murder was standard.

Kelly had given her pound of flesh to the capital city. She'd dreamt of joining a murder squad in the Met. Now she was thankful that her job wasn't overwhelmed by evil. All crime was challenging to police, but back in those days in the capital city, she'd lived, breathed and consumed murder. Here, they were more used to burglaries, domestics and road traffic accidents. That wasn't to say they weren't prepared. They'd had their share of serious inquiries, but they weren't faced with it every day. A murder changed the flow of the office. Suicides just depressed them.

Today they potentially had both.

'I'll start with the death of Jamie Robbins because there's more to go on,' she said.

'Because it's more fun that way?' Kate lightened the load and everybody relaxed.

'I heard the roads around Rydal were choked this morning,' Dan said.

'Rubbernecking in the extreme,' Emma said.

'I don't think they're there just for the coffin trail,' Kelly added.

'And they're decamping to that posh castle in the middle of nowhere?' Fin asked.

He referred to Tilda Dent's intention to take her executives to the huge estate of Dow Bank House near Grasmere to recover from the shock.

'Why don't they just fly back to the USA?' Kate asked. 'Why hang around?'

'Respect? I don't know. They don't strike me as sensitive types,' Kelly said.

'Was he drunk, boss?' Fin asked.

'Apparently not but we'll have to wait for the tox results.'

'What kind of party was it?' Dan asked.

'It wasn't a party,' Kate replied. 'It was a conference for health and wellness.'

Dan snorted into his coffee and Emma covered her mouth. Kelly recalled how she felt when she got a whiff of the stuff when she'd been pregnant and the nostalgic feeling of nausea caught her by surprise. Cigarette smoke had the same effect. Now she quite liked it when Kate came in after a sneaky smoke.

'The coroner still hasn't made a decision on cause of death, because we didn't find anything concrete yesterday, so we don't know the circumstances surrounding Jamie's death. So I'm treating it as suspicious because the coroner is. He'll be autopsied this afternoon. The evidence suggests a scuffle, either in his room or in the corridor, or both, but we're sitting on this information for now. None of the guests mentioned hearing it so far. I'm going back there today if nothing else comes up.'

Jamie's picture was projected onto the whiteboard behind Kelly's head. The photo they used was a professional one. In it he beamed at the camera, as if preparing for a high-level meeting about funding for his first big gig. He looked innocent and earnest. His teeth shone, his hair was neat, his shirt was crisp, and he looked as though you could trust him with anyone's daughter, or half a million pounds. The squeaky-clean image didn't marry with the porn haul though, and it worried her. Something about his character didn't add up.

'Don't let looks fool you,' Kelly said. 'His bosses suspected significant recreational drug use, also he was ruffling a few feathers in the industry.'

She tapped a few keys and links came up behind her on the whiteboard. One of them was the solicitor's emails referencing several litigation claims about corporate manslaughter. Another was a photo of Joe Folly.

Kelly considered the jobs she'd dish out to her team today and studied her little band of trusty combatants. Within budgets squeezed as tight as a courtesan's corset, and morale as low as the tide in Morecambe Bay when the cockles come up to feed, anyone willing to commit to the task was, in her book, a hero.

Emma Hide was her young feisty terrier, but she was intelligent too and that surprised and disarmed people. Dan was her Glaswegian hound who couldn't be knocked off a scent. Fin was all Irish charm (didn't she know it), with a serious underbelly of grit. Kate held them together like the mother hen she was, and Kelly steered the ship.

'Meet the DiggerMan,' she said.

They stared at her.

'You know him?' she asked.

Dan and Emma nodded.

'He's brilliant, he talks about the most amazing stuff and he's got millions of followers,' Emma said.

Kelly felt old and out of touch and wondered where her youth had gone. Earning a wage and raising a child, she guessed.

Perhaps the DiggerMan was somebody she might have followed before she grew up, when she lived in London with her flatmates in Bow Wharf.

'I was researching all these influencer types and he popped up. He's got a lot to say about Hampton-Dent and I think he's worth looking into. On one of his YouTube videos he publicly appealed to Jamie Robbins to be a guest on his podcast.'

She waited for the information to sink in. They were beasts of a different realm nowadays, with the onslaught of the digital space, and policework couldn't ignore it.

'Dan, Emma, I have no idea how to find a podcaster who is a digital nomad and could be anywhere in the world, and who might not want to be found. This guy is almost invisible. Litigators can't even pin him down and Hampton-Dent are eager to silence him for some reason. I want you to find him.'

'On it, boss,' they said together.

'Fin, I'm leaving it to you to chase forensics; there are a few results I want ASAP.'

'Didn't you say people heard him cry out, boss?' Fin asked.

'Yes, exactly. The coroner wants a full picture before he'll rule one way or the other. I'm expecting results for fibres from the hotel bed, fingerprints from items in his room as well as his luggage. The smashed glass has been dusted and we need to trawl through any CCTV to look for anyone wearing a purple scarf during the event. And then there were the muddy shoe prints inside his bathroom that didn't match his own, they looked like CAT Boots to me. Jamie was a size eight and these were much bigger; the SOCO thought about a size ten or larger. The porn has been sent to specialists. We're hoping to find some kind of source for the hefty collection. It seems like overkill to me. Why drag all that to a hotel for a four-day event?'

More additions popped up on the board as she tapped her computer.

'How long are we expecting the tox results to take, boss?' Emma asked.

Kelly shrugged. 'The coroner has called the lab to expedite. I'm heading off to chat to him after he's finished with the autopsy.'

She drew breath.

The lack of sleep and the buzz in her head about her research made her twitchy and she fiddled with the ruby ring on her right hand. Being so close to a pregnant woman, and the fact that Water Nymph had carried a child too, made her sentimental.

'So. Water Nymph.'

A picture of a grey squirrel appeared on the whiteboard alongside the young woman with porcelain skin and stained fingers. It was greeted by a ripple of good-natured laughter.

'This is Skippy. Found alongside the deceased.'

A sachet of *YouthBlast* popped up at Kelly's bidding and she tapped on her computer keys.

'No ID. She was dressed plainly and could be waiting staff. We're appealing to all Lakes hotels for missing person reports, starting with ones in a ten-mile radius. Autopsy confirmed sexual assault. She was also pregnant.'

She let the news sink in. Emma hadn't officially informed her of her pregnancy yet but there was silence and Kelly saw Dan reach under the table to find Emma's hand.

'Now, you should have all received a separate brief on the business interests of Jamie Robbins. This is his product.'

She turned their attention to the bright green and orange sachet of *YouthBlast* on the screen and Kelly told them about the wonders of the supplement industry.

'That's all bollocks, boss, excuse my language,' Dan said.

Fin laughed.

'Language excused, Dan,' Kelly said. 'The point isn't if it's bollocks or not, the point is this. Skippy here was found dead next to Water Nymph, and he was lying on top of one of these sachets.'

She held a sachet of *YouthBlast* up for them.

'Skippy and a sachet of this stuff have been sent for testing. My gut is telling me they're linked to the Heron Hall incident, because it's not yet on the market for public consumption, so whoever dropped it for Skippy must have been at the conference. But first we need to find out who this woman is.'

'That girl is Millie's age,' Kate said. Nobody told her not to bring her personal life to work. Nobody told her to concentrate on the job and not make it emotional.

Everybody understood.

Death was personal and it was emotional.

That's what made a good copper: compassion. Gallows humour aside, they were good at what they did because they kept a healthy distance while at the same time caring.

Life taken when it was so ungrown, so unlived, was such a shocking tragedy. It wasn't that any death mattered more than others; it was just that somebody so full of potential and so innocent made more of an impression because she was so helpless. Young female victims always presented as powerless. No weapons, no defence, nobody to protect them. Alone. Vulnerable. Hunted.

'Has the public appeal flagged up anything?' Kelly asked.

'There is news, boss,' Emma said. 'We might be on to something. There's a hotel that contacted the incident room just an hour ago. It's a small place over at Skelwith Bridge. A guesthouse. The owner rang in after seeing the story on the news, and said he's worried about a young woman who checked into the hotel on Friday and her room is empty. A young Caucasian woman, around twenty years old, with black hair. The manager said she looks like the girl from the sketch. She's also an artist; it's what she told him she was there for, to draw. With charcoal.'

It was hopeful news but they were cautious.

'Transient workers walk out of shit-paying jobs in the Lakes all the time,' Kate said.

'Exactly, that's what I thought, but the owner said that a man had escorted her there and asked him to keep the girl safe and, I quote, "anonymous",' Emma said, reading from notes.

'That's odd,' said Kelly. 'Who was the man?'

'He didn't know but said he can describe him.'

'And?'

Emma checked her notes. 'White, late twenties, business-looking type, fancy car.'

Kelly's stomach felt full of clay. 'What type of car?'

She thought of Jamie Robbins' M4 coupe BMW sitting in the carpark at Heron Hall Hotel.

'This is where he got excited. It was a very expensive beamer. Grey. Red interior. He remembers it so well because he poked his nose in through the window when the woman was dropped off on Friday.'

'If you were after anonymity, why would you drop her off in a top-of-the-range beamer?'

'You know it, don't you? I know that look,' Dan said.

Kelly brought up a picture of Jamie's car on the whiteboard. 'This is Jamie Robbins' car. Emma, can you check with the owner of the hotel to see if he recognises it? What's it called?'

'The Old Man Guesthouse.'

'Cute.'

Skelwith Bridge was a base for climbers wanting to tackle Coniston Old Man. Kelly had been up there countless times. It was one of the most beautiful and interesting walks in the Lake District. The roads were narrow but an M4 could navigate them. It would also stand out like a sore thumb. People who drove cars like that usually stayed in the higher-end establishments like the Lodore, or the Gilpin. Tourists who arrived in such style rarely sought out the havens of hiking and were more interested in the fudge parlours of Windermere. If it was Jamie Robbins' car and he was concealing somebody – perhaps a lover – why did he show it off?

'Things just got interesting,' Kelly said. 'As far as my inquiries go, Jamie Robbins wasn't dating anyone, but let's keep our options open. It could turn out to be a coincidence. Emma let me know if the guesthouse owner recognises the car. In the meantime if anybody has a burning desire to observe an autopsy, the bus is leaving in half an hour,' she added.

She had no takers. Most coppers avoided them like the plague. If she was honest with herself, if it wasn't Ted Wallis conducting it, and he wasn't her dad, then she probably wouldn't attend either. She dismissed the briefing group and made a quick fresh coffee before she left. As she waited, she googled Jamie Robbins on her phone, but this time instead of concentrating on his business history and his impressive CV and climb to power, she searched his private life. Lovers, escorts, socialites, artists.

His family. They'd picked up a few details from witnesses, and they knew he'd spent his early life in care. Wikipedia pages were always sanitised versions of true life, but Kelly read between the lines. He was born in Slough, and his parents were civil servants, but they'd died in a car crash when Jamie was seven years old.

Then, bingo.

He had one sister, but there was no name, so she googled 'Jamie Robbins' sister'.

A single photo popped up, with a name. Jamie looked so young in the image, and he had his arm around a young woman with black hair, who stared at him adoringly.

They looked ecstatically and unapologetically happy and Kelly felt a sudden gut-sapping punch of grief as she stared into the face of Angelina Robbins.

The caption said it was a photo of the 'business entrepreneur' Jamie Robbins with his sister, Angelina, at Nobu, three years ago, celebrating the takeover of FairGro by Hampton-Dent for twenty million pounds.

She marched back into the incident room and called everyone together. She connected her phone by Wi-Fi to the whiteboard and brought up the snap of Jamie and his sister, Angelina.

'What do we think?'

'Holy fuck, that's her,' Kate said, speaking for all of them.

A searing muteness caught them unawares until Emma said quietly, 'That's Water Nymph.'

Jamie Robbins' autopsy could wait. Kelly needed to get over to the Old Man Guesthouse in Skelwith Bridge.

Chapter 18

'How's Lizzie?'

Kelly drove and Fin kept her company. It was his turn to support the boss. Her morning plans had just changed dramatically, and they headed to Coniston. It was a good opportunity to check in with Fin and make sure he was content with their new arrangement but her mind was on Angelina Robbins and why two siblings had met violent ends a day apart.

She'd resisted introducing her daughter to Fin for months, but it had been a chance meeting in Keswick when she'd been out with Ted that had finally led to it. Lizzie had been toddling along talking about dogs and ducks – the most important topics to a toddler on a day out to a lake – and Fin had happily chatted with her. In fact, he seemed to get along with her daughter better than he did her in the end, despite saying he didn't like kids. His irritation was perhaps a ruse to protect himself from commitment, she decided in the end.

She concentrated on the road. 'She's good.'

She filled him in on the milestones her daughter had reached and bored him with the details of mushed-up food and hilarious mishaps that had happened since they'd called it a day.

'You know you can come and see her anytime,' she said.

'Yeah, I know. I always think of it and then I get another shift at work. My boss is a bitch.'

'Is she now?' She side-eyed him.

They were comfortable in each other's company. It had always been that way. It was calming listening to his southern Irish lilt. He had a beautiful voice. He was handy to have around for a tricky arrest. He always knew how to disarm even the most aggressive pricks they had to deal with. His size helped too.

They chatted about other cases, and he filled her in on the timings of expected results from the labs they used around the area. They were spread far and wide across Cumbria depending on what they required. It wasn't every day that they sent forensic evidence off for testing – that process was wildly expensive – but sometimes, to progress an investigation, they had no choice. All departments were surviving on the skins of their bare arses, but until Carleton Hall shut her down, she'd carry on investigating the way she'd been taught.

'Have you seen many suicides, Fin?'

'My fair share, like. Fecking selfish if you ask me.'

'Really?'

'Yeah, I get that it's awful and tough for somebody with nothing left, you know, but it's worse for those poor bastards left behind.'

They heard a notification ping, and Kelly recognised it as her email.

'Can you check my phone? I'm waiting for the passport office to get back to me about Angelina Robbins.'

Fin reached into her bag, and she told him her password.

'Anything on here I shouldn't see?'

'Fuck off.'

'Righty-ho.'

He opened her email as Kelly navigated her way around Ullswater. They would be over the Kirkstone Pass soon and she tapped the wheel impatiently. It was moments like this that she felt lucky to do what she did. Having to travel around the Lake District was one of the best aspects of her job. Catching bastards was better.

'Yep, it's her. They sent her photo and address.'

'Well, well. So, now we need to find out what she was doing there at the same time her brother was twenty minutes away at a conference.'

'So, he flies in from New York, let's say they haven't seen one another for a while. They catch up and he deposits her in a hotel in secret.'

Fin referenced the owner of the Old Man Guesthouse telling the police helpline Angelina checked in anonymously at the request of the BMW driver, who handed over a wad of cash for his silence.

They both said what they were thinking at the same time.

'He gave her something to hide.'

'Says here she lives in Chapel Stile,' he said.

'That's five minutes from Skelwith Bridge, so why stay in a hotel?'

Kelly reflected on how easy it was working with Fin. He'd made six months of her life more bearable, and they'd had fun. She had no idea how or when she and Johnny had ever lost that, but they had. With Johnny she'd become a woman who worked pretending she wasn't a mother, and parented pretending she didn't work.

Kelly's foot pressed a little harder on the accelerator. Coniston was a beautiful drive, but the lanes were narrow and wound like a spring. The trees were tinder-box dry, and the lake was woefully low, like they'd all been last summer when they'd found the body in Thirlmere, exposed by the drought.

Fin called the SOCO who'd been appointed, and they chatted on speaker; it was the same SOCO who'd processed Heron Hall. The forensic team was already at the guesthouse.

'I've had ID confirmed. The victim is the sister of Jamie Robbins,' Kelly said on speaker.

'What? Did I hear you correctly?' the SOCO asked.

'Yes, you did.' Kelly gave the SOCO the details and warned her she might be walking into a murder scene. Angelina could have been abducted or held against her will. The woman's room could be a treasure trove of evidence. Jamie had wanted her there in secret for a reason, and she'd been found out. Perhaps. Kelly's mind raced. 'A squad car should already be there. The owner only reported her missing this morning after the appeal went out so I have no idea who else might have been in her room.'

She ended the call and silence sat between them. Scenarios filled her head, and she was aware of Fin deep in thought too.

'Just because they were siblings, and he was trying to hide her, didn't mean they loved or even liked each other.'

She nodded her head. They couldn't jump to any conclusions.

One image kept coming back to her, though. The sight of Angelina's body and what Kelly knew she'd been through in her final moments. Life hung across such a delicate balance of minutes and seconds. If only Angelina had gone for a walk. If only she'd taken a lover back to her room. If only…

If only Jamie had stayed with her.

But it didn't work like that.

Maybe Angelina did take somebody back to her room, and it turned out to be her killer. Then it struck her that Angelina's body had been found on Monday and Jamie jumped from the second floor of the Heron Hall atrium on Tuesday.

He could have been her murderer. But first, they must discover why he was hiding her.

Chapter 19

The Old Man Guesthouse turned out to be an old water mill sitting abreast a pretty stone bridge over the River Brathay. This part of the Lake District was quieter due in part to its inaccessibility and tiny little narrow roads which led to the Furness Fells. The houses there were built from local slate, which had been mined since the twelfth century. Coniston Old Man still had scars of the mining industry and Honister was a working mine selling about ten million pounds worth each year. It left the surrounding countryside nestled inside a bygone era. Building was difficult because of the protected status of the land and the rugged nature of the surrounding forests and hills.

In short, it was a stunning getaway, and it jarred Kelly to be here for a murder case.

The Langdales were just along the valley, past Chapel Stile, and Angelina would have known this part of the Lakes well.

They knew little about Angelina Robbins, and that's what they hoped to change today. She'd instructed Kate to lead a team to her private residence too.

The guesthouse was privately owned, which made it uniquely intimate. Kelly guessed that's why it was chosen.

They were expected, and Kelly saw a forensic van parked in the small carpark. The SOCO was already here, having a head start on them from the scene in Grasmere, and she and Fin got out of the car and made their way to the entrance. A young receptionist looked worried and was trying to balance guest queries with managing the movement of forensic officers around the communal spaces. A couple of uniforms had done a great job managing the situation, but the young woman looked tense. She promised to find the manager and Kelly chatted to one of the uniforms in the meantime. He told them that they'd taken a statement from the staff on shift today and they'd secured the contact details of others who weren't here today but who might have come into contact with the young woman in room 13.

A man older than Kelly expected approached and held out his hand.

'Sorry about the intrusion,' Kelly said. She introduced herself and Fin and the man told them the whole thing was bringing on his eczema.

Kelly apologised again.

He introduced himself as Tommy and explained that room 13 was upstairs.

'It's a beautiful place you have here, Tommy,' Kelly said. They followed him out of reception and upstairs. The floor creaked and the ceilings were low. 'Did you meet Mr Robbins, who checked his sister in on Friday?'

'I did. I admired his car. It was a limited edition. We get wealthy folk here, but he was on another level.'

'Really?'

'He paid in cash, and he gave me brand new-notes, in twenties. He paid for the room for six months, upfront, no questions.'

'Right. That's a long time. Were you aware of why Ms Robbins was staying so long?'

'I told your lot on the phone. She was private. Secretive, you know? My wife thought she was pregnant.'

When he said the word, he hushed his voice, like old people did when a woman was with child out of wedlock. Kelly's mum used to do it. That generation were almost gone now, and it saddened Kelly that some of their sayings were too.

'So, she didn't work for you?' Kelly asked.

Tommy laughed. 'She didn't need to work, the way her husband flashed around the cash.'

'Her husband?'

'The guy in the flash car.'

'Oh.'

'He had work to do and was coming back for her. Has he been told she's missing? Poor sod.'

'Actually, Tommy, I've got terribly sad news. The young woman was called Angelina, and she was found dead in Grasmere on Monday.'

Tommy stopped. 'Oh, my Lord, that's just awful.'

'And Jamie, the man who paid for her room, was her brother. I was hoping you could help us piece together her time here.'

They carried on walking, but Tommy's shoulders sank a little lower. Then he stopped.

'*Was* her brother?'

They paused in the corridor; there was no easy way to say it.

'That's how we found her. He passed away yesterday and it led us here.'

'How terribly sad. I thought they were a couple. Here we are,' Tommy said, stopping outside a door, a little less bright than he was outside. Bad news did that to people: it let air out of them and made them smaller.

'He told me she was here to paint. She was an artist. That's what he said.'

Kelly recalled the dark inky substance on Angelina's fingers.

Room 13 was open and the SOCO was inside. Tommy glanced around and shook his head. They thanked him and he left the same way he'd come, no doubt to deal with inquiries about why the police were crawling all over the hotel. She hoped he didn't lose business over it but there was little she could do.

They pulled on gloves and masks and covered their shoes.

Their first impression was that room 13 was a mess. Drawers were pulled out, the bed was in disarray, glasses were smashed, the contents of a wardrobe were scattered all over the floor, and the TV was cracked. The SOCO stepped over some of the detritus and greeted them.

Kelly spotted a heavy lamp stand on its side and knew she'd found the assault weapon. Remnants of what looked to her like human tissue clung to the base and Kelly reckoned the broken shaft might be responsible for the hole in Angelina's hand. Her throat constricted and her stomach tightened as she imagined a sustained aggressive attack on Angelina in here where there was nowhere to hide.

'This would have caused a hell of a noise,' Kelly said. 'And yet nobody heard a thing.'

'The interesting stuff is in the bathroom.'

Kelly's heart sank. She followed the SOCO to the small bathroom and was shown pooling stains in the shower cubicle. They were brown and dried.

'I've done prelim swabs. Kastle-Meyer test was positive,' the SOCO told her.

The test was the most common indicator of blood at a scene when it couldn't be seen easily with the naked eye. It was obvious to Kelly that some form of liquid had been spilt and smudged all over the bathroom, but they must be certain. It could turn out to be coffee.

They all knew it wasn't.

'Did you see the lamp?' the SOCO asked. Kelly nodded gloomily.

'I've given it a cursory examination and it's also positive for blood protein, and somebody tried to wipe it off. I guess whoever did it panicked. It's not clean and tidy. It's not professional. She fought back. She crawled here and here.'

Kelly wracked her brain to see if there was any scenario that would make sense to her that Jamie had done this and then killed himself.

There wasn't.

The SOCO walked her through the trauma blow by blow.

'Then she fell here, hitting something on here.' She pointed to the bathtub. 'Then there's handprints here and here. Finally leading to the inside of the shower cubicle where blood pooled significantly.'

'This explains why there wasn't much blood at the dump site,' Kelly said.

'Poor bugger. It looks like she died here. All the splatter and drop patterns suggest the same thing.'

Kelly glanced at her feet. 'She wasn't dead when she was dumped. I attended the autopsy yesterday. She drowned.'

'Oh Christ. Bastard.'

Kelly stared at the floor.

'Are those prints?' she asked. The SOCO nodded.

'They look similar to our prints at the Heron Hall Hotel, but then generic men's boots are notoriously common at crime scenes,' Kelly added.

'We've scanned them,' the SOCO confirmed.

'Anything else? I'm looking for a paper trail; it's a possibility she was hiding something here and died protecting it.'

The SOCO nodded. 'No laptop or electronic equipment, that explains that then. No phone. We'll continue looking. Thanks for the heads-up; we're taking down the panels on the wall.'

'What panels?'

'Look.'

The SOCO led Kelly back to the bedroom where Fin was chatting to an officer. They were peering under the bed and the forensic officer had pulled it up, supporting it with his strength while Fin looked underneath. There was a large hole in the mattress and Fin pulled something out and held it up.

'What is it?' Kelly asked.

'It's a slim box file.' Fin opened it, and inside he found several neatly arranged folders. Kelly followed the SOCO, who removed a panel in the wall closest to the bed.

'How did you know that was there?'

'The owner.'

'Tommy?'

The SOCO nodded. 'Tommy told us that the room was booked specifically because of the legend of the place.'

'Which is what?'

'Skelwith Bridge is haunted by those who travelled by coach through it on the way to steal mining secrets for Queen Elizabeth the First, four hundred and fifty years ago. They bunked here for the night on their way back and their whole coach fell into the river, and they drowned.'

Kelly blinked and spread her hands. 'Who knew? I suppose this story is on their website, luring unsuspecting tourists to pay for a tour and buy merchandise?'

'Obviously,' the SOCO chuckled.

'So, what has that got to do with this room?'

'Tommy told us that one of the mining experts got away but was tracked down by German mercenaries and shot with a pistol and buried in these walls. There you have the legend of Skelwith Bridge.'

'So, this spy stayed in room 13?' Kelly asked. Her voice dripped with scepticism. 'Next you'll tell me he consorted with witches too, who stayed in room 666.'

The SOCO shrugged. 'Some people believe anything.'

'OK, joking aside, Tommy told you Jamie Robbins knew about this legend when he booked?'

'That's what he said.'

'And have you found anything in there?'

'We did.'

It was said with triumph.

The forensic officer showed Kelly a bagged suitcase. It was almost identical to the one found in Jamie's room, but she guessed this one wasn't full of porn. Now she wondered whether the one in Jamie's room was a decoy. If anyone went to Heron Hall looking for Jamie and his secrets, they'd find a bag full of porn instead of what they were really looking for.

'Did you look inside?'

'Yep. We haven't had time to look closely. Loads of scientific papers and some letters that mean absolutely nothing to us but I'm pretty sure they'll be valuable to you. Also, we reckon about five hundred thousand in twenty-pound notes. Oh, and some incredible artwork.'

'Nice,' Fin said.

'Well done, good work. God, what a mess,' Kelly said.

She looked around the spacious room and peered out of the window. In ordinary times, this room – except for it being haunted by a Tudor spy – would be a perfect getaway to relax surrounded by the beauty of the Lake District. Today it was a murder scene.

And they now had a potential motive.

Before she left, she went to find Tommy, who was sitting in the pretty garden at the rear of the hotel, staring across the river.

'Hi, Tommy,' she said gently.

He moved up and she sat next to him on the bench.

'I hate being the bearer of bad news,' she said.

'Poor lass. It's so sad.'

'I was wondering if you saw or heard anything strange in the village recently? Anything. If you think of anything, please give me a call. You know, a stranger acting nervously or loitering, that kind of thing.'

Tommy shrugged his shoulders. 'We have tourists from all over the place; they're all a bit weird.'

She laughed. 'I believe you.'

'But I guess there was one thing. There was a bloke who was walking Potter at the weekend, Saturday I think.'

'Potter? Is he a local chap?'

'He's a dog.'

'A dog?'

'The post office dog.'

Kelly was puzzled.

'On Saturday, I saw him with a bloke I'd never seen before. I shouted out, because Potter wanted to come over here, I could tell.'

'And that was strange?'

'Yes, because when I went over to the post office on Monday, I asked Bill, and he said Potter had gone missing for most of the day on Saturday and they'd never heard of the bloke I described.'

'And who was he?'

'No idea. Big bloke. It was difficult to see his face because he was wearing a baseball cap.'

Chapter 20

The mortuary at the Penrith and Lakes hospital was characteristically chilly not simply because it was effectively situated underground, like a morbid cave, but also due to the industrial-grade steel which never heated up, along with the fridges and freezers which stored body parts. But Kelly looked forward to it as she parked in the central carpark of the hospital, which got more expensive by the week; she'd left Fin at the Old Man Guesthouse, evidence gathering, and he'd agreed to hitch a ride back with the SOCO.

Kate was at Angelina's property in Chapel Stile. So far there was nothing to report. It was a typical abode of a tidy and organised woman with an art studio, full cupboards of organic food, and no evidence of foul play.

The café in the hospital foyer was bustling like always but recently she'd also noticed that the corridors were filling up with people waiting on wheelchairs, trolleys and mobile gurneys. The hospital was at breaking point, but doctors and nurses walked around the place as though it was normal now. The whole affair was depressing.

Ted had once told her that the unhealthiest places on earth were hospitals, and fit people should avoid them like the plagues they spread. She held her breath until she got past a man who was coughing loudly and headed to the lift which took her down two levels to the bowels of the building.

She greeted several of her father's assistants who she'd seen only yesterday. Cadavers generally arrived here because of unexplained fatalities, and it was the coroner's job to give the families an answer. Too many people were dying of flu, especially for summer. She knew it bothered her father, who wasn't getting any younger. But today was different.

She kept her jacket on and had brought a thin sweater from the car which she'd slipped on underneath it. Too many times, she'd been caught inside the mortuary freezing her nuts off. In summer it was an escape from the furnace-like heat above ground when a flash heatwave took hold. Britain wasn't built for heat and the mortuary provided a welcome blast of refrigeration.

She'd spent the journey to the hospital listening to a podcast from the young Londoner who called himself the DiggerMan. She felt behind the power curve after discovering the young podcaster's fame and status and it spurred her to do some catching up.

Joe Folly, originally from Clapham, had dropped out of college to travel the world, then he'd got into conspiracy theories and interviewed big names about clinical negligence, political corruption, globalist elites and official scandals.

He rubbed lots of important people up the wrong way.

Kelly liked him.

Dan had singled one episode out and sent it to her, telling her it was a must-listen. It featured several guests talking about Hampton-Dent and they'd mentioned the new thrusting executive, Jamie Robbins, and how they thought he was selling out. They had to be careful with their language because of slander laws but she got the impression from the guests that they'd been told (and this was where it became simply hearsay) that Jamie was known for possessing more respectable ethics than the ones held by Hampton-Dent. Kelly thought about it and wondered if Jamie had listened to what was said about him. Had he felt ashamed?

Did his work for the supplement industry jar his moral code?

She'd also learnt that Jamie was on record questioning the safety of mRNA vaccines (short for messenger ribonucleic acid). Apparently, this was highly controversial because conspiracy theorists said it manipulated DNA and caused cancer. But that wasn't all. Joe and his guests discussed other less well-known technology that was hidden in the injection that was made up of nanoparticles of plastic that could assemble inside the body. From there, it could be remotely controlled from outside the human body with a 5G network.

It was sci-fi worthy stuff, and Kelly was highly sceptical. It was the kind of theory you'd find in a dystopian novel, but she was also open to persuasion, and nothing was off the table now, given she had two bodies in her father's mortuary. These were very clever people and the DiggerMan had gone to ground for a good reason. If the police found it impossible to trace him then he must have hit some raw nerves. In her experience, investigative journalists didn't put themselves in danger for the fun of it; they knew something.

Secret technology was a motive for murder, that much was for sure, but the story was fantastical. A professional hit was a consideration she must bear in mind. But in front of so many people? In Kelly's mind, it would be so much easier to take out somebody like Jamie in a back street in Miami, than in a hotel full of adoring guests in a tiny little village in Cumbria. It didn't make sense. She also must consider if Angelina's murder was connected to her brother because of what he did, and what he was hiding. Joe Folly might be able to tell her.

She also noted Joe's tone when he talked about Jamie, as if he knew him, even as if they were buddies. There was affection and humour in his voice, then he said, 'I'll ask him next time I see him.'

It was a throwaway comment that was hidden in the banter of the moment. Easily missed. As if it wasn't there.

But Kelly had heard it and it mattered.

It mattered a lot.

Kelly found herself sucked into a world of intrigue and high-stake lies. Mysteries worth dying for. By the time she walked into Ted's theatre, she was mulling over NGOs and how they paid off local corrupt officials in faraway lands and got away with it. There was a whole world out there she didn't understand and discovering it was like being sucked into a huge hole.

One thing she did know was that Joe Folly was a likeable and highly articulate rogue with a platform which gave people a voice.

And that made him dangerous.

She kissed her father.

'Dad, have you heard of mRNA?' she asked.

'Yes, it's being used in vaccines, isn't it? I don't trust it, I'm afraid. Many of my colleagues think it's gene altering and should be well avoided.'

'I think it's a bit late for that. It's in circulation already.'

'I know.'

'You know?' she asked.

'I keep up to date with my journals. Why?'

She looked at the cadaver under a sheet, assuming it was Jamie.

'Because he was on record saying exactly the same thing as you.' She pointed to the sheet.

'Oh,' Ted said. 'Brave man. Do we think that's why he "slipped"?'

'It's possible. Have you heard of nanotechnology?'

Ted stopped his prep and stared at her oddly as if warning her of something.

'What?' she asked.

'Be careful,' he said.

'I am.'

'You know what I mean. Hampton-Dent? That's money we can't imagine. It's government-level wealth.'

'Not our government, Dad, we're broke, remember?'

He chuckled. 'Right-ho. But seriously, the things you're talking about have been developed in secret – some say – and used as population control.' He lowered his voice.

'What?' she said. She was incredulous. They sounded like a pair of co-conspirators, like the DiggerMan. People who broke the establishment. People who were in danger.

She looked at her father.

'Do you believe all that stuff, then?' she asked him.

'What stuff?' he asked as he prepared his kit. Goggles, saw, cutting equipment, GoPro camera, blocks, probes, forceps and needles.

'That it's true? That some vaccines have bits of tiny plastic in them capable of being activated by wireless 5G towers?'

She grinned but her face slowly fell as she saw the seriousness of her father's face.

'There's little proof but I've seen all sorts of things found inside the dead in this room, Kelly.'

'You can see it?'

Kelly imagined her father pulling a remote control out of someone's artery.

'No, not like that, just clots that shouldn't be there. Long strings of plastic that don't belong in bodies. The embalmers see it all the time now.'

'Why didn't you tell me?' she asked.

'I didn't think you'd believe me,' he said simply.

Then he got to work.

Chapter 21

The sight of Jamie naked and exposed was a sobering reality check. It reminded her that we're all the same when we die.

Kelly perched on the same steel stool as yesterday and watched Ted switch on his mic. Their conversation sat between them.

'Ready for this again?' Ted asked.

She nodded. 'I'm good.'

'You don't look well; are you feeling a bit peaky?' he asked as he looked inside the horrific wounds to Jamie's upper torso.

It was her father's way of telling her she looked like shit.

'I'm not sleeping,' she told him.

'Par for the course in an investigation like this,' he said.

She nodded.

She'd seen mangled bodies plenty of times before but having just listened to Jamie being discussed so vividly on a podcast made her tremendously uncomfortable. She felt as though when alive, he had been a player on a stage, like somebody's puppet, and he'd walked blindly into danger. Or perhaps it wasn't blind. Why else hide his sister with a huge suitcase full of documents?

Kelly was a realist. Some might say a cynic. Her mind was analytical and logical. She must be convinced of something before believing in it. She was a fan of conspiracy theories because most of them were entertaining and scandalous to contemplate, but that didn't mean she believed them, not because they didn't make sense but because they were often debunked by experts. Conspiracy theorists were treated as nutcases, outsiders, charlatans and weirdos.

But the DiggerMan didn't come across that way and neither did the people discussing Hampton-Dent.

They were convincing.

So was her father.

She acknowledged that the Twin Towers turning to dust when they were made of solid steel was weird, and JFK being assassinated by his own government was shocking, and chemtrails were real, but the moon landings being faked and flat earth theories discredited themselves before they had a chance with a mainstream audience. But she'd always had affection for loners. Those with enough courage to stand up to the crowd. That was what DiggerMan did. He used his voice for the people who couldn't. That was what was so special about the internet. Social media allowed ordinary people to be part of the conversation without the establishment interfering, and that was what appealed to most people with a rebel inside them, like Kelly.

But was there more to it other than clickbait and sensationalism?

'Are you all right?' Ted asked her, jolting her.

She realised she was staring at the body.

'It's such a waste, isn't it? He was so successful and clever.'

Ted stared at her. 'You know a fair bit about him already then?'

'Somewhat. It's a reminder that life can be snuffed out any minute.'

'Isn't it just? I have no idea how I've lasted so long,' Ted said.

'Don't talk like that, Dad. You are everything to me and Lizzie.'

They shared a rare moment of emotional exchange. It wasn't that their relationship was sterile, anything but. Ted threw Lizzie around screaming, onto sofas and rugs, and she chased him around the park in Keswick on market days. Their life together was vital and growing in energy by the day as Lizzie became a toddler. But these quiet moments where Kelly told Ted how precious he was were rare. She understood how little time he had left compared to what had gone before, and they were playing catch-up.

She'd only discovered her true paternity a couple of years ago. For forty years she'd believed another man was her blood father. They'd lost so much time. Which was one reason she turned up to so many of his autopsies. It might seem macabre, but it was time she could spend learning from him, watching him, loving him.

The man on the slab told them everything they needed to know about how transitory life was.

'And this is the young woman's brother, you say?' Ted looked at Jamie. She nodded.

'How terribly sad. Is it a domestic do you think?' he asked.

'I'm not sure. She was hiding away in a hotel in Skelwith Bridge for a reason.'

'Ah, the German spy of Skelwith Bridge!'

'You know it?'

'Of course!'

'Apparently she asked to stay in the exact room.'

'Do you think it's significant?'

'I'm not discounting it. Anybody who hides something purposely in the room occupied by the ghost of a spy deserves attention to me,' she said. 'Not because I believe in ghosts but because they did.'

'Quite. Well, he hid out in Rydal Caves if that means anything to you. I read local histories when I get the chance.' He winked over his mask and she smiled at him. They got back to the man on his slab.

'Falls are brutally violent,' Ted said, beginning his examination of the body. He walked around it and observed the corpse. Kelly watched him and imagined Jamie in life, persuasive, cogent, winning.

A brother.

Ted spoke into his mic. Two assistants busied themselves.

'Extensive blunt force trauma. Multiple injuries consistent with a fall from height of approximately thirty feet. Impact site appears to be the cranium and left shoulder. Visible evidence of defensive preservation wounds on both hands and wrists, indicative of trying to break his fall.'

He looked up at Kelly.

'Is that conclusive?' she asked.

'Not one hundred per cent. However, it's what I look for in suicides, because genuine ones give up and don't try to break their fall.'

'Christ, is that true?'

'We can only go on the data. On average, accidental falls are more survivable because people try to protect their heads. I'm sorry, it's not a very pleasant conversation for a Wednesday evening is it?'

Kelly listened to the list of terrible wounds, and it was moments like this that she knew a spirit – the essence of somebody – had left a body. Jamie's body was simply a pile of flesh and bone lying on the gurney.

'Does what you know about him lead you to see this as a desperate conclusion to a psychological problem?'

She considered his explanation and decided that no, from what she knew about Jamie Robbins so far, he showed no signs of mental disorder.

'Three in four suicide fatalities have tried before,' he said.

'Jesus. He doesn't fall into that category either.'

Discussing suicide stats was probably one of the more rigorously cheerless topics she'd contemplated lately.

'Forty-four per cent have a mental illness,' he carried on.

'This is where your psychological autopsy comes in?' she asked him and he nodded. He'd explained to her that though you couldn't prove without doubt that somebody did not actually jump from height, the behaviour of the person in the run-up to the incident often was the biggest indicator.

'Subarachnoid haemorrhage, cervical spine fractures, rib fractures and numerous fractures of upper body appendages.'

She found Ted's voice soothing despite the topic of the monologue.

'It's as if he dived off the banister,' he said.

She waited for him to explain.

'If he fell over the lip of the wooden rail, his body would have flipped, like an acrobat. It indicates that he had no time to do that. He went straight down.'

'Witnesses heard him shout out.'

'Are you sure it was him?'

'Not one hundred per cent.'

'Because that would indicate him being conscious and further support the defensive injuries. He landed awkwardly, but then thirty feet isn't a long time to think about what's happening. We both agree that the banister was almost impossible to fall over, especially if you've stayed in the hotel three nights already, and the items indicating a scuffle, I think, give you your answer. I'd treat this as homicide unless more evidence comes to light. That's what I'll write in my report, so you have my verdict, for now.'

Kelly chewed her lip and nodded.

Two homicides, three if she counted the baby.

'If there was a scuffle inside or outside his room, and he fought with someone, perhaps that explains why the Clem Allins meditation he was listening to was paused? He wasn't expecting somebody. The conference was busy. Anybody could have entered the hotel and gone up to the second floor.'

'Quite. OK, let's turn him over.'

An assistant helped him turn the body and Kelly looked away. It felt improper for her to watch as Jamie's exposed flesh was dumped so unceremoniously on its front, like a wet seal. When she looked back, she could see huge blood pooling and discolouration and was reminded just how quickly a human body deteriorated once it had expired. It was in the process of consuming itself right now and Ted's job was to investigate the clues left behind before it turned to biological mush. Nature sure did a fine job of cleaning up after itself, but when a human soul was involved it wasn't easy to appreciate.

She turned away again as Ted took samples from crevices and orifices, then examined Jamie's nails and hair. She found it incredible that Ted still knew what he was looking at when he rummaged through Jamie's broken scalp.

'Did you see this?' he asked.

Kelly went to the body and Ted showed her Jamie's right hand. His forefinger and middle finger seemed to be welded together with glue.

'He grabbed something before he died.'

'Or as he was dying?' Kelly asked.

Ted prised apart his fingers and revealed a small torn strip of purple material.

'Gold dust,' Kelly said.

It looked as though it came from the torn scarf they found outside his room. The purple one which had been tossed aside, as if by accident, but now Kelly knew that the wearer had contact with Jamie as he slipped.

Or was pushed.

Chapter 22

The following day was Thursday but weary as she felt, Kelly pushed on with the investigation, as did her team. She drove back to Heron Hall with Emma first thing and they faced a full day of interviews there.

The VIPs from Hampton-Dent had decamped to the glorious estate of Dow Bank House and Emma said it was a pity they weren't going there to conduct interviews. Kelly agreed.

'I imagine it to be like Downton Abbey,' she said as Kelly drove.

'How are you feeling?' Kelly asked.

Emma hadn't officially announced her condition. Now was her chance.

'You've guessed?' Emma said.

'I'm thrilled for you both. I just want to keep an eye on you, that's all. How far are you?'

'Fourteen weeks.'

Kelly smiled. 'Past the big scan then.'

'I couldn't sleep last night. It was too hot; I feel as though I'm giving birth to a pressure cooker not a baby.'

Kelly laughed.

Ever since she'd discovered Emma's secret, she'd looked at her in a new light. The rosy cheeks, the thick waist, the hot flushes and the sprints to the toilet.

'But you don't need to worry about me. I'm pregnant not broken,' Emma said.

Kelly recalled her own pregnancy spent rushing around the Lakes chasing leads. The only change to her routine was waddling into an ice-cream shop for a fat cone dripping in caramel and raspberry sauce.

Nothing else changed. Except she was dog tired.

'Is Dan excited?' she asked.

Emma smiled broadly. It said everything. She changed the topic back to the case.

'What struck me most about the people I interviewed at Heron Hall on Tuesday was their air of certainty. They're not easy to read. They've been striking deals their whole working lives and I guess it's hard to just be themselves. They're real hardballers,' she said.

They parked up outside the entrance and noticed the lack of cars compared to last time. Jamie's M4 was still there, and it'd be towed to the compound for forensic examination on Monday if they were lucky. The hotel looked different somehow, though nothing had changed. But without the buzz of people milling about down by the lake, or lights on above the atrium, it seemed abandoned, but it could just be her imagination.

Sandy Cooper should be waiting for them.

Doctor Cooper was a scientist, not a sales rep, so Kelly expected to get straighter answers from her; however, a check of her work history showed that she'd been employed by Hampton-Dent for thirty years and she also liaised with legal and HR. It was an odd collection of hats and Kelly assumed it was one of those situations where a very experienced employee is trusted with more than the remit of her exact role. It happened less nowadays but Sandy was in her fifties and a product of the market before over-regulation.

Her role fascinated Kelly and she wanted to get to know more about her. There was no doubt of her value to the company, and she'd left her stamp on patents going back to the 90s. She'd also been one of the only two people to try to help Jamie in his final minutes. Even though she'd been useless in her anguish, she'd at least shown she cared for him and Kelly wondered if they'd been close. In the footage of the incident, Sandy had been covered in Jamie's blood.

Emma was tasked with finding Lee Lovett and Kelly found Sandy Cooper in the conference room, sitting alone, looking out of place. Kelly didn't see a wedding ring, though that was none of her business. Sandy struck her as somebody who played fast and low. Kelly smiled and thanked her for meeting her for an informal interview. Kelly sat down.

'Coffee?' Kelly asked.

'I've had enough coffee to send me to the cardiac ward,' Sandy said.

Kelly got a whiff of cigarettes and thought it was a good job Kate hadn't returned with her – she'd be envious, for sure. Kelly was surprised Sandy was a smoker. These days, especially being a supposed health expert, it was hugely unpopular. But apparently coffee was bad for you too. Kelly already knew that if you took every piece of advice offered, you'd not only cease to exist, but also suck every last bit of joy out of life to boot.

Kelly possessed a healthy dose of scepticism when it came to wellness advice. She'd noticed in the few years she'd been back from London that her health had improved. It wasn't as if she'd been unfit in London, just her skin had brightened, her pallor shone, her personal bests had improved and she breathed easier and slept soundly, even with a two-year-old waking her up at odd times. There was definitely something to be said for the Cumbrian regimen of fresh air, exercise and local food. But she knew that the sort of backward beliefs that provincial folks spouted wouldn't convince these cutting-edge corporate animals wanting to sell pills and gels over Keswick cheese and butter.

It wasn't worth arguing with these people who spent their lives on synthetic pick-me-ups.

'Can you explain to me your role in Hampton-Dent? You're a scientist, is that right?'

Sandy Cooper nodded. She told Kelly that it was her job to oversee the efficacy and safety of the myriads of supplements marketed by Hampton-Dent.

'So, you legitimatise the product with scientific backing?'

'If you want to put it like that, yes.'

'Did you encounter any problems with *YouthBlast*?'

'No, all standard stuff, I've been doing this for years.'

Kelly got up and walked to the flip chart and stood next to the poster that Tilda Dent had showed her yesterday.

'It just strikes me as significant that Jamie was doing so well, especially with this new product that was being championed here, and that drew your most senior execs from across the pond. I guess I'm looking for a reason Jamie might abandon his dreams.'

She held on to Ted's assessment that Jamie's death was a homicide for a little longer.

Sandy shrugged. Kelly reckoned the woman was more used to running meetings than being the subject of them. Tough luck. She'd come across tight-lipped interviewees plenty of times in her career and most of them didn't like her. But that wasn't why she was here.

'How well did you know Jamie?'

'He was a colleague. I get to know my colleagues on a needs basis. If I need some information, I associate with them. If not, I don't. We weren't drinking buddies.'

'I watched the footage; you were hysterical over him.'

'Footage?'

'Somebody recorded it, after he fell.'

'What the fuck? Give me a name; they'll be off the Christmas list by close of play today.'

Kelly didn't like the woman's attempt at grim humour. It was inappropriate.

'I'm afraid I can't. The investigation is ongoing.'

Sandy Cooper looked mad. Kelly changed the subject.

'You gave a lecture yesterday?'

'I spoke to the delegates at around three p.m.'

'And did you see Jamie?'

'No. He was busy preparing for his own keynote speech.'

'I've been told that he watched your speech.'

'Yes, he did but I had no interaction with him. It was busy; we had things to do.'

'Of course. You were launching *YouthBlast*, right? And you're a hefty shareholder in FairGro? I did my research.'

In fact it was Dan who was compiling the money trail and collecting the information on Hampton-Dent employees.

'I have chosen a maximum pension pot, yes. I have no husband or kids to think about, just my retirement to a villa in the Caribbean.'

'That sounds nice. Is it a tight unit? Hampton-Dent? Are people close, or is it typical of a large corporation where people don't recall names?'

Sandy laughed. 'It's global; we employ around twenty thousand people.'

'Got it.' Kelly got a pad out of her bag and began to take notes. 'I'm getting the impression Jamie had everything to live for, career-wise.'

'Yes. He was happy. Or at least I thought he was.'

'So the keynote speakers didn't interact much? What did you do at night? When I've been to conferences we sit in the bar chatting, getting to know our colleagues,' Kelly said.

Sandy eyed her. 'I knew Jamie well enough. He was in his twenties; he wouldn't want to hang out with oldies like me.'

'Right. Did you stay in your room all morning, then, on Tuesday, preparing for your talk?'

'I stopped for a few breaks. I avoided the communal eating spaces. I didn't socialise with anybody really. I talked to the catering manager a few times; we had a few cigarettes together outside.'

'Oh yes, Lee Lovett, the conference and banqueting manager?'

'Yes. We went for a walk around the lake, to the caves.'

'Rydal Caves?'

Sandy nodded.

'You said you were practising your speech.'

'It's not far; I needed a break.'

Kelly sensed a shift in the air. The room suddenly felt stickier and the atmosphere close. Why a scientist would go for a walk to a beauty spot with a catering manager was a mystery.

'Was Mr Lovett off shift then?'

'It was before he started.'

'You got close during the conference? Sharing cigarettes, visiting tourist spots?'

Sandy smiled. 'I'm a free woman. Lee is a gentleman.'

'Of course. I'm just trying to place everyone. So, after the caves, you went back to your room alone?'

'No, Lee came with me.'

Kelly watched the scientist. For somebody so measured and in control, her behaviour struck Kelly as risky, but the woman had an alibi. If they were working on an assumption that Jamie was pushed after a fight, then whoever did it had left clothing in the corridor and wore muddy boots too big for Sandy Cooper, who had been busy shagging the conference and banqueting manager. But it also didn't escape her attention that whoever pushed Jamie would have left trace evidence on him, and Sandy Cooper had that covered because she'd thrown herself at him when he was dying on the floor.

Cute.

'So, you gave your speech at three p.m. How did Jamie seem after?'

'Snappy.'

'Example?'

'I saw him arguing with Tilda – she's a CEO of Hampton-Dent.'

'Yes, we've met. What time did your speech end?'

'Four.'

'Long speech.'

'It was well received.'

'Did Jamie congratulate you?'

'Yes, he did. He said it helped his vision immensely. He wasn't a man bent on killing himself. He was hungry for the future. You think you know someone…'

Kelly nodded in understanding. Enough people had told her exactly the same thing.

'So, what happened after four o'clock?'

'I was hungry so I thought I'd grab something from the buffet. That's when I went downstairs.'

'And that was what time?'

'About five.'

'And you were in your room all that time?'

'Yes.'

Kelly noticed no flicker of hesitation. Not one sniff of vagueness.

'Right. And so you went downstairs.'

'That's when it happened.' Sandy looked up at the ceiling as if she might find answers there.

'Did you notice anyone missing from the conference during the day at all?'

Sandy looked at her suspiciously. 'I didn't see Paul.'

'Paul Burlington, Jamie's partner?'

'Yes, they were inseparable. He wasn't here when the police came. When everybody was screaming and running around, trying to figure out what the hell happened. He wasn't here.'

'And Joe Folly, have you heard that name? Or the DiggerMan?'

'The what?' Sandy chuckled.

'It's his podcasting name,' Kelly said.

'Oh. No, who is he, is he here? He could have been invited as media.'

'I doubt it; he was digging, excuse the pun, into the damage pharmaceuticals cause people. Were you aware you were facing litigation from several sources?'

'At our size, somebody is always suing us for some unfairness.'

'Oh, my mistake, I thought I saw you listed as a liaison for the legal department during a couple of personal damages cases over the last couple of years.'

'Oh, yes, right, that. I give advice on the scientific bit.'

'Jamie was dealing with a few litigation cases; I've seen the emails. He cc'd you?'

The vagueness was back but the demeanour was just as tough. However, Kelly saw that her foot was curled around the chair leg so tightly, the skin around her ankle was changing colour.

'I work for a pharmaceutical company; people sue us all the time.'

'Sure. Was Jamie worried about any of them?'

'The cases? Not that I recall.'

'Right. Can I ask you one more thing. Did you know Jamie's sister?'

'His sister?'

'Yes, Angelina.'

Sandy shook her head and kept the rest of her body very still. 'He had a sister?'

'Yes, she was staying not far from here, in a hotel, paid for by Jamie. So, you never met? He never introduced any of your colleagues to his family?'

'No.'

'It's just that Angelina was found murdered on Monday afternoon and I was hoping somebody in the company might be able to cast a little light on who might have something against both brother and sister.'

Kelly saw the colour in Sandy's cheeks change.

'So, you're saying they were both murdered? Dear God.'

It was the first indication of true emotion Kelly had seen from the scientist.

But it was unconvincing.

'I've got a couple more questions. I believe Mr Hampton and Ms Dent have headed over to Dow Bank House?'

'I believe so.'

'Did any delegates go over there this week? Security staff, admin staff? Anybody?'

Sandy shrugged. 'There is a skeleton staff kept there to get it ready for events like this one. I'm also heading over there this afternoon, I think. I can ask.'

'And will the close protection detail for Hank Hampton be there?'

'The heavies?' Sandy laughed.

Kelly remained serious. She didn't find it funny, not since one of them was a person of interest to her. Mercedes man.

'They come everywhere with us.'

'Is there any reason one of them might have been anywhere else? Like Skelwith Bridge, for example.'

'Where?'

'It's where Jamie's sister was staying.'

'Oh. I doubt it. They stick to Hank and Tilda like glue.'

Chapter 23

The hotel was down to a skeleton staff and Kelly thanked a young waiter for bringing more coffee. The server worked silently as if he was being paid overtime at a funeral wake. Kelly decided she didn't give a stuff what the experts said about coffee, she wasn't giving it up anytime soon. The smell of the recently ground beans filled the room and comforted her with renewed strength. It was a good job Emma was elsewhere. A call from her father grounded her further after feeling unsettled from her chat with Doctor Cooper. It wasn't that Kelly was intimidated by the older woman whose presence sucked the air out of a room, more that she got the impression that Sandy Cooper was lying.

'How's Lizzie?' she asked her dad.

'She seems hot, but she's in my arms and sleeping,' he told her.

The contrast between their jobs and their personal lives couldn't be more brutally on display in that moment, she thought.

'You spoil her; she deserves you.'

'Don't be too late,' he said, but he knew as well as she did that it was out of her control. She would leave when she was done.

Ted always managed to cheer her up. He helped her out in all sorts of ways without even realising he was doing it. He helped her financially on occasion, though it hurt her pride. He eased her burden without her ever asking for it. He saw her struggling on her copper's wage and spoilt her. She'd put the money from the sale of her mother's house into her current property and she loved it there. Since Johnny had moved out, she'd shouldered all the bills, and it was tough. Ted stayed over regularly and insisted he was merely paying his way, but he left little gifts around the place, replaced firewood and arranged workmen to fix things.

They were a small but tight family and Josie – Johnny's daughter from his previous relationship with Carrie – still visited during her university holidays. They were truly modern and blended. Now all they needed was a dog. A pooch like Melvin Stone's would do nicely, one that sat and grinned all day, and was a constant companion.

They said goodbye and Kelly turned her attention to Paul Burlington, Jamie's business partner.

She smarted at how much these people were worth on paper. Kelly couldn't imagine spending millions of pounds, or even having it at her disposal. A holiday a year might be nice. A decent car, a new kitchen would be lovely, but at the moment all she could hope for was managing to pay her gas bill, which had gone up again, feeding Lizzie real food without going bankrupt, and paying her ever-increasing mortgage.

These people had so much money they must get lost in counting it, she thought and it begged the question yet again why the conference was held here in the first place. Highflyers usually chose places like New York, Hong Kong, London or Singapore. They could have gone anywhere. The reason she'd been given was that the UNESCO status of the Lake District promoted connection to nature, which was spot on trend for their brand. There was also the Dow Bank House association. It made sense but something still nibbled at her.

She turned when she heard a noise, expecting Paul for his interview, but instead Emma joined her in the conference room.

'How are you doing?' Kelly asked her.

'This is my least favourite part of an investigation,' Emma confided.

'You have a favourite part?'

'I mean talking to witnesses in an enclosed space like this. It's impossible to know who's telling the truth and they've had a few days to make up fiction.'

Kelly nodded. It was unavoidable. Discovering the ID of Water Nymph had drawn their resources elsewhere.

'Who've you spoken to? Some of the staff?' Kelly asked.

'The awful American woman giving orders out, it wouldn't surprise me if she's told them all what to say.'

'Tilda Dent? I thought she'd gone to Dow Bank House.'

Emma shrugged. 'Well, she's still here.'

'There's a lot at stake; she must be nervous,' Kelly said.

'They act so sycophantic around her, like they're celebrities. Something about this feel-good conference doesn't sit right with me,' Emma said.

'What exactly?'

'I spoke to a couple of YouTubers who just left for Manchester Airport and I saw they had sachets of *YouthBlast* tucked into their bags. I asked if they found it effective. They laughed and looked at me as if I was an idiot. "We don't drink this stuff," they said, "it's just for Reels" and walked off.'

Kelly perched on a table next to her.

'And that old guy, Melvin Stone? He's back with his dog. He's waiting for you, he said.'

Kelly raised her brows.

'What I don't understand is why they came to an average hotel in the middle of the Lake District for a conference attended by so much wealth you could write off the debt of an African nation between them,' Emma said.

'Average?' Kelly asked.

'Not for us, but to them, this is so… basic.'

Kelly contemplated what she said; Emma was right. It chimed with her earlier misgivings.

'Do you think it's a bit hidden away for a reason? Why not hold it at Dow Bank House?' Emma asked.

The mention of the luxury estate got Kelly thinking.

'Because it's all a façade? They don't need the money or the exposure,' Emma said.

'But they need the legitimacy,' Kelly said. 'Why?'

'Did you see the catering? I mean, I know the staff have tried hard but these people are used to private jets flying crab a thousand miles for a snack. You know I once heard Barbra Streisand actually does that; she has this favourite crab place in Miami and she flies it to LA.'

'Goodness me, that's true?' Kelly asked, incredulous.

'It's true.'

'I can't even afford bay shrimp bussed in from Morecambe,' Kelly said.

They laughed.

'What were you watching when I came in?' Emma asked.

'Clem Allins.'

'Who?'

Kelly turned her phone around. She'd googled the guru as she waited for Paul Burlington.

'The spiritual guide Jamie was watching before he died.'

'Ah, him.' Emma nodded.

They looked at the screen and Kelly pressed play. The sage was a small thin man with tiny spectacles and messy hair. He looked of Indian origin.

Kelly informed Emma of the man's background as they watched him practising meditation whilst in a distinctly impractical yoga pose.

'Born and raised in Canada, to an Indian mother and American father, he travelled extensively and dropped out of his engineering degree at Stanford. After wandering for ten years, he wrote a book and it sold ten million copies.'

'I think there was a poster of him up in the lecture hall,' Emma said.

Kelly raised her eyebrows. 'He's done some work for Hampton-Dent too, group wellness retreats, according to their website.'

'It's such a cliché isn't it?' Emma said, which took Kelly by surprise because she thought, unlike herself, Emma was the type to buy into this stuff. They watched him on screen and Kelly felt her eyelids grow heavy. Clem Allins spoke about contemplation, his voice was calm and demonstrably zen, he wore loose clothes and changed position like an elegant leggy giraffe gliding across the plains. He lurched and dipped.

'That's quite beautiful,' Emma said.

Kelly stared at her. Hormones got to every mother in the end. Even ultra-fell running legends weren't immune and Kelly felt rather relieved that it wasn't just her who turned to mush because she was pregnant. She put her arm around her junior and squeezed her.

'Has this case changed your view of all this wellness stuff?'

Emma laughed. 'Dan's always telling me they're full of crap, these self-styled teachers. And their supplements have the same additives in them as kids' sweets, but I take them mainly on long endurance runs, which I'm not doing at the moment because I feel so shit. I'm a sucker for a good ad campaign, what can I say, but yes I think it's made me wary.'

'Answer me this,' Kelly asked. 'Why do fit and healthy people like you, and all of these people here, need reminding to keep fit and healthy when you already do it?'

'Because they sell health, they don't practise it,' Emma said. 'We're millennials; we fall for branding and believe we need something else to make us whole.'

Kelly stared at her. Now she understood why Sandy Cooper didn't practise what she preached. The reality of a fairytale was never the same as the promise.

Did Jamie's rose-tinted spectacles fall off?

'What does that make me? A dinosaur? I thought I was a millennial.'

'I think you're the tail end of Gen X. You're... sturdy.' Emma winked.

Kelly pretended to slap her playfully. She hopped off the table and looked at her notes.

Then her phone buzzed and it was Fin.

Kelly answered it chirpily.

Fin had returned to Skelwith Bridge this morning to continue the inquiries around the local area.

'I'm at Angelina Robbins' cottage in Chapel Stile,' he said.

'Something come up?' Kelly asked.

'Well there are photos of her with Jamie everywhere; I think it's safe to say they were close.'

'Good, anything else?'

'There's a photo attached to the fridge with a magnet that I think you should see; I've sent it to your phone. Jamie bought this place seven years ago. Her studio is full of incredible work,' Fin added.

'It sounds like it's a tough visit,' Kelly said. She acknowledged that rifling through the detritus of somebody's life after they'd been brutally murdered wasn't easy. 'Wait, I've just got it.'

Kelly switched screens and opened the text from Fin.

She stared at the photo and called Emma over, who joined her.

On the phone, staring back at them, smiling, happy, ecstatic even, were two friends – more than friends – hugging and carefree like two young lovers on holiday at the height of their passion. The stage of a relationship when each laugh at the other's little annoying habits that with age grow divorce-worthy. It was two people who looked as though they were about to spend the rest of their lives together.

'That's the DiggerMan,' Emma said. 'With Angelina.'

'I know. It's Joe Folly.'

Chapter 24

Tilda Dent was packing her own suitcase to take to Dow Bank House. Her personal assistant had gone ahead with the bodyguards. She hadn't wanted to join the others just yet but the detective downstairs needn't know that. She was tired of answering questions. It was all so confusing and the female policewoman seemed to think they were all hiding something. In New York, nosy cops were paid off with trips on yachts and tickets to Broadway. Here, the female cop seemed to be fixated on digging deep like that fanatical podcaster who refused to disappear.

A light tapping on the door made her pause and sigh. All she wanted was a minute alone. The conference had ended in disaster and she'd have to explain to the board of directors if their stock price took a hit. The best policy was keeping it quiet. In a backwater like this, only local journalists would be interested in the story; it was in everybody's best interests to make sure that's how it stayed.

'Come in!'

Paul Burlington opened the door and poked his head around it.

She smiled. 'It's you.'

He closed the door behind him and walked to the window.

'You know, it's only five weeks until launch now we can go ahead,' she said.

He looked depressed, like a puppy who can't jump high enough to get on the sofa.

He came close to her and put his hands onto her face. She couldn't stand it. It was a habit of his to enclose her, to capture her, and to consume her. At first, his enthusiasm had intrigued and seduced her but now she found it suffocating. She shrugged him off.

'You're upset?' he asked.

'I'm still at work, Paul; I need to figure out how to contain this thing before it goes viral. Did we request a media blackout?'

'Yes, but the police have requested some of the phones. Apparently, there's footage of the lobby when he fell.'

'Jesus Christ, really?'

Paul nodded.

'Who has it?'

'The police, at the moment.'

'Who recorded it?'

'Don't worry, she's been blacklisted already, and she's in trouble with the police.'

'Good.' Tilda sat on the edge of her bed and put her head in her hands.

'I believe it's police protocol to wipe any evidence they find. I've got people working on it,' he said.

She got up and paced up and down and he smiled at her. She stopped.

'How can you be so nonchalant? You're as chilled out as Clem after a pill, for God's sake.'

'I wouldn't know,' he said, still smiling.

'Oh come on!' She laughed. 'You'll try anything, but I guess you don't need it when you drink so much of that disgusting drink. Give me strength! Stop staring at me like that. Sex is out of the question.'

'Is it? We've nothing else to do but fuck. What better excuse do we have other than we're trapped here together until it's time to leave? Hank has gone, the heavies have gone, Jamie is gone…'

'Has she interviewed you yet?'

Paul shook his head.

'Surely you're needed down there? Are your hands shaking? How much of that have you had?'

She referred to the sachets of *YouthBlast* he guzzled as if it were going out of fashion. A part of her felt guilty for what they were doing to him, but her job was to monitor not mother him. A tiny shaft of lust filtered through Tilda's groin, and she found herself reciprocating his grin.

But a phone call pierced the mood, and she hesitated for a second before answering it. Paul walked to the balcony and opened the sliding door. The view from Tilda's room was spectacular. It wasn't the Alps, but beauty didn't always have to be big; it could be small and quiet, like this minute little lake hidden away from everything. 'What a place to die,' he whispered.

Inside, Tilda listened carefully.

'Yes, I understand that, so pay them more. Everybody has a price. Failing that, threaten their families.'

She hung up and joined him on the balcony.

'You love it here?' she asked him.

'It's so peaceful. Who was that?'

'London. They're sending a couple of suits up here to make sure we get NDAs from all the delegates and media-bots before they leave.'

'Good idea. What about the ones who've already left?'

'I spoke to each one personally.'

'So, we have several hours to kill,' he said.

She pressed a button to close the blinds, and darkness fell upon the room. Only a shaft of sunlight and a warm bedside lamp illuminated their bodies as they came together and silently began to undress.

Paul's skin was already wet with perspiration, and she slid her hand up his back.

'It makes me sweat,' he said.

'Not much longer now,' she said, soothingly.

Chapter 25

'Mr Lovett, please sit down. I'm sorry we're meeting under these circumstances; I've always wanted to come and stay here,' Kelly said.

Paul Burlington was nowhere to be found so she decided to speak to the conference and banqueting manager, who was next on her list. Emma had gone to locate Jamie's business partner in the meantime.

'I'm assuming you don't want a cup of your own coffee?'

She smiled and saw him visibly relax. He was nervous. Lee Lovett looked stressed, as he might. A man had died horribly on his watch. The general manager seemed to expect a lot of him in his absence, she'd gathered.

Lee Lovett sat down and examined the folds on the tablecloth, then he peered underneath at the carpet. He seemed to be looking for signs of vacuuming that met his expectations. It seemingly did because he was happy for a moment, until a shadow returned to his brow and he looked at Kelly.

He wrung his hands and Kelly remembered in the video that Jamie's blood was all over this young manager. It was the kind of traumatic event that haunts dreams.

She would know.

Blood smelt like iron, like the earth. Like the lake. It was fresh, alive and viscous – everchanging. It felt oily and warm. She watched him and he confirmed he didn't want coffee. They chatted about how long he'd worked at Heron Hall and what he knew about the guests and generally about Hampton-Dent. Which wasn't much.

'It's all mumbo-jumbo,' he chuckled.

He was charming and good-natured.

She wondered how he was treated by the elite. Was it Elon Musk who took potential employees for lunch to see how they treated service staff? It was an excellent judge of character. She recalled summer jobs in hotels and how vile a few of the guests were to her. On the whole, they were generous and engaging but some could be tricky and rude, as if they were superior to those attending them.

'Have tips been good?' she asked.

He looked caught off guard which was exactly what she wanted.

'Yes, actually. Very good. Some of the guests are very wealthy.'

'I know.' She paused. 'It can be overwhelming. You were the one who held everything together, by all accounts. We have specially trained officers you can speak to about the things you saw. I know it can wreak havoc on your mind.'

He stared at her.

'I bet you've seen plenty,' he said.

She nodded.

'Do you get used to it?'

'No.' She answered honestly. His transparency was disarming and she could see why Sandy Cooper might show interest in him. Doctor Cooper was a rebel; that much was clear from the fact she wandered around at the edge of the lake puffing on cigarettes at a health conference. But she doubted somebody like Sandy Cooper would be serious about this gentle man in front of her, and Kelly felt a pang of maternal protection towards him. Doctor Cooper would eat him for breakfast and by her own admission, she already had. She had no idea how many times these two had snuck away from the conference to jump into bed.

'What did the coroner say?' he asked her suddenly.

'He'll reserve his findings until he's completed his report.' She remained tight-lipped.

'Of course. I was in shock. I said some things perhaps I shouldn't.'

'Don't worry, your statements on the night will be investigated in context. Witnesses say all sorts of things in the moment.'

She knew he referred to his initial statement to the first uniforms on the scene when he told them he didn't believe Jamie Robbins jumped, which was what got their attention in the first place.

'Some witnesses have reported a noise before Mr Robbins hit the floor, like a shout or a cry.'

'Yes, I think he did shout. It was like a wail, as if he was scared. I suppose I would be if I fell like that.'

'And you saw no one upstairs with him?'

'No.'

'Anyone acting strangely?'

He hesitated before he said no this time.

'And you took Ms Cooper to the Rydal Caves that morning?'

He coloured and looked down at his hands. 'Erm, yes. It's the biggest attraction around here.'

'I know; I'm from Penrith.'

'Oh.'

'And, after the caves, you returned with her to her room?'

Lee looked uncomfortable. Considering he was happy to bed hop with guests, he wasn't used to explaining himself.

'Yes. We took the back stairs via the kitchen.'

'The back stairs?'

'Yes, this is an old building. I know the renovations make it look modern, but the original house stands at the core of the central building and there is a network of stairs and corridors behind the walls.'

'Can you show me?'

'Of course.'

Lee stood up and looked relieved to be getting out of the conference room. He led her towards reception then behind the main desk and through a curtain which led to a storeroom. At the back, he took her through a door, and they stepped into a cool and dark concrete corridor. He pointed either way.

'That goes to the pool. That goes to the stairs and bedrooms.'

'Let's go this way.' She indicated the stairs. They passed old fridges, cupboards, storage boxes, piles of clothes and laundry bins, as well as other doors leading to various rooms. Lee opened each one for her. Finally, they came to some stairs, and he led the way.

They went up to the first floor and he showed her the way out to the guest area then they carried on to the second floor and he took her out onto the landing. She stared at the atrium lip, where Jamie Robbins had gone over. Then she retraced her steps behind the wall, down the stairs and turned towards the garden at the bottom, instead of the reception. It led to a fire exit.

'This isn't alarmed,' she said.

'No, it never has been,' Lee confirmed.

She went outside and saw that the door led to the staff carpark.

'Do you have CCTV covering this area?'

'No, I don't think so,' he said.

'Would you know if somebody random, who wasn't on your staff and whom you didn't know, parked up here in your staff carpark, came in through this entrance, spent time in the hotel and left? Is there any way of knowing who comes and goes through here?'

He didn't answer straight away. She could tell that he was figuring out if he could put a square peg in a round hole. In the end he admitted what she suspected.

'No.'

'That's what I feared. Is there CCTV at the front?'

'Yes, but I don't think it works. It's one of those fake ones, I think.'

'That's not helpful, is it?'

'We don't get trouble here; it's just a decoy.'

'Maybe you should rethink that.'

'You don't think it was suicide, do you?' Lee asked her. 'You know he tried to tell me something before he died.'

She stopped walking and looked at him. They'd gone outside and she was peering under cars and kicking leaves, hoping to find evidence of somebody loitering out here.

'What did he tell you?'

'I don't know. I said he tried. I couldn't understand him. He whispered something to me; it was two words, like a name, but it could also have been something else.'

'Did he move his mouth?'

'Yes, he was staring right at me. God it was horrible. This gurgle came out of his throat and he said two words, but I just can't get them fully formed in my head. I'm sorry, I had no idea what he was saying. Then he stopped moving.'

Lee looked down at his hands. He looked utterly helpless. Kelly put a hand on his shoulder.

'I'm sorry you had to go through that. It must have been awful for you. You did all you could. I've been told you kept everyone calm. Come on, let's go back inside. Did you get to know any other delegates?'

'Is that a euphemism, Detective?'

She smiled. 'It wasn't actually, but if you did, this is the time to tell me.'

'I didn't sleep with anyone else, but I think I got a good impression of their characters over the four days. They put on this pally façade as if they love life and preach wellness and kindness but in reality, they're all after the killer deal. They'd stab anyone in the back to get the next bestselling product.'

The detective stared at him. 'Thank you for your insight. And your honesty. It's valuable.'

'I'll take you back inside,' he said.

'Do you know where Paul Burlington might be? He was Jamie Robbins' partner.'

'Yes, I think I saw him outside with Melvin earlier.'
'Melvin Stone?'
Lee nodded. 'The old chap who lives across the lake?'
'You know him?'
'Kind of, he's got dementia; he wanders around a lot.'
Great, thought Kelly, *there goes another witness.*

Chapter 26

Kelly watched Lee Lovett go back inside then went to the shore of the lake where two men sat chatting. The younger of the two looked very happy indeed, as if he'd just had a quickie behind the boat shed. A shadow across her path made her look up and she saw movement in an upstairs window. It was where the VIPs stayed in the swanky penthouse rooms, and she assumed the maids were cleaning up there.

She recognised Paul from a company photo and she guessed the older man sitting with him was Melvin Stone. She'd get to him in good time but after what Lee said she doubted she could use any of his testimony. She approached them and introduced herself.

'I've been looking forward to meeting you,' Melvin told her. He was alert and lucid and she'd heard that about dementia sufferers: their attacks came and went depending on severity and how long they'd had the illness.

She leant over and petted his dog.

'This is Acorn. I brought her back with me today because everyone has fallen in love with her. But it's so quiet now!'

Kelly smiled.

'I have seen you on TV and in the paper. You're the reason this area is getting cleaned up. Did you have something to do with closing down that hotel in Ambleside? They were racketeering everything out of that place, drugs, poor women, animals, you name it, they made money from it.'

'No, that was drugs squad. They did a good job; those women were lucky to escape when they did.'

'What will happen to them?' Melvin asked.

'They'll be treated medically, then they'll go through an interview process, then I guess they'll be eligible to go home or seek asylum.'

Melvin shook his head. The other man got up to leave.

'Can you stay? It's Paul, isn't it?'

The guy looked jumpy and his earlier bravado disappeared. Melvin laughed.

'Don't worry, mate, this is a good'un. Answer her questions and she'll leave you alone, unless you have something to hide, then I'd run for it.'

Kelly watched Paul Burlington for his reaction and Melvin giggled to himself. He seemed happy with himself and came across as overfriendly.

'Can I speak to you after?' Kelly asked Melvin. 'I know it's been a very long couple of days for everyone; we're almost done.'

'Of course, I'll be getting a cuppa inside.'

Melvin walked away and called Acorn, who trotted after him. Kelly sat down.

On closer inspection, Paul Burlington appeared flushed and sweaty. She didn't want to shake his hand but she did so and introduced herself properly. He appeared to be the polar opposite of Jamie, who'd been described as suave, polished and charismatic. Paul was bulky, rough and shy.

She noticed his hands shaking as he reached down into a bag at his feet and brought out a sachet of *YouthBlast*. As she looked down, she saw that he had very large feet.

'I had a chat to Sandy Cooper about that stuff. It's your star product, isn't it?'

He nodded and smiled.

'What's so special about it?' she asked.

'It's a compound Jamie and I worked on for years. It enhances performance and energy, encourages muscle bulk with fat loss and is generally an all-round fantastic product.'

The marketing speech was impressive but Paul didn't look to her like a man winning at life. He looked ill.

But she did notice that he became enlivened by talk of profit. She clapped her hands after he'd finished telling her how the powder could save her life and prevent disgusting degenerative diseases.

'That was quite a sales pitch. I'm impressed. Is it safe?'

She watched him pour the contents of a sachet into a bottle of water and shake it up, then he gulped at it as if his life depended on it.

'It's been passed by the FDA.'

'Ah, so it must be.' Kelly winked.

'You don't believe it?'

'Sandy Cooper said it's not quite ready for public use yet.'

Paul stopped sipping and stared at his bottle. 'I get to try these things out.'

'It's your privilege as the creator of the brand, I guess. Can I ask you a personal question about your partner?'

'Jamie?'

Paul looked away wistfully and Kelly saw affection and possibly regret.

'It's come to my attention that some people think he struggled with substance abuse. Did you know that?'

Paul's face told her everything she needed to know.

'Jamie? Never,' he said.

'This next one is quite intimate,' Kelly warned him. 'We recovered extensive pornographic material in Jamie's room.'

Paul's immediate response was to laugh. 'Jamie? Why would he need porn? He had women falling over him!'

Kelly watched him. She got the impression that despite having a close bond with the deceased, Paul was also envious of him.

'What size shoe are you, Paul?'

'Eleven, why? Jamie always said somebody could row the Channel in my trainers.' He laughed but stopped suddenly.

'Do you own a pair of CAT boots?'

He hesitated and appeared puzzled.

'Do you?'

'I did.'

'You *did*?'

'I can't find them.'

'When was the last time you had them?'

'I can't remember, I must have left them down at the lake when I went swimming.'

'Have you visited Skelwith Bridge while you've been here?'

He looked at her oddly. 'I don't think so,' he said.

Kelly maintained her cool exterior and nodded to his drink.

'And that's just vitamins and juice?' she asked.

He smiled. 'As well as some hidden treats,' he said. He held his finger up to his mouth in collusion, but she wasn't impressed.

'Such as?'

He shrugged.

'You don't know?' she asked.

'Jamie and Sandy took care of that.'

'Are you compelled to test it, or do you like it?'

He stared at her dumbly and she reckoned she'd caught him out.

'What's it like?'

Paul looked down.

'If the company coerces you to take it, you should tell me.'

He smiled again and the moment was lost. A faraway look descended over his face and he looked melancholy, depressed even. He certainly didn't behave as if he was in control of all his faculties, but shock did funny things to people.

'So, why don't you explain your relationship with Jamie to me, and your role in the company.'

Kelly listened as Paul Burlington gave her a precis of his career history with Hampton-Dent. He told her how they met and how they clicked instantly. Their shared love of technology and health and fitness.

'They're a great company to work for. I have share options allowing me to retire soon; that's my plan.'

Dear God, she thought. Retirement for her on her police pension would likely be at seventy the way she was going. Paul was twenty-eight.

'Was Jamie happy at Hampton-Dent?'

Paul looked at his hands and Kelly saw emotion stir in him again. He ran his fingers though his hair and rubbed his eyes. 'It was everything.'

'What was everything?'

'The deal with Hampton-Dent. We came up with this idea five years ago. Now, the market is saturated with products promising miracles, but this one is different. It makes you strong. And I mean so tough you can stay up all night working, you can stand up to a boss, you can walk out on bullshit, you can bench press another fifty pounds...'

She watched as he transformed before her eyes. Then she looked at the sachet which had blown off the table onto the grass. He truly believed in this stuff. Some things were simply too good to be true.

'Fuck, I can't believe he's gone. He had vision. This was his product really. I designed the branding, but he had the original innovation. He was a genius. He could have gone all the way and been a director of Hampton-Dent one day.'

'Did he want that?'

Paul stared at her. 'I don't know.'

'Do you think he wanted out? Do you think he was disillusioned? Bored? Scared?'

Paul's head snapped up and he stared at her. His eyes looked like those of a drug user and Kelly wondered why Tilda Dent would accuse Jamie of drug taking and not Paul, who clearly was high on something.

'What's your relationship with Tilda Dent like?'

That's when she knew.

His neck reddened and his head turned to the hotel and the penthouse suites.

'Erm, she's fine.'

He didn't elaborate so she tried another way in.

'Are you aware of the staff corridors behind the hotel?' Kelly asked. She didn't expect his answer.

'Yeah, it's how I got around.'

'Really? Why did you need to get around without others seeing you?'

'Erm, I was seeing somebody who I shouldn't have been.'

He smiled but it was more of a grimace, knowing he'd been caught out. But Kelly also noticed a creeping energy boost inside him. His body wouldn't keep still, and she couldn't help thinking the juice had done it to him. She'd almost completely disarmed him.

'Who?'

'I don't really want to say.'

'OK, you're not under arrest, but if it becomes important later and you withheld information then that might be a problem for you.'

He stared at her. 'Will it be confidential?'

'I can't guarantee that.'

He looked up to the hotel and she followed his eyes. He gazed at the suite in the middle with a balcony; it was designed like some kind of castle with the lord's manor at the top. But it wasn't a lord who was checked into that suite. It was Tilda Dent's room. Her hunch had been correct.

Paul blushed.

'So, you're screwing your boss? Did Jamie know?'

'Kind of.'

'Kind of? Did it cause a problem between you?'

'No, not at all, we always used to share... I mean, oh, God.'

'Thanks for being honest. Were you sharing Tilda?'

'No, he wasn't interested.'

'Did *that* cause a problem?'

He shrugged. 'I have no idea.'

'Is that where you were Tuesday evening when Sandy couldn't find you?'

That bewildered look again.

'She said she thought you were outside?'

'Oh, it was a hot day.'

'It was,' Kelly agreed. Too hot for boots, she thought. 'When did your boots go missing?'

Paul looked embarrassed. 'On a walk. Tuesday night.'

'A night walk?'

'It was cooler.'

'I see.'

'I took them off to go for a swim in the lake and couldn't find them after.'

'Fair enough.'

It wasn't fair enough. It was too convenient.

'When did you last see Jamie before he fell?'

'Only after his speech.'

'And?'

'He went back to his room.'

'Alone?'

'I think so.'

'Are you sure?'

Paul examined his fingers. Kelly got the impression he was losing concentration as he zoned in and out of reality.

'This feels like an interrogation. I thought he killed himself. Is this all necessary?'

It was a curious question from a man who was supposed to be a partner and dear friend of the deceased. She ignored him.

'Where were you when Sandy and Jamie gave their speeches? You were reported as absent for those events. And afterwards, I might add.'

He gaped at her. 'Asleep.'

'In your own room?'

'No, wait a minute. I wasn't. Yes. I went for a walk, around to the caves. Sandy told me about them; she said they were amazing.'

'She'd seen them before?'

'Yes, she said she went at the weekend with Jamie. So, yes, that's where I was. They're beautiful.'

Lee Lovett had said they visited on Tuesday before her speech. Sandy hadn't mentioned the weekend. Now it appeared Sandy had been to the caves with Jamie too. The dynamic between these people was intriguing, and Kelly struggled to keep up. She wondered how they had time to make any money at all when all they did was run around after each other. Why were the caves important? Something tugged at her memory.

'Did you take photos?' Kelly asked.

'Sorry?'

'Come on, you must have taken some photos for Instagram?'

He froze.

'I can look on your socials for myself. Sandy sure likes those caves. When did she tell you about them?'

'I can't recall.'

'Her speech was three until four o'clock. You said you went to the caves before that, while they were both speaking; why so long?'

'I got mixed up.'

'You should watch what you drink,' Kelly said. She tapped his water bottle. 'Which was it? Morning or afternoon?'

'I can't remember.'

'How long were you at the caves?'

He scratched his head.

'Did you have your boots then?'

He looked genuinely perplexed. 'I think I did.'

'Tell me, Paul, you are, or were, Jamie Robbins' partner, and this product is going to get you those share options you need to retire before forty, so why would you miss his presentation?'

'I've seen it a thousand times; we wrote it together.'

'Doesn't that look bad though? You're both the face of *Youth-Blast* aren't you?'

He didn't answer.

'It's an odd time to go sightseeing when your partner is trying to impress influencers who will make it go viral. It's a pivotal moment of the conference.'

'We had a few issues with the product I was trying to iron out.'

'Such as?'

'The chemical profile is delicate. There is some evidence that the balance of the diuretic and testosterone can lead to side effects.'

She eyed his water bottle. 'Like what?'

'We don't know.'

He wiped his brow.

It was bewildering trying to make sense of Paul's erratic behaviour.

She suspected he did know, and it wasn't good.

'Sweating? Irritability? Lack of concentration?' she asked. He didn't answer. 'So, on the back, where it lists fruit and vitamins and compounds which sound natural and healthy, actually there's some alchemy going on which doesn't have to be declared.'

'Not quite, we abide by all laws dictating the supplement industry.'

'Do you suffer any side effects? You seem jumpy.'

He paused. She waited.

'There's a compound called Neurohydroxy-14. It's new. It changes mood regulation. I actually love the way it makes me feel.'

She studied his face. More sweat droplets had appeared on his forehead and he looked stressed. More so than one might expect in a casual interview. She recognised the name of the chemical; it was the one that was hidden in the small print, denoted by an asterisk. She didn't even attempt to pronounce it.

'How does it change mood regulation? Does it behave well with – what did you say – testosterone and a diuretic? How do they behave together?'

'We're not sure.'

'But in your experience?'

He looked down. 'If I'm in the gym, it's cool.'

'And if you're not?'

'I get pretty angry.'

'Angry?'

'Furious, actually.'

She looked up to the hotel and back to Paul. 'Were you angry on Tuesday, Paul? Is that why you didn't attend the speeches?'

He grimaced. 'I...'

'Are you sure you didn't see Jamie after four o'clock on Tuesday?'

Paul's eyes darted quickly to the balcony then he recovered himself. 'No. I didn't.'

She'd lost him.

'There's something else I must ask you about.'

'Of course,' Paul said. He was relieved to be off the hook for now but Kelly logged him as a person of interest.

'Did you know Jamie's sister?'

'Angelina?'

'Yes. You knew her?'

'Erm, kind of. I mean we had a few drinks when Jamie was in London. That kind of thing. Why?'

'So, she had a property in London?'

'I don't know. Jamie was private. The last time he told me, I think she was in London, yes. Is everything OK?'

'Angelina was staying in a hotel near here, paid for by Jamie.'

'Really? He was incredibly generous.'

'Her body was found on Monday. She was murdered.'

Kelly thought Paul might throw up.

It was a visceral, overwhelming and violent reaction that could have been true. It seemed natural and honest. But she had yet to decide if he was a good actor or not. Or if he'd just drunk too much *YouthBlast*.

'Do you recognise this man in the photo with her?' she pressed on, seizing the moment.

'Him?'

'Yes, you know him?'

'That's the guy who we're suing.'

'The podcaster?'

'Yes, Jesus, why is Angie with him?'

'Angie? You knew her well?'

Paul stared at her. 'I think if you want to take this further, I'll need Hampton-Dent to arrange a legal representative. Excuse me.'

He stood up and she watched as he walked into the hotel and didn't look back.

Chapter 27

Lee found Sandy in her usual spot, smoking a cigarette down by the lake. He'd avoided the detective talking to Paul on one of the benches and skirted around the treeline, keen to avoid further questions. He found Sandy watching them from the shoreline.

She heard the noise of his footsteps and swivelled around. She didn't exactly smile, it was more of a resigned grimace, but he approached her regardless.

'How are you doing?' he asked.

They both watched as first Paul, then the detective, went back inside.

'I'm looking forward to getting out of this place. I didn't want to hang around, but, you know, boss's orders.'

'Who's your boss? I didn't think anybody could boss you around.'

'Flattery won't work with me; I'm beyond it. That's why I'm not married.'

She stared at the lake. He lit a cigarette and inhaled deeply. The lake was as placid as ever, despite what had happened here. He didn't suppose lakes had feelings. If they did, it might be a tempest out there. That's how he felt inside. After talking to the detective, he felt a fool and his ego was damaged, but now he was standing next to Sandy, he felt all that melt away and all he wanted to do was hold her and go back to before Tuesday when the horror started. He was intoxicated by her, despite her hardness.

'Your speech was excellent on Tuesday; I didn't get the chance to tell you.'

She threw her cigarette into the water and Lee looked disapprovingly. He hated pollution, especially of somewhere so beautiful.

'What does it really matter now?'

'Well, I thought you'd like to know, that's all.'

She stared across the lake, and he heard the faint shouts of children playing in the water across the beach.

Everything had gone back to normal, but nothing had.

'Did you speak to the detective?' he asked.

She side-eyed him suspiciously and he could tell she was working out what he knew.

'What did you tell her?' she asked.

'The truth. Well, kind of. Not everything. I didn't tell her that we found your friend Paul naked up Loughrigg Fell, raving like a lunatic.'

'Keep your voice down,' she whispered. 'And he's not my friend.'

'Of course, sorry, your guinea pig.'

She turned to him angrily and flared her nostrils, but to him, it was another turn-on.

'Don't worry, I didn't tell her that either.'

Sandy looked around and he reassured her that he wasn't followed.

'You have no idea,' she said.

She stormed away and lit another cigarette. He walked after her.

'Sandy, I didn't mean to offend you; I just thought we got on well; I wanted to see you again.'

She didn't answer, but blew smoke heavily and the wind caught it and blew into his face.

'What's going on? I don't understand.'

She turned to him then and tutted.

'You already knew about the caves, didn't you?' he said.

'What?' Her voice was bored now, which was even worse than simply being rejected.

'That night, when we found Paul and took him down the hill and found shelter in the caves, which I suggested, you were already familiar with them, even though you said you weren't. What's really going on? Now his partner is dead, and you're involved somehow, aren't you? I saw you.'

'What do you mean, you saw me?' Now she was interested.

'I saw you come from outside, when Jamie fell. Or at least they're saying he fell, or jumped, but he didn't jump, did he?'

'Get the fuck out of my space,' she seethed.

'I don't think the police believe it now either.'

She backed away.

'I showed the detective the corridors behind the hotel. She knows how somebody can slip around them unnoticed.'

Sandy's eyes flared and her skin turned pink. Lee backed away further.

'You came from outside and rushed to him as if you expected him to be there, lying on the floor in agony, dying, like a stuck cold fish on the end of a line, pinned there and caught by your hand.'

'How dare you!' She took one step towards him and struck his face. It stung like hell. He stood his ground, and she did it again. He didn't flinch.

'There's CCTV in those corridors that I didn't tell her about.'

She paused with her hand mid-air as she went for another blow, but she lowered it. 'Where?'

'What do I get?'

Sandy looked up to the hotel and back to him. 'They'll pay you thousands.'

'How many thousands? I want to get out of this game forever and leave. That'll take a good few thousand.'

She smiled. 'Bargaining now? I knew there was something about you.'

'Everybody has something about them; you just have to find it.'

'I'll get back to you, but how do I know you're telling the truth?'

'How do I know you are?'

She walked away, throwing her second cigarette onto the grass. Lee tutted and jogged after her, picking it up.

'I'll upload a taster onto my phone and send it to you, then you can take it to your masters, and they can pay me what I want. I've watched it already and I think it should go for a high price.'

He glared at her and walked away towards the back of the hotel. His heart was racing, and he wished the meeting had gone in a different way. What he really wanted was to keep her on side, impress her, make her see that he was more than a temporary lover. Yes, he was younger than her, but he didn't care. She'd got under his skin.

He didn't care much for her speech, really. It had been loud, borderline arrogant, and patronising too. He'd thought that scientists weighed up all sides and produced analysis based upon facts. Sandy wasn't like that at all. She spoke like a dictator, a despot forcing home their point, regardless of the truth.

But from what he'd pieced together so far, that was the whole point.

Chapter 28

It wasn't difficult for Kelly to relocate Melvin Stone.

He was showing Acorn off to a small group of young women who were waiting for a taxi. The guests had almost all gone now. Kelly stood behind him and waited for the cooing to stop.

'We've got a lot to talk about,' she said. He spun around and gathered himself, draining his tea.

'Excuse me, ladies, duty calls,' he said. 'Pleased to meet you,' he said, introducing himself all over again. Kelly noticed his sincerity and it dawned on her that the man she'd met earlier wasn't there now. The realisation saddened her immensely and she thought of Ted and worried about his future. Surely he wouldn't lose his mind? He used it too keenly.

'How is your wife?'

'My wife?'

'Yes, I thought you cared for her? Forgive me, I was told you looked after her.'

'Of course. Let me introduce myself.'

The three young women left the table and Kelly sat down. He did too and they shook hands, then as quickly as the mist had descended, it lifted, and Melvin was lucid again. That's what dementia was like, she supposed. It was dreadfully wretched. She wouldn't keep him long.

'I can feel the stares in my back,' she said. 'My presence makes people feel uncomfortable.'

It was an ice breaker. An ex-army man would understand. She'd briefly read the notes on him; like all witnesses, their context might come in handy.

'It doesn't matter that the dreadful incident was nothing to do with them; you represent the law. Rules. Authority. It puts anyone on edge.'

'Is that your military training talking?'

He smiled a warm and generous smile.

'Shall we go to the lake and get Acorn some air?' she said.

He followed her and Acorn trotted behind.

'So, you're in charge?' he asked.

'I am.' She quickly got down to business as they walked, not wanting to lose him again. 'Where were you when you heard the screams?'

'Over there.' They stopped and he pointed to the beach access.

Kelly turned back to the hotel and then back to the lake. 'It carried that far?' she said to herself more than anyone else.

'It was horrendous; I haven't heard screams like that for years.'

'What's your story?'

'My story?'

'I can tell you've seen your fair share. Which regiment were you in?'

Melvin put his hands in his pockets and stared at the lake. The surface was flat calm, like glass. Not even the trace of a duck's wing broke the magic. Clouds reflected off the lake and the sun had baked relentlessly into the mud around the edges. They heard a shout and Kelly looked across the lake, making out an almost imperceptible splash as a couple of tourists waded in and frolicked.

Sound really did travel when the world stood still.

'I started out in the Royal Engineers, but I was attached to different units. I finished in intelligence.'

Kelly side-eyed him. That explained a lot. 'Do you always walk Acorn this way?'

'Yes. It's our favourite route. It is glorious this time of year and they don't mind me using their beach. I came up here as fast as I could, then I saw the lights and heard the sirens, and I knew it was serious.'

'You have experience with disaster scenarios?'

'I do, sadly. I could reel off all the combat zones I've been sent to but I don't want to bore you. Suffice to say that my first aid skills weren't needed here. The fella was beyond help.'

'When you got here, can you recall the people who were aiding him?'

'Of course. The manager, Lee, was superb, poor sod. He slipped on top of him. Terrible.'

'You're good with details. Have you ever worked with the RMP?'

He nodded. He had a critical brain – when it worked – and Kelly suspected he might have had some experience with investigative cases. The Royal Military Police was just a good guess. He could even have been MI6. She reckoned he was in his late sixties. Too young to suffer from such a horrible disease.

'Are you retired?'

'Yep. That's why we came here.'

'You and your wife?'

'Yes. Ursula, my wife, loves the Lake District. The idea was that we would live here and walk every day and do all the things you dream about before life takes over.'

Kelly allowed him to expand. It didn't seem to her as if things had quite worked out as planned.

'We discovered Ursula had early onset dementia shortly after coming here. I'm her carer.'

They sat at a bench.

'I'm sorry.' Life surely was cruel, but she got the impression Melvin was unaware he was struggling too. He seemed to drift in and out of cognisance. He'd make an unreliable witness but that didn't mean he wasn't valuable.

'It changed our plans somewhat.'

They watched the couple swim out to the centre of the lake and pretend to sink one another. She was reminded of when she and Johnny used to do that and found herself wandering away from her job here at Heron Hall and back in time when things were simpler. She gazed at her ruby ring and touched it for some kind of support. She felt silly.

'Do you need to get back to her?' Kelly asked.

'I do, but she also needs to maintain her freedom else it will get worse quicker, or that's what we've been told. I don't really trust doctors, do you?'

'Erm, I suppose I do, yes. My father is the coroner, and I trust him with my life.'

'The old chap?'

'Same.'

'Now I see the resemblance. Nice fella. I bet you two are the dream team.'

Kelly smiled. 'Why don't you trust doctors?'

'It's a long story,' he said. Kelly found Melvin Stone cryptically fascinating. She'd like to share a pint with him to learn all his stories.

'All this lot,' he added, pointing his thumb at the hotel. 'At the end of the day they're all in it for the money, aren't they? I spent all day yesterday chatting to them and none of them talked about Jamie Robbins. I know more about him because of asking questions than any one individual could tell me. They're corporate animals.'

'What has that got to do with doctors?'

'They're all cut from the same cloth, aren't they? This lot mess with food and drugs, doctors deal them.'

Kelly thought about his synopsis and couldn't argue with it. She found herself smiling. He sounded like her father. Ted never used to be cynical, it was only in the last couple of years that she'd watched him become less tolerant of bullshit.

'To be fair, they're not personal friends, they're colleagues. I know the army is different. You live with your work mates, but civilian life isn't like that,' Kelly said, offering some defence.

'I know, but look at what they're peddling here. This shit.' Melvin produced a sachet of *YouthBlast*. 'They've got these kids fighting one another to show that this crap works. They've lost the plot. Health is just a business, and the docs are all in on it. They're glorified drug pushers. When was the last time you went to your GP, and they tried to get to the heart of what was wrong with your body? Or did they just send you away with a prescription?'

Kelly thought about it.

'Fair point.' She sighed. 'And I came out here to have a straight conversation.'

They laughed.

'I know I'm a grumpy old sod at times.'

'Just tell me your version of the events of Tuesday evening and you can get back to your wife.'

'The two in charge,' he said. Suddenly, the razor-sharp coherence was back.

'Tilda Dent and Hank Hampton?'

Melvin nodded. Then he mumbled something incoherent and looked over his shoulder.

'They stood and watched the whole thing unfold. They didn't move. I know shock plays a part, but they were about as useful as tits on a fish – excuse me – they just remained rooted to the spot as if Jamie's death was… inconvenient.'

Kelly watched him. He'd got to know more about some of these delegates in two days than she reckoned they knew about each other over a four-day conference.

'Anything else?'

'The lad I was speaking to earlier, Paul.'

'Paul Burlington?'

'He came to see what was going on and he had a coat on as if he'd been outside. I expected him to smell of cigarettes, but he didn't, and he had exactly the same look on his face when he was desperate to get his mouth around this rubbish. Do you know what's in it?'

Kelly stared at the sachet and back to Melvin. Sandy Cooper had told her she couldn't see Paul that night either. She felt deep sympathy for his situation and the fact that he was trying to help, but he was hypothesising wildly, and she wished he'd slow down. But more importantly, if Paul was outside, he might have got his boots muddy. Kelly recalled looking at the floor around Jamie's body on Tuesday night. Somebody had mopped. Badly.

'They handed out some messed-up shit in Iraq, and I always wondered what it really did to people. I asked young Paul what is in it, and he told me it's a mood booster apparently, but it doesn't perhaps work well with testosterone and a diuretic at the same time.'

Melvin spoke technically and took Kelly by surprise. He knew a lot.

'It sounds like you know what you're talking about,' Kelly said. He described it exactly as Paul had done and it struck her that if Melvin suffered from some kind of mental deterioration, then it was normal for him to recall trivia but not be able to explain links.

Melvin turned the sachet over. 'I've read the ingredients,' he said, proudly.

Kelly nodded, humouring him.

'They all take weird stuff now, these young 'uns,' he added.

Melvin looked over his shoulder again and called Acorn, who'd wandered down to the water's edge.

'You must be getting back to your wife,' she said.

'My wife?'

She stared at him. Then she got up and he did too. As they walked back to the hotel, Kelly looked towards the rear, to the staff carpark, where she knew the back door was concealed. The door which led to the network of private corridors that could take somebody directly to the guest floors.

'When you first arrived on Tuesday night, did you see anyone upstairs?'

'Yes. Paul, that lovely fella who drinks this rubbish like it's going out of fashion, he eventually made an appearance from upstairs about half an hour after I got here. No one else noticed. But I did.'

'I thought you said he came in from outside with his coat on?'

'Did I?'

Kelly knew from living with an army man for six years that Johnny saw everything. Even if they were in a toy store, Johnny would clock every person inside, what they were wearing, and if he deemed them a threat. Melvin had just given her some breakthrough information. However, if he was suffering from a progressive loss of mental acuity, then his evidence wouldn't be worth much to her. Also, he could have imagined it. His recollections were conflicting and unhelpful.

Kelly stretched and took in the wondrous lake air to recharge her batteries.

Perhaps she wouldn't need to visit Dow Bank House after all. If Tilda Dent was right here at Heron Hall. Also Dan had passed on a message from Carleton Hall police HQ that the bodyguards were protected by diplomatic immunity and if Kelly wanted to interview them she'd have to get embassy approval, which she knew would never happen.

She'd need to think of an alternative means to get access to Mercedes man.

Chapter 29

Kelly knocked on the door of the loft penthouse suite.

Her witnesses were leaving Heron Hall for good. This was her last opportunity to nail a few details that perturbed her. It was also an opportunity to catch Tilda Dent unprepared and ask her how long she intended to stay at Dow Bank House.

Tilda wasn't pleased to see her and Kelly could see she'd come at a bad time.

'Can I help you?'

'Yes. Can I come in?' Kelly asked. 'I'll be quick.'

Kelly had come across people like Tilda before. They thought they owned the place. They believed that their superior wealth gave them more moral fibre and thus more entitlement to the air in the room. But she also appreciated it was a byproduct of privilege and not necessarily personal.

Tilda opened the door and Kelly went inside following the jangle of Tilda's jewellery. The room was untidy. Expensive handbags and clothes littered the sofas. Kelly looked around for scarves similar to the purple one taken into evidence, but couldn't see any or stolen CAT boots either. It was a suite overlooking the lake, but the curtains were drawn. People who discarded beauty just because they could afford it were people Kelly didn't generally care for. Tilda went to the wall and flicked a button, opening the heavy drapes. Kelly noticed a pair of lacy pants on the floor before Tilda could pick them up and stuff them into a suitcase, and she tried to push the thought of Paul Burlington pulling them off out of her mind. They made an odd couple.

Tilda was wispy, stylish and an heiress; and Paul was a working-class English boy. Her Mellors perhaps. She couldn't help wondering if they'd enjoyed a quickie after Jamie died too and the thought shocked her. It was an unsavoury and disturbing image, and she didn't know why it had popped uninvited into her head.

'I want to pass on the constabulary's appreciation that your guests have been so willing to give us statements. It'll help get to the bottom of what happened here.'

Tilda laughed.

'What's funny?'

'Oh, these Southern boys from Texas, they're very religious, you know, they take their morals very seriously. It was Hank who insisted we all stay. He's very noble.'

'And I take it Hank is now at Dow Bank House?'

'He is. He adores it there, so tiny and cute.'

Tilda smiled wolfishly and Kelly thought the severe and edgy tough act slightly overdone and ridiculous. They weren't in a boardroom and Kelly wasn't her gofer. It was also mildly depressing that a woman of Tilda's status demeaned herself to a caricature. Kelly would like to get to know the true person behind the bullshit but she doubted she ever would. Body armour was an important part of the corporate illusion.

'Do you think Jamie was an addict? Paul doesn't.' She got down to business. The question caught Tilda off guard.

'I was merely pointing out that Jamie wasn't pure as the driven snow.'

'Hank was quite adamant you called Jamie an addict. Paul is convinced he wasn't. There's inconsistency there.'

'Well, it depends how you define an addict doesn't it? He drank too much and enjoyed recreational drugs. Are you going to arrest him posthumously?'

'That's a tasteless joke,' Kelly said.

The two women stared at each other.

'You like power, don't you?' Kelly said. She didn't expect an answer. Tilda's face was a picture of indignation and intrigue.

The woman was touchy. 'You're rich, beautiful, clever – I assume – and powerful. I know you're sleeping with Paul Burlington.' Kelly held up her hands. 'I know, it's none of my business, but it certainly smacks of favouritism between two partners. Did it affect business?'

Tilda folded her arms. 'Last time I checked, it wasn't a crime. Are you from the 1970s or something?'

'It's not about that. Help me understand why you're sharing your bed with business partners. They were childhood pals. Is that part of your plan? To pit them against each other? Is it about control?'

'It's none of your fucking business.'

'I know. Just woman to woman, you're worth more than that.' Kelly walked to the door.

'Is my sex life on trial or have you got a fucking job to do?' Tilda shouted. She was rattled and Kelly wasn't bothered.

Kelly smiled and reached for the handle. Tilda lit a cigarette. Kelly stared at it.

'Are you going to arrest me for smoking now?'

Tilda stood in front of her, indicating for Kelly to challenge her and see what happened. She behaved as though she was above the law, and something told Kelly that she was.

Kelly opened the door.

'Can I ask just one more question?'

Tilda sighed.

'Did you know Jamie's sister?'

'Angelina?'

'Yes.'

'I know he has a sister. I don't think I've met her.'

'But you knew of her?'

'Jamie talked about her.'

'And you're sure you've never met her? She was staying at a hotel near here, paid for by Jamie.'

'Really?'

'Really. Her body was found on Monday. She's dead.'

Tilda didn't react for a minute, then she made a cruel joke. 'Suicide too?' Her face barely changed.

Kelly's stomach tightened.

Tilda softened. 'She was an incredible artist, I recall. We have some of her work in the head office in New York.'

Then Kelly realised what had been bothering her. She'd seen Angelina's paintings hanging in the offices of Hampton-Dent online, and one had stood out because of its familiarity.

'You were saying?' Tilda said.

'Sorry, yes. I know her work is quite exquisite,' Kelly said. 'Did you manage to visit the caves? Everybody else seemed to.'

'That's two questions.'

'Is it?'

Tilda stared at her. 'What caves?'

'Rydal Caves. The award-winning painting hanging in the atrium of Hampton-Dent HQ, isn't that what you were talking about when you admired Angelina's work? I didn't make the connection till now. It's special, this place,' Kelly said.

'Is it? I find it cold, bleak and damp.'

'You didn't want to come?'

'Like I said, Hank loves it here in the UK.'

'Was it him who commissioned her work?'

'I have no idea.'

'You know you're free to leave. I got a call from your lawyers reminding my department of the fact, just in case I tried to detain you. Overkill, don't you think?'

'We're a pharmaceutical company; we leave nothing to chance.'

'Indeed. I know Dow Bank House. I'll come to you if I need anything else.'

'Of course. I'll look forward to it.'

Kelly didn't know how to take the comment, so she decided to ignore it. She hadn't gone to Tilda's room for confrontation, but it had turned out that way.

'How well do you know Hank's bodyguards?'

'That's three questions and I'm growing tired of your interrogation.'

'I could ask more; I have an endless stock, such as do you own a purple scarf or what are the chances Hampton-Dent will be able to silence critics like the DiggerMan? Or, why it is that you're covering for Paul Burlington's drug habit but were so keen to flag up Jamie Robbins' non-existent one? Diplomatic immunity is a wonderful thing when you're on the right side of it.'

'And now you can fuck off out of my room,' Tilda said.

Kelly smiled. The meeting couldn't have gone any worse but she was frustrated and angry.

'We'll get answers for you very soon, I'm sure. I know how valuable Jamie must have been to Hampton-Dent; you all must be grieving.'

Kelly didn't wait for a come-back. She'd had enough of the prickly hostility of the woman from New York and it was time she headed over to Chapel Stile.

She left the room, and Tilda slammed the door shut behind her.

Chapter 30

Sandy stared at her phone. She acknowledged the number. It was the same one again.

Furious, she decided to answer it and deal with it once and for all, for the last time.

'What?' she answered.

'Sandy?'

'What do you want?'

'You. I'm coming for you.'

The voice cracked. He sounded unhinged. Dangerous. But she was still tempted.

She was tired. Weary. Ready to walk away from it all and leave the fuckers to their own demise. Without her.

This man was the only person who had any hope of helping her yet still she was reserved.

'Give me five minutes, that's all, I promise. No recordings, no threats, no lies, just time. I'm still here, at the hotel. Meet me by the lake and nobody will know who you are talking to,' the caller said.

His voice recovered and returned to its masterful confidence she knew so well.

'Do you think I was born yesterday? Your disguise is shockingly bad. My seven-year-old nephew could do better.'

She liked playing games with him.

'Acid tongue like your acid rain, as always,' he toyed with her.

'Fuck off,' she said.

'Whatever, I'll explain everything when I see you.'

He hung up.

Sandy stared at the handset.

Her heart raced. She needed a cigarette, but she'd just put one out. Her smoking had got out of hand this week. No wonder, she thought. She tucked her phone into her jeans pocket and left her room, looking up and down the corridor. She should have gone to Dow Bank House with Hank and the others. There they were safe. It was a slice of US territory tucked away from the rest of the world. Nobody could touch them there.

But first she had something important to do.

One more week wouldn't hurt, then she was officially retired. One more trip into the wilderness wasn't going to kill her, though drinking anything made by FairGro might. The things she knew could sink them and they all knew it.

She could be bought. She had a price. Everyone did. She'd been doing it all her life. But her priorities had changed. Money no longer interested her. It was helpful, sexy even, and she'd rather have it than not, but it no longer sent her heart racing. Her fees were different now.

Anonymity.

Peace.

Safety.

Who knows, she even might just run away with Lee Lovett.

Happy there was nobody around, she went downstairs. There were less people in the foyer now, and the police were nowhere to be seen except guarding the hotel entrance. She assured herself it was to keep nosy journalists from getting in rather than to keep them caged in here. They were free to leave anytime they wanted, and the company lawyers were on standby to represent anyone who had hassle from the police. It was the way business was done. Jamie might be dead, but reputation and profit were everything, not necessarily in that order. And Angelina was dead too. So, it was true. Jamie knew the risks. It was a shame because his sister's paintings were beautiful. Sandy recalled Angelina's ethereal vulnerability and the way Hank looked at her when she came to reveal the Rydal Caves piece in New York.

She headed down to the lake, where she saw a lone figure sitting under a tree near the pebble beach, watching her. She stared at him, and he raised a hand slowly and waved at her. She looked around, checking for company.

She was quite alone.

She gazed up at the hotel and saw no one checking on her from the windows of the grand suites, and no VIPs stalking her from the upper floors. The thuggish bodyguards had gone to Dow Bank House. The detectives seemed to have cleared out.

By the time she got closer to the beach, she realised that this part of the garden was entirely private, and she could no longer see any hotel doors or windows. The awareness was a double-edged sword because if she couldn't see anybody then they couldn't see her either. And she had yet to decide if she could trust this man entirely. He'd been useful, for sure, but he played a good long game, and Sandy didn't know where it would end. As she got closer, she took in his disguise. It had been superbly convincing to everyone but her and she admired his balls. He'd been at the conference all along, recording conversations, taking notes and stealing samples.

He'd fooled them all, except her.

Sandy recalled his face when Jamie fell from the upper floor.

It was unforgettable.

Regretful. Woeful.

They were close.

She greeted him by clapping. In praise of his performance. High praise indeed. He'd fooled them all.

'Nice outfit. Shit disguise, but you had them eating out of your hand. I saw you.'

He bowed. 'You're welcome,' he said, lifting his lanyard. 'I had to gain access to the snake pit somehow.'

'You've got balls. Given what's happened to Jamie and his sister.'

At this, the young man flinched and Sandy realised that he must know Angelina. There was something else. Grief.

'You knew her?'

He nodded.

'Will you at least walk with me?' he asked. He made it clear he didn't want to discuss Angie.

'No. I'm close enough.'

'Fair enough,' he said, wiping sand off his jeans. He faced her and kept his distance.

'People know where I am,' she warned him.

'I doubt that. I know the kind of people you work for. I imagine you do too.'

'Get on with it.'

'Jamie gave me your personal number before he died. In fact, it was last week. He was scared.'

'Scared? I know he trusted you.'

Joe nodded. 'I'm trying to keep this brief. He thought you'd be open to talking to me.'

'Really?' Sandy side-eyed him and smiled. 'Well, well.'

'His story was that five years ago, when he first had the idea for *YouthBlast*, he approached some industry reps who promised to represent him at fairs and suchlike. Long story short, they didn't. They stole his idea, however. Tilda Dent being the terrier she is, once she poked around in Jamie's business and saw the potential, she called off all competitors and undercut them. With me so far?'

Sandy nodded.

'Her funding came with certain conditions.'

'I know.'

'But do you know which ones?'

Sandy shrugged. 'I think so. Jamie told me his worries.'

'Really?' Joe asked.

She looked at the pebbles under her feet.

'He was under contract to develop three more products to sell by next year. He withdrew from two of them and the third was ready for market last week. So, he was in breach of a very watertight contract with one of the richest companies on earth.'

'Tell me something I don't know, Joe. Surprise me.'

'You already know every move Hank Hampton makes.'

Slowly, she smiled. 'And this is what you want to tell your followers on your podcast? You think I'm going to help you? You really are a nutcase.'

She began to walk away but he grabbed her arm.

'Get off me!' She shrugged. He let his hand fall. She hesitated. 'I'm going to report you to security. Have you seen Hank's bodyguards?'

'I have; they look thoroughly decent and friendly chaps.' He grinned. 'And they're not here, are they?'

'But the detective is.'

'She's gone too,' Joe said. 'I watched her leave. She looked so fed up but so would I if I'd been amongst your lot all morning.'

'They know who you are.'

'I know; why else would Jamie have been murdered?'

'They'll ruin you if they don't kill you. You'll be ridiculed and blacklisted from all mainstream media. Your reputation is in tatters.'

'It already is. Good job I don't care about the mainstream media. You know what they say about conspiracy theorists?'

She didn't answer.

'We're just a year ahead of the news.' He grinned again. 'If the mainstream hates me, then isn't that the perfect reason to trust me? Aren't you a scientist? Jamie said you were a believer in truth once upon a time.'

'I find money pays the bills better than truth,' she said.

He grinned at her and she knew she wouldn't be here at the lake talking to him if she wasn't interested in blowing the lid off.

'I used to think this was all about the Neurohydroxy, but it's not, is it? That's just a primer. It's about the electronic messaging Jamie told me about.'

'Ah, the infamous nanotechnology injected into the subject. Fascinating. There were rumours that mRNA vaccines were capable of it but papers on it are, understandably, suppressed. Nobody will believe you,' she said.

'They won't have to because I know where the asset is.'

'You're bluffing.'

'Now I know I'm close.'

She walked away.

'So, it's true?' he asked her.

He didn't follow her. Instead, he sank into the shadows behind the treeline and headed for the road. The buses to Chapel Stile were like rocking-horse shit and he was late already.

Chapter 31

Paul's hands shook as he packed his bag. He could kick himself for hanging around to wait for the police, but Tilda told them it's what everyone should do. The last thing he wanted was to be flagged as a person of interest because he showed too little concern over the death of his partner. Or too much interest because he was freaking out.

Jamie's death had been gruesome.

He felt lost. He'd always been sure about what action to take. Certain of his convictions. Master of his destiny. Now though, he wasn't so sure. The sensation of ambiguity troubled him. He didn't know what to do with it.

And now Angelina. He'd genuinely almost vomited on the copper when she told him Angie was dead.

Beautiful, small, delicate and clever Angie. His first love. Unrequited. Taunting him from afar, reminding him how he wasn't in her league. The artist, the ethereal untouchable sister of the man he envied to such an extent that he'd let resentment cloud his judgement.

He examined his behaviour towards the detective microscopically, and thought he'd done a pretty good job, all things considered. He'd managed to pull off shock, grief and compassion all in one, he thought. He'd given it his best shot. He wasn't an actor; he was a salesman. He'd made mistakes and he'd told the detective about his affair with the CEO. It looked bad. That was his problem, he couldn't keep his mouth shut.

He laughed at his own stupid thoughts. Salesmen *are* actors!
The first law of selling was to tell a story to your audience.

Being a sociopath also helped.

But it wasn't necessarily a derogatory term these days. Most professionals accepted that the attributes of somebody with a personality disorder were the same ones desirous for the world of hard-nosed commerce. Buyers only wanted to see the illusion of empathy, reliability and trust. Sellers could acquire these things a variety of ways. Charisma and charm were but two examples. Manipulation and risk taking were arguably more valuable. Paul thought he possessed a healthy balance of all of them.

But he'd never been as good as Jamie. That was why he'd accepted Hank's offer so readily. His offer to work his way deeper into the core of Hampton-Dent. It involved becoming a lab rat and he'd willingly done it because he had nothing to lose.

Until he did.

Now, he understood they were obliterating his mind.

He glanced over at the remaining sachets of powder on his bedside table. He was drinking too much of the goddam stuff. He knew it. He was a grown-up. He knew when he was becoming addicted to something because he'd been hooked on most substances available on the open market (as well as the illegal ones) at one point or another in his life, and he could sense the slippery descent into losing control, but that was the whole point. The chemicals made the nanotechnology work better. He'd signed up for it. He knew what was at stake.

So did Jamie.

Until the night in New York that changed everything.

Jamie's biggest mistake was introducing Angie to Hank Hampton. He loved her work; he admired her fine talent. He spent a fortune on her genius. But he wanted more in return than she could give. Hank Hampton thought he could own anything.

If it wasn't for sale then he'd just take it anyway.

But Angie hadn't been for sale.

And Jamie was appalled that Hank thought he could win somebody like Angie with money and status.

Some people don't have a price tag and Angie was one of them. Which was what attracted Joe Folly to her.

Theirs was a fire that Paul thought he'd never get to feel in his lifetime. It was like an inferno of pure respect and trust, and all the goddamn things Paul had sold off years ago.

He could taste it but never attain it.

For Jamie there was no going back. There was no choosing between his sister and his bosses. Since then he'd become insufferable. Noble suddenly. The seller of dreams. The purveyor of honour.

He heard a noise on the other side of the door and looked up briefly before stuffing the rest of his things into his bags. They were leaving to go to the huge pile in the country, to lie low and recover from the shock. Paul was resigned to the fact that he might never make it out again. But it wasn't as bad as what had happened to Jamie. He at least hoped that if he succumbed to the toxic side effects of Neurohydroxy-14, then he'd slip away in a drug-induced coma. It must be better than slamming into a hard floor at breakneck speed. He'd never forget the sound of Jamie's bones breaking and the colour of his blood seeping out of his body as he lay broken and destroyed.

The poor bastard.

He didn't know how Angie had died and he didn't want to. But he knew they were framing him for it, why else would his boots disappear and end up at a crime scene? Unless…

Paul stopped packing for a minute and thought about his best friend. They'd shared everything. Except shoes, he thought affectionately. He still hadn't found the damn CAT boots.

Starting out in London, with nothing but an idea to make the health industry more about proper fitness, they'd shared a flat in Shoreditch. Then they rented an office and took turns on the one computer they owned. Their phone line was manned in shifts. Their stationery was thieved from the library. They shopped in food banks supposed to be for those struggling to make ends meet. But they were both consummate storytellers and so the women on the door let them in. They went dressed in jeans and baggy jumpers, telling anyone who'd listen how they were brothers whose parents had died, and they'd been made redundant and were both struggling to find work. Hustlers even then.

It got to the point where they used to go just to tell new stories. Their audience was a captive one and they took more and more food each time. They studied the women who volunteered in the tiny shed in Queensbridge Road, and practised their fiction on them.

They eventually shared some of them in bed too.

It was a thesis in mind control. A psy-ops campaign in social engineering.

They moved on when they got bored. London was never short of charities and do-gooders desperate to make connection. That was where they learnt how to sell. And how to profit from others. But when somebody wins, somebody always loses.

This time it had been Jamie.

There was a light tapping on the door and Paul froze.

Then he heard it again.

He went to it and peered through the spyhole and saw that it was Tilda.

He opened it and let her in and she strode into the centre of the room.

'Ready?' she asked him.

He nodded. 'Nearly.'

'Get a move on, Christ we've been here long enough.'

She stared at him, and he got the impression that she wasn't here to jump into bed with him. She had her game face on. He finished packing and looked around the room, noticing his charger was still plugged into the wall.

'Did the police search your room?' she asked.

'No, why? Should they have done? I thought you said they had no right to enter anyone's room,' he said.

She smiled. 'You can stop panicking. I never had you down as somebody who lost his nerve.'

'I'm distracted, that's all. I don't know what the future looks like without him,' he said.

'Don't concern yourself with things like that,' she said, softer now. Her voice made him wary. Tilda spread her affections thinly and this level of attention made him cautious.

Paul eyed her suspiciously. She thought she was in control of them both the whole time, over everything. Like a master puppeteer. But she wasn't.

She grew serious again and looked cross. 'Was it really necessary to tell the police that I'm shagging you?'

'You're shagging me? Am I not shagging you?'

'Paul, stop being an arse; you know what I mean.'

'Not really. Words are important. You're implying that you're in charge, as always, Tilda.'

'Stop psychoanalysing me, for God's sake!'

'She worked it out! What can I say? She's smart. Maybe here wasn't the best place to wash dirty laundry,' he said, smirking.

She scowled at him.

'OK. You win. I'm ready. When are we leaving?'

'The car is here.'

Paul wiped his brow.

'Calm down, Paul. Didn't I tell you I'd protect you? We must find out who did this and then we can go home.'

Her words didn't make sense. Paul was sure they knew already who did it.

'But Sandy told me…'

'Never mind what Sandy told you. She twists things to get what she wants; Christ, we all do that, don't we? You must stop believing people just because they make promises.'

She went to him and stroked his temple, just the way he liked it when the red mist descended in his head.

'I don't want to drink it anymore. I've had enough. I'm tired, I get blackouts…'

'Oh, Paul, you're in good hands. You're the strongest of all of us. We've learnt so much from you and you will be rewarded like we said. It'll all be over soon. You shouldn't believe Sandy; she's lost her youth, and she resents the company's new direction. She's worn out. Tired of it all. She'll be retired soon. We're getting rid of old wood.'

Paul stared at her and she glanced at the bottle by his bed.

'How many is that now?' she asked.

'I don't know. Three or four bottles a day over two weeks.'

She smiled. 'And no side effects!'

'I just told you…'

It was as if she was ignoring him on purpose, but then he questioned if he'd told her anything at all; perhaps he'd dreamt it. His head felt thick, and he knew he needed to get off it. He stared at her and his eyes felt heavy, then he felt an overwhelming rage throttle him from the inside.

'Paul…' she said. She held her hands up and he stepped towards her. She slapped him across the face, and he stopped, then questioned what he was doing so close to her and her face looking as though he'd hurt her.

He stopped and held his hands up to his face, which was burning up.

'I need to get off this shit, Tilda, it's killing me.'

'Don't be dramatic, Paul; have you been drinking with it again?'

'No… I never drink with it; I don't drink booze anymore, I swear…'

'Don't worry, I won't tell them.'

She patted his hand and then held him in her arms, and he allowed her to keep him there. Suddenly everything felt normal again and the welling up of destructive energy inside him subsided.

Paul thought her voice was funny. It was as if she was accusing him of something. Jamie warned him about this. But he wasn't guilty. He hadn't done anything. She was making him think he had.

And whatever was in the drink.

Chapter 32

Before leaving Heron Hall, Kelly and Emma had watched some of the footage that Dan had uploaded from the USBs found in Jamie Robbins' room.

They discussed it in the car on the way to Chapel Stile.

The tiny hamlet was a gem of nostalgia nestled in the Langdales. It still boasted a red telephone box and the local shop sold scones, toffee and maps.

Despite the images being personally repugnant, they weren't illegal and the porn angle was a dead end.

Jamie Robbins, it would seem, was merely a pervert, but on the spectrum of deviance Kelly had witnessed in her eighteen years as a police officer, he was most definitely at the 'normal' end of the rainbow.

The images were all very similar. In the business, they might be deemed as vanilla, or bland. But it was still a distraction and Kelly wondered if that might be on purpose.

'Do you think they were planted?' Emma asked.

'A diversion if anyone searched his room?' Kelly asked back.

'If somebody was looking for the suitcase that was actually in Angelina's room?'

'Which is virtually identical.'

'Exactly.'

For a man of Jamie Robbins' means, the haul wasn't sophisticated or unique. What was unusual though was the idea that a man of Jamie's influence, and one who was so busy, needed to drag this amount of porn around with him in a suitcase, when he could have used the hotel Wi-Fi. He could have easily gained access to better quality films and media content by simply hooking up to the internet. And who printed out real photos anymore? Even if he didn't want the front desk to see his search history or his downloads, he could have firewalled his VPN, or used a remote one.

Emma caught up on the team's progress and fed Kelly information as she drove.

'Kate just texted me,' Emma said.

Kelly waited.

'She says *YouthBlast* doesn't have a separate certification from the MHRA,' she said.

'MHRA?'

'Medicines and Healthcare products Regulatory Agency.'

'Ah, why?'

'Because it uses ingredients already passed for consumption. Allegedly.'

'What about a patent?'

'Yes, in the USA.'

'Where was it tested?'

'Like I said, it wasn't required to be officially tested because it allegedly uses ingredients already deemed safe.'

'So, they got a patent to protect their secrets essentially.'

'Looks that way.'

'How long until the lab tells us what's in it?'

'Another couple of days.'

'And what if they lied about what's in it?'

'It's illegal to trade in a product that makes medical claims without MHRA approval.'

'Interesting. Anything else? Do we know if Skippy met a natural end or a chemical one yet?'

Emma laughed. 'Not yet. We've had an email from Manchester Airport security,' Emma told her as she navigated the winding roads towards the Langdales. 'Jamie had a return first-class ticket back to New York scheduled for next week on a private flight. Tilda was scheduled to take the same one. The same for Paul Burlington. In answer to your inquiry they've confirmed that Hank Hampton and Sandy Cooper are booked on it too, as well as their security detail.'

'Please tell me we have names for the heavies?'

'We do. From what I can tell from the scanning of boarding passes and the time stamps, our main man, the big one who likes baseball caps, is called Kevin Streeting; he's a Brit. Ex-Special Forces. Worked with A-list celebs.'

Kelly didn't normally handle cases involving private jet travel across her desk in Penrith. That world was unfamiliar to the Lake District. They had helipads and fancy yacht moorings but that level of wealth was uncommon around here.

'Has he got a UK passport?'

'Yes.'

'So maybe we can get to him without ruffling too many feathers.'

'They've attached the CCTV of Jamie passing through Manchester airport security with the others.'

Most ports were accommodating when it came to investigations. All it took was a few clicks of a mouse and they had their answer. Together with what the small group ordered to eat on their way from New York to Manchester, it was confirmed that the suitcase full of porn was not part of anyone's luggage.

'Jamie travelled light; on the security footage he's carrying a holdall and a suit carrier, neither of which are the right size for us.'

'So, what's the likelihood of him picking up a case containing porn from a secret address in the UK, after he stepped off a plane and between Manchester and Cumbria, or that it was already in his room. Or his sister gave it to him?'

'Not likely,' Emma said. 'I'm just checking Paul Burlington's luggage list, and he didn't have a suitcase matching the size and weight either.'

'When I spoke to him he looked shaken up. Scared. Worried about something more than losing his friend and partner.'

'Did he seem upset at all?' Emma asked.

'Upset, yes, but not emotional, does that make any sense?'

'Heaps,' Emma said.

'Maybe the stash was supplied by the hotel. You know some of these finer establishments cater for some highly unusual requests for the right price.'

Emma screwed up her face.

'Guv,' Emma said to her. 'Joe Folly posted on his Instagram last night. I follow him and I've been keeping an eye on his activity so me and Dan can hopefully work out where he is.'

They were almost at Angelina's address and Kelly pulled into a parking spot and stopped the car. Emma showed her the post and Kelly watched it. The Reel was fresh and slick. The graphic was edgy with catchy modern music giving the impression that the podcaster challenged the system and won, every time. They'd tried to locate the address of the account holder, but some social media providers could be slippery fuckers, and anybody could run an Instagram account from anywhere in the world. They'd got nowhere and no closer to locating the DiggerMan or finding a contact for him.

The DiggerMan gets to the bottom of everything... the Reel promised to expose anything that was being hidden from sight. Joe Folly's face was posted at the top of each slide and Kelly saw the same young and handsome guy from the podcast. The same man who appeared to know Angelina Robbins very well. He was charismatic in a US-jock kind of way, with a broad, confident smile, even though he was English.

He was immediately likeable. She'd visited his site several times to check out posts about Jamie and *YouthBlast*, as well as general podcast episodes about the supplements industry, and each time she listened to him, she was convinced more by him. He had two million subscribers. Emma, an avid podcast listener, told her that Spotify alone had over 170 million users. Mainstream media didn't matter anymore. Anybody could create an account like this, and if they were clever and committed, they could connect with millions of people around the world directly, bypassing the establishment. They were the news now. The mainstream was being squeezed out by these digital wizards who accessed people's lounges and bedrooms as friends. They projected their own investigations onto ordinary citizens in their homes. It was no longer filtered by corporate giants with only money in their hearts. Companies like Hampton-Dent, who had everything to lose if they let go of the narrative.

These kids provided instant access to independent news with no filter through the establishment, which was why governments wanted them shut down. It was as scary as it was genius.

She watched as Emma flicked through Joe Folly's last posts. It seemed as though he was in the USA when he'd last connected with his millions of fans, but then at the bottom, and easy to miss because it was the only one like it, was an update posted last night, like Emma said.

> England is so beautiful, guys, more news very soon. I'm home! You're not gonna believe this one.

The Reel was a compilation of Lake District locations and Kelly stared dumbfounded as Emma tapped through it.

'Is that…?'

'Rydal,' Emma said.

'He's been here all along,' Kelly said.

Chapter 33

Angelina's house was chocolate-box pretty.

Fin greeted them and showed them round. They'd managed to get a forensic officer to the scene and the house was being processed so they wore coveralls, masks and gloves.

It was hell-hot and Angelina's studio was a conservatory with windows on all sides. It was like an oven in there. Photos of Jamie were everywhere.

'She loved to paint him. He was a common subject in her work,' Fin told them.

They stood in silence in the middle of an active work room which was not in any way abandoned.

Angelina was planning to come back here.

'It doesn't look like she was a natural portrait artist; she preferred landscapes. There's a magazine of her famous pieces over there and the one hanging in the Hampton-Dent HQ in New York is valued at two million dollars.'

'Bloody hell,' Emma said. 'Who says what a drawing is worth?'

'Supply and demand,' Kelly said. 'There's only one like it. It's virtually priceless if somebody is willing to pay limitless amounts for it. It's a crazy world.'

'Everything about this case gets crazier,' Emma said.

'Look,' Fin said. He directed them to a series of sketches of Rydal and Grasmere.

'Is that Heron Hall?' Emma asked.

'It is. She studied it, why?' Kelly asked aloud.

'The photo of Joe Folly is in the kitchen. I didn't bag it; I waited for you. There's an ultrasound pinned up there too.'

They followed him and walked through where Angelina lived her life. Kelly recalled Water Nymph and her smashed-in head, and her broken hands, and the sexual assault and it jarred with this haven of tranquillity and creativity.

The photo of Joe Folly was vibrant. Phone copies could never capture the original and he beamed out of the satin-finish photograph. It was a different man to the professional one. He was open, happy, in love.

'Anything else?' Kelly asked.

'Everything seems in order, as you would expect a happy home.'

'A happy home expecting a baby,' Kelly added.

Emma went quiet and Kelly felt clumsy.

'Sorry, Emma. That was insensitive of me.'

'No, we're here to do a job. My pregnancy is incidental,' she said.

'I needed to see this place for myself,' Kelly said. 'I feel I know her a bit better now. And Jamie.'

Her eyes were drawn to a large painting in the corner of the kitchen.

'Is that a self-portrait?' Kelly asked.

'It looks like her,' Emma said.

They were drawn to the large eyes, the black hair and the way the subject peeked from a shy stare to seduce the onlooker.

'God, she's good,' Kelly said.

'Thought this might be interesting too,' Fin said. He handed them a magazine which featured a piece about the Rydal Caves original and there was an accompanying photo that wasn't in the Hampton-Dent magazine. It was of Hank Hampton beaming and standing close to Angelina in front of the painting.

'They met,' Kelly said. 'I need to get access to his bodyguards. They might all wear Mercedes baseball caps but I doubt it.'

'There was only one in the footage,' Emma said.

'Kevin Streeting?'

Emma nodded.

'HQ isn't budging on protecting their special status as VIPs. The embassy is stalling and my hands are tied. Technically, Tilda Dent invited me to Dow Bank House so I could just turn up. Emma, do you want to come back now or with Fin?'

'I've finished; we can all go together,' Fin said.

'Right, I'm getting out of this suit, I'm dying. Meet you out front in ten minutes? I need to make a phone call.'

Kelly left and ripped off the protective coverings from her body and rolled them up as she left the house, placing them in a black bag in the back of the forensic van.

She must call Johnny to arrange his visit to see Lizzie this week. Her pulse quickened unexpectedly and she realised she was looking forward to seeing him, as if he had gone away for a weekend trip and was coming back to her bed.

Stop it, she told herself.

As she went back to the car a shape caught her eye and she peered across the road to an old barn. The figure darted behind it and she ran across the road, trotting around the grassy patch to where she'd seen the individual.

Round the back she saw a person walking quickly away.

'Stop!' she shouted. 'Police!'

He carried on walking, head down, hood up, hands in pockets. Perhaps it was a sullen youth with nothing better to do, but something told her to not let him go. She followed him and caught up with him. He turned and confronted her behind the post office where they sold a local author's crime books that were very good; she'd read them all.

Her breath caught in her throat.

She'd seen him before, but only on a screen. In a photo. But in the flesh, he was unmistakable.

'Joe Folly,' she whispered under her breath.

She felt her lanyard blowing across her chest and she stilled it with one hand and pushed her hair away from her face with the other.

'You're a difficult man to find.'

She studied him. His face was unmistakable, but it was broken. She saw pain, anguish but also anger, rage…

'You came back to be close to Angelina's home?'

'You're the detective,' he said quietly. 'Forgive me, I don't trust many people,' he said.

It was a curious introduction, but Kelly understood. These people were paranoid. She looked about.

'There's no one here,' she said.

'You're here.'

'Your Instagram post. You posted a picture of the lake.'

'You recognised it?'

'Of course. This is my backyard. What are you doing here, Joe Folly?'

'Research.'

'Into the death of Jamie Robbins and his sister?'

He smiled and she noticed dimples in his cheeks. Joe Folly was more good-looking in the flesh. He wore casual denim shorts and a T-shirt, over which he'd spread a knitted top. The dark hoodie completed the disguise. He looked like a regular tourist.

'What was your relationship with Angelina?'

'I can't talk about her in the past tense,' he said. His voice cracked and Kelly saw the love he had for her.

'Should we talk about Jamie instead?' Kelly looked around and lightened the tone. 'Behind a cowshed is not really the interview I had planned for you but there we go.'

'What do you want from me? I'm not related to your investigations into anything.'

'But you are. You knew both victims well.'

He backed away.

'I know Jamie shared information with you. Was he worried about his safety?'

'Let me see that ID again.'

'You really are worried, aren't you? Who do you think I am?'

'You have no idea who you're dealing with, do you?'

It sounded like a threat to Kelly, and she didn't like his tone. It was dark and menacing. She recalled teenagers like Joe Folly at school. They were obsessed with inverted reality and drama. She smiled.

'Would you like to tell me?'

He peered across the road to Angelina's house. 'Are you in charge of Jamie's murder investigation?'

'Why do you think it was murder?'

'You don't?' He laughed cynically.

Kelly waited.

'He wasn't toeing the line. They wanted to own him. He wasn't playing along.'

'What do you mean?'

'He believed in his product, but they wanted to use it as a vehicle for something else.'

'Who's "they"?'

That smile again. 'Hampton-Dent. They're not a wellness company; they're a chemical company. It's very different. Pharmaceuticals shouldn't go anywhere near food.'

'I notice that's the theme of a lot of your material.'

'You listen to my podcast?'

'I became interested in it because of Jamie.'

'And what's your theory? He jumped? He had everything to live for.' He parodied a sycophantic voice.

'OK, let's rewind a little. You think Jamie was pushed because he was about to reveal some high-up corruption inside Hampton-Dent, linked to medical approval?'

Joe smiled again. Kelly felt like an amateur every time he did so.

'You need to help me out here,' she said.

He walked towards her and stopped about a foot away. Kelly heard footsteps and was distracted, turning sideways.

'You need to watch your back. If you get too close, they'll come for you too,' he warned her.

'Is that what Jamie told you? Were he and his sister about to go rogue?' she asked.

The footsteps got closer.

Joe went pale at the mention of Angelina again.

'Why did Jamie move her to a remote hotel?'

'He wouldn't tell me.'

'You didn't know?'

'If I did, do you think she'd have been killed?'

Kelly hesitated. She was gobsmacked. Not only had Joe lost his love, he'd been prevented from protecting her.

Or at least that's what she was being told.

'We need to talk properly, Joe. Come with me; I can protect you,' Kelly said but even as she did she knew it was a promise she couldn't see through. HQ was breathing down her neck and how the hell could she keep someone safe when she couldn't even gain access to vital witnesses?

Joe laughed.

'Who do you think you are? The fucking Sweeney?'

'You're too young to remember *The Sweeney*,' she said.

'That's the problem with you institutionalised lot, isn't it? You underestimate everyone else who's outside of the system.'

Kelly held his gaze and she felt small. Ridiculed. Insignificant. Irrelevant.

'It's important I understand what Jamie and Angelina were about to expose before their deaths.'

Joe backed away.

'Am I under arrest?' Joe asked.

'Of course not,' Kelly said. 'Don't go. Wait. Take this,' she said, holding out a card.

He took it.

'Contact me anytime. Be forewarned that I won't hesitate to arrest you if I find out you were involved.'

He skipped backwards, almost tripping, and then disappeared as a lorry roared past and whipped up dust into her eyes.

'Fuck,' Kelly said.

'Boss?' she heard Emma shouting and went back across the road to her car.

'Where were you?'

'I've just spoken to Joe Folly,' she said.

Chapter 34

Back at Eden House, Kelly held a late afternoon briefing. It was five o'clock already and they didn't have a distinct lead or a suspect yet. Apart from Mercedes man, Kevin Streeting, who was, as yet, off limits thanks to the 'special relationship' between the UK and the USA.

It stank.

'I followed the money trail,' Kate explained. 'Dan got me going on a software program Rob developed.'

Rob Shawcross had been their numbers man. Dan had big shoes to fill, and they all felt Rob's absence keenly when they had a fraud case or a money trail like this to follow. Rob crunched numbers for breakfast, and they missed him dreadfully. His legacy was sitting inside the office and his software program, which they'd affectionately named the Shawcross Redemption, and it had helped to crack several cases since Rob's untimely death.

They sat around the incident room table and even with all the windows open and a couple of old fans whirring, they were melting in the heatwave.

'Hampton-Dent have been involved in a few very public and messy takeover moves,' Kate said.

She'd been digging into the VIPs at Hampton-Dent all day.

It had been a long one and Kelly was looking forward to seeing her daughter and her father. Ted grounded her after work pulled her in every direction and she lost herself to the grim realities of the horrible things humans did to one another. Lizzie distracted her like only babies can, with mindless chatter that soothed the soul. Her sudden haze of sentimentality caught her off guard and reminded her of when she was pregnant with Lizzie. Maybe it was the proximity to Emma and her growing bump that was having an effect on her. Or the loss of Angelina's child.

'There was one in particular that stood out. The CEO of Dent-Whalley bid to take over the Hampton corporation back in 2015 for – get this – seven billion dollars.'

'Holy shit,' Emma said.

'Who was the CEO of Dent-Whalley back then?'

'Tilda Dent.'

'Shit, she'd only have been thirty?'

'And the company being taken over, who was that run by? Who were the negotiations with?'

'Hank Hampton, what a name,' Kate said.

'Yeah, he's all-American, for sure. They were both at the conference with their entourage of bodyguards. They're staying at Dow Bank House not far from Grasmere, as if nothing has happened,' Kelly said.

'Wow, I know that place; I thought it was private?' Kate asked.

'It is; it's owned by Hampton-Dent. They use it for meetings when they're in the UK. Aren't we lucky? So, there's bad blood between them?'

'I'll say. Hank Hampton lost his family fortune. His family lost virtually everything and even though the takeover saved his name, it can't have been easy to go and work for the company that waltzed in to pick up the pieces.'

'Right, so Hampton is beholden to Dent. So what?' Dan asked.

'I'm coming to that. Part of the takeover was FairGro. It was purchased the year previously and it was the biggest point of contention between the two. It's their main pharmaceutical arm and negotiations took six months.'

'Wait a minute, I'm sure I read FairGro was taken over a couple of years ago, and it was owned by Jamie Robbins; that's why he was so wedded to the company.'

'No, my information is that it was taken over ten years ago. I have the documents here in front of me,' Kate said.

Kelly was confused. 'So, according to your information, FairGro was owned by Hank Hampton?'

'Yes.'

'So back in 2015, Jamie Robbins was nineteen years old. He had nothing to do with FairGro or Hank Hampton. OK, so why is this important?' Kelly asked.

'Well, this is where it got me stumped, so I dragged Dan in to help. Dan found eleven different companies, all separate, all called FairGro.'

Dan mimicked a seated bow.

'So, every time they redevelop, they do it under the same name, but they are really different companies?' Kelly asked.

'Yes,' Dan said.

'Why?' Kelly asked.

'They do it when they want to hide history,' Dan replied.

'Is it legal?'

'It's all legal, but that's not the point. We found that what it enabled FairGro to do was apply for multiple patents on medical products which had failed under successive applications. Then finally, they got legitimised last year.'

'What were they trying to get passed for human consumption? Medical supplies?'

'A compound called Neurohydroxy-14,' Dan said.

'Really? They've been trying to get it passed for decades?' Kelly asked.

'You know it?' Kate asked.

'It keeps popping up in our inquiries. It's in *YouthBlast* but I'm not sure exactly what it is. I found it in the small print as an added ingredient,' Kelly added. She googled the page and scrolled down.

'Bugger,' she said.

'What?' Kate and Dan asked.

'It's not there anymore; I swear it was there. I must have the wrong page. Go on.'

'It has got a general patent dating from 1989, when it was first catalogued in the Journal of Modern Science. I've contacted the Home Office, and they've searched their records too. Nothing. It's as if it disappeared from the public domain,' Kate said.

'Why?'

'Because it was referenced as a biohazard,' Dan said.

'A what?'

'A biological weapon. If you google it, you get blank after blank, except a few references to YouTubers who are on several watchlists at Interpol.'

'Interpol are involved?'

'They have watchlists for people who are deemed to be a threat to national security across the agencies.'

'The agencies?'

'Worldwide. Joe Folly is on there. He did a podcast on Neurohydroxy-14 last year.'

'Was Jamie Robbins mentioned?'

'Yes and the DiggerMan went for him as one of the bad guys.'

'So, we have a multinational using a biohazard but it's completely legal because its patent is general and still in use but there's no law to prevent it from being used in food for general consumption?' Kelly asked, bewildered.

'That's right,' Dan said. 'Because its component parts have been passed for general consumption.'

'So if it's legal and above board, why is it a problem?' Kelly asked.

Dan and Kate looked at one another.

'We don't know yet, boss.'

Chapter 35

Sandy stared at her phone.

Her view was of a mountain called 'the Lion and the Lamb'. They'd been told by one of the staff at Dow Bank House that the mountain was given its name because if you look up at the peak from a certain angle, it looks like a small lamb sitting meekly in front of a fierce, huge lion. She took the barman's word for it. She wasn't about to go and test the statement. She believed him. From this angle, it looked like a small hill. It still amused her, after years of living in the US, how her native Brits still thought they were Great with a capital G. She'd driven up bigger hills in the Smoky Mountains.

The house was stunning, and Sandy expected nothing less. The plot had first been developed during Elizabethan times and it still had a topiary garden. It had been fortified, rebuilt and extended over centuries and now stood as a fine example of a classic historic home. But this one wasn't open to the public. The Dent family had purchased it twenty years ago when the owners ran out of money to maintain it. It was also where she'd discussed the first trials of Neurohydroxy-14, over several brandies. She had great affection for the place.

It was consummately private, unlike the hotel, and the grounds were more extensive. There was a lake and island in the middle, with a funny-looking bandstand-type structure on it, added by the Victorians. It was barely five miles away from Heron Hall, and part of her wished she could sneak Lee in for the evening. She was bored. But his threats to her were still fresh in her mind and she hadn't yet decided what to do about him. If Hampton-Dent got wind of potential blackmail, things wouldn't end well for Lee Lovett.

Her whole career had been shaped by the belief that the early bird catches the worm. It had been a saying her mother used. It meant coming first. There was no other option. Staying ahead of the game was as much about science as it was about wit. Sandy liked to think she had both. Which was why she'd called the detective and left a message. She'd called just after five o'clock, thinking the female copper would be enjoying her privacy with her man. Perhaps she had a family, and they were swimming in some lake to cool off, or at a big party, laughing and being normal, like she imagined people doing. But no, the detective turned out to be a workaholic and had called her back.

She let the phone ring five times, then answered.

'Sandy?'

'Yes.'

'It's Detective Porter.'

'I know.'

'You know?'

'I never forget a voice.'

'Right. Are you settled in? I know the estate; it's beautiful. You called me.'

The detective sounded breathless and Sandy recalled her keen eyes and terrier-like stare.

'It is and I am. It's peaceful here, just what we all need after what happened.'

'Exactly. Take time to look after each other.'

Sandy didn't know if the detective was genuine. DI Porter was hard to read.

The copper sounded upbeat, and she reminded Sandy of one of those annoyingly happy people who breeze through life with a smile. Then she checked herself and realised that the detective had seen death too. But the detective's motives couldn't be further from the science. The police were on the right side of justice, and they sought the truth. Science, Sandy reflected glumly, stopped doing that years ago. What was the saying? *Scientific studies find that 99 per cent of scientists agree with whoever provides their funding?*

She smirked to herself. But it wasn't funny. Plenty of old colleagues had lost their livelihoods, reputations and futures for sticking to the truth, which was why she'd chosen not to. Truth was relative.

'I was keen to stay in touch regarding what happened,' Sandy said, aware she sounded insincere. But if morality – or rather the lack of it – bothered her she'd be in a different job.

Jamie had once been a similar beast, until Hank got handy with his sister, then suddenly he'd discovered a moral backbone.

'The company is keen to resolve the matter for damage limitation,' she told DI Porter.

'Really? You called me for that?'

Sandy looked across the estate from the grand hall windows. Tilda said they must avoid attention.

The detective was a Joan of Arc type, she could tell. Which was exactly why they should be on a jet out of Manchester heading for New York and not still in the English countryside waiting for the police to work out what Angelina Robbins was up to.

But she was feeling rebellious over the commands Tilda had given them. They weren't to leave the grounds, nor should they explore the beautiful surroundings they found themselves imprisoned in. And they couldn't call anybody. Rule breaking felt deliciously awful to Sandy.

'I hoped you were calling with extra information,' DI Porter said. 'But I'm glad you called, as I wanted to talk to you about *YouthBlast*,' the detective said.

Sandy's stomach tightened and she was impressed with DI Porter's progress.

She peered across the gardens at the bodyguards who followed Hank wherever he went. The detective was closer than anyone could imagine.

'In particular a compound I've been told is in it but shouldn't be.'

'Really?' Sandy instantly regretted calling. It was too soon. Her aim was to find out more about Jamie and Angie. Some news on their postmortems perhaps. A reassurance that Jamie tripped and fell over the banister, even though she knew that wasn't true. Or how much they knew about what his sister was up to.

'It's called Neurohydroxy-14.'

Sandy didn't answer straight away. But she did wonder how on earth a small-town Cumbrian detective had figured out they used the compound in their laboratory which was five and a half thousand miles away in San Diego. She stayed on the phone out of fascination with the woman who was in charge of seeking the truth. How much she discovered was up to Hank Hampton, and Sandy's money was on the Texan.

'I'm asking your professional opinion as a scientist, Sandy. I just want to learn a little more about it.'

'Who told you it was in *YouthBlast*? That's a lie.'

'Is it? Oh, well I stand corrected. I'm all ears. Perhaps you could enlighten me on which active compound is in it, if it isn't Neurohydroxy-14.'

Sandy couldn't think of anything to tell her.

'I can't find any information on the compound online. Isn't that unusual?'

'Not for something that doesn't exist,' Sandy said, feeling clever.

'How do you know it doesn't exist?'

'Pardon?'

'Well, you seem very sure. I thought science was about gathering data and making observations about something that we don't understand. If you have never heard of Neurohydroxy-14 then how could you possibly say it doesn't exist?'

Sandy was trapped.

'On the *YouthBlast* website it lists it in an appendix.'

'I have heard of it.' Sandy backtracked.

'Oh, so can you tell me what it is?'

'From memory, I think it's a hormone combined with a few other elements to make a diuretic-like energy boost.' Sandy walked towards the garden making sure nobody could hear her. Her heart raced.

'So, why isn't it banned?'

'Why should it be banned?'

'An article from 1989 in the Journal of Modern Science called it a bioweapon and stated that it should never be used for human consumption.'

'Right. Well, you have done your homework. But the ingredient listed on the website must be a derivative.'

'Did Jamie know how dangerous it is?'

'We didn't discuss it.'

'You're sure?'

'Yes.'

'Were you aware that it is considered a bioweapon?'

'That's ridiculous,' Sandy said. The space under her ribs hurt. She needed a cigarette and an alcoholic drink. She was on private property now, and she was safe, but she didn't feel it.

'Why do you say that? I thought scientists considered evidence. You're dismissing claims without examining them first.'

Sandy wanted desperately to hang up. This woman was incorrigible.

'I mean I don't deal with biohazards, so I can't help you with that. Like I said, I've heard of it because I know its elements are made up of testosterone, glutamate, lactic acid and a thiazide diuretic.'

'That's quite specific.'

'You're the one who asked a scientific question. I'm being specific.'

'Thank you. Can you repeat those so I can write them down?'

Sandy did as asked.

Detective Porter thanked her again and apologised for disturbing her. 'Try to get some rest. Do you have the same security there?'

'Pardon?'

'The big guys, the close protection blokes who look like heavyweights?'

Kelly Porter chuckled but Sandy sensed something loaded in the question. She puffed out her chest towards the Lion and the Lamb, as if they might help her. But she felt hunted right now, and very alone, like the lamb, not brave and strong, like the lion.

Jamie had accused her of lying to him about Neurohydroxy-14.

She'd told him they changed the formula to make it safe.

He hadn't believed her. Just like Kelly Porter didn't. But who was the biggest liar? The scientist, or the profiteer?

'I have no idea,' she said, and the detective said goodbye and hung up.

Images flooded her brain. Pictures of white rats killing one another. Blood against their white fur covering the floor of the cage. One rat started it, then the others joined in. She imagined them now with tin hats on, carrying weapons, lining up in military formation. Trained killers. Chemical killers. They'd chewed, scratched and gauged each other until they were all dead. The compound would change the face of modern warfare.

But that was never their original intention.

In the doses they'd used, Neurohydroxy-14 should be a superpower without being a lethal superweapon. It created a euphoric feeling of invincibility and strength. The rage must be activated separately, and they thought they'd perfected it.

But as she'd witnessed this week, perhaps they'd got it terribly wrong.

Paul was showing signs of irritability and stress like the rats had in week five.

That's when it had all gone wrong. It's why they'd chosen the Lake District. Now, they had to wait it out, here, together, until the effects of the hormone compound had worn off inside Paul's blood, so they could see if he remembered what had happened in Jamie's room before he died.

Chapter 36

Kelly took a phone call from the SOCO at the Old Man Guesthouse later on Thursday night.

She was having dinner with Lizzie and Ted and excused herself to take the call. The SOCO had been at the hotel in Skelwith all day, and she told Kelly she'd sent over some drawings by email.

'They were inside the suitcase, and they stood out; I thought you'd want to see them.'

Kelly opened her phone. There were six attachments.

'Have you found her phone yet?' she asked.

'Negative. There's a lot to get through,' the SOCO said.

'Sure. My office has checked her known number for a signal and the phone company has confirmed that it last pinged off a tower close by. Jamie phoned her several times on Monday, and it was still there.'

'We'll keep looking.'

They ended the call and Kelly opened the email.

Watercolour had been added here and there on the intricate sketches, making them rather beautiful. Kelly's first thought was that these were blueprints for future projects. Didn't some artists sketch out their ideas first before they composed the final piece?

They exuded mystery and romanticism like much of the Lakeland virtuosity. They couldn't be placed in time but if she had to guess, Kelly would say they depicted images from hundreds of years ago. Renaissance perhaps. But she was no connoisseur.

Looking closer and zooming in, Kelly saw the initials AR in the corner. Something stirred inside her and she appreciated the skill of the creator. They already knew Angelina was a fine artist, and it was no surprise that she was drawn to the Lakes. Artists had been lured here for centuries to draw, paint and craft the landscape into legend.

Angelina, it appeared, had done the same. It was probably what made her choose a house here to settle in. Her passion for the area stretched back at least to the Rydal Caves painting that hung in Hampton-Dent's New York office, and the magazine told them the reveal party was three years ago.

Kelly examined the six drawings found in the suitcase in the walls of room 13. One painting was of the Skelwith Bridge, and it re-imagined the legend Tommy had told her. There was a horse and cart and inside, a black figure, hidden from view. It felt as though there was movement in the paint as the carriage rushed across the bridge, presumably, away from Queen Elizabeth's spies.

Next was a painting of the largest Rydal cave. The cavern wasn't natural, but carved from centuries of slate mining. What was left was a cathedral-like structure which drew visitors in a steady stream all year round. Kelly's eyes were pulled to the stepping stones, the famous entrance to the cave. Like the other visual, there was extraordinary movement in the piece. A lone figure walked across the stones and was hidden from view like the stranger in the carriage, but this one carried something. He or she wore a cape, placing the era long ago, and faced away from the painter. Kelly smiled but she didn't know why. It evoked something in her. Wasn't that what good art did? It was different to the grand painting in New York, it was simpler somehow, with a message.

The package under the figure's arm looked like a pile of papers, just like the ones they'd pulled out of the mattress in Angelina's room. But it could have been anything. Kelly's romanticism and sense of drama was heightened the wearier she became, and it was late.

She refocused.

There was a similarity between them. A flow, as if they belonged together.

She opened the other attachments and studied the other four examples of Angelina's work.

Then she saw it.

They made a pattern. They told a story.

The carriage on the Skelwith Bridge, the stepping stones in Rydal cave...

Kelly thought back to what Tommy had said about the legend of the spies who'd perished in the water. The legend said there was one traveller left in room 13 and he'd hidden in the walls but had been discovered. She flicked around the paintings and found one of what looked like the inside of room 13. There were four beautiful flagstones on the floor.

Stone.

The walls were stone, the bridge was stone, the steps were stone...

She opened her MacBook and arranged them differently on the much larger screen.

The stone bridge had six flagstones on the roadway passing over the bridge. There were five stepping stones. Four stone slabs on the floor of room 13, three keystones in front of the carriage, two boulders at the entrance to the cave, and a single rock in the water.

Numbers 1 through to 6.

It meant something.

She rubbed her eyes and held her head in her hands.

Whatever it meant – if anything at all – she wasn't going to piece it together tonight. Her head was too fuzzy.

She yawned as she googled the cave at Rydal, that Hampton-Dent was so taken with. And she saw that the single stone in the final painting was exactly as it was when Angelina had painted it. It was off to the left of the stepping stones, next to the hollowed-out wall of the cave, on its own, beckoning her somehow. Kelly zoomed in.

But her brain was blank.

She heard Ted playing with Lizzie and her daughter scream in delight.

She switched off the light and headed back to cold fish pie.

Chapter 37

On Friday morning, Kelly felt fresher, but this case was taking over her every waking thought and some of her unconscious ones too.

Last night she'd dreamt Lizzie opened a sachet of *Youth-Blast* and sucked it dry, and started foaming at the mouth and convulsing. She'd woken in a sweat and had to pad next door to her daughter to check on her. She'd started checking food labels too.

Everybody at work had.

Kelly was first into the office and she examined the footage of the fall again. The influencer's video had been isolated in parts so the audio and visual were now separated at Kelly's request. It had been sent to a specialist here in the Lakes who'd forensically isolated the talking off camera that Kelly had heard. At first, without isolation, she'd heard an American accent, and when she'd met Hank she'd known it was his voice. Now, she rewound it several times to make sure.

She compared it to the visual which was on a different file. She watched the footage a few times, concentrating on where Tilda Dent was looking. And she focused on the background. The YouTuber who'd recorded it was American and had argued that the laws of the UK didn't apply to her, so she'd been reminded that the UK and the USA had a mutual legal assistance treaty (MLAT). So far, the footage hadn't been shared again, as far as Kelly's team was aware, and Meta and X had blocked it. They relied on Emma to police activity like it. She knew how to do a quick check of viral posts, as well as for individuals. She was quicker than their digital department. The other matter that must be dealt with, via the US Embassy, was the fact that private security had cocked their weapons on British soil. The bodyguards were presumed currently resident at Dow Bank House, but they'd been filmed and that *had* been shared on social media. It made the Cumbria police look like fools.

The woman had started filming after Jamie's body had hit the floor, but only by a matter of seconds. Kelly guessed she was used to whipping her iPhone out at a moment's notice to get a potential post that might attract more financial endorsement for her channel. She'd been investigated. The woman was harmless enough. No criminal record, no link to the victim apart from the obvious invite to the conference, and she had clearly been downstairs when the fall happened. What interested Kelly more was the footage itself. The woman's hand was steady as a rock as she filmed. She didn't comment, indicating her experience when it came to filming live disasters unfolding in real time. She whipped around the scene like a pro.

Each time Kelly watched it, she scanned people's feet for large CAT boots, and their necks for pretty scarves. But she hadn't spotted them yet. Then she saw Sandy and registered the scream she'd heard and seen dozens of times. The woman's face was etched in horror. She saw Lee trying to give Jamie reassurance and witnessed him slip in the blood and fall on the victim. It was desperately shocking even though she'd seen it dozens of times now. Jamie's body twitched and jerked. She watched as pairs of feet ran away, stopped dead, or shuffled around. Nobody knew what to do. Disasters were uncommon for most people.

Then she saw Hank look to the side and she started the audio alongside. This was what she was looking for. From the position of the camera and the direction of Tilda's face, Kelly knew that she was nodding towards Hank. Then he said it.

The words chilled her soul.

He'd said, *'I told you this would happen.'*

It was resolute. There was no mistaking the words.

She moved past the frame and allowed the film to finish.

The YouTuber panned out to the rest of the foyer and Kelly got a glimpse of Hank. He was about three feet away from the phone, which made him about four feet away from Tilda.

As the footage took in a 360° Kelly let it run to the end. In total it was five minutes long and it was their best piece of evidence so far. It was rare to be in possession of real-time footage of a homicide and Kelly experienced a weird sensation of privilege. She turned to her notes on the two siblings.

Neither was on the police national computer system. Nor were they on any databases flagging up deviant behaviours, including minor ones. Fin had found contact details for foster parents who'd looked after the pair when they were teenagers, but apart from that, they seemed to have zero links to family.

The camera zoomed in on Jamie's face and Kelly shut her eyes. She was staggered at the macabre desire to do such a thing to a dying man. She fought the urge to allow tears to fall from her eyes and she caught them in a tissue just in time. The moment of somebody's death, especially such a violently dramatic one, was something so intimate that being a witness to it was something Kelly didn't get to see very often.

It was repulsive.

She forced herself to watch again to the very end.

Emotion did curious things to memory and several people had been through the same footage since Tuesday night. But coppers weren't machines. And video couldn't be analysed by robots, yet. Things were missed. Shock and personal bias dictated what the human brain focused on.

And that's when she saw somebody in the background who wasn't there before. A man wearing a hoodie with casual shorts and his hands in his pockets. He'd also turned away from the camera.

Chapter 38

Tilda's grand room overlooked the seven acres of private land leading down to a woodland. She breathed easier than she had all week. The place was deserted, just how she liked it. It had been Hank's idea. He could have easily disappeared off back to Dallas and hidden. Some backwater UK detective had no jurisdiction where they came from. But they had unfinished business here. The colour of dollars and old-school political allegiances were the best currency in the world when it came to protection from legal complications. They must stay close to the source of their stress, for now. Hank had explained they couldn't leave their patient. Paul was a big enough liability without the added complication of another asset they'd neglected for too long. There was too much cleaning up to do and Hank insisted they do it.

Hank had never been one to shy away from getting his hands dirty, Tilda recalled affectionately. She didn't know what compelled her to limit her sexual experiences to colleagues; she guessed it had something to do with opportunity. She did little else but work, and men were readily available, and none of them said no, because she was the boss.

But Hank was old news. It had been exciting a decade ago, when the oil and cattle tycoon had yielded his company to hers. The triumph turned her on. Conquering him in the boardroom and the bedroom had been deliciously hot. But now she sought young blood.

She stood in front of the window and peered out at a sizeable hill which guarded the road in the distance. England was so quaint, she mused. Her home in Boston would cover this entire house and gardens and probably take in the little mountain too. English people didn't appreciate space. They lived on top of one another like ants in a tunnel. But certain things were cute. It had been Jamie's idea to hold the conference here. She didn't even know where the English Lake District was until this weekend. She'd just read about it in documents, and been told how beautiful Dow Bank House was, and she simply must visit. It kept UNESCO happy, as Jamie had explained, and it gave them cover. Plus, they were close to the asset. And only Sandy understood the science.

'How far from London is it?' she'd asked Jamie. He'd laughed, his beautiful open chuckle, and said in his perfectly small voice, 'Boston to Brooklyn.'

She sighed and spotted two runners making their way up the rocky slope in the distance. Their bright jackets stood out and Tilda thought English people were crazy for lots of reasons. Their obsession with fresh air was one of them. Their love of dogs was another. Their reticence when faced with change was another. She could go on.

Terrible food, the stiff-upper-lip thingy that she didn't really understand, lack of imaginative sexual prowess…

'We have to move with the times,' she'd said to Jamie.

In his standard stuffy English way, he'd screwed up his face and told her that they didn't have to follow the field like sheep.

Jamie was one man she'd never conquered and now never would, and the fact irritated her.

The science was solid, according to Sandy, the market was ripe for a new health product, and the funding was there for them on a plate. They'd be stupid not to jump at the opportunity. But Jamie still had reservations.

He wasn't yet part of the inner circle. He wasn't old money, and he had no family name.

It was that simple.

Jamie had been a decent player. He told her that when you're brought up in foster homes you become an expert in reinvention and dissociation. He'd had years of therapy, but Tilda never would have guessed. He came across as a confident and sturdy character. Intelligent, passionate and clever. She'd never met anyone like him who was so good at making money but such fun with it. The two were usually exclusive qualities in her experience. But not Jamie. In the end, he allowed emotion to cloud his judgement. As it turned out, Hank wanted young blood too but he coveted the wrong woman and everything changed.

She folded her arms and forced herself to hold back her own emotion. She'd kept it hidden for so many years that another couple weren't going to hurt. She must stick to the programme and ride the storm. As long as Jamie's death didn't cause a ripple effect in the market, they'd be home and dry within days.

Damage limitation.

And they couldn't afford to fail.

The contract was too big.

She grabbed a thin cardigan. English people called this their summer, but to her, only 95 degrees was anywhere near hot.

She walked along the corridor and took the sweeping stairs down two floors and approached Sandy's room. She knocked and Sandy appeared within seconds to greet her.

'Waiting for me?' Tilda asked.

Sandy smiled and backed away from the open door.

Paul was already inside, in bed, asleep.

'How is he?'

'Suffering.'

'Can you do something for him?'

'I'm trying. We're dealing with addiction here. I did warn you.'

'That's enough, Sandy, I really don't want to hear any more whining. I've enough to deal with.'

Tilda approached the bed. Paul looked fairly stable, though his skin was pale, and he was sweating profusely.

Hank came out of the bathroom and closed the door.

'What's that?' Tilda asked Sandy, pointing to a syringe in her hand.

'It's your choice,' she said. 'We end it here and now, or we try to get him out of here.'

Chapter 39

Downstairs, in the ballroom, where there was a decently stocked bar, Joe Folly sipped a brandy. He was watched over by the hawkish threesome who followed Hank Hampton everywhere he went. The big fella with the Mercedes baseball cap watched him from under the shade of the hat.

Joe didn't like his eyes.

They were the stuff of nightmares.

What he was doing was commonly known as playing with fire.

He hadn't seen Hank Hampton, or Tilda Dent since he'd arrived.

He was here to see Sandy and nobody else. She'd seen to it that he was allowed into the devil's lair. He was taking a huge risk in trusting her. That in itself put him in grave danger. This manor was essentially US territory, despite being in the middle of the English countryside. That didn't matter. He could easily disappear when they were done with him. He knew what they were capable of. He'd had colleagues in the business of journalism – whistleblowers in science, medical doctors, nurses, research assistants and politicians – end up seriously harmed, terrified or dead when they'd pushed too many buttons. 'Suicides' from two bullets to the back of the head. Falls from height…

Anything could be buried. Information, secrets, lies, bodies…

Which was why he couldn't grasp why Jamie's death had been so public. But with these people, there was always a plan.

Two friends. A lover. Gone. Because they got in the way.

He must make himself indispensable, and he thought he knew how to pull it off. Without him, they'd never get what they wanted.

Access to Angie's hiding place.

The gloves were off. He had nothing left to lose. These people had taken everything from him, but he had one more card to play.

Like his hero, Milton William Cooper (no relation to Sandy), he knew he must watch his back. He was safest close to the nest, which he was now. Even the heavies in dark clobber hadn't worked out who he was, but they were just mindless thugs, not paid to think. It reminded him of a story Angie had told him. Jamie had told her when she was walking through London alone at night to walk with purpose, do something familiar, stride confidently or talk to an imaginary caller on her phone. People are less likely to suspect somebody who belongs.

Hunters seek the vulnerable.

Bodyguards weren't employed to figure out the danger, just eliminate it.

Sandy's trials had just been the beginning.

He'd dug, like his podcast handle suggested, until he'd struck gold. He'd proven beyond doubt that Sandy was employed to test Neurohydroxy-14 and what it did to lab animals. By following the data, he'd proved she was paid to smudge the outcomes by Hampton-Dent. He'd thought he was going crazy on some days, as he spent months in dark rooms, rented in anonymity, for short-term leases until it was time to move on again.

But the problem hadn't been finding the evidence, it was finding people to listen. In the end, they didn't, wouldn't, couldn't.

They were too scared.

Too rich already. Too far into the Great Lie.

His name was in tatters. He was dismissed as a quack. Once an investigative journalist or podcaster found the truth, even if they had compelling evidence that damned a whole sector of corruption, it was up to the mainstream media to get the word out. And they were owned by the same people who controlled the funds behind the politicians. It was one oversized club for gods who toyed with people's lives. Real lives. Real people who paid taxes and struggled to make a living, never knowing they were trapped in the same kind of slavery they thought civilisation had eradicated.

Milton Cooper knew it and had paid the ultimate price.

If Joe thought about it too much, it depressed the hell out of him, and he was tempted to sink several shots of brandy, not just the one to warm his senses and give him the courage he needed to move forward in the direction he'd chosen to.

It blotted out the memory of Jamie's face. And the memories of Angelina and her paintings.

He heard a sound behind him and turned to see Sandy standing at the wide-open entrance to the ballroom bar. She walked towards him and placed an empty glass on the bar.

'Let's walk,' she said.

It was an order. One he'd grown used to.

He knew he was in trouble, but he needed time to explain that he'd done everything they asked. He'd slipped into the conference unnoticed and had coached Jamie and recorded his testimony loyally. And sent it to Angie for insurance.

Nobody else knew Jamie was a whistleblower. Just the three of them. And that was his last card to play. He'd hidden the USB in a place so safe it would never be found without him.

They walked across the vast lawn and Sandy stared into the distance. They stopped next to a huge rhododendron bush. She poked her nose in to smell and she was virtually covered by it.

She took a packet of cigarettes out of her pocket and lit one, offering him one. He took it. They smoked together. Clandestine opposites of the same partnership. Bonded by the death of a man who was about to do the right thing. Not the thing that made him more money than his wildest dreams. Not the thing that would bring him fortune and financial freedom for the rest of his life. Not the thing that was easiest. But the thing that would ensure the end of his life as he knew it.

'He was ready to tell me the truth,' he said.

'I know, and it had implications for the rest of us,' she said.

'I know.'

'You made the right decision, Joe.' She sucked hard on her cigarette.

'Just answer me yes or no,' he said. 'The trials were halted because the rats killed each other in rage.'

'Yes.'

'Neurohydroxy-14 was never declared.'

'Yes.'

'Hank Hampton bought the patent for it to use in military contracts.'

'Yes.'

'Bioweapons are being developed offshore in Nigeria in labs funded by the Whalley foundation.'

'Yes.'

'The Whalley foundation is a not-for-profit NGO subsidised by the EU and registered in the USA.'

'Yes,' she said.

'You have been busy,' Joe said.

She turned and stared at him.

'You know who these people are. Now you know what they do. Now you know what to do with the information you have. And then you'll be richer than you've ever dreamt of, which, I guess, you already are. Selling your soul is the easiest thing in the world once you accept it doesn't hurt,' she said.

She had no idea how right she was.

She winked at him and he likened it to how he imagined a cup of cold sick.

She stared at him and blew her last breath of dirty fumes, as if symbolising the toxic nature of what was at stake.

'You can't go against these people and win,' she said. It was a last warning as if she hadn't made it clear enough. 'Jamie tried, and look what happened to him. Don't be a martyr, Joe. You've done your job. Now let us do ours. It's time to let it go.'

She waited.

'I'm sorry about Angelina,' she said. Her voice softened and Joe saw a flicker of a different side to her. 'Jamie knew he would be obliterated by dirty money. He always knew it would be made to look like something else,' she said. She reached out and patted his arm. 'People who get mixed up in this do so knowing they are risking everything, including Angelina.'

Joe gazed across the gardens.

'There's one more thing we need you to do,' she told him.

He stared at her.

'Then you can fuck off and live however you want to at our expense.' She grinned. 'If there's anyone who is going to find Angelina's paintings, it's that female detective who has taken on Jamie's case.'

Joe stared at her.

'I can sense it from her. She's not going to let this go. They investigate murders sensibly here, don't they? Our English police like to tick boxes and tie off the fraying edges. It's cute but a pain in my ass. Angelina knew what she was doing, Joe. You couldn't get it out of her. I will.'

'She's dead.'

'I know she's dead. But she was clever. That's one thing you didn't predict. She didn't even tell you what she did with the information Jamie stole.'

She patted his arm again and threw her cigarette away. He didn't feel her petting. He was numb.

'You tried,' she said. 'We'll find what we're looking for and this will all be over for you.'

She walked away and Joe felt his stomach hit his toes.

Chapter 40

First thing Saturday morning, Kelly stood in front of her team in the incident room at Eden House. Her first job was to get the team's view on what she'd spotted in the video from Jamie's death. She'd watched it so many times now that she questioned her sanity.

'I want fresh eyes on this because mine have stopped working.'

She brought up the end of the footage and froze it on the character she'd seen in the foyer. The male in the hoodie.

'Any takers? Dan, did you trawl through the attendance list?'

'I did, boss, and there was only one who wasn't accounted for. A guy called Greg Minda. He's down as an Instagrammer from Chicago but I can't for the hell of me find him on any other literature, no passport record, no paper trail. He was in room 7.'

'Greg who?'

'That's what it says here, but I've been able to trace and account for everybody who was there except this laddie.'

'Could we have an imposter?' Kelly asked. 'When I saw Joe Folly on Thursday he was wearing a hoodie like this. Look how he turns away from the camera.'

'Little fecker,' Fin said.

Kelly brought up a picture of Joe Folly from their records and the man in the video had a similar build.

'Why would he go there? To the lion's den?' Emma asked.

'To infiltrate?' Dan suggested.

'To work on Jamie?' Kate proposed.

'Aren't podcasters just another kind of journalist? They dig for info,' Dan said.

'The little fecker.' Fin repeated himself.

They turned to him impatiently.

'I mean the little fecker,' he said again. 'Years doing the Simplex crossword in the *Irish Times* weren't in vain,' he added.

They looked at him, utterly puzzled.

'It's an anagram. Greg Minda. DiggerMan.'

Kelly felt her lower jaw sink down to her chest and it was a curious feeling because she was stuck in a moment of being aware she looked an idiot but being so gobsmacked that she was unable to control a part of her anatomy. It was an unwelcome realisation.

'Fucking hell,' Kate said.

'Let's release this comedian's name, boss.'

'I agree, let's bring him in,' Kelly said. 'In other good news, Angelina's phone has been found. She had few phone numbers stored, and Jamie's was the one most used. They were close. Apart from that, her internet search history was sporadic, and recently it had been about the trimesters of pregnancy.'

Kelly's memory of those days made the woman's death more poignant. She remembered Lizzie wriggling in her belly those middle months. The rollercoaster of emotions as her child grew and the day drew closer when she would meet her.

Angelina was on Instagram but not Facebook or X. Her page was full of her artwork, and they'd learnt she was a successful teacher too, running workshops from the studio at her home in Chapel Stile.

Kelly brought up several of the artworks from Angelina's Instagram onto the whiteboard. 'That's Aira Force,' Fin said.

The team chuckled with affection at his recognition of one of the most iconic scenes in the whole of the national park. He spread his hands.

'What about this?' Kelly asked.

'Lone tree, Buttermere,' Kate said.

The team appeared refreshed. Morale was buoyant. They felt as though they were getting somewhere. Emma looked radiant and Dan sat close to her protectively.

'And this?' Kelly asked.

'The screes at Wastwater,' Emma said.

'The cradle of the storms,' Dan added.

'Indeed. And these?' Kelly said. She tapped a key and the six watercolours that she'd received from the SOCO at the Old Man Guesthouse popped up.

Her team studied them.

'Are they a set, boss?'

'I think so. Each seems to be indicating a number from one through to six. Look – one rock, two boulders, three keystones, four stone slabs, five stepping stones and six flagstones on the bridge.'

'They're stunning,' Emma said. 'I wonder why she didn't paint them in oil, you know, larger canvases; they'd be worth a fortune.'

'More importantly, I want you to get your heads together and consider why she would have concealed them. Why are they so important to her? Is there a pattern to these numbers?'

Everybody took a minute to scribble notes.

'Which brings me to the fact we've got to release her name to the press. It'll cause a stir in the art world and I would imagine a media frenzy, given her reputation.'

Kelly clicked a few more keys and several articles on Angelina Robbins flashed up. In art circles, Angelina was a celebrity.

'The DNA results are back and the coroner told me this morning that Jamie and Angelina shared 50 per cent familial DNA. They're siblings from the same parents and the coroner is satisfied that this gives us official ID for Angelina. We did consider asking somebody from Hampton-Dent to ID her but we decided against it given our inquiries around Jamie.'

'What about dentals, boss?' Dan asked.

'Yep, they've been sent off for confirmation.' Kelly took a deep breath. 'Kate, did you call Tommy?'

'I did. He doesn't recall ever seeing anybody after seven o'clock on Friday the eleventh but he was told by a member of staff that she told him she heard voices from room 13 on the Saturday morning.'

'Emma, do you have the blood results?'

'Yes, guv. There are two profiles. Angelina's blood is a match for the stains in the bathroom, the pooling in the shower, the lamp stand, and the bed sheets. There is a second profile, and it doesn't match anyone on our database, but it is male. It's not a match for Jamie either; it's not familial.'

'Fin?' Kelly asked.

'Initial reports from the lab which is testing the prints from Jamie Robbins' room tell us that the footprint we got from the bathroom in Angelina's room matches the one left in mud in Jamie's room. Again, they weren't Jamie's. They were too big. Size eleven. They're assessing it now, but they did tell me that first impressions have it as a CAT boot.'

'On a side to that, do either of the prints have any workable DNA in them, placing the wearer there at the time of the attack on Angelina or in Jamie's room?'

'Yes. The one at Angelina's does. There was blood splatter disturbed by the shoe, so that proves the wearer was there before and after the time of the attack.'

'So the CAT boot is solid. That's our first concrete lead. Let's get up the footage from the Heron Hall scene.'

They watched as the video played back and forth and they all studied the feet of those in the video carefully.

'No CAT boots. I was looking at Mercedes man,' Kelly said.

'OK. Next, DNA samples. Our hands are tied on this. Hampton-Dent won't authorise blanket DNA samples of its staff. It's a dead end. To get them we need warrants or at least something to convince the US Embassy with and that's not happening today.

The VIPs have moved to an exclusive stately home owned by the company, here.'

Kelly brought up a website on Dow Bank House.

Dan whistled.

Kate said, 'Fuck me.'

'At the moment I've got no reason to go over there to justify an interview, but I received a call from Doctor Sandy Cooper on Thursday which I returned. I thought she had further information for me but it was a strange general fishing exercise for knowledge. She talked about damage limitation to the company as if Jamie's death was an inconvenience. She really pissed me off. Anyway, I started to ask her about this stuff.'

Kelly tapped a key and an information document came up about Neurohydroxy-14.

'Dan, you were right, it is a biohazard but it depends how it's used. Sandy Cooper explained the difference to me. To be fair, it was all nonsense to me, but it must be more important than they're letting on because she denied it was in *YouthBlast* at first. Why would she say that if it wasn't important? She's covering for something. Fin, can you get on to the lab about Skippy the squirrel ASAP?'

'Yes, boss.'

'Dan? The suitcase found in the walls of room 13.'

'I'm making my way through the scientific papers. There's lots of information about clinical trials, additives, American food standards law and lots of recognisable names; however, I admit, I haven't pinned them together with anything obvious yet. And so far no mention of Neuro-whatsit-14; can we please call it N-14 from now on?'

'Do you need help with big words, Dan?' Kelly asked.

'I'm giving him a hand, guv,' Emma said.

They laughed and Kate patted Dan on his head.

'Fin, help me out, mate, I'm surrounded by feminists.'

'I love it, mate, wait until you have a daughter,' Fin said.

'It's a girl?' Kate asked Emma.

Emma blushed and Dan beamed at her.

'God help yer,' Fin said, laughing.

'Oi!' Kelly said. 'You big Irish oaf, you can't say things like that anymore.'

'But you can call me an Irish oaf?'

'Because it's true, mate,' Dan said.

'Emma, how far did you get with Angelina's bank accounts?' Kelly moved on. None of them had time for new directives from HQ unless it affected their work.

Emma tapped a few keys and lists of debits and credits appeared, from a statement courtesy of Barclays bank.

'It looks like she was paid huge amounts by a company affiliated to Hank Hampton, but I haven't found what they were for. Private commissions perhaps?'

'Dan, you have some news?'

'We've got the CCTV footage from the Old Man Guesthouse, boss, and Jamie is clearly identified as there on Friday afternoon as the person who dropped her off,' Dan said. 'There's no evidence of Angelina leaving after that. However, the side entrance to the hotel, which leads to the garden, and the river, is not covered by CCTV.'

None of them had forgotten how violent Angelina's death had been: one that started in room 13 and didn't end until she inhaled lake water because she didn't have the strength to lift her head out of it. And nobody had been there to protect her. Or her baby.

Dan flicked a few keys on his laptop and footage popped up behind Kelly's head. They watched the video clip. It showed the carpark at the Old Man Guesthouse, and Jamie arriving in his M4 coupe. It was sleek and stunning, and Kelly knew it was a top-of-the-range edition costing in the region of a hundred thousand pounds. She'd got her love of cars from her time in London, when her lover and boss, Matt the Twat, pointed them out. Dan forwarded the footage, explaining that he'd trawled through it to flag up the incidents of note.

'This is where Angelina and Jamie turn up,' Dan said.

'But look she stays in the car while he goes inside.'

'What was he doing for an hour inside?' Kelly asked.

'Chatting to Tommy about cars?' Fin suggested.

'I watched the rest of the footage from the afternoon – eight hours of it – thank you.' Dan took a bow. 'And I found this.'

The room fell silent again and they watched another car pull up. It was a taxi. A figure got out of it but it was difficult to see her face. Then a tall shape of a male got out of the other side. His face was covered by a cap.

'Does that look like Sandy Cooper to you?' Kelly asked.

'I was just thinking that, boss,' Emma said.

Dan rewound the footage but it was impossible to ID the faces of either visitor.

'Dan, why did you flag up this car arriving?'

'I went through every piece of footage for last Friday and then ticked off those checking in with the list of guests provided to us by Tommy. Nobody checked in after seven o'clock and this is almost eight p.m. They're in there for ten minutes, look.'

They watched as the taxi waited and the woman came back and got back into the car. But the man didn't.

'Did Tommy mention this when he was interviewed?'

'I couldn't find any reference to a late arrival,' Dan said.

'Kate, get Tommy on the phone and ask him.'

A knock on the door focused their attention away from the whiteboard and a young uniform came in and told Kelly that a man named Lee Lovett was downstairs asking for her.

Kelly raised her brows and got up.

'Anything else?' she asked.

She received murmurs of a collective acceptance that everybody had said their bit, so she got up from her chair to leave.

'I'll report back soon,' she said.

Chapter 41

Lee Lovett looked nervous.

Kelly greeted him warmly and noticed his hand felt tacky. She took him into a free interview suite.

'How can I help, Lee?'

She studied him as she waited for him to collect himself. She appreciated that just being inside a cop shop was at best intimidating and could be downright terrifying. Especially if you had something to hide.

Which Lee Lovett clearly did. He looked like a child who's caught pilfering pudding before main course. She relaxed into her chair.

'How are you holding up?' She broke the ice.

On a serious note, Lee had witnessed a horrific scene and the longer she sat with him and watched him, the more she realised that he was conflicted.

'You're here for a good reason; tell me what it is.' She put on her most charming manner and opened her body. She waited patiently.

'I was thinking about leaving the area and taking a new position.'

'That's good. It's a positive step,' she said. 'A fresh start. What will happen to Heron Hall?'

'I've heard rumours that a big American buyer is interested. The Nirvana Project.'

'It's being sold?'

'It's been on the cards for some time. Everybody is struggling in hospitality. Especially the independents.'

'And this American buyer, do you know how long they've been interested?'

'Months. I think there have been negotiations.'

'And this incident. The very public death of a guest has spurred on the owners to sell?'

'Looks like it.'

'Does that strike you as fortunate for the buyers?' Kelly asked.

Lee looked at her and it dawned on him what she was getting at.

He relaxed and smiled at her. 'Christ, I didn't even think of that; you don't think…'

Kelly shrugged. 'I'm a police officer; I don't assume. I wait for the evidence to come together.'

A whiff of respect blew Kelly's way and she knew she'd earnt his trust. He wouldn't be here otherwise.

'I have some information for you,' he said. 'But I think I might have committed a crime.'

'Really?'

'I withheld evidence.'

'What evidence?'

'The CCTV from the back corridors of the Heron Hall.'

'I thought you said there was none. You lied?'

'I wasn't sure. I double checked after you left. I was astounded it had a battery in it to be honest.'

'You've seen it?'

He nodded.

'And?'

'There's hours of it. All sorts of people used those corridors that I was unaware of. Staff sneaking about in the middle of the night. Guests thinking they were being clever.'

'And the night of Jamie's death?'

'I didn't watch it all.'

Kelly didn't figure Lee to be a voyeur but neither did she believe him that he hadn't scoured the footage to within an inch of his life. Otherwise he wouldn't be here.

'Have you got it with you?' Her heart raced.

'I thought I'd better keep it safe.'

'Safe, where?'

'In my room.'

'And you've driven all the way to Penrith to tell me that you want to give me something that is back in your room?'

'I didn't want to lose it.'

She glared at him but corrected herself. She'd get nowhere by hounding him. 'Why did you withhold it?'

'Because Sandy asked me to.'

Lee looked at his shoes and Kelly checked they weren't CAT boots.

They weren't.

'Did you give her a copy?'

'No.'

'Did she ask for one?'

'Yes.'

'Did she offer to pay?'

'Yes.'

'So I'm guessing she didn't come up with the goods so now you've come to me?'

'I thought it was the right thing to do.'

'So how can I get it?'

'If you'd like it I can email it to you when I get back.'

Kelly realised that this was his insurance. She'd have to let him go if he promised her something.

'Is there something else? You could have told me this over the phone.' Her hands twitched and she was desperate to see the footage but she mustn't rush and scare him off.

'We can overlook your timelines,' she said.

'I saw Sandy come in from outside just as he fell.'

'Tuesday evening?'

A nod.

'Had she been smoking?'

'I don't know. I guess she could have been.'

Kelly's heart sank. Lee Lovett was suffering. Now paranoia had kicked in and he was grasping at anything he could to assuage his desperate abandonment at the hands of a predatorial woman. Sandy had wounded him and so he wanted to repay her in kind by pinning something on her.

She understood.

'I hadn't seen her go out,' he said.

Now Kelly paid attention because this was more interesting. Lee was in love with Sandy, that much any fool could tell, so he'd pretty much stalked her the whole conference. This detail was significant to him.

'When did you see her before then?'

'In the conference talking to the American in the cream suit.'

'Hank Hampton?'

'Yes, Mr Hampton.'

'So are you telling me, then, Lee, that you suspect that Sandy could not have gone from talking to Mr Hampton inside to being seen outside?'

A nod.

'You're telling me you think she used the back stairs?'

A nod.

'Why would she do that?'

Lee's face showed her that he was confused, yes, but also unsure, worried.

Troubled.

He was fighting with his conscience. He'd fallen in love and when that happens, hope emerges strong and clear. That hope had been dashed by Sandy's callousness. She'd dumped him. Now he wanted to offload.

'Do you think the timing of her being outside at that moment was important?'

'It seemed odd. Like her behaviour afterwards. She and Mr Robbins didn't seem close, but she was hysterical over him.'

Kelly had seen the footage. People reacted in different ways to trauma but Sandy's was more like a performance, she had to admit.

'Thanks for telling me, Lee. It's a big step when you've been so close to somebody to go behind their back and reveal the truth.'

He smiled weakly.

Her words wouldn't help him heal his broken heart. To Doctor Cooper, this man had been a quick lay. A bit of rough sex on the side. Exciting, clandestine, thrilling.

To Lee it meant so much more.

'There's something else,' he said. 'Paul Burlington went missing from the hotel last Tuesday night. Sandy asked me to help search for him. They were worried. Panicked, you know? Like they knew he couldn't look after himself.'

'Go on.'

Kelly recalled seeing the physical signs that Paul Burlington was unwell. Perhaps there was more to it.

'We found him in the caves.'

'The caves?'

Lee nodded. 'He was in a real state. Like hallucinating or something. He'd lost his clothes, ripped them off apparently and Sandy calmed him down.'

'He's a big bloke,' Kelly said.

'She was able to relax him. I got the impression it happened a lot.'

'You said "they". Who else knew this?'

'Hank Hampton knew because he waited in the bar for them to return and he sank about seven whiskeys. One of the bodyguards came with us.'

'Which one?'

Lee shrugged.

'Did he wear a baseball cap?'

'No I don't think so.'

'What was he doing in the caves?'

'Sandy said he was obsessed with them.'

'Obsessed? That's an unusual thing to say.'

'Maybe he was sheltering in there? Sandy said he'd liked to walk on the fells, maybe he got lost, but then that doesn't make sense because he told me he hated exercise and all this "health crap". That's what he said. He was drunk at the time.'

Lee stopped talking suddenly. 'I think that's everything, can I go?'

'What time on Tuesday night?' She couldn't help herself imagining Paul Burlington's bulky frame inside Angelina's room, turning nasty and forcing himself on her.

'It was late, about midnight.'

'And was he injured?'

'I don't think so.'

'Did he have boots on?'

Lee looked at her oddly. 'I can't remember looking at his feet. I just recall him being undressed.'

Kelly thought it was worth a look around Rydal caves for a pair of boots because if they were to turn up it might corroborate Paul's story.

'OK, Lee, thank you.' Kelly stood up.

'Will you email me the footage as soon as you get back?' she asked. 'Are you intending to stay in the area for the time being? We may need a formal statement from you,' she said. She didn't add 'depending on the footage' because that might encourage him to tamper with it.

Lee looked forlorn. That hadn't been part of his plan but reality was something that, once faced, couldn't be put back in a box.

She walked him out and headed back to her team upstairs.

But she didn't make it past the door.

Chapter 42

It was a call from Carleton Hall.

'The chief constable wants you to head over here ASAP,' the PA said over the phone.

'I'm busy,' Kelly said.

She didn't like the woman. Kelly saw her as the snooty gate-keeper to hell. The PA thought her role above law enforcement. As a result, anybody who was a real copper was beneath her.

Timings were everything and the woman persisted.

'He's got a window of fifteen minutes so if you don't head over now you'll miss him and of course I'll have to tell him that you decided something else was more important.'

Something else is more important, you stupid bitch, she felt like saying, but didn't.

Sighing, she said she'd be there.

She called Kate on hands-free as she drove over to Carleton Hall HQ, filling her in on what Lee Lovett had told her.

'There's only one thing that is more urgent than a murder inquiry,' Kate said. 'And that's you heading for a bollocking.'

She parked her car at Carleton Hall and walked slowly to the entrance to the 1960s concrete façade that had been plopped on top of a rather nice nineteenth-century home. Inside, the modern had conquered the historic and it felt like she was inside any cop shop. It was a pity, but most grand public buildings used for the services were now crumbling shadows of their former selves.

Kelly nodded to a few colleagues she knew. The atmosphere at Carleton Hall was different to Eden House. The pace was slower, the dress was more formal and the mood less urgent. It felt like what it was: an admin centre.

There was a new kid on the block. Chief Constable Derek (Del) Booker was approachable, firm but casual, and fair. He had a worn but kind face, like a young Clint Eastwood, and he'd worked in the Manchester Met both with Dan and Fin at various points in their careers. He'd also worked with DCI Craig Lockwood from Barrow-in-Furness, who she rated highly. He was one of the good guys. It still wasn't a woman, but that was fine by Kelly, if the best candidate got the job. She knew from her days in London that female bosses could be just as brutal as male ones.

She knocked on his door and he shouted for her to enter. He smiled broadly at her when she did and beckoned her to relax and take a seat.

'Sir,' she said, sitting.

'Kelly, I'll get straight to the point. Your Grasmere case.'

'Sir?'

To her, the chief looked uncomfortable, but she could have just imagined it.

'Grasmere? Rydal?'

'Ah, the double homicide, sir?'

'Exactly. Where are we?'

'In what way, sir?'

Del sighed and got up out of his chair. He walked to the window and peered out. His side profile was terribly handsome, but Kelly forced herself to focus on the job at hand. It was a sad situation that the only men she ever came across were at work. She'd met Johnny in a bar in Pooley Bridge and she recalled those days before she had Lizzie fondly. But now she didn't get out. She was either at work or at home. Her attraction to colleagues – senior or junior – was indicative of her narrow pool of choice, and nothing to do with coppers being especially attractive.

'She was a famous artist wasn't she?'

'I didn't know you were up to date on your artists, sir.' Kelly grinned and Del smirked. It softened the tone a bit. 'We're releasing both their names today. And that of a podcaster who has gone to ground.'

'Good God, there'll be a frenzy.'

'Yes, sir, but that's kind of the point.'

She had prepared a whole speech about where they were in their inquiries and what they were doing. That's usually what she came to Carleton Hall for but what he said next threw her.

'Hold off on that.'

'Excuse me, sir?'

'I said, hold off. We don't need a media circus right now. The Home Office is adamant that relations between us and the US remain solid.'

Clearly conversations had been had behind closed doors that Kelly had no idea about. And they weren't just cosy chats; they were taking place in the highest offices of the land.

'Is there something you wish to share with me, sir?'

He walked back to his desk and leant over it. Kelly felt disadvantaged and very small.

'What have you got on them?' He sat down and waited.

She recovered herself. 'As you know the coroner has ruled homicide for both. They both had some kind of relationship with a famous podcaster which we haven't worked out yet. The CCTV from the guesthouse in Skelwith has flagged up some interesting leads but we're still in the thick of it, sir. His sister was hiding a suitcase full of documents, presumably for him as he was the one who checked her in, and there was a decoy suitcase in his hotel room.'

'So, nothing concrete then? What about the bodyguard? Can I assume you've let that idea go now?'

'No, sir, the opposite in fact, it's urgent we speak to him, if he's still in the country. I'd appreciate your backing to put a bit of pressure on the VIPs at Dow Bank House.'

'Anything else?'

It was abrupt. Distracted. Fucking rude.

'They were close as brother and sister, and I'm tracking down their known associates, who weren't many in number. Jamie's business partner seemed to know her well, judging by photos in her camera phone, which we only discovered this morning. Also, she was pregnant, sir.'

'Oh dear, that's nasty.'

Kelly nodded. 'We don't know who the father is but we've taken DNA tests from the foetus just in case so they can be informed down the line. My suspicion is that it's the podcaster.'

He stared at her and looked away, somewhere over her shoulder. She hated when people did that, not only was it unsettling and made you feel utterly irrelevant.

'Look, I'll get straight to the point,' he said. 'It's sensitive.'

'What is, sir?'

He sighed again. She felt as though it was code for her not being able to read his mind and she felt as though she was supposed to feel inadequate. But she didn't. She was mad.

'Give me a clue, boss, I'm struggling here,' she said.

She could be open and candid with Del, despite having to call him 'sir' now. They had previous form on cases going back to the London Met when he'd been involved in a fraud case years ago when she was a junior detective. She'd been fond of him back then. Memories flooded back of her partner, Seb Crook, and a young Del Booker swooping in to handle a corrupt colleague whose betrayal left everybody blindsided. You always had to watch the ones who worked in professional standards because they were picky about detail and made ruthless officers. Del had a soft outer shell but was remorseless when it came to nailing the perp. He'd been an outstanding officer.

'The company Jamie worked for is of vital importance to foreign trade agreements,' he said.

'What?'

'You heard.'

'Hampton-Dent?'

'Yes.'

'They don't want to be embarrassed, is that it?'

'You got it.'

'Christ, Del. Sorry, sir.'

Del wafted his hand around. 'Call me what you like behind closed doors, Kelly. I know you have impeccable standards when it's important. Between us, this rank means very little if we can't communicate.'

'Yes, sir.'

'I read in your brief report that you sent me that it's rumoured that Jamie Robbins was a drug addict, and his suicide is a potential embarrassment for our partners at Polar Rock Global. You know they were in Downing Street last month. The PM is about to sign a deal on climate change, apparently.'

'Our partners, sir? Since when are we politicians on the side of any government?'

'Kelly, I shouldn't need to remind you about optics. It's not political; it's common sense. Damage limitation.'

She'd heard that phrase before from Sandy.

'And that has what to do with my investigation? By the way, for the record I don't believe he was a drug addict. That's a fallacy designed to throw me off a serious investigation, and now you've just confirmed it. And he didn't kill himself.'

He stared at her.

'Del, when did you grow scared of corporate suits? Are you telling me to back off because I might just find out the truth?'

He smiled. 'Oh, Kelly Porter. I remember you in London, Major Investigation Team EAST. Your ambition hasn't dimmed at all has it?'

'I would call it passion for the truth.'

'I know you would.'

'Is this where you tell me that as we climb the ranks, our burdens become heavier and the little people at the bottom don't understand the pressure from above. The load we carry is directly related to the responsibilities we take on. Have you become an establishment pawn, Del?'

The room suddenly felt very silent.

Kelly felt anger burning in her chest. If she was going to be promoted this year, she'd just fucked her chances.

'Think carefully about your next move, Kelly,' he said.

She got up and turned to the door, then back to him. 'This is above my pay grade. You'll have to remove me from the case if you want a cover-up.'

'Be careful, Porter.'

'Porter? Jesus, Del, when did you sell your soul?'

'That's enough.'

He got up again and paced back to the window and she stood waiting, folding her arms. She'd gone too far but so had he. But then he was paid more and could sack her on the spot. He must do a lot of staring out of that window, she thought.

'Am I dismissed, sir?' she asked finally.

He turned to face her. 'Can you just be a little less noisy? Can you dig around without digging around?'

'I can try,' she said. 'I'll keep you in the loop so you can warn the dogs off when they come for me.'

'I'm serious, Kelly. This is bigger than both of us.'

'What is? I will not massage it to make it look pretty. I simply cannot do that, Del. Sir.'

'I expected that from you. But tone it down. Don't go public just yet.'

'The press is all over it, sir. The media department is going crazy.'

'I know. That's why you're here. Just tone it down. It's no different to dealing with any other high-profile case; certain parameters need to be in place.'

'Gagging restraints?'

He grinned. 'We don't have the resources for you to go charging all over the world to investigate this. And there is no will from above.'

'I know. Justice is expensive.'

She walked to the door, and this time she didn't look back.

'Sometimes politicians make decisions that we don't like,' he said to her back.

She stopped with her hand on the door handle. 'And sometimes they get away with it because money matters more than people. I'll send you the autopsy photos and you can look at them before bed tonight.'

She opened the door and closed it gently behind her and left the building. When she got back into her car she hit the steering wheel several times and swore loudly until her throat hurt. After she'd finished her tantrum, she saw a female officer who'd been smoking behind the carpark staring at her with concern. She smiled and waved and started the engine.

Chapter 43

By the time they finished up for the day, Lee Lovett still hadn't emailed Kelly the CCTV footage from the back stairs at Heron Hall and she'd called him seven times, each time not being answered.

Saturday evening should be the best of the week. For most normal people with nine-to-five jobs, it was. But for Kelly's team, it was just another evening. Lab results were non-existent at the weekend and Kelly insisted they leave at a sensible hour to go to their respective homes. Jamie's toxicology results were being reviewed and might possibly be ready for Monday.

Kelly drove home and picked up a bottle of red wine from a local merchant's and a bunch of fresh flowers to cheer the house up. The last thing she wanted was for Lizzie to grow up conscious of what she did for a living and how it affected her. She wanted the house to be a place of tranquillity and stability, no matter what she was dealing with at work.

When she pulled up, Johnny's car was in the driveway. It was his turn to have Lizzie, and she found she was looking forward to seeing him. It had been three weeks. She opened her front door and went in to the sound of *In the Night Garden*. Lizzie was bathed and dressed in a fresh all-in-one and sucking happily on a cup of milk. Johnny held her on his lap and smiled widely. He was tanned. Her stomach lurched but she told herself it was just the pull of familiarity at a tough time. Sometimes all she wanted was somebody who understood her to hold her and listen to the shitty week she'd had, and Johnny had always done that. The wounds left from his lies still smarted, but they were healing. He'd finalised his divorce from Carrie and they'd split their assets, but the secrecy regarding the whole thing was something that she didn't need in her life at the time.

'Hey,' she said. She went to kiss her daughter and Lizzie held out her hand to stroke her face.

'Mama,' she gurgled. 'Dada,' she added.

Johnny was thrilled.

'Clever girl!' Kelly praised her. Lizzie's favourite words were 'Nana', short for banana, 'nee-nor', chorused whenever they played with vehicles, 'Gang', for Ted, and 'Lee-lee', for Millie.

Her repertoire was growing.

'How was Scotland?' Kelly asked.

'Epic,' he said. 'The weather was perfect.'

'I heard a climber died on Stob Dearg.'

'Yeah. He fell. He was sixty years old, with his family. It was horrendous. It was across the valley from us.'

'Good, I'm glad you didn't get involved; you need time off too.'

Johnny was an experienced mountain rescue volunteer and had worked with the Lake District teams for seven years. Now he split his time between here and Glencoe.

'Have you eaten?' she asked.

'I was thinking about going to the van for fish and chips, fancy joining me?' he asked.

'Sounds wonderful, let me change and put these flowers in a vase.'

She left them and went to the kitchen. She arranged the flowers and corked the wine ready for later then she rushed upstairs to change. Getting out of her work clothes, even though she had a casual dress policy around the office, was still a luxurious feeling of freedom. It was like shedding old skin. A quick shower revived her, and thoughts of Angelina and Jamie Robbins left her for a moment. She touched up her make-up and went downstairs.

'We could take Lizzie out for a walk first then grab some food on the way back.'

'Perfect.'

'Will you stay tonight?'

'If you don't mind. I got your message; thanks, it helps. The traffic will be hell tonight, so I decided to hang around here for the weekend. I'll probably stay next week too if you want to give Millie some time off; I'll pay her.'

'It's hard prising her away from Lizzie but she'll appreciate that, I'm sure. She was telling me this week that her mates were swimming in Grasmere, and I could tell she wanted to go. I've had a hell of a week; I'll tell you about it on our walk.'

They got Lizzie ready and plonked her in her pram. She cuddled a teddy bear and looked almost ready for sleep. Kelly put a thin blanket over her to keep the night air off her even though it was still warm. The sun was going down over the western fells. Helvellyn was clear and dominated the other end of Ullswater. Kelly's house was a haven of peace with the terrace sitting over the River Eamont, but she knew the contours of the sky like the back of her hand. She closed the terrace doors, and they left the house. They wandered along the road to the steamer launch. There was a boat coming in and they stopped to watch so Lizzie could point to it, but she soon grew tired and fell asleep, so they turned back to the village.

'I heard about the woman in Grasmere,' he said, confident his daughter was asleep.

Kelly looked at Johnny's sure hand on the pram and imagined the warmth where the veins stood out. He smelt good and he reminded her of a safe place. It wasn't that she wanted to throw herself at him and start all over again – they'd tried that so many times – it was just that he was a harbour for her. She liked to be anchored to him. She missed him. He was still her best friend.

'Yeah, she was killed for something she was hiding, we think.'

'Mysterious,' he said.

'It's not in the news; it's a blackout. Her brother died the next day.'

'That's terrible for the parents.'

'They didn't have parents; they were foster kids.'

'Were they connected? Why the mystery?'

'Yep, he was staying at the Heron Hall.'

'I heard something about that. A suicide? I always wanted to take you there,' he said.

She side-eyed him and he smiled.

'You're flirting with me again,' she said.

'I know, but I will always keep trying, Kel.'

She put her arm around his waist, and he held her close and kissed the top of her head.

'You smell good,' she said.

He squeezed her.

'It's probably a good thing they had no parents. Their deaths were violent.'

'He was murdered too?'

'It presented as a suicide, like the rumour mill is saying, but the circumstances are off. He was launching a hot new health supplement that is worth a lot of money to a huge American pharmaceutical. The whole thing stinks, but like you always told me, I can't catch all the bastards, just one at a time.'

He laughed. 'Did I say that? I'm a veritable modern-day prophet.'

She laughed. 'You know, I had the oddest meeting at Carleton Hall this morning. I haven't told a soul. I was warned off by the new chief.'

'Warned off?'

'This case. Don't dig too deep, he said. International relations, can you believe it? The corporate masters are valuable to British trade interests, and we wouldn't want to rub them up the wrong way, would we? I can't be responsible for ruining the special relationship.'

'Special relationship my arse. If the Americans say jump, we say how high, and rightly so. When I was in Iraq, their kit was supreme, and our families were sending us body armour bought off the internet. We are the poor cousin. If this has come from Downing Street then they've been warned by the embassy, which to me says everything. Be careful. I know you too well. You'll go charging in and scratch the scab off and it won't be welcomed. You've got a daughter now, Kel.'

Five years ago, she would have hit him for being so conformist and easily bought, but today she knew he was right. The value of her life and that of her daughter was more important than anything in the world. Whatever Jamie and Angelina were up to, she couldn't single-handedly expose a trail of corruption and dirty money that led to the heart of Big Pharma and, ergo, the American government. That was above her pay grade.

'You're right. I haven't decided exactly how I'm going to handle this. I reckon there's a trail leading to market share leaders who are so rich they buy economies. I've looked into them. These families have been billionaires since the Rothschilds and Rockefellers won the First World War.'

'Woah, what have you been reading?'

'I've been following a podcaster. He's controversial. Many would say he's a conspiracy theorist. He's got a whole series on the Twin Towers, Princess Diana, Epstein. My God, honestly, it blows my mind.'

'You know what they call a conspiracy theorist?'

She nodded. 'A year ahead of the news?'

'But seriously though, what is all this about? Do you need me to take Lizzie away for a while?'

'That might not be a bad idea. I found documents relating to clinical trials in the woman's personal items – hidden in a bloody wall – I know, you can't make this shit up. Have you heard of the legend of Skelwith Bridge?'

'The spies?'

'You know! How did I not know?'

'No, I'm pulling your leg, tell me. It was just a guess because you've gone all cloak and dagger on me.'

She told him what Tommy at the Old Man had told her and Johnny chuckled.

'Blimey, you really must be careful.'

'It all points to them using an untested compound in a health drink.'

'What is it?'

'I don't know yet; I'm having it tested. If it's harmful what the hell do I do? Nobody takes on the food and drug industry and wins. It's got some silly name. Neurohydroxy-14. I think the two victims were going to go public with the information.'

'No one takes them on and survives. They can ruin anyone who gets close, I've seen it with whistleblowers in the army. The arms trade is dirtier than Blackpool beach. I've seen it from the inside. Sierra Leone. Bosnia. You don't want to get anywhere near big business that is funded by governments.'

'How do I know it's funded by governments?'

'Why else would you get a warning through channels that presumably came through the Home Office, via the Foreign Office, via diplomatic comms? Follow the vested interest and sooner or later you get to a boatload of money.'

'Why is this planet run by megalomaniacs?'

Johnny smiled. 'To test the little people. We always win in the end. Empires never last very long, only around a thousand years, and then they have too many wars and they implode.'

'Great. Let's celebrate the end of the world as we know it.'

'Let's get food. What are you having?'

'Large haddock, chips and mushy peas.'

'I'll get the same.'

They walked to the van and said hello to Ned, the owner. His enterprise had brought another food outlet to Pooley Bridge to cater for the tourists and locals alike. The van was extremely popular. Ned wrapped up their food and placed it in a plastic bag and Johnny carried it while Kelly pushed the pram. The smell made her hungry and when they got back to her house, it didn't take long for them to unwrap and begin to devour them. Kelly put some ketchup on the kitchen table, and they loaded their plates and took them onto the terrace. They didn't need blankets just yet but there was a definite cooling of the sky.

'How's Ted?' Johnny asked.

'He's great. Sharp as ever. He misses you.'

'Do you miss me?'

Kelly glanced at him. This was the question she didn't want to answer because she was terrified of it failing again.

Lizzie gurgled from her pram in the hall. They hadn't risked moving her while they were eating; that could wait – she was more than comfortable in there.

'Of course I do. I miss the best times. I miss swimming on a hot day after work and talking about our jobs. I miss you next to me when I wake up and when I go to sleep.'

They munched quietly, each contemplating what the other meant to them.

When they'd finished their food, Johnny tidied the plates and Kelly put Lizzie to bed and when she came back downstairs, Johnny had poured them a glass of wine each and taken blankets out to the terrace. The sun was dipping, and the day was almost done. The week had thrown Kelly some curveballs but now Johnny was there, and even if it was only for a couple of nights in her spare room while she tackled whatever this case threw at her next, she knew that she'd feel safer.

Chapter 44

Sixteen miles away, in the town of Keswick, on Derwent Water's north shore, Emma parked her car.

She'd been following a podcast on a corporate manslaughter case, related to FairGro, and paused it to gather her things and finally relax at home with Dan for the evening. They were looking forward to turning in for an early night. The case was making them all scratch their heads. Until they had solid forensic analysis, they couldn't tie anything together.

She and Dan had been seeing each other on and off for over two years now and they'd had the conversation about what their future looked like.

They fitted together. That was all that mattered to them both. In many ways, they were opposites, but that's why it worked. In the office, they were soulmates; at home, they dovetailed.

Kelly Porter was a brilliant boss. A superb operator but she was also human. She had warned them in the early days about interprofessional relationships. They were tricky. They knew that. But their boss said personal lives only became important if they encroached on performance. Besides, since losing Rob, they all valued life a little bit more.

Emma's pregnancy had made them even closer. At only fourteen weeks, she'd had to tell Kelly because her body had begun to show signs of mutiny. Sickness, weird swelling, nausea towards tea and coffee, irritability and a short temper. It also made her terribly emotional and it had been tough looking at the autopsy photos of Angelina Robbins.

She walked towards the door of the grand old Victorian terrace that was divided into four flats, laden with kit from her car.

The podcast was part of a series she was following. It was hosted by Joe Folly.

This one told a story of corruption and money grabbing that was worthy of a Netflix show. Emma hardly believed it was true and if she hadn't seen the evidence for herself, she wouldn't have believed it still. Over the last week, she and Dan had grown to regard the young podcaster as an important voice in the case. He showed integrity, he treated his sources with respect, he never revealed his witnesses without their permission, and he was endorsed by some big names across the pond and in Europe. It had become quite a thing for Emma and Dan to listen to him in the evening. They'd discovered Hampton-Dent had a history of covering up insurance claims and illegal use of toxic ingredients. They got away with it, according to Joe Folly, because Tilda Dent's uncle was a congressman, her cousin was a Supreme Court judge and Hank Hampton's father was a senator. There were governors, attorneys and a litter of names in the house of representatives too.

They were like the Kennedys. It was the UK equivalent of being related to the royal family, with the access to their cash, as well as having chums in the Houses of Parliament. The dark shadows of power were a mystery to her and her mind was open to anything, if it was backed with enough evidence. Joe Folly was convincing.

Medical negligence claims against Hampton-Dent were hushed up, paid off, or the plaintiff disappeared.

She got to the door, but her key didn't work. It happened sometimes because it was slightly twisted from being crushed under a car wheel when she drove over it. She swore and thought about calling Dan. She could see lights on in their window on the first floor, but she took a deep breath and picked up her things again and went to the rear of the building. It was dark back there and she had difficulty finding her keys again. She'd put them in her bag and now had to put down everything and search for them.

'Fuck.' She dropped them.

'Emma.' The voice was male and unfamiliar, and she jumped out of her skin, falling over backwards into a bush.

A figure in black came towards her and leant over, holding out his hand, which was gloved. She looked at it and then at his face, which was half covered with a face mask, as if he were afraid of some invisible virus, but her innards told her that he wore it to prevent her recognising him again. Her body went into high alert.

'Do I know you?'

He didn't answer but came closer and she went to shout at the top of her voice, but as soon as she did, he moved like lightning and was on her, covering her mouth with his hand, stifling her cry.

She couldn't move. Her heart raced and her body stopped fighting. They were taught to appease an attacker and use their intellect not their strength. In most cases of assault, the victim was overwhelmed because of poor decisions and panic. The element of surprise made up for 80 per cent of the power. Emma felt vulnerable and tried to think her way out of the situation. He released his hand gently and whispered. 'Don't shout else I'll hurt you, understood?'

It was a London accent.

She nodded.

'This is a warning, Emma. Don't be a hero. I watched Dan come home, he's waiting for you, but next time it might be me up there not him. You understand, don't you?'

She nodded vociferously.

Then he disappeared.

Chapter 45

Across town, Ted watched a couple taking their dog across Hope Park for the honour of his last toilet stop of the evening. They were about the same age as him and he felt nostalgic as he recalled the two loves of his life. His wife, Mary, was a fine woman before the drink took her mind. Then Wendy, the woman he should have been with all his life, was taken too soon from him. He missed companionship.

Their daughter, Kelly, had been conceived not far from here, on the shore of Lake Ullswater, under a moon like this one, as the guests of the Earl of Lowesdale partied the night away at Wasdale Hall.

Wendy had been married to John Porter.

She hadn't told him about the baby until Kelly was forty years old.

Better late than never.

He stared at the couple and wondered if they were late to love or they'd been together forever.

His relationship with Wendy, rediscovered again just recently, until her untimely death, felt like a lifetime, it was that precious. But now she was gone, and he lived for Kelly and Lizzie. He'd be with them now, but he knew that Johnny was here for the weekend, and he secretly hoped they'd get back together. They were a great couple, but modern life was harder than in his day. They had so many decisions to make and it was too easy to give up. He liked Johnny and treated him like a son-in-law. He stayed out of the way not because he wanted to but because he thought they needed time, that was all. In time, they'd realise their relationship was a good one, and not one to be thrown away.

He smiled as he made his way home, with a takeaway Chinese in a plastic bag. He shouldn't eat so late because it gave him indigestion, but he was ravenous after a busy couple of days. Two autopsies – and such detailed ones – which were terribly important to Kelly, had taken the puff out of him. Tonight, he'd eat and open a bottle of fabulous red and then have a good night's sleep.

Then tomorrow he'd see Johnny, Kelly and Lizzie all together.

Life was good.

He was almost home and about to cross the road at the traffic lights when a jogger came towards him pretty fast and ran straight into his path. Ted tried to move but they smashed together, and his Chinese food went all over the pavement. Ted tried to put out his hand to break his fall, but he couldn't get it out of the bag's handle in time and his head hit the concrete of the pavement hard. He heard a din in his ears and thought his brains were rattling. He rolled close to the side of the road and lost his vision.

For a second, he thought he was about to be run over as a car screeched to a halt three inches away from his head.

He peered up. The street was deadly quiet.

The runner leant over him but instead of asking how he was, or trying to help, he just grinned. His hood was pulled tight over his head so Ted couldn't make out his face.

'You need to be more careful, old man.'

Ted stared at him and then the pain hit. His head pounded and his wrist felt on fire as an electric bolt shot through it. He reckoned it was broken.

Another pair of feet came to a stop next to him and Ted reckoned it was the driver of the car.

'Tell that daughter of yours to stop nosing around, or she might find herself without a father to babysit.'

The voice was low but powerful and it took Ted a little while to make sense of the words. But when he did, he realised exactly what had happened to him. It was no accident. It was planned. These two fellas had ambushed him and knocked him over on purpose.

And Kelly was in danger.

Then the driver and the runner climbed into the car, and it sped off before Ted could even see what make it was. He wasn't even sure of the colour.

He peered around the street wondering if CCTV covered it, but he saw no cameras. Perhaps one of the shops over the road might have footage of the street. He was thinking like Kelly. Panic gripped him as he thought about her alone with Lizzie in her home. No, he recalled, Johnny would be there by now.

An aroma of Chinese food wafted over to him, and he looked forlornly at the mess on the road, which could have been his body, if he'd gone under the wheels. He wasn't stupid. He knew that if they'd meant to kill him tonight, they would have, and it would be considered a terrible accident.

He went to fish his phone out of his pocket but the pain in his wrist made him howl.

Then the couple with the dog rushed to his side and helped him up.

'Are you OK, fella? Jesus, he ran straight at you. I thought the car was going to hit you.'

'You saw it?'

'We did; he was aiming straight at you!'

'Please, go into my pocket and take out my phone,' he pleaded with them.

The woman did so and handed him his mobile and he called Kelly. They fussed over him as the call connected.

Kelly picked up and he breathed into the handset.

'Dad? Are you OK? Dad?'

'Kelly? Thank God.'

'Dad? What is it?'

Chapter 46

Kelly took the call in the kitchen.

Johnny was upstairs seeing to Lizzie, who'd woken up. She was coming down with a cold. Another one.

Kelly couldn't hear her father properly and moved around the downstairs to get better reception. But she still couldn't make out what he was saying. It was late and it was unlike her father to panic so she knew something was up.

'Dad?'

'Kelly?'

Then an unidentified woman came on the line. She told Kelly her dad had been knocked over.

'Knocked over?'

Kelly went into overdrive and gathered shoes and a jacket to throw on. She prepared to rush upstairs to tell Johnny she was leaving and hopped about from one foot to the other, trying to get socks on. She managed to get a location out of the woman. He was lying on the pavement in the middle of Keswick near Hope Park after his ordeal. As far as she could tell, he'd been knocked clean over by a jogger then nearly run over by a car which drove straight off.

A potential hit and run.

A hollow feeling crept into Kelly's stomach, and she looked towards the terrace, as a noise drew her attention.

She peered up the stairs and flicked off the lights.

'I'm on my way; have you called an ambulance?'

'Yes, but your father is trying to get up; he won't stay still. He's saying you must be careful.'

Kelly tucked the phone under her chin and her eyes focused.

The lounger outside had moved.

She had left both of them close together when she and Johnny had brought in the blankets.

They'd kissed.

She'd regretted it but loved it at the same time. He was doing it again. No, she was allowing him to do it again.

Thoughts of Johnny's lips on hers melted into insignificance as she sank back into the shadows of her own home. Then she thought of her daughter upstairs.

Her head tingled with alertness.

The tiny hairs on her arms stood up and her breathing slowed.

A movement on the terrace caught her eye and she saw a shadow cross the space and enter her lounge from the open door. She pressed her back into the wall and found the curtain with her hands. She manoeuvred her body into the alcove near the front door, where she hung coats, and covered herself with one.

And watched.

A figure, dressed in black, wearing a mask, crossed the floor and peered upstairs.

She heard a door open and close above her and tried to make a decision based on what was best for Lizzie. Should she scream and alert Johnny, thereby forcing him downstairs and leaving Lizzie exposed? Or should she tackle the intruder herself, thereby putting herself in danger but protecting her daughter?

There was no contest.

She felt behind her. Her hand made contact with an umbrella stand. Inside it was a spare walking cane for Ted. It was made of oak and had an enamel duck on the top. She'd bought it with Johnny, at an antique market in Ambleside. Her hand clasped it, and she waited for the figure to appear in the hall. It didn't take long, and she held the cane as tightly as she could, poising her body for attack.

The figure looked upstairs again, and she could tell he was figuring out the floorplan.

For a split second she refused to believe this was happening to her and her brain told her she was hallucinating, but then she saw him approach the stairs.

She grabbed the cane with as much force as she could load through her body and swung it towards him. It connected and she felt a splat where it hit his head.

He went down and she stood over him, but then he recovered and rolled away.

'Who the fuck are you?' she seethed.

He rolled and rolled and sprang up, then shot towards the terrace and jumped over her balcony. She chased him and heard him enter the river with a faint splash, but when she looked over into the dark water, there was no trace of him.

Her chest heaved up and down and her eyes darted every which way. Her heart pumped hard, and she willed herself to calm down.

Johnny came down the stairs and flicked on a light and she held up the cane.

'What the fuck?' He backed away.

Then she sank to her knees and mumbled some words that didn't make sense.

He came to her and held her.

'Kel, what happened? I heard a noise.'

She sank into his arms and allowed herself to be embraced wholly. In that moment she surrendered everything because she knew she was safe.

In the same moment, she realised that she wanted him home. It wasn't the same without him, and that wasn't to do with the fact that he might be able to deter an intruder or comfort her in her hour of need. It was because his presence soothed her. It was like they were two parts of the same whole.

She calmed her breathing and told him about the phone call from Ted's phone.

'Jesus! Is he OK?'

Kelly's heart glowed because she knew how much he cared for her father.

Then her phone rang, and it was Dan.

Johnny answered and stared at her.

She knew exactly what Dan had told him.

Her team and her loved ones had been warned.

This was no accidental invasion.

Chapter 47

Sunday morning felt otherworldly. Not only had Kelly not slept, but she was still wearing the same clothes she'd had on last night.

She'd driven to the Penrith and Lakes hospital, where Ted had been admitted for observation. He'd railed against his treatment, saying being mollycoddled wouldn't help anyone.

He'd been embarrassed. It would take his wrist six weeks to heal in a cast. In the meantime, he wouldn't be able to perform surgery but he'd already announced loudly that he could type one handed and tell other people what to do.

'Twenty years ago, I would have seen them coming,' he'd told her.

'You might not have done, Dad. It was organised; it was a warning,' she'd told him.

He'd stared at her, incredulous that the arm of hidden violence from an unknown source could reach as far as the peaceful Lake District.

She stopped short of telling him her true theory, thinking it'd be too much for him. Sometimes being awake to something awful wasn't designed to be shared with everyone. She must choose her moments carefully to announce what she suspected. But that provided her with another problem, because she was unsure exactly where the threat originated. She had no doubt it was connected to the warning she'd had from HQ, but exactly who she was dealing with was a mystery, and she hated surprises. But there was no doubt in her mind that whoever it was would lead back to Hampton-Dent.

Emma had been stalked back to her home and pushed over. Ted had been badly hurt and could have been killed. And she had been invaded. None of it was coincidence. Serendipity and policework did not get along. Chance was a children's game. Providence wasn't on hand to intervene in a murder case to make it fit neatly with a whole other agenda, which just so happened to be primarily about financial profit.

And Emma and her baby had been put in danger. Dan had almost gone out of his mind with rage, and their joy, along with the euphoria surrounding it, had been ruined by thugs. Kelly was mad.

There was nothing quite like injustice to get Kelly's back up and her mind wandered to when she'd first worked in London as a newly qualified detective in Bethnal Green CID. Her dream had been to work in a murder squad, thinking it noble and virtuous. If she'd known then what she knew now, after too many respectable people had let her down from within the service, would she have seen it through? Would she still choose the same career path?

She didn't know.

After some routine treatment for shock, Ted had marched out of the hospital with his head high, and his arm in a temporary cast, thanking all the staff and insisting they treat people who were seriously in need of their help.

In the car, he'd been silent, and she'd allowed him to disappear inside his thoughts. Until they reached her house. Johnny had greeted him with open arms, and Ted had snuck upstairs to give his granddaughter a kiss.

Lizzie had slept through the whole thing.

They'd stayed up all night, the three of them, drinking strong coffee – and Ted and Johnny something a little stronger – trying to figure out who'd sent the heavies.

They kept coming back to the money trail. Her original plan of keeping Ted out of it had hit the wayside straight away and he was ahead of her the whole time.

'People only protect one thing like that,' Johnny said. He'd experienced corruption on a biblical scale in Africa and inside the Pentagon during a stint there on an MOD secondment. And it all led back to money, every single time.

'Tax dollars pay for foreign aid from the USA and Europe, and it's funnelled through non-government organisations and industry contracts, then the top is skimmed off and cleaned and sent back to handlers in the origin country. Politicians, CEOs of Big Pharma and civil servants looking the other way all get rich. You disturb this gravy train at your peril,' Johhny announced. 'Hampton-Dent are not to be messed with.'

Ted and Kelly had stared at each other. All they were trying to do was solve a few murders in one of the quietest and loveliest parts of the national park. They didn't ask to take on the world; the world had come to them, suddenly, brazenly, and unannounced.

'It all seems very dramatic,' Ted said.

'Which is why nobody ever believes it's what goes on, but I've seen it with my own eyes, Ted. I know people who've been hurt trying to spill industry secrets, but the media is in on it too, because they're owned by the same people.'

'My head hurts,' Ted said.

'You need to rest, Dad, you've had a nasty bang, and the lady said you hit the ground hard. You should have stayed in hospital.'

'There's nothing wrong with me. I mean my head hurts because of what Johnny said, not because I banged my head. It hurts because of the badness in the world, going on out there, all the time while good people just try to do the right thing.'

It was a grand statement and one that neither Johnny nor Kelly could disagree with.

They'd watched the sun come up behind Pooley Bridge and the orange welcome kiss the lake. Only then had Kelly become tired as her adrenaline dipped.

Then she'd taken a nap, but now it was time to get to work and rally the team.

The thing was, she didn't know what to say.

She didn't want to alarm anyone further.

But equally she didn't want to go back to HQ and tell Del Booker what she knew. He'd clearly been warned by somebody higher up, so he already had an inkling of corruption, but would he believe the extent of it? Perhaps she was being naïve and he knew more than she did all along.

She must figure this out on her own. Her priority was keeping her team and her family safe, and she'd already arranged for squad cars to sit outside the addresses of her team.

Johnny would stay the weekend in her house, and Ted had agreed to stay there too.

A quick shower had freshened her up and woken her sleepy brain, but a weariness sat on her shoulders. She had an overwhelming desire to speak to Joe Folly and she wished she'd arrested him on Thursday when she had the chance. But what crime had he committed?

This was just the type of thing he warned about. His lack of social footprint, his vigilance, and his wild theories all seemed to be coming to fruition right here in the tiny Lake District.

Which led her to her original question. Why here? Why had a huge multinational billion-dollar company chosen the shores of Rydal Water to hold a conference that stood to make them crazy profits?

Was it the anonymity? The secrecy? The fact they could hide it if anything went wrong?

Was it the caves?

Maybe that was it. Perhaps they were expecting trouble. Perhaps Jamie was a loose cannon.

She'd hugged Lizzie extra tight this morning and was more vigilant than normal on her journey to work. She checked her rear-view mirror and locked her doors and windows.

When she arrived at Eden House for the unusual Sunday morning brief, she looked up and down the street for anything suspicious.

The office was silent, and she expected to see nobody there, but everybody had beaten her to it. She found them sitting in their chairs, working seriously at their computers.

Wordlessly, they looked to her for strength and for her to decide their next move. It was unprecedented. They'd never been attacked as a team before. And Kelly had never felt so vulnerable and exposed.

She sat down at the head of the incident table and one by one, her colleagues took position around her. Kate sat down first. She looked tired and Kelly smelt cigarette smoke. Kate had started up again, and no wonder. Dan sat next to her and fiddled with his fingers. Emma pulled out a seat and Kelly had never seen the young woman appear so pensive. She was usually full of life and vibrancy. But now she had a new life to protect. It was an added worry.

Finally, Fin sat to her left and he had shadows around his eyes.

A quick check had revealed that Fin had stayed at a mate's house last night so was absent from his usual address and Kate had been woken in the early hours by their new dog going nuts. Minor incidents took on new meaning and they peered at one another, waiting.

'We have several choices,' Kelly announced. 'One, I go to Del Booker and tell him everything, and my guess is he'll want to avoid the heat and I'll be removed from the case. Two, we quietly drop the investigation and come up with some bullshit spurious causation and file it away. Three, we throw everything at it and nail these fuckers.'

Their shoulders lifted a little and then a lot. Kate smiled. Dan put his hand over Emma's. Fin clapped.

'Ladies and gentlemen, I'm exhausted. I didn't sleep. My father is recovering from a serious head wound which he is denying even exists. He's also got a cast on his arm. An intruder came within twenty feet of my daughter's bedroom. My faith is in us, here in this room. I'm not convinced this is a global intrigue that has invaded our beautiful space here in the Lakes, but if it is, and I'm open to persuasion, then I'm throwing everything behind chasing them out. I'm told what to do sometimes, I'm told what to eat, what to wear and how to speak. I've never been told what to think. And I don't intend to start now. This investigation is open and we're going to finish it, like we do all the others.'

She looked around the table and there was no dissent, just glances of admiration from her team. She wasn't asking anyone to put themselves in danger. She was simply asking for hard work.

'We work from here. The risk is mine. We'll direct uniforms to gather the detritus, and our job is to find where this all leads. Nobody is to leave this office without explaining when and why.'

The atmosphere in the incident room transformed from unsure and cowed to upright and energised and she slapped the table.

'Dan, I believe we have some lab results to share?'

Dan nodded. 'Poor little Skippy the squirrel was poisoned for sure. He was overcome with a toxin that isn't isolated on our databases, so I can't give it a name, but nonetheless we have similarities with other chemicals and that means we can best guess the sample. It behaves like a neurotoxin, and I've been told it presents most like something called glutamate, which is an amino acid essential for normal life. It's actually produced by the body and it's vital for a healthy nervous system. However, in high doses, it's lethal. The lab is working on it further.'

He looked around the room and was reassured that his colleagues were just about keeping up. 'This sample was unique because of what it was attached to, a diuretic called hydroxy-11 and a testosterone compound known as androstene-3. The lab said they had never seen a real example of the compound under a microscope, though they had read about the existence of such drugs, mainly used for performance enhancement.'

'Did they give you a name?'

Dan smiled. 'They did. My old friend, N-14. During initial rounds of testing it destroyed the neurotransmitters of rats' brains. The lab technician said she'd only read about it, she'd never seen it, neither had anyone she worked with. She was quite excited about it in a scientific nerdy kind of way.'

'Holy shit. Do we have confirmation on the contents of *YouthBlast*?'

'I received a definitive yes from the lab in Dublin. The sachet contains the compound; it's unequivocal. And I wonder if it's linked to what happened to some of us last night. The lab made some inquiries outside the area to several other labs in London and the one in Dublin which specialises in metabolic disorders. These things get around, it's a small world, and I wonder if their calls triggered a chain of information that got back to those wanting to keep its use hidden.'

Kelly googled the ingredients list again, sure now she hadn't made a mistake. The asterisk and the reference had gone.

'Do we know what links those labs have with parent companies and funders?'

'Emma?' Kelly asked.

Emma stood up and Dan squeezed her hand. She went to the front of the room and stood next to where Kelly was seated and tapped the computer screen. The hush in the room demonstrated what everyone was thinking: that if they got their hands on the bastard who'd threatened Emma's baby, they'd better run for the hills behind Penrith or get battered.

Information on several pharmaceuticals popped up on the large white screen and Emma sat back down so the others could absorb what they were reading.

'These four companies are all owned by subsidiaries of Hampton-Dent,' Emma said. 'What's that one?' Kelly asked. 'I recognise it.'

'The Nirvana Project?' Emma asked.

'Yes. Lee Lovett told me that an American company had shown interest in buying Heron Hall. I'm sure he said it was The Nirvana Project.'

'Hampton-Dent wants to buy Heron Hall?' Fin asked.

'Yes, and the fact that somebody died there deflated the selling price and made the owners desperate.'

'That's illegal fixing,' Dan said. 'Do you think this could be motive?'

'It's a bit dramatic just to get a hotel at a knock-off price,' Kelly said. 'But it's important nonetheless. It shows that we need to forensically examine each of these trading partners. Which company linked to Hank Hampton paid Angelina? Was it one of these?'

'None of these, no, but that doesn't mean there aren't more we haven't found yet. It's easier to follow the names rather than the products. That's where we've found dead ends,' Emma explained. 'Hank Hampton sat on the board of all four of these companies at some point. He has also hosted conferences on the efficacy of new and experimental drugs which disrupt biomarkers and immune systems. He is also linked via money to some of the funding for the clinical studies into the components of N-14, amongst others.'

'Amongst others?' Kelly asked.

'Yes, that's what I've discovered. N-14 is just one very minor cog in a huge wheel. Experimental drugs and compounds are being released onto the market all the time. Some are endorsed by celebrities and politicians both sides of the pond, and some don't make it. N-14 falls into the grey area in the middle, along with about four hundred others. Officially, for our purposes, what this means is that it is still under the umbrella of those drugs and additives without rubber-stamped safety regulatory caveats. So, for example, when a drug is passed as safe, it can then be added to the food supply or consumed via medical prescription or over the counter, depending on its grading. There are thousands though which are "deemed safe" that don't have to be tested. This is where the shady links come into play, because if they were safe, why have the cloggy bureaucracy confusing anyone trying to sue them for negligence?'

The room was silent.

Considering Emma had been threatened just last night, it certainly hadn't dimmed her focus. The team looked at her with a mixture of confusion over where she sourced her energy, and admiration.

'And that's where it gets really interesting,' Emma continued. 'Hampton-Dent, or companies trading under its parent name, and I've only scratched the surface of how many of those there are, pay out millions in litigation per year. But that is nothing compared to how many claims they reject. Some estimates range from them paying out to only 5 per cent of claims against them. And the cases literally get swept under the carpet, ignored, or lost in paperwork. Claimants can't afford to hire good legal teams, the paperwork is too complicated, or the judicial system is rigged against them, or all three.'

Kelly stared at Emma for a few seconds and the injustice of it all stuck in her throat. She could see the rest of her team thought exactly the same. These huge corporations poisoned ordinary people and got away with it. It was that simple.

'And where does N-14 sit in all of this? Is it dangerous or not? Because the way you and Dan have explained it, if I'm getting this correct, it is toxic, and can cause huge damage, even fatal, but there is no existing certification, or even any acknowledgement that it is in the food supply?'

'Correct,' Dan said.

'OK, so we're dealing with an additive that doesn't exist on paper, but its components do, so before we can prove that Jamie knew this and died for it, along with his sister, we have to prove that Hampton-Dent are covering it up?'

Silence.

Kelly sat down.

'We start with the lab,' she said, sitting up straight. 'We need them to state categorically that this is a compound that is toxic and untested, with potential lethality. Once we have that, then we can start the process of confronting the manufacturer. I don't need to warn you all that we might not get very far. The product is made in a lab in San Diego, shipped to factories in the Republic of Ireland and then packed in another factory in the Netherlands. By that time, it's legal, so liability will rest on us proving Angelina and Jamie were killed for it, and at the moment I have no other suggestions.'

Kate indicated she had something to add. They shifted their attention to her.

'I looked into the scientist, Sandy Cooper. She has written plenty of scientific papers for Hampton and Dent companies. When Emma flagged up the links, I began to pay more attention to who funded her work.'

'Hampton-Dent?'

Kate nodded. 'Without exception. If you follow the names of the companies and their stocks, they all come back to Hampton-Dent. Like Emma and Dan, I started looking at the small print under the articles in scientific journals. You can do a Google search of any of the companies listed underneath her title and they all go back to the same lab in San Diego. However, I looked further into it, and I managed to track down a couple of ex-employees and one was willing to answer a few questions. They didn't know much about the structure of the company or the names of CEOs or that kind of thing, but one was extremely angry about the way they'd been let go and she had lots to say about Doctor Cooper.'

They all listened intently as Kate read from her notes.

Kate took a deep breath and Kelly knew there was something important coming. She was so proud of her team, and it went some way to softening the shock of last night.

'She called Cooper a quack, which could be sour grapes, of course. But then she accused her outright of being responsible for the long-term illnesses of hundreds of people who'd been paid to take part in trials. Now, bear in mind this is a disgruntled ex-employee, we don't know if we can trust her, but I asked about the studies, and she said they were testing diuretics and hormones and how they could be used to control behaviour. Ostensibly they were told that it was for breakthrough medicines for behavioural syndromes like ADHD. But she heard rumours it was for the military. She couldn't name the compounds, but she did say that a couple of people were given huge pay-offs for their injuries and sent to recuperate in random places all over the world.'

'What sort of injuries?' Kelly asked.

'Neurological. She said the test subjects were called assets.'

'That's an intelligence term, not a commercial one,' Kelly said.

'Right? She alleged they suffered bouts of uncontrolled rage and Alzheimer's-like symptoms. There were several accidents involving violence and the whole project was shelved.'

'Paul Burlington said he felt angry when he drank too much *YouthBlast*,' Kelly said.

'The point is, she told me an interesting location for one of the "recuperation centres", as she called them. There's one right here in the Lake District. They choose remote and obscure locations for the assets who survived.'

'Survived what?'

'Whatever they were given, I guess,' Kate said.

Chapter 48

Kelly checked in with Johnny at home.

She was getting jumpy.

She'd tried several times to locate Lee Lovett, but his phone had gone to voicemail each time and now it was switched off. She'd called Heron Hall and she'd been informed by a cleaner that it was still closed. He still hadn't sent her the CCTV footage of the back stairs.

Last night had spooked them all but more than that it had lit a fire in Kelly's belly, and she was more determined than ever to nail the people behind the web of lies and the layers of deceit. Del Booker could go to hell. This was her investigation, and she didn't take intimidation lightly.

She was still buzzing from the brief with her team.

'You should come home,' Johnny said. 'If you feel unsafe then you shouldn't be there. You need to get some protection guarantees before you pursue this, Kel.'

'That's why we're going to do as much work here as we can at Eden House. Everyone knows not to go charging round until things have settled down. It's being taken seriously here.'

'Good.'

'How's Lizzie?' She fiddled with her ruby ring as she spoke to him, and she found comfort in his voice.

'We're both good. Your dad is under strict orders to sit and do as he's told. He's a cantankerous old codger and I know where you get it from.'

Kelly laughed.

'Funnily enough I was contacted by a very old army associate of mine. I had no idea he was here in the Lakes. We go back years; he was intel when I was in Iraq. He's only in Rydal. I was thinking of taking Lizzie over there, for a change of scenery.'

'No, please, Johnny, don't take her out.'

'Hey, it's all right, if that's what you want, I'll pass, it's no problem. I'll do whatever makes you feel safe.'

'What's his name?' Kelly asked him.

'Mel. Melvin Stone. He was a colonel when I was a major. He was a stuffy old geezer but a good sort.'

Kelly's stomach hit the floor.

'Kel? Maybe you should come home?'

'Maybe.'

'Look, how about you come home for some lunch?'

'The Sunday tourist traffic is crazy.'

'So, we could meet over there,' he said.

'No!'

'OK, don't bite my head off, Kel.'

She felt awful. Cruel. Bad tempered. Unhinged. But she knew if she told him the truth he'd rage and get involved and that was the last thing she wanted. She needed him taking care of Lizzie. He was the only person on the planet she trusted to do that one thing right now. Ted was hurt and Millie was too young.

Indecision gripped her. Suddenly she missed him, and she stared at a photo on her desk of Lizzie. She was in her carry backpack, though she and Johnny were cut out of it and it was zoomed in on their daughter. Kelly recalled the day, the hour, the exact spot it was taken. It was summer last year, and they enjoyed a moment of isolated abandon, one where no one else in the world could penetrate.

If only life was like that. A series of moments that could remain forever separate. *Instead, we must navigate everything all at once and together*, she thought. It muddied the water and took away the special nature of those snippets of perfection.

But perhaps that was the point.

Life was messy and one couldn't expect it to be a staccato series of events in order, organised around individual feelings.

Kate poked her head around her door and twisted her head to one side, indicating she'd seen that look on Kelly's face before.

'You OK?' she asked.

'No. I've put everyone in danger, including my own child. Your children. God, who are these people?'

'It doesn't matter who they are. Nobody is above the law. Everybody needs to be accountable for their actions, including this lot. Put it this way. Whatever it is that you've uncovered, they don't like it. To gain access to Carleton Hall like that is disgusting and we're all united on this. Emma and Dan, Fin, me – all of us. This makes me want to get to the bottom of why Jamie and Angelina are dead all the more, and I know that lot is with me.' Kate thumbed behind her towards the incident room.

Kelly reached out her hand and covered Kate's. Kate squeezed and Kelly smiled.

'I thought you might like to see this,' Kate said, distracting her. She turned her police iPad around and showed Kelly some stills from the CCTV at the Old Man Guesthouse of the two strangers arriving in a cab.

'This is the result of the digital enhancement; the digital forensic team has done an amazing job. I'd say it's quite clear who these two are,' Kate said.

'Holy shit,' Kelly said.

'That is Sandy Cooper and that is Mercedes man.'

'Kevin Streeting.'

Chapter 49

Kelly spoke to Ted's office when she was alone. She'd tried to absorb the information from the brief with several strong coffees. Ted's lab technician had accessed his notes for her and the lab results were back for Jamie Robbins' bloodwork. The technician read them out over the phone and Kelly made notes.

'Blood alcohol zero. No recreational substances. Positive for toxic levels of glutamate and we're trying to isolate the source.'

'Is there any mention of elevated hormones or dehydration?' Kelly asked. It was a long shot. She had no idea what she was asking for, or if these things showed up on toxicology results. She'd worked with plenty of scientists on cases and she was told if something killed or not. She didn't get into the chemical structure of hidden poisons, and she'd never thought about doing so either. She'd not come across a case where a substance wasn't even recognised and therefore potentially missed on a tox screen.

'I'm interested in a compound called Neurohydroxy-14, but I doubt it will be categorised as such. It's made up of glutamate, hydroxy-11 and androstene-3.' Kelly read from notes and stumbled over the pronunciations.

She heard the woman use her mouse and clicks punctuated the quiet.

'Here we go. They've flagged up three elements of unusual levels in his tox results and, here we go, yes, they've highlighted a toxic mix of those three compounds. Somebody has written here by hand with a question mark your Neurohydroxy-14 as a possible source. They've also tagged the information as suspicious because the combination of the elements is not something that should occur in human bodies. So, there's a question mark over how it got into his system. I've heard of it but only at college; I've never seen evidence of it in tox results before.'

'Thank you,' Kelly said. They hung up.

They had their proof.

But she didn't understand why, if Jamie Robbins knew the dangers of the compound and had told Joe Folly as much, he was drinking it? The only sensible answer was that he was forced to before he died, or he was addicted and kept it a secret. Long-term use suggested hallucinations and mania, if Paul Burlington's behaviour was to go by and Lee Lovett was telling the truth. He'd said Paul was manic when they found him above Rydal Caves. But if Jamie and Paul were both taking the substance, then did they do it willingly?

She tried Sandy Cooper's mobile again and this time, to Kelly's shock, the scientist answered.

'I need to ask you a few more questions, Sandy. A few issues have come up which we need clearing up. You might need a lawyer.'

'Really? That sounds ominous, and highly dramatic. I'd better get on the phone to Hampton-Dent in New York, I'm sure they can recommend a good attorney.'

Kelly didn't like the scientist's tone, but it was expected. She'd love to hop into a car and fly over there to Dow Bank House but she'd promised Johnny she'd sit tight and it would also draw attention from Carleton Hall.

'Head over here anytime,' Sandy said.

'We can speak over the phone,' Kelly said.

'It's perfectly safe over here, it's private land, and we have those burly bodyguards.'

Sandy was toying with her, but Kelly didn't bite.

Kelly tapped her pen. She could feel an opportunity slipping away from her and she was tempted to call Del Booker to demand a warrant for the arrest of all of these Hampton-Dent fuckers. She was tired of playing around and her loved ones had been threatened. Maybe she could take a squad car as back-up.

'I'm a bit tied up here. And it'll take time to arrange an attorney from the US. So, I guess you'll just have to wait. I'm assuming I need an attorney before I answer any of your questions.'

Kelly imagined Sandy Cooper flying out of the UK by private jet this afternoon and the opportunity to interview her properly slipping away from her.

'What if we agreed to meet informally. Under English law, if I don't arrest you and you're not interviewed under caution, I can't use the testimony without your permission.'

'Isn't English law ludicrous? Who is it aimed to protect? Law-abiding citizens or those who'd do them harm?'

'Good question. The more I discover, the more I feel it's designed to protect those who are in charge, rather than the little people who need the protection in the first place.'

'Now we're talking. It's all becoming clear.'

Kelly felt a little nauseous. She knew the scientist was correct because she'd seen it before. Free law was cheap for a reason. She'd found herself in the middle of a game she wasn't controlling, and it felt horrendous.

'You're on CCTV at the Old Man Guesthouse on Friday, Sandy. There's no need to lie anymore. I know you knew Angelina well. It's blatantly clear you were familiar with each other. What were you doing there? And why did you lie to the police?'

Sandy sighed. 'None of your cosy chats at the hotel were formal interviews. I didn't lie about anything. I was bereaved and confused. Jamie wanted a chaperone for his little sister.'

'And he chose you?'

'You sound surprised!'

'What happened to her?'

'I have no idea.'

'What about the bodyguard? Kevin Streeting? He's the tall one with the Mercedes cap isn't he? He's on the passenger list we received from Manchester Airport. Why was he there?'

'Security. Jamie was jumpy.'

'I wonder why. Did you take him there as a recce?'

Sandy hesitated. Kelly could hear the trepidation in her voice as well as something behind it. Fear.

'Meet me at Rydal Caves at two o'clock and I'll tell you both everything.'

'Us both?'

The line went dead, and Kelly stared at the photo of Lizzie on her desk. She'd never come across a case like this in her career before. She was being played by people who held no regard for the law at all. They didn't have to. They were beyond its scope.

HQ had warned her off explicitly.

She was in uncharted territory.

But her curiosity was incorrigible. Being commanded to do something often had the opposite effect on her. It made her want to investigate the puzzles of this inquiry even more. Del Booker might have rolled over like a lapdog, perhaps he'd been paid off too, but there was no way she was bowing down to whoever was pulling the strings. Then her stomach sank.

She was desperate to find out what was so special about Rydal Caves. What was there? It was remote, sure. It was hidden away, but full of tourists. Then Kelly recalled it was entirely devoid of a mobile signal. It was a Wi-Fi blackspot. Perhaps that was the reason.

She checked the images on her phone again of Angelina's artwork. It didn't matter how many times she stared at the brush strokes or focused on the stones and rocks, or rearranged the numbers, they still meant nothing to her. But yet they still tugged at her, appealing to her to do something about it. Try harder.

Concentrate.

The six images were a key. A message.

If only she could figure it out.

She paid Fin's desk a visit and found him with six printouts on his desk. She tapped him gently on the shoulder. 'You're trying to do the same as me.'

'You gave me a puzzle, what do you expect? Have you cracked it yet?' he asked.

'No. Have you?'

'I think it's a six-digit code that is unique to Angelina. That's what we have to find.'

Chapter 50

Melvin checked on his wife. But she wasn't there.

He searched every room and ended up where he'd started, on the terrace.

'Ursula,' he called.

Acorn padded to his side and placed a paw on his trouser leg, then he remembered that Ursula was dead, and they were all alone.

He gazed at where Ursula's hospital bed and the medical equipment used to be, then out of the window to the lake which he recalled she loved. That's why they'd moved here. He wondered where all his things had gone. And when he went to look for her photos, he couldn't find them. It was as if they'd all been taken away. Or never existed before.

It was then that he noticed his hands swelling. It looked like good old-fashioned water retention to him, and he racked his brain to see if he could recall eating or drinking anything that might have produced a histamine response. He was well hydrated, or at least he thought he was. He wasn't hungry and he didn't feel unwell, though it had been quite a hectic couple of days.

Perhaps he should tell the doctor.

But he didn't like doctors.

His memory was worse, but he recalled today was a special day because it was the anniversary of something.

He went to the calendar and had to walk past where Ursula's bed had been, and he placed his hand on the imaginary sheets and said good afternoon to her. He stroked the linen and watched his swollen hand glide up and down and for a moment he was back with her.

But then a crash jolted him back to his current reality and he realised that he'd knocked over a vase. It had been hers and it contained dead flowers and no water. They lay broken into a thousand pieces on the floor; the brown withered leaves like paper now covered the floor like confetti and it reminded him of their wedding day.

He looked around him wondering where the bed had gone and if it was ever there in the first place.

Where was she?

He glanced around the room and wondered where she was but then tutted as his memory flooded back.

The slipping in and around time was one of the scariest things he'd ever experienced. It was worse than a battlefield. It was more terrifying than combat. It was like being trapped inside some cruel game that he had no control over. There was no end. No victory. Just torture. He checked the calendar and saw that it was the fifth anniversary of her death.

It was all a blur now, but he vaguely recalled them discussing the plans for the sunroom and an extension out the back, edging down to the lake. But now, as he reached for a packet of soup from the cupboard and flicked the kettle on, he stared out of the window and looked at a single figure in a canoe, paddling right up to the shingle shore which was at the end of his garden.

A memory of Ursula walking towards the beach with something in her hand took him back to the night they'd moved in.

They'd been dropped off with their luggage and everything had gone to plan, except this wasn't the house they'd chosen, and Ursula wasn't his wife. They'd been introduced to each other as part of the experiment. He and Ursula were going to pretend to be husband and wife. The fiction was designed to keep them safe. Keep them legitimate. Ursula was an asset too.

They'd met through their shared desperation. And ended up falling in love. Or had they?

He didn't know what was real and what was fantasy anymore.

He turned to the door when a sound interrupted his train of thought, but he was annoyed, because he very much wanted to imagine Ursula as his wife. He looked out of the window again but the figure in the lake had disappeared.

There were no photos of them together, and the smells he imagined that lingered on cushions, soft furnishings and chairs were no longer there when he pressed his nose against them.

It was as if she never existed.

The noise turned to a knock, and he turned to the front door.

Nobody came to visit. It was an extraordinary turn of events.

He'd been given strict instructions on what to do, which procedures to follow, if anyone ever dropped by, like a postman, or a counsellor, or a lost tourist.

There was no questioning the routine.

It was not up for discussion.

He walked backwards, unsure of whether he could recall the exact order he was supposed to follow, and eventually he came to Ursula's bed and sat down. Though when he felt for it, it was a lot lower than he remembered and as he turned, he realised that it wasn't a hospital bed at all but an ordinary one, and his things were laid out on it.

His head hurt and he reached for a cup of water on the bedside table, and the knocking got louder.

Acorn barked and alerted him to his current situation, but it still took a minute or so to evaluate if it was real or imagined. So much of his life was dreamlike at its edges that he was constantly unsure of what was real and what wasn't.

Like the Heron Hall Hotel, for example.

Had he really been there?

He felt for Acorn, and she nuzzled his hand.

She was real, at least. But she'd lost her silk scarf. He'd tied Ursula's purple scarf around Acorn's neck, for comfort? To remind him of her? He couldn't remember, but it wasn't there now.

The doctors had told him that this might happen. He was expected to go the way of Ursula. They were the same. What were the chances? Their brains were designed to disintegrate over time, and that was what would eventually realise their value. Their legacy was their future. Their value to medical science. Their riches were not for them but for their future selves, as yet unacknowledged. They'd both known what they were signing away when they'd been called to volunteer on a rainy afternoon in Chicksands in Bedfordshire. For Ursula, it was her elderly sister, who lived in Brighton, who would be the recipient of their savings. For Melvin, it was his daughter who lived in London. But she had no idea who he was. One day, when Melvin finally succumbed to this awful disease, then his daughter would get a letter from his solicitor informing her of her father's existence and she would receive everything he owned.

At least that's what he hoped.

He'd chosen an executor carefully.

Everything was arranged.

And he'd been paid well.

The knocking was rude now and it threatened to derail the wonderful dream he liked to have about Ursula being his wife and not simply an asset murdered by a clinical trial.

Fat chance.

All he wanted was to be left in peace.

He went to the door and the sound of the banging hurt his temples. As his hand reached the knob and turned it, a hand came around the frame, and he stepped back in shock. A man stood in the doorway and Melvin shook his head. He was baffled at first, but then sanity returned once more, and the man stepped into the kitchen.

Melvin's familiarity with the man was a mixture of pain and relief.

'Hello, Doctor,' Melvin said. 'Have I got worse?'

The man closed the door behind him and took out an iPad from his satchel that was strapped across his chest. He tapped the screen and Melvin watched him.

Then his pain went away.

Chapter 51

'You're not going to Rydal Caves on your own. Ted, tell her.'

Ted was lying on the sofa in Kelly's lounge and Johnny fetched him some paracetamol. He refused anything stronger, saying it didn't help the healing process. The body was designed to heal itself, he told them. He was a stubborn old mule, and Johnny knew where Kelly got it from. It was one o'clock in the afternoon and Kelly had surprised them by walking through the front door and telling them her plan.

'It'll be heaving with tourists,' Kelly said in her defence.

She glared at him as if to ask how dare he talk over her as if she was some pathetic female in need of male assistance. Johnny knew the look, but he didn't care. They weren't together anymore. His actions now had different consequences and one of them wasn't being kicked out of her bed.

He stood his ground, and he could see she was livid. She went to speak but then glanced at her father and walked out of the room.

Johnny shrugged and Ted raised his eyebrows.

'You're going against your own instructions you gave your team,' he said.

'This is different,' she shouted back.

'I agree with you,' Ted said to Johnny, 'but it is her job, and you know she'll go anyway.'

'But she should at least take someone else. I'd go, but what about you?'

'I have Millie looking after me,' Ted said.

'It's not good enough; I can't let any of you be here alone.'

Millie came back downstairs after putting Lizzie down for a nap and looked worried.

'I've got somebody changing all the locks this afternoon,' Johnny told her. 'You can go home, if you like,' he said.

'No, that's not what I was thinking. I don't want to leave Lizzie here. What about I take her to my house?'

Johnny tried to think of a way he could tell Millie that wasn't a good idea without letting on that her home was just as much in danger because of her mother's job. Kate had been spared last night, but that might not be the case tonight. Kelly had assured them that squad cars would be patrolling their respective addresses all day, but she couldn't guarantee they wouldn't be called away in an emergency.

They were on their own until the coppers had something to investigate; in other words, until somebody got seriously hurt. Ted didn't count because he wasn't filing a complaint. He was set in his ways and couldn't be moved on it. It wasn't the first time he'd been in harm's way because of his job, and he reckoned it wouldn't be the last. But he could see that Kelly was riled.

'I'll get a squad car here,' she said, and left the room. 'And Millie, you go home, take some time off,' she said over her shoulder. Millie got her keys and smiled at them. The day was a corker and the thought of having a day off was a nice surprise.

'Stay local and in a group,' Johnny told her.

'Yes, boss,' Millie said. She said goodbye and left.

Johnny stared at Ted.

'She's so bloody pig-headed,' Johnny said.

'That's what you love about her,' Ted told him.

Johnny smiled and nodded, giving up. He'd tried blackmail, emotional manipulation, and good old brutal truths, but Kelly saw through it all. Only the notion of Lizzie's safety being compromised made her stop to think about her own actions.

She walked back into the room.

'You're right,' she said.

Ted and Johnny stared at her.

'I've got a couple of uniforms coming over here. My guess is they won't hit the same address twice. They've done what they set out to do, which was letting me know they're watching. Next time will be somewhere or someone different.'

Johnny folded his arms. He had no need to say anything else. All he cared about was her and Lizzie's safety and sometimes her sense of justice blinded her own self-preservation. He was happy she'd seen sense.

'I'll take Fin,' she said.

Instantly, Johnny's stomach dropped, and he felt powerless to respond. He'd told her she shouldn't go alone, and now she'd hamstrung him. He knew Fin was the bloke she'd been involved with after they'd split because he'd got it out of Emma one night at the pub, months ago, just before he left for Scotland. It wasn't nasty; he simply wanted to know if anybody else was involved in Kelly's decision to dump him.

It didn't distract from the fact that losing her was entirely his own fault, but for some morbidly masochistic reason, he wanted to know if she was safe.

'Fin?'

'Do you want him here looking after Lizzie or there looking after me?' Kelly asked.

'Excuse me, I am more than capable of looking after my own granddaughter,' Ted said defiantly.

They looked at him and he sat up.

'Look,' Kelly said. 'This is getting out of hand. I'm going to meet somebody who may or may not have something to tell me. Nobody else knows.'

'Or it could be a trap,' Johnny said.

'You're paranoid because of last night.'

'And you're not!'

'Come on, you two, you both want the same thing, which is for Lizzie to be safe, and with a couple of strapping lads in uniform, or lasses, obviously, I will be absolutely fine here and so will Lizzie.'

Johnny and Kelly looked at each other.

'It is broad daylight,' Johnny said. 'But I'm not leaving until the uniforms get here.'

The doorbell rang and Kelly went to answer it. She'd already had a text on her phone telling her that a squad car was on its way, and she peered out of the window to confirm it. She recognised them and opened the door. Two coppers nodded at her and Kelly introduced them to Ted and Johnny, then showed them into the lounge. Then she went over instructions. One of the coppers asked if she could take a look at the layout of the house and Kelly showed her around.

Meanwhile, Johnny gathered some things for his outing to Rydal Caves. He didn't have the time or inclination to analyse if his decision to leave with Kelly was because of his ego or his sense of loyalty to her, but one thing was for sure, the opportunity to spend some time with her and be useful in her life, even if it didn't last long, was something he knew he wanted more than anything else.

Thoughts of meeting up with an old military contact were forgotten.

Chapter 52

The Rydal Caves were created by quarrying in the nineteenth century. Now a popular tourist attraction, Kelly had little hesitation about meeting Sandy Cooper there. It was public, busy and open. But she was also fully aware that Sandy Cooper would likely have another agenda. The woman wasn't straightforward and she wouldn't be easy to catch out.

And she'd been at a murder scene without giving Kelly any explanation as yet. She'd blatantly lied about how well she knew Angelina.

However, Johnny's mindset was elsewhere. In some ways, she thought his Superman impression was heartwarming and touching, yet his need to protect her came a year too late. If only he'd have tended to her better when they were together, they might still be two halves of the same life.

But they still shared a daughter and when Kelly looked across at him sitting in her passenger seat, vigilant as ever, watching over her, she couldn't help but feel contented. Even just for a moment, it was enough. It was like before. But thinking about the past was a slippery slope into nothing. She'd made her decision to quit on their relationship because he'd lied to her about still being married to Carrie. He had long standing debt with her and splitting it put Kelly's financial security in danger for a time.

It was sorted now, he told her. Carrie had disappeared for good this time, along with half his money.

'You owed her,' she told him. 'You should have done it sooner.'

They'd been over it a thousand times and neither wanted to flog a dead horse. Sometimes leaving stuff in the past was the best place for it.

In fact, she was enjoying his company. Seeing him with Ted warmed her heart and watching him with Lizzie made her appreciate deep inside that Lizzie would always have a great father. She reckoned that was what she always wanted, for her daughter to have more paternal security than she'd had.

Her relationship with John Porter had been tricky. He'd been an old-school cop, impossibly strict and arrogant, and it had meant that what he brought in discipline and firmness he lacked in warmth and nurturing.

It left two women feeling inadequate in their different ways. Kelly suffered a pang of guilt when she counted the months since her last meeting with her sister, Nikki. It wasn't her fault they'd had John Porter for a father. But it was too late for them. There was no way back. Nikki had her own life with her husband and the kids. Discovering they had different dads lessened the guilt.

'What are you thinking?' Johnny asked.

Kelly had been holding the wheel tightly and she relaxed, knowing she'd been caught out.

'This case is bugging me.'

'That's not all,' he said. He knew her so well.

She turned into the carpark nearest the road that carved its way through the valley from north to south between the great mountains either side, parked, and they got out. The weather was stunning and perfect for a trip to the caves. They provided a welcome and cooling break on a hot summer's day. Water gathered at the foot of the caves and in the spring, it was so full one had to jump over it or wade through it to reach the back of the main cave, but in summer it was almost dried up. The water reflected incredible colours across the roof and the cavernous nature of the space reminded Kelly of big churches. The feeling of spirituality was the same.

She changed the subject and told Johnny about the people she was meeting. She explained that Sandy was the scientist responsible for the legal arm of the company's products, and that she'd said 'both' to her over the phone, indicating somebody else was coming.

'And now you tell me?'

She grimaced. 'It might be nothing.'

He stared away across the River Rothay for a moment. She knew he'd gone to a place where plenty of comrades had taken their last breath, either in battle or afterwards at their own hand. In the short time she'd known him – about seven years – she'd been to more than ten funerals of soldiers and officers with him, all by suicide. He looked back to her and she knew that he was back with her.

'I don't trust any of these people. I'll be watching you like a hawk. Don't forget whoever broke into your house and hurt your dad work for the same people. Has it crossed your mind that they could have planted the stories by the podcaster, what was his name?'

'Joe Folly, the conspiracy theorist?'

'Him. He could be a plant. A very convenient one who just so happened to be in the area podcasting when an important drug rep jumped off a banister.'

She glared at him. He'd grown in confidence since they'd split up and she liked it. He made her laugh. He was less uptight too. It was as if he tried less hard to please her and in doing so, was more natural at it. His openness was welcome whether they were together or not. Too many exes fought against one another, and it was only ever the kids who suffered. If they could get along like this for Lizzie, she had no complaints.

But he'd also hit a raw nerve. Because Joe Folly – or Greg Minda – had been an imposter at the conference and easily could have been planted there. She didn't know one way or the other.

'Maybe that's what's bugging you,' he said. 'When people don't behave how they say they're going to. Has he made a fuss of Jamie's death on social media? Has he sounded the alarm?'

'No,' she said. 'He's gone to ground here in the Lakes.'

'He's here?'

'Yes. He was Angelina's lover, we think.'

'Well then it's obvious he's the other one meeting you. The scientist wants out and he's her ticket. You're the rubber stamp.'

It irritated Kelly how straightforward men were. Johnny thought in such a linear fashion. They were black and white. No mushy in-between with emotional baggage to consider. But she had to admit he had a point.

Johnny raised his eyebrows as they got their things out of the car.

'And he was at the hotel, what, just by accident? Why did he hang around? Who else was he meeting there?'

Kelly thought in silence. She'd missed Johnny's analytical brain. And he was right. She'd assumed Joe Folly was a good guy and had been sucked in, but was that a mistake? Just because he'd fooled Angelina and they looked good in a photo on her fridge. But maybe he was a bad guy.

'I'll hang back and pretend to be a tourist,' he told her.

She looked at her watch. It was ten minutes before 2 p.m.

She walked ahead and Johnny hung back.

Up ahead, groups of walkers chatted and spread across the path.

Kelly peered through the trees and saw Heron Hall from the path. She imagined Sandy coming up here with both Lee and Jamie and she wanted to know why this place was so special to them. Was it a hiding place for something? Was it something else? Was it a trap? And why had Angelina loved it so much?

A few people stared at her attire, but people hiked up here in all sorts of gear. She wore comfortable trousers and a thin top. She left her lanyard in the car, but she had no backpack. She and Johnny were used to the fells, and they knew where to stop for fresh spring water. She marched ahead and ignored everyone else, knowing Johnny had her back.

When Kelly arrived at the opening to the cave, there was a queue of people trying to get in to take photos. She peeked in and shaded her eyes. The entrance was just like Angelina's painting. The two boulders stood like guardsmen welcoming them in under their watch. Then the five stepping stones led away from the sunlight towards the back of the cavern. And she spotted the rock on its own, proudly dominating the area under one of the magnificent arches. An order started to form in her head, and she found herself immersed in the arrangement of the visuals. Angelina had created a code.

Kelly opened an email on her phone from Emma, just before she entered the cave, before she lost all Wi-Fi. Her internet was still working but it whirred a little as it struggled to connect with whatever mast was powering this side of Loughrigg.

A visual of Paul Burlington wandering around almost naked and raving caught her attention, and she wondered if he'd been taking drugs, or, as Lee Lovett insinuated, there was more to it. Until she had permission to enter the grounds of Hampton-Dent property, or the basis to arrest any of them, they'd remain safe and hidden away in their ivory tower, and she'd be unable to interview any of them under caution, and Kelly knew that was their intention all along.

There was no sign of Sandy.

She found the email she was looking for and it was an attachment of Angelina's bank account, the one which had received hefty sums from companies associated with Hank Hampton.

The numbers sat latent in her memory bank for this exact moment.

The sort code of the bank account caught her eye. 43-62-51.

Rearranged, that was 123456.

She checked the paintings again, but this time looked at them in the order of 43-62-51. It made sense in that order. It was a journey from Skelwith to here. It started with the four flagstones on the floor of room 13, then the three keystones in front of the carriage travelling across Skelwith Bridge, then the six stones across the roadway of the bridge itself, then the two boulders guarding the entrance to the cave, followed by the five stepping stones, finishing with the single rock, at the wall of the cave. She stared into the darkness at the lone rock.

A child's shriek surprised her, and she turned to see Joe Folly at the entrance staring at her.

A woman beckoned to her. It was her turn to cross and she looked away from Joe, taking the stepping stones across, making her way into the cave, towards the back where there were less people.

Johnny was right. She looked back and searched for him but couldn't see him.

What was Sandy playing at? She waited for Joe, and he smiled at her when he finally approached. Behind him she saw Johnny hovering at the cave mouth, keeping an eye on her and blending in with the tourists and her heart rate calmed.

'No sign of Sandy?' she asked him when he was standing beside her.

'I don't think she'll come; I think this was her way of bringing us together,' he said.

The statement took Kelly by surprise.

'Really?' she asked him.

'I see you brought a bouncer,' he said.

They looked at Johnny, and Kelly smiled. His face was cross, and she could see he was ready to pounce, but she signalled to him to hold off. She saw nobody else out of place and certainly none of the close protection she'd expected to accompany Sandy.

No sign of Kevin Streeting.

'I met with Jamie here a few times. I guessed that's why Sandy chose it.'

'Do you trust her?'

'No, I don't trust anyone,' he said.

Their voices echoed slightly in the cavern.

'I've been up here enough times to know this is where Jamie and Angelina hid shit they didn't want finding.'

'What makes you say that?' Kelly stared at the lone rock, wondering what was under it. It was a ridiculous thought because nobody could lift the thing in the first place, never mind hide something under it, and replace the stone. She must be mistaken. Kelly looked around. 'It's all very clandestine. Are you expecting me to believe that they met here like spies and dropped documents for one another?'

'That's exactly what they did.'

Kelly became wary.

'Why didn't Jamie tell you where he was taking Angelina?' she asked him.

He was taken off-guard. 'To protect her.'

'But I thought you two were close. The baby was yours, right?'

It was a low blow. Cruel, cheap. Effective.

His face crumpled.

'You didn't know?'

Joe looked around and recovered. It was the action of an alpha male. No emotion. She was disappointed because she'd imagined a love story. She thought about what Johnny said.

'It must have made you mad when Jamie wouldn't tell you where she was. Did you speak to him the night he died? About Angelina? About where she might be? You were at the hotel as Greg Minda. We have you on video footage in your hoodie. You're not that clever, DiggerMan.'

He stared at her, having regained his cool.

'He wouldn't tell you where their hiding place is either,' she said.

She watched his face tick and his eyes darted to the mouth of the cave.

'I know it's in here,' he said.

'Why here?' she asked him. She saw Johnny from the corner of her eye scouring the place for threats.

'It's the only place close to here that cuts off 5G, and there's no rear exit so it can't be set as a trap.'

'But why here in the Lake District? It's… random.'

Joe smiled.

'I'm missing something?' she asked.

He nodded.

'The injured patients?'

He looked surprised.

'Survivors, assets, whatever they're called. It's not just podcasters who can dig around, Joe Folly.'

They moved aside for a family to squeeze past to take a photo.

'Tell me why you are still here.'

'Before Jamie's death, I communicated with whistleblowers via Instagram posts. I posted something with a message and then the people who "liked" it sent me affirmation I was correct.'

'So, you used Instagram as a code?'

'Yep, exactly. I was in touch with Sandy for a long time before Jamie's death. This was one of the places I posted about, and we had quite a conversation going until Jamie died. Then it all stopped.'

'So, you pretended to post about a beauty spot, and it was actually a secret conversation?'

He nodded.

'Is Sandy ready to become a snitch?'

He smiled.

Bingo, Johnny was right again.

Kelly was impressed; they'd missed that in their searches of his social media accounts. It was clever. Everybody must stay ahead of technology, she guessed.

'And you communicated with Sandy like that?'

He nodded.

'Behind Jamie's back?'

'No, he knew. He trusted her too.'

'Which was why she was at the guesthouse with Angelina,' she whispered under her breath.

'What?' Joe asked.

'What is Sandy hiding? What is she so scared of that she can't come here today?'

'She confirmed the use of Neurohydroxy-14 and what it does to people. Read that.'

He gave her his phone to read, and she did. It was a medical profile of a patient.

'He's right here. Why else would they send their kings and queens here, if not to protect the crown jewels?'

'That's why they held the conference here?'

'Of course. Sophisticated criminals always choose the places you're least expecting. What do you think they're hiding in Antarctica? Yetis?' He laughed.

To Kelly, this was a new world, untouched by her kind. She had trouble keeping up with it and believing it was another ball game entirely. She hadn't decided yet. She glanced at Johnny and knew he was losing patience. She was supposed to be meeting a woman and she'd been chatting to a young man for almost ten minutes.

'Jamie tried to tell me, but he was compromised before he had the chance to confirm the location. He became obsessed with the patient. At one point he thought it was Paul, his partner.'

This was new to her. 'How did he know it wasn't him?'

'He didn't. He suspected.'

'Paul was close to Angelina, how could he have let anything happen to her, if he knew what was going on?'

'Perhaps he didn't, or not at least willingly. I know the methods of these people first hand. I went into hiding because I had a visit from some unpleasant men in black balaclavas.'

'Ah, I had that last night, but just one.'

'You get used to it. You're still here. That means it was just a warning.'

'Do you have proof that Jamie and Angelina were murdered because of what they were going to reveal?'

'He does.' Joe nodded to his phone that Kelly was still holding.

'This address is near Rydal,' she said, reading the details.

'It was here all along, right under Jamie's nose. He was just too late.'

'Did he go there to see if it's true?'

'It is true.'

'How do you know? Have you seen it for yourself?'

'No. Angie did though.'

A couple of hikers muscled in on the queue and caused a stir for pushing in. Kelly saw Johnny watch them closely and follow them towards the back of the cave. He'd spotted something. Then Joe moved away. He'd seen something too. Kelly searched the cave for signs that some of the people there were not tourists, but she struggled to identify any imposters.

She saw Joe leave and turned back to Johnny, who was suddenly behind her. He blocked her with his body and the two hikers passed by. He pulled her arm, and she went to the entrance, and as she looked back, she saw one of the hikers staring at her and give a signal to her of a slit throat.

She was still walking beside Johnny when she turned away from the stranger and walked out into the bright sunshine.

'Jesus, how did you know?'

'Their trainers were too clean,' he said.

'Damn,' she said under her breath. 'Did you see where Joe went?'

'Joe? The fucking podcaster? That's him? Jesus Christ, you were set up. He's down there, getting into his car. Has it crossed your mind why he's still walking around freely and they're not following him? He's playing both sides, Kel. I'd bet my life on it.'

They walked back to her car and watched as Joe got into his and drove away.

'When you are forced to gather intel like this, Kel, perhaps it's a sign that it won't end well and you're dealing with people who are more powerful than your job.'

'We need to go here,' she said, showing him the address in Rydal on her phone.

'Don't you think it's time you requested some back-up? You have no idea what you'll find there.'

She slammed the car door shut without getting in and peered back up to the caves.

'What are you doing?' he asked.

'I need to find something,' she said.

As she thought, when they got back to the entrance, without Joe Folly there, the imposters had disappeared.

'I think maybe you were right,' she said.

'About what?'

'Joe Folly.'

'Why would you trust a podcaster called the DiggerMan anyway? What kind of name is that?'

'Look, they've gone. It was a dramatic set-up to try to scare us away again. Idiots.'

'Now what?'

He followed Kelly into the cave once more and she walked around the lone rock.

'Johnny, can you see a way of hiding anything under this?'

He laughed. 'No, but I'd say that if that was your intention then I'd look around the back and see it's a manmade trig, to hide an old electric supply when this place was modernised as a quarry before it closed.'

Kelly stared at him.

'Here,' he said.

She walked around the rock and saw what he was pointing at.

It was a small hatch, and she tapped the rock, shocked to hear a hollow sound.

'Fuck me,' she said.

He grinned. She hugged him and her face fitted into his neck perfectly. She pulled away but he held her tightly before letting her go.

He found a rock and slammed another against it to break the lock and Kelly reached inside and pulled out a plastic bag containing a USB.

'You can thank me later,' he said.

Chapter 53

Joe's exit from Dow Bank House had been surprisingly unproblematic.

He'd imagined all sorts of scenarios where they wouldn't let him leave. Before doing so, he'd peered up at the grand staircase and imagined himself hurtling down, headfirst, from the top, smashing into the Italian marble below. As he'd walked to his car and two burly blokes in military-style gilets peered at him from under caps, he'd suffered a vivid visualisation of what Angelina might have felt as she met her end. He didn't know for sure but he assumed she'd put up a fight. The police investigation was ongoing. Angie gave her life for what she knew.

That's what they all risked.

The short drive down the long private road that led to the gates felt like an eternity.

Did they believe him?

Now, as he drove from Rydal towards Ambleside, he remained unmolested, and still alive. He could hardly believe it.

So far, so good.

Sandy had been true to her word. The detective had come, and now she'd discover the truth and they'd both be safe.

Or at least that was the plan. He had no insurance, only that he'd involved the police.

Ambleside was a walker's paradise, and cheap. The Airbnb was hidden away, and he'd rented it months ago. He kept moving to avoid exposure.

Joe knew how to stay offline.

The drive into Ambleside was claggy and frustrating but thoughts of what he would say on his next episode of the DiggerMan podcast kept him distracted amidst the traffic. It was already part recorded and this one featured Jamie Robbins himself.

From the grave.

The same grave of his unborn child.

Stop it.

He focused on the podcast.

A reveal was so called for a reason: it gave information to the public that was shocking because it had been concealed. Pure and simple.

The problem was that those who wished important information to be hidden were usually the ones who profited from its secrecy.

So, he was careful.

And that's why he'd chosen to play both sides.

And he'd promised them what Angie hid in the caves.

Problem was he couldn't find it.

The flat was anonymous. All the kit was rapidly dismantled. The surfaces were easily wipeable, and the neighbours weren't the sort to give evidence to the coppers. The street was a long row of terraces, forgotten by time, and all the windows were either covered with drapes or full of flyers for climbing experiences and clubs. He set up his monitors, mics, headphones and soundproofing equipment easily. He'd done it a thousand times before.

He ran through his notes a few times before he started. He took a deep breath and then warmed up his lips and mouth.

'Bladder, bone, belly, blubber.'

He repeated the mantra a few times, making sure to enunciate the vowels and consonants. He exercised his mouth and put his head back and gargled, warming up his throat.

He began.

Then the lights went out and his screens went blank.

He froze.

The blinds were blackout, and the room was plunged into instant darkness, despite it being only late afternoon.

He tapped the mic, but it was dead. He checked the feeds behind the screens, and they seemed fine, then his eyes began to accustom, and he looked around the room.

There was no movement, no sound and no shift in energy.

He heard the traffic outside and a heated argument in the distance. His eyes adjusted and a sliver of light caused a shadow to dance across the first-floor window, and he slipped out of his seat and went to it and held the curtain back.

A sinking feeling crept through his guts, and he rooted around the room for his mobile phone.

He found his phone and saw he had reception and Wi-Fi.

Damn.

That's how they'd traced him.

He hadn't turned off his phone. What an idiot. He'd made a vital mistake because he was rattled.

He had no idea if the copper was toying with him when she told him about Angelina's baby. His baby. He was going to be a father.

He had a decision to make, and quickly. Either call somebody to alert them or switch off his phone and disappear, risking oblivion. He wrote a text to a trusted friend but then quickly deleted it. The indecision galled him. He wasn't used to it.

But it was too late. He couldn't get his thumbnail to slip the button up to turn it off, because he heard somebody in the hall and his hands suddenly turned greasy with panic.

The door handle turned, and he looked around him, in no doubt about what was going on. He went to the window and opened it, peering down into the alley below to see how far the drop to the street was. It was too far; he'd twist his ankle at the very least, and worse if he landed badly. He thought about Jamie's smashed body on the atrium floor and Sandy wailing over him. The prospect of pain immobilised him.

The only other option was to hide.

But that was pathetic. If the person on the other side of the door was sent by the same people who'd killed Jamie Robbins for speaking out, he'd have to fight. But he was only a keyboard warrior not a real one. Inside his head he said a silent apology to Jamie. And to Angelina. And his dead unborn child.

'I'm sorry,' he whispered.

He crouched under the table and pulled a rug his way to cover his body.

All his kit was on top of it, and he made a last-minute decision. He crept out from under the table just as the door opened fully and a figure stood in the doorway. He removed a USB from the main MacBook and swallowed it, as the light flipped on and he covered his eyes, then he felt something slam into his head and he hit the floor like one of the wrestlers Jamie used to show him on WWE network. They'd laughed at them, but the serious side was too awful to ignore. He'd written a piece on the drugs they took to make them look that big. Drugs endorsed by Hampton-Dent.

As the blows came thick and fast down on his body, all he could think of was Angelina's face and the last thing he said to her.

'I won't let anything hurt you,' he'd promised. Hoping she'd tell him where it was. Then the look Jamie gave him the last time he saw him, rifling through his stuff in his room at the Heron Hall Hotel.

The look of a broken promise.

Betrayal.

As his head hit the floor, curiously he felt no pain. He'd gone numb with submission. Anaesthetised by guilt.

And now he was happy he'd never found what Angelina had hidden because his death would be worth nothing to them.

Chapter 54

Paul searched the wardrobe for something to wear. He had no idea how long he'd been in bed for. He turned on the TV and saw that it was Sunday afternoon.

He'd lost several days of his life, and he felt familiar anger rushing up from his toes.

He pulled on a pair of shorts and a thin sweater and looked around. His mind whirred and he no longer knew what was true or false. He couldn't distinguish reality from fiction. He looked through the closed curtains and saw where he was.

All he knew for certain was that he needed to get away.

He *must* get away.

He went to pull on some trainers, but he felt the overwhelming desire to throw up and he made it to the bathroom just in time to retch over the toilet bowl. When he stood up, he felt dizzy, and he doused his face with water from the tap. His face was hot, and he looked at his reflection in the mirror. His eyes were sunken and dark, and his cheeks were grey-looking. He looked fifty years old. Sweat covered his brow and his hair was scruffy. The worst part was the mental questioning. His head was never quiet. It was as if an alien had invaded his brain and spoke to him constantly, telling him he was useless, weak and phony.

He went back to the bedroom and took a swig of fluid from his water bottle, scrunching up his face. He knew what was in it and he was aware that it was harming him, but he couldn't help himself. He'd seen addiction in many of his friends, but he'd never thought it would grip him again so easily. He believed he was stronger than it.

In control.

But their product was poisoned.

It had been a game-changing creation. The balance of vitamins, special isolates and plant additives was a momentous step forward – no, a leap – for the industry and they were charging ahead with the new revolution in supplements.

But FairGro wanted to go one step further.

Paul wiped sweat from his forehead, and he couldn't tell what was tears and what was perspiration. The feeling of complete hopelessness overwhelmed him, and he wished Jamie was still alive.

He'd been outside at Heron Hall when Jamie's body hit the floor, but he hadn't been able to recall how he got there. The night air had been cooler than the previous few days and he'd worn a loose jacket. He was out there getting some air after their argument.

Another one.

He'd passed the assassin on the stairs and recalled being struck by how ordinary he seemed.

Now, he heard movement outside his door and wondered if they were coming for him. He felt rage building up inside him.

It was working.

The door opened and all he saw was enemies.

And the iPad.

They were here for one of two reasons: either to end the experiment and release him of his duties, thereby frying his brain and locking him up in a safehouse somewhere, like the other assets, or complete the set up for Jamie's murder, which they'd already begun. The pieces fell into place. He'd be the fall guy this time. He'd walked straight into it. Thinking he could get rich from taking a few drugs like a lab rat had been beyond stupid. It was reckless. They'd played him all along.

'You should have taken me back to the USA,' he told them.

They closed in.

'It'd be easier to kill me there,' he said.

They were slow.

But Neurohydroxy-14 made him quick, agile and terrifyingly strong. He took them by surprise and produced a heavy glass globe paperweight from behind his back with expert precision. He brought it down on Tilda's smug face first and rather enjoyed the feeling it gave him.

The long nights spent in her bed meant nothing, he realised now. Hurting her felt good.

Next, he caught Hank's iPad and it thundered out of his hands and into the wall, then he swiped at the big Texan and caught him square on the ear, and he went down like a sack of Texan cattle feed. Then he dropped the paperweight and dashed out into the corridor.

They had no one else with them. Fools.

From there, he leapt over the balcony and landed on the soft grass underneath the ballroom, and he sprinted away towards the woodland on the edge of the property. He felt superhuman.

He knew exactly where he was going. Because Jamie had told him.

His priority wasn't just to seek justice; perhaps it was too late for that. It was finding the other patient and stopping anybody else from getting hurt.

Chapter 55

Kelly and Johnny were driving around Rydal Water when they heard the crackle of Kelly's radio reporting a 999 call from Dow Bank House.

'That way,' Kelly said. She turned the car and headed to the manor estate, which was only a couple of miles along the road.

It was Johnny who saw the man running away from the grounds first.

'Look,' he shouted.

She pulled into a narrow layby off the road and from there they could just see through the woods to the house beyond. She recognised the size and gait of the man.

'That's Paul Burlington.'

Kelly shot out of the car and shouted at him but he didn't hear her. He didn't look back as he continued running. He looked like a crazed madman.

'Damn.'

'Is he one of the people you're looking for?' Johnny asked her.

'He's Jamie's business partner. He looks like he's lost his mind.'

'He looks like he's being chased,' Johnny added.

Iron railings prevented them from giving chase themselves and Kelly tried to hoist herself up but they were too high. They watched Paul disappear then Kelly spotted Hank Hampton shuffling across the gardens in the same direction, closely followed by his bodyguards, who soon overtook him.

'They're after him,' Johnny said.

'The inmate has escaped the asylum,' she said.

She felt helpless standing outside and rushed back to the car to call Eden House for back-up.

'Get in.'

She drove the short distance to the main entrance, which was deserted.

In the distance, along the driveway they could make out several figures running towards the main house and they knew something was seriously wrong. Her radio crackled again, and they heard medical assistance was on its way to the address. Johnny jumped out and pulled at the gate, expecting it to be locked, but it opened.

She drove through it and Johnny jumped back in, then she sped up the drive, parking outside the grand house.

'Jesus, look at this pad.'

They jumped out of the car and followed the screams. The front door was wide open and they had no time to stop to admire the beauty and craftsmanship of the house. Kelly never thought her first visit to the famous house would be like this. Inside, the screaming echoed off the walls and seemed to come from upstairs. They took the stairs and Kelly ran her hand up the marble balustrade. It felt cold, abandoned and unwelcoming.

She felt like an intruder and as though the house didn't want them here. As if the screams were meant to remain here forever.

In the distance, through the countless open windows and doors, they heard the whine of sirens. The screams turned to sobbing and when they stopped at the room where all the noise was coming from, they saw why.

A figure was slumped on the floor and Kelly instantly recognised her as Tilda Dent and a housemaid sobbed over her.

But Tilda was lifeless.

Anybody could see that.

Nothing could be done. Her head was caved in and a large glass object covered in blood sat motionless but still potent somehow, as if it could hurt them too.

Kelly went to the body and pressed one finger to the woman's neck but as she suspected there was nothing. She and Johnny backed away and agreed to check the rest of the house.

There was no sign of anyone else. So the killer had escaped.

Downstairs, they saw Hank returning from the garden nursing a wound on the side of his head.

He looked more stunned by her presence than his situation.

'Why on earth are you here?' he asked her.

'Who did this?' Kelly asked.

'Will she live?'

Blood made repellent patterns on Hank's cream jacket, like raspberry ripple ice cream.

Kevin Streeting appeared behind him, wary and alert.

'I hope you're not armed,' Kelly said.

'This is private property,' Hank said.

'On English soil,' Johnny said.

'Diplomatic immunity,' Hank said.

'Since when did you become an envoy to the USA?' she asked him. 'We've got an emergency situation here and you've got a lot of explaining to do.'

The Texan slipped back into his Christian, concerned and dutiful persona, and Kelly recognised the switch. The ease with which he flipped made her question everything. She studied him and decided to hold off on questions until she worked out what had happened. The air in the imposing entrance hall was solid with pressure.

The sirens grew louder.

Hank muttered something inaudible under his breath.

'What did you say?' she asked him.

He stared at her.

Her radio crackled.

Kevin Streeting's hand moved and she felt Johnny manoeuvre beside her.

'Leave it,' she whispered.

Streeting's fingers on his right hand twitched and disappeared behind his back.

'I wouldn't if I were you,' Kelly warned him.

Her heart raced and thumped in her chest. Her mouth was desert dry.

'Don't,' she muttered under her breath to Johnny.

From somewhere outside, Kelly heard the sound of a crow, or at least she thought it was. Was there some kind of ancient tale about the significance of crows? Wasn't a group of them called a murder? It was something to do with the scavengers gathering around carrion and being associated with death.

It cawed again.

Was it calling to its pals?

Her body felt taut with anxiety.

Then Hank raised his hand and Streeting relaxed.

Now perhaps wasn't a good time to arrest him for the murder of Angelina Robbins but she was tempted.

It was the first time they'd come face to face properly and they eyed one another. She felt Johnny staring at her from the side and sensed his shift in alertness. In that moment she wanted to hug him for his chivalrous display of protection. He had no chance against a gun but that wasn't the point.

They heard squad cars entering the property and scream up the driveway and officers and paramedics rushed into the main house.

But Kelly couldn't allow herself to breathe just yet.

Two brawny six-foot uniforms looked to Kelly for a sitrep and she indicated towards Kevin Streeting.

'He's armed. How quickly can you get armed response here?' she asked.

But as she turned to watch Streeting's movements, she saw he'd disappeared.

She put her hand on one of the officers' vests. 'Don't,' she ordered. 'Wait for the ART. It's too much of a risk.'

Johnny was at her side and they walked together into the sunshine as the uniforms ushered everybody outside.

'The only time I've ever witnessed anyone dying from a single blow to the head like that was in Cyprus when a squaddie punched a civvie in the head and he went down. He died the next day. That's some weird strength there, Kel.'

'I know. This drug, is it possible it's being trialled for the military? Do you know anyone you could ask?'

'That's some serious shit, right there. I can ask, but whether anyone will tell me is another story. If the MOD is using something that changes a soldier's strength to the extent where he can become a human weapon, well, that's got to be worth a crazy amount of money, but…'

'But?'

'It'd be unethical.'

'Since when is war ethical?'

'There are rules of engagement, Kel. We have strict protocols.'

She stared at him oddly. 'Protocols like that shit you took in Iraq that gave you vomiting and headaches for seven years?'

'Fair point.'

'How many did you lose to that?'

'We'll never know. It turned men crazy.'

'Wasn't that the point? Turn them into deranged killers? And who benefitted from that experiment?'

'What are you asking me?'

'Think about it. Who might gain from unleashing something so powerful that men are no longer scared to walk into battle and straight at the enemy?'

'Are you serious?'

'You saw what that man did. Paul isn't a convict, nor is he a soldier. He's a sales rep, for God's sake.'

'So, how…'

The penny dropped. Johnny looked back to the hotel, and then to Kelly.

'What's in this stuff?'

'We don't know yet, but you can bet your bottom dollar that I won't get my hands anywhere near an investigation into it, which is why I need your help. Nobody will own this. I have a lab report telling me that it induces rage, but I have no evidence that links it directly with lethality. You know where this is going. Those people who threatened Emma, Ted and us – our daughter – these are the people who are protecting this stuff.'

'You need to leave this one alone, Kel.'

'I can't.'

'You have to.'

Her phone buzzed and it was Emma back at Eden House. They'd heard.

'Boss, are you OK?'

'I'm fine.'

'We found Lee Lovett.'

'What?'

'He was in a road traffic accident. We think he was on his phone.'

Kelly's mind whirred. 'Is he OK?'

'Unconscious. He was airlifted to the Penrith and Lakes.'

'A bad smash then?'

'We received an email from him around the time the folks on the ground estimate the RTA impact.'

'He sent it when he was driving?'

'Witnesses say he was being pursued at speed by another vehicle.'

'Oh God, he must have panicked.'

'Yes. It's the CCTV from the back stairs at Heron Hall. I'm sending it to you now.'

Chapter 56

Kelly watched the footage over and over again. Emma and Dan had isolated the range that concerned their inquiry. It was five minutes long.

It was all she needed.

Sandy and Paul sneaking along the corridor, past the old fridges, cupboards, storage boxes, piles of clothes and laundry bins. She felt the cool interior as if she was back there with Lee, as he showed her this way to the pool, that way to the guest bedrooms.

They came from the direction of the upstairs bedrooms.

The time said 5 p.m. exactly.

Then another figure emerged from the gloom.

Upright, purposeful, a little in a rush perhaps.

A man who got a little confused. A man who tied his dog up outside the hotel even before he heard a commotion.

Acorn had sat there for a good while before Jamie Robbins hit the atrium floor.

Because Melvin was already inside.

The time was 5.07 p.m. when Melvin lumbered through the dark corridor to make his way back to Acorn, and wait for an appropriate gap before he entered as a concerned civilian.

Suddenly Kelly felt her body betray her and she recognised the first signs of shock. Her hands shook and she felt terribly thirsty as if she was about to suffer a migraine attack. Flashing lights assaulted her peripheral vision and she sat down on the grass. Johnny was there to catch her and prevent her from falling over. He reached into his pocket and brought something out, unwrapping it and putting it into her mouth. She tasted sugar.

Images of Emma scared out of her wits, her dad falling in the street, alone and terrified, Jamie crashing into hard tile, Angelina terrified and abused by thugs, Lee run off the road and how many others rubbed out and haunted for the greed of the few?

She recovered slightly and smiled at Johnny.

'You are invincible, Kelly Porter, but everyone needs a Murray Mint occasionally.'

She passed him her phone and told him to watch the footage.

'Is that your colonel pal, Melvin Stone?' she asked him.

His brow furrowed in bewilderment as he pressed play.

'Colonel Stone, yes, that's him,' he said.

'My God, they almost got you too,' she said.

She scrambled up to her feet and marched towards where they'd left her car.

'Kelly!' he shouted after her.

'Come on, let's go.'

'Where?'

'This isn't over,' she said.

'Think of Lizzie,' he said.

She glared at him.

'You've taken enough risks for one day.'

'I don't want my daughter to grow up thinking I walked away from justice because I was scared,' she said.

'Do you want to be here to see her grow up at all?'

It was a low blow, but Kelly admired his tenacity. He was trying everything. It made her admire and respect him. It was an equal fight.

She looked up at the Lion and the Lamb, as if for inspiration, but the mountain gave her none.

'Just take a minute to calm down,' he said.

She nodded and leant against a low wall as they watched an AR team arrive and get out of their response car, looking for Kelly to update them on the whereabouts of the armed man. After she'd done so, she used some of her nervous energy to open emails from Eden House but the knowledge that Streeting had scarpered and was out there somewhere changed everything.

She sought out Hank Hampton but instead of finding him handcuffed and in the back of a squad car, he was walking around freely, talking on his phone. Johnny pulled her back.

She shrugged him off and walked right up to the American and confronted him. He had the temerity to grin at her.

'I know you think you've won. I know you think you're above the law. But I also know what you're doing.'

'Ma'am, I admire your enthusiasm, but I have a job to do. Excuse me,' he said, pushing past her.

'Sandy Cooper, the scientist. *Your* scientist,' she said.

He stopped and stared back at her.

'Any idea where she is? I know she was here with you, so where is she now?'

Hank stared past her as if longing for the opportunity to get into a car and disappear, but that luxury wasn't something she was going to allow him just yet. If he was going to be allowed to board a plane out of here, due to some kind of reciprocal love-in law with the US, then she wanted to get as much out of him beforehand as she could.

'She left before Paul attacked us.'

'What do you mean, she left?'

'I don't know; I heard her talking on the phone. They argued.'

'Who argued?'

'She and Paul, I don't know. Perhaps they were lovers?'

'That's a convenient get-out clause, isn't it? You all seem to be bed hopping when it most suits you. I don't buy it.'

'Ma'am, you seem to have a growing grudge against me, and I'm at a loss to understand why. As far as I can see, I'm the victim here, and my associate, Tilda Dent.'

Kelly stood her ground. He had some neck.

'I'm just trying to work out, Hank, how many people fall for your charm.'

He grinned.

'Exactly that. I wonder if that's why Jamie was selling you out, because he saw through you. Was it you who arranged Angelina's murder too?'

He shook his head. 'Angelina was an angel indeed. Her work was exquisite. I bought a lot of it.'

'I know. I've seen the pictures.'

'You think you're very clever don't you, ma'am? Too clever for me.'

She leant in close, her nose almost touching his now cream and brown suit where the blood had dried. It was now more barista coffee than ice cream.

Bitter not sweet.

'I have what you've been searching for,' she whispered.

Then she walked away.

Johnny lingered behind her and Hank eyed him suspiciously.

'Who is this guy?' he shouted after her.

Chapter 57

Johnny called his pal at the MOD as Kelly drove them back to Rydal Water.

They caught up on their lives briefly. They talked about kids and life in and outside the army. They shared news about old pals, some who'd since passed away. Some at their own hand.

Then Johnny asked about procurement.

It was the department within the armed forces that tested, sold and bought weapons and equipment from reputable sources. The trade made up about 20 per cent of the total defence budget which was around 2.5 per cent of the UK's GDP, estimated at around sixty billion pounds.

Twenty per cent of that could buy a lot of weapons.

And it was a sensitive topic.

Most of the deals were in the public domain, such as submarine building in Barrow-in-Furness, but some of it remained top secret. Johnny had no access to that kind of information anymore, but some veterans owed him favours.

He'd been to the MOD main building on the Embankment in London many times. It was a standout construction, architecturally speaking, that dominated the gardens overlooking the Thames. The neoclassical white stone of MOD Whitehall gave a nod to the once glory days of empire when Britain's standing in the world meant something. Johnny saw it now as a dying façade, which was one reason he was glad he'd left when he did. It had been designed during the run-up to World War Two, but unlike the fate of that lengthy event that was responsible for killing off millions of citizens, the mecca of British warmongering had survived intact.

Johnny reckoned that the medals worn inside the place could sink one of the few remaining battleships the country had to her name if they were all loaded on at once. He smiled to himself cynically.

Those days were long gone but he still remembered how it all worked, and he knew for a fact that some shady figures inside the MOD weren't above trading with less savoury dealers of lethal armoury around the globe, if their cut was attractive enough. British Forces wages were abominable, and their pensions were under attack. Loyalty was no longer about king and country; it was about paying bills.

'The sort of information you're looking for would be kept at Winterbourne Gunner near Salisbury Plain,' his pal said.

'I thought so.'

The science and defence campus in Wiltshire experimented in bioweapons, drug use and nasty things such as nerve agents that the mainstream media didn't talk about. The facility had been housed at Porton Down before that and it was the arm of the forces that was responsible for bio, chemical, nuclear and radiological training and experimentation. It was where the drugs came from that had been injected into him in 1991, when Johnny had been just nineteen years old, in preparation for Gulf War One, courtesy of Stormin' Norman and George Bush senior.

But Johnny wanted to know what they were up to nowadays. He didn't like to dwell on how his own body had been abused.

'Do they deal in viruses and additives?'

'Of course. What's all this about?'

'I want to know if they're interested in a chemical element called Neurohydroxy-14,' Johnny said.

'You selling?'

'Very funny.'

'I'll do my best. I don't have the same access I used to; they're touchy about these things now more than ever. Everybody thinks the next war will be fought using AI and germs.'

'What about mood-altering substances?'

'They've been in play for decades.'

'OK, pal, let me know.'

'Will do. What is it?'

'It makes people vicious and superhuman strong.'

'Sounds perfect for the infantry, mate.'

'This is where it gets weird, and I'm not sure I believe it, but there's a rumour self-assembling nanotech can be implanted to intensify the results.'

'You're not going mad, mate. I've heard of that. The Americans and Chinese have had that kind of technology for decades. My wife thinks it's in vaccines.'

'At least you're still married, pal.'

They laughed for old times' sake and ended the call and Johnny stared out over the lake. The concept of it was terrible and depressing at the same time. Conventional warfare was a thing of the past. Drones, poison and cyber-attacks were the norm now. To him, though, the idea of using a combination of chemicals and nanotechnology to turn soldiers into cold-blooded animals was terrifying.

He'd seen war first hand, and he knew that the men who started it were always the ones who survived it and somehow got richer.

'Theirs is not to reason why, Theirs is but to do and die.'
Tennyson's words haunted him. He never thought he'd become a pacifist, a conscientious objector, a war denier... not after what he'd done. But it was true. He hated war. But what he hated even more were those who started it. War was never unleashed on human populations innocently. Whatever Neurohydroxy-14 was, somebody somewhere had created it on purpose, and something had gone terribly wrong.

Chapter 58

Kelly answered her phone on hands-free as she drove. Johnny sat in the passenger seat. He'd relayed his conversation to her and was now refusing to leave her side. He'd found a nut bar in the car and they'd grabbed drinks from a tiny shop along the A591. She felt revitalised.

The caller was Sandy Cooper.

'Sandy! Don't hang up!' Kelly said. The phone was on speaker hands-free.

'Why is my photo all over the internet?'

'We need to talk to you. Tilda Dent is dead.'

'What?'

'Paul Burlington assaulted both her and Hank before he went missing. Tilda didn't survive. He's somewhere near here; you're in danger. Tell me where you are, and I'll come and get you.'

Sandy laughed. 'I'm not scared of Paul.'

'You should be; you have no idea what he's capable of.'

'Yes, I do.'

'Why don't you tell me?'

'You wouldn't believe me.'

'Try me.'

'No thanks, I've got another idea,' Sandy told her. Her voice was icy, final and far away. Kelly suddenly thought she might have left the country already.

'Where are you?' she asked her.

She clasped the steering wheel and Johnny glanced sideways at her.

'Let me come and get you and we'll talk this over.'

Kelly heard crackles on the other end of the phone, so she knew Sandy was still listening.

'It's too dangerous; you have no idea who you're dealing with.'

'I do. They came for me, Sandy. You're not the only one. I need to find Paul, and I think I know where he's gone. Was he the only one?'

'The only what?'

'Patient from the trials to survive? He's hidden here in the Lake District, isn't he? That's why the conference was here, to keep an eye on him? He's worth so much money that even Hank Hampton and Tilda Dent had to make the journey to come all this way to see him in action. But it didn't quite work out, did it? I'm heading over there now. I know where he is, and I have the thing that you were so desperate to get from Angelina. She outsmarted you.'

'I've no idea what you're talking about.'

'Why did you send Joe Folly to meet me at the cave? Was it to see if he could piece together the code? From Angelina's paintings?'

Johnny pointed up ahead. They were almost there. The tranquillity of Rydal greeted them, and Kelly felt peace spread across her body. They were almost at the house and Kelly would have missed the small turning into the lane had Johnny not tugged her arm. It was almost invisible from the road.

They both saw her at the same time and Kelly stopped the car.

Sandy was sitting on the side of the lane, almost hidden by the bushes, hunched on the floor, talking on her phone. When she saw them, she hung up.

Kelly cut the engine. They got out and slammed the doors.

They approached Sandy carefully.

'Who's he?' Sandy asked suspiciously, nodding sourly at Johnny.

'This is Johnny Frietze; he's a specialist mountain rescue volunteer. He's a colleague.'

Sandy eyed him and Johnny smiled warmly.

'We're not up a mountain.'

'No, but Johnny has training in emergencies of all types. Is Paul in the house?'

'I guess so. How did you work it out?'

'Work what out?'

'This address?'

'I got your message from Joe Folly. You want this all over the same as we do.'

'What message? I didn't give Joe Folly anything.'

Kelly stared at her. 'We met at the caves, and he gave me this address.'

Sandy shook her head. 'He thought he was contacting me on Instagram, but he never was.'

'Who was he talking to?'

'The people in suits who listen to everything,' Sandy said.

Kelly thought she'd lost her mind and been sucked into an espionage vortex. It was too outlandish. Too silly.

'CIA?' Johnny asked.

'He gets it,' Sandy replied.

'What have you done?' Kelly asked her.

'Me?'

'You allowed all this to happen.'

'If it hadn't had been me they would have found someone else.'

Sandy looked away from them towards the lake. They could see the twinkling of the water beyond the treeline.

'Does Joe know he was tricked?'

'You'll have to ask him, though I think you might be too late. He uses a place in Ambleside. You should try there.'

'Jesus, Sandy, you signed his death warrant? Who did you tell about his place in Ambleside?'

'Like I said, you don't know who you're dealing with.'

'Yes, I do. The military? They want a product to hide Neurohydroxy-14?'

Sandy began to laugh.

'Now's not the time for jollity, Sandy,' Kelly said.

'Why not? Things are too gloomy around here. You know I am retiring next week?'

'Something tells me you might be otherwise detained,' Kelly said.

She glanced beyond the trees and spotted a small house. It was hidden from the road. And Kelly had never known it was there all the years she'd been coming here running, walking and swimming. The Lake District was like that. It kept secrets from prying eyes behind private gates and thick trees.

'How long has he lived here?'

'He was monitored.'

It wasn't an answer.

They heard sirens in the distance.

'Stand up,' Kelly demanded.

Sandy looked up at her, docile now, and Kelly felt impatience bubble up inside her. They were losing time.

'Get up,' she repeated firmly.

Sandy sighed and did as she was asked.

Kelly turned her around and slapped cable ties on her hands, then she read her rights, and marched her towards the house. In her book, they were all guilty of beating Angelina close to death and also of killing her baby and pushing Jamie over the banister; whether they were bystanders or active players, they all deserved to rot. But if this was the only one she could arrest, then so be it. Sandy didn't look the type to take to prison very well. Kelly reckoned she'd do a deal in exchange for her knowledge.

She watched Johnny approach the house and peer up at the windows. There was no noise from inside, no vehicles close by and no sign that anyone was home.

'Is he home?' Kelly asked.

Sandy didn't answer.

'Jamie trusted you,' she said to Sandy, pushing her forward, trying to find an entrance to the property.

'No, he didn't!'

'Watch her.' Kelly stopped at the back door and indicated to Johnny.

'No way. Wait, they'll be five minutes, max,' Johnny pleaded with her.

Sandy laughed. 'You're going in there on your own, without a gun or a radio. Have you got your little taser or a truncheon in those pretty pants?'

Kelly grabbed Sandy and shoved her into the wall without thinking and Johnny winced.

Kelly let go of Sandy's arm and looked towards the house then back at Johnny, working out what to do. She knew he was right. She could delay for a few minutes. After all, she had no idea what she'd find inside. There was no harm in keeping a cool head, but every fibre of her body wanted to rush into the little cottage. Her head filled with questions. What if Paul had killed again? What if Kevin Streeting was in there?

She made her way around the windows at the rear, but she was still in sight of Johnny and Sandy. She peered through and saw an empty kitchen.

'How stable is Paul?' she asked Sandy.

She shrugged.

'How does it work?'

'What?'

'Don't play games, Sandy. For fuck's sake. Level with me. Who controls the nanotech?' Kelly forced her to look into her eyes. 'This isn't a game,' she said.

Sandy grinned. 'Paul was taken off the programme months ago, but he was already addicted.'

'To *YouthBlast*?'

Sandy laughed.

'What am I missing?' Kelly asked.

'We couldn't put something so powerful on the open market,' Sandy said. She was serious now. 'Mass distribution was designed to prep the population for incremental progress.'

Kelly stared at her, gobsmacked. 'Incremental progress?' It sounded so matter of fact. So emotionless.

The woman's arrogance bypassed the deaths of thousands of people. Her own narcissism trumped the morality of murder. She wondered if Sandy had always been like this, or she'd been trained over time, like a circus cat, doing tricks for treats. She saw that Sandy had no soul left. Zero humanity. Like all killers, whether they got their hands dirty or not, she was an empty vessel, devoid of life itself.

Kelly glanced at Johnny.

'You're too late,' Sandy said.

Johnny took Sandy's tied hands and forced her to stand up straight.

'That was the worst thing you could have said to her,' he said.

Chapter 59

Paul sat in a corner of the kitchen and rocked forward and back.

His body was covered in a layer of sweat but it wasn't ordinary perspiration; it was sticky and grimy and synthetic. It was as if he was covered in a diet soda drink. He felt it clog his pores and struggled to believe he was still breathing.

The kitchen fixtures morphed into blobs, and he pressed his thumbs against his temples.

In his hand, he held a large kitchen knife, and he pointed it out in front of him, even though his eyesight had begun to fail him.

'What are you pointing that thing at me for?' the other man said.

Paul wiped his eyes and felt them burn as if he'd poured chemicals in them.

'Are you feeling hot?' the man asked.

Paul tried to ignore him. He didn't trust anyone.

All he wanted was to go back to before, when everything was normal and their future was so bright, it blinded them. Now he knew that what really dazzled them was greed.

'Do you get headaches?'

Paul looked up and nodded.

'Do you remember when it started?'

'We felt like kings. They flew us first class. We stayed in the Mandarin Oriental in Manhattan.'

'Ah. I know it well. I stayed there too. Could you see Central Park and the Hudson?'

Paul nodded. His face reflected in the blade of the knife and seemed to sharpen his memory of that time. But try as he might, recalling what he did an hour ago was impossible.

Hank told them they could sell anything.

They were invincible.

'You two can sell water to fish.'

It was exactly what Hank had said.

His blood boiled and he grabbed the knife.

A noise at the door startled them and their attention shot towards the door.

Paul opened his mouth to speak but no sound came out. He felt as though his jaw had been hijacked by little workers intent on sealing up the great cavern that had once been his throat. He no longer had the power of true speech.

But he realised that it had gone a long time ago.

The night he agreed to help Sandy rather than Jamie. That was the turning point.

It was all his fault.

'No, it isn't, son,' the man said.

Paul didn't realise that he'd spoken out loud. The lines between reality and fantasy had blurred and he didn't know if his words were manufactured or real. He blinked and stared at the man.

'It's the detective,' he said.

Paul tried to think who he could be referring to. Detective? He couldn't place anyone matching that description.

Then he heard banging that hurt his head.

It reminded him of the thump of Jamie's head hitting the floor when he'd fallen from the second floor.

He hadn't pushed him, though that's what he'd thought about doing to stop him ruining everything they'd worked so hard for.

'We don't own anything, Paul,' Jamie had said.

'Value is nothing when it's given by the devil,' Angelina said.

Now when he remembered Jamie's face, it was too painful a memory. He couldn't bring himself to relive the full reel of images. They always stopped midway through, like some incomplete slice of remembrance.

He recalled somebody else wearing his shoes, his CAT boots, thinking it was peculiar. He also recalled his body lying on Jamie's bed. It was more comfortable than his own bed in the hotel, and he had felt offended. It fuelled his paranoia that Hank had favoured Jamie all along. Jamie was the brains behind their success. Jamie was defter with the sales teams. Jamie was the one who understood the science. Jamie had been the one to pull the plug.

Sandy had been sent to placate them and offer more money. Money which Paul was desperate to accept. His habits had begun to cost astronomical sums.

The breaking of a window caught his attention and Paul looked to where the noise came from. He covered his face and reached out to feel around the floor to see if he could find something to drink. His thirst was killing him. But he found nothing. His whole body seemed filled with noise and then he felt fingers clawing at his hands.

'Paul? Paul?'

Layers of reality converged inside his head and his eyes flickered open, and he was able to stare at the light above his head. Beneath that was a man's face, and he knew he'd seen him before.

'Paul, it's Melvin, remember me? Can you hear me, Paul?'

He stared at the older man, who had the same look of paranoia in his eyes as he did when he stared into the mirror in the mornings.

'Who the fuck are you?' he asked, but he wasn't aware of his mouth moving.

'Woah, fella!' the stranger said, as he grabbed his hand and took a large knife from him. Paul watched him remove the weapon but couldn't figure out how it had got there.

He'd roamed around this place, trying to break free. He remembered bits of his journey. The caves. The podcaster, was he called Joe? Jamie's face before he fell.

The face of the man who pushed him. A robot. A man possessed by another's hand.

This man.

The man called Melvin.

Chapter 60

Kelly hammered on the door, but nobody answered. She peered through the window which was to the side of the porch, but she saw nothing. Johnny climbed on top of a wood store and reached another window, and he said he could see no one either.

That was when Kate contacted Kelly from Eden House and said she had a warrant for the property and the tactical entrance group was on its way.

That meant she could break the fucker down.

She and Johnny hammered the door with a log each until they exhausted themselves. It wouldn't budge. It was an oak construction that looked as though it had been standing since King Arthur, who was responsible for supplying the indefatigable Welsh timber.

Nobody was getting through it.

Then somebody shouted from the other side.

The door opened as they stood back and Kelly breathed so deeply that her chest heaved up and down.

An older man stood in the doorway and Kelly squinted as the sun was dipping over the tree canopy and shone straight into her eyes.

'Melvin? Is that you?' she asked.

'It is! I wasn't expecting you. How can I help? Come in, come in! Both of you, and who is that? Sandy! What a nice surprise.'

Kelly watched as Sandy retreated as much as she could before she backed into a stone wall. Johnny shielded the two women as was his instinctive response and Kelly peered behind Melvin into the home.

'Is your wife OK, Melvin?'

'No, she isn't here. I don't know where she is.'

'What about Paul, is he here?'

'He is!'

Kelly didn't know if she was dealing with a man who suffered from dementia and his mental acuity was dissolving before their eyes, or if Melvin Stone was an automaton being directed by an invisible force inside his head, via 5G. None of the people she'd met since Jamie Robbins' death were who they said they were; none of them were capable of telling the truth.

'We need to come in, if we may,' Kelly said, waiting for Melvin to make good on his invitation.

He did, and he stood back to allow them inside.

Kelly was wary and eyed Johnny, who took the lead.

The sirens had zipped straight past the hidden entrance and they no longer heard the whirring in the distance and Kelly realised that they weren't the ones they were waiting for. Some other emergency in the Lakes had needed an ambulance this afternoon. Her stomach felt like stone, but she walked into the house and found herself in a small kitchen. It was an L-shape but she couldn't see around the bend. She felt Johnny near her. Sandy hung about at the door.

'You want me to cut those off? They look painful,' Melvin said to her, noticing the cable ties.

'She's good, she can keep them on, Melvin,' Kelly said. 'Where's Paul?'

'I'm here,' a voice said from around the wall. He emerged and stood in the space, way back from them. The faint whine of sirens started up again in the distance and Kelly prayed that this time it was for them.

'And Kevin Streeting? Is he here?'

'Who?' Paul asked.

Her eyes darted around and she caught Johnny looking for a trap too. Her nerves were threadbare. She twisted the ring on her middle finger on her right hand. How many times had she wondered what it would have been like to have it on another finger on her left? It felt heavy, and she always said she'd stop wearing it to work but she couldn't bring herself to leave it at home in a box when it symbolised something quite different to that. It attracted her energy for good reasons, and it never got on her nerves; even when she and Johnny split up and she considered taking it off, it was a source of comfort. The sturdy nature of the gold and the never-ending lustre of the rubies provided a silent strength that kept her going and she rubbed it now.

The gesture gave her reassurance and Johnny noticed what she was doing.

Paul and Melvin were on opposite sides of the kitchen space, and they were now stuck in the middle. In no man's land. Like the lone tree at Buttermere, exposed. Vulnerable.

'It's OK, Melvin, you can stop with the story now; I know who you are,' she said to him.

He looked at her with a confused look and she almost fell for the innocent old man trick, but something in the way he held his body, which was not quite without intent, put her own body on high alert.

'Melvin, it's me, Johnny Frietze,' Johnny said. Kelly wanted to stop him from becoming involved, but he was doing it to buy time. In that moment, she wanted to kiss him. He was doing it for her, but she was still angry with him for taking so many risks. That was her prerogative.

'We served in Iraq together, years ago, pal. I couldn't place you, but now I do.'

Johnny got nearer but Kelly wanted him to stop. She looked at his feet and watched them inching backwards as Johnny moved forward. Then she saw that Paul was wearing just socks and Melvin boots. CAT boots. Melvin saw her and followed her stare and looked at his own feet, then smiled.

'I borrowed his boots,' he laughed.

'You do that often, Melvin?' Kelly asked.

'I do!'

'Our most successful subject,' Sandy said from behind them.

'I knew you were somebody I recognised!' Melvin said.

'Sandy, what are you doing?' Kelly asked.

'She's controlling them. It's straight out of the military playbook.' Johnny stepped forward and blocked Sandy's view of the others. But it was too late. Something had triggered Melvin, and he looked down at his trouser pocket and pulled out a large kitchen knife.

Chapter 61

'She's their handler,' Johnny said. His voice was monotone. Disarming. Neutral.

'I need you to take these off,' Sandy said to Kelly, holding up her bound hands.

'Are you nuts? Why should I trust you? Just stay over there and shut up or I'll have to take you outside.'

'Because your back-up won't get here in time. I'm the only one who can stop these two from continuing their programming.'

Now Kelly was jammed against a cupboard as Melvin held the long knife up to examine it. She watched Johnny out of the corner of her eye inch towards him, but she also noticed Paul doing the same thing.

'Paul, stop,' she said. 'Don't get into any more trouble. I know you didn't kill Jamie.'

It was a delaying tactic in the hope that Johnny wouldn't get trapped between them, but like a pair of vultures, they'd encircled them, and they were indeed stuck.

The sirens got louder but as Kelly got her hopes up, the noise whizzed past the end of the tree-lined driveway. She kept her face set in stone and Johnny did the same.

'Melvin, I think you should put that knife down. You're not the type of man to have a handler, are you? She can't tell you what to do. You're dispensable, Melvin; they've hurt you, haven't they? We can make you well again.' Kelly tried to appeal to the human inside the shell.

'They're using you,' Johnny chipped in. 'Take it from me. From one military man to the other.'

Melvin laughed. 'Of course they are! Isn't that the point? Were you ever a free soldier, young man?'

Johnny grimaced and Kelly looked curiously between the two of them. She glanced at Johnny, who blinked ever so slightly at her, and she took it as a sign that he was somehow in control. Did they really know one another, or was Johnny just bluffing and playing along? Was he playing along to buy time?

'How do you know this pretty lady?' Melvin asked, nodding to Kelly, but still lovingly toying with the knife.

'Paul, perhaps you should sit down on the floor; you look as though you're having a rough time detoxing from that crap they put in you,' Kelly said.

'Don't try to be my friend,' he said. His eyes narrowed and Kelly stepped closer towards the door. There was enough distance between all four of them that nobody had a stabbing chance without making a run for it, but that didn't mean they were safe.

They performed a kind of macabre dance together. A quartet, wary and ungraceful, tense and taut.

Kelly cocked her head as the sirens returned and grew louder.

Thank God, this time they were here.

Her eyes darted about for any sign of Kevin Streeting. His orders would surely be to come here, to eliminate the witnesses to Jamie and Angelina's murders. She didn't see any sign of him, but she did sense a shift in the mood.

'I know you didn't kill Jamie, Paul,' she tried again. 'Or Angelina.'

Paul shook his head and covered his ears. She could tell he was struggling with whatever substance they'd forced on him, but that wasn't her concern right now, only her safety and that of Johnny focused her attention. She could tell that Johnny was thinking the same thing. It was also eminently clear that whatever had been controlling these two men was not simply a powder mixed into a shake; it was much more than that.

The sirens deafened them now and they heard car doors slamming. Kate had sent the cavalry and Kelly rarely found herself in this situation where she was on the inside of a building about to be entered by the task force. She knew that the sensible thing to do would be hit the deck, but she looked at Johnny.

Then she saw Sandy say something to Melvin, and he lunged forward with the knife.

Chapter 62

Kelly felt her face hit the floor and a body on top of her, but she could tell by the smell that it wasn't an assailant's; it was Johnny's. She heard him grunt and saw Melvin's feet, wearing over large CAT boots that didn't fit him properly, right next to her head, as the kitchen filled with screams and shouts to get down and hold hands in the air.

She was so winded that she couldn't move at all.

And Johnny was a dead weight on top of her.

'That fucking hurts,' he said under his breath, and she could hear that he was holding it in for her. Then she felt the warm liquid on her trousers and looked down as far as her neck would twist and saw the blood. She wriggled and fought so hard that eventually she was able to turn around and get Johnny's weight off her so she could move. She saw Paul on the ground, Melvin struggling with uncharacteristic strength, though still in vain, with an officer who had to resort to punching him in the ribs to restrain him, and Sandy crying. Kelly saw that she'd decided to play the innocent woman act.

'It's all a mistake,' she whimpered. 'They'll tell you! It's those two you want, not me.'

'Medic!' somebody shouted, and calls of 'Clear, clear,' rang out in the small house.

She looked at Johnny's side where Melvin had plunged the knife in, and he slumped onto her.

'No, Christ, Johnny, stay with me.'

Two paramedics took over and she crawled out of their way as they found the wound and began checking Johnny's vital signs. He held out his hand for her to take and she knelt beside him and took it. He squeezed it and she smiled at his face. But his eyes closed, and the paramedics yanked his body upwards and onto a stretcher.

Then he was gone.

She was left sitting on the floor, with her trousers covered in blood, staring at the ruby ring he'd given to her years ago, when they'd been in love and before Lizzie had been born. It was the most precious thing she had, after Lizzie.

The rubies were the colour of his blood.

She clasped her hands together and stared at the scene. Johnny's blood was on the floor and her professional brain tried to assess if he'd be able to survive the loss of volume, and perhaps where on his body Melvin had stabbed him. A millimetre could make all the difference. Things paramedics said flashed through her mind. Their calculations, their assessments, their sucked-in teeth when all was lost.

She got up, keen to avoid touching anything lest she contaminate the scene.

Paul had been arrested for the murder of Tilda Dent and taken outside to a waiting squad car. Sandy was bundled into a second one and the ambulance carrying Johnny had already left.

'Nobody else in the house, ma'am.'

'Are you sure?' she asked.

'Yes, ma'am.'

An armed response officer offered her a towel and she took it gratefully.

But Kevin Streeting was still at large, with a loaded weapon.

And she had no idea if he was a patient too.

A loud pop-crack made them all duck, then all Kelly heard was radio crackle and the rushing of feet through bushes. Then a shouting match and a single round firing off into the trees.

Then silence.

She raised her head, and the firearms officer called the all-clear. The second in as many minutes. She stood warily.

She looked to where the commotion had taken place.

It turned out Kevin Streeting wasn't all that great a shot after all. Paramedics were called over to assist and she saw him put up a fight, even though he'd been shot.

Her phone buzzed and she answered it but couldn't speak.

It was Kate.

'Kelly, everything go to plan?'

'No,' was all she could say.

Then she began to sob.

Chapter 63

The contents of the USB found inside the trig point, retrieved by Kelly and Johnny inside Rydal Cave, were examined back at the office.

The mood was sombre and quiet.

When Kelly walked in, everybody stared at her.

'You shouldn't be here,' Kate said, holding her arm.

Kelly released her arm and held Kate by the shoulders. 'I'm fine.'

'But Del said you are on leave; you need to go home. We all understand. It's not your fault.'

'I should have handled it differently,' Kelly said. She glanced at her team, who looked away one by one.

She'd let them down. She'd let them all down. But most of all, she'd allowed herself to cross the line between professionalism and love.

Johnny wasn't here because of her.

She sniffed and wiped her face and walked to the front of the incident room.

They stared at her clothes.

Johnny's blood had cleaned off in places. But her shirt was still heavily stained and the cardigan she'd pulled over barely covered it. Her hands and face were clean but she was aware she looked like what Wendy, her mum, would call the wreck of the *Hesperus*.

'Everything is ready?'

Kate nodded and beckoned the others to sit down.

Kate flicked a few keys, and a recorded video flashed up on the screen. Kelly stared at it in dismay. Kate put up the sound.

Angelina Robbins' face filled the screen.

'If you're watching me then I haven't made it,' she said.

It was the first time anybody had heard her voice.

It was small. Perfect. Inoffensive.

'It might also mean that my brother didn't make it either, in which case, we're together again.'

Angelina gave a little laugh and Kelly scanned the people sitting around the table. They were transfixed by the petite but mighty artist of talent.

'This is my testimony. They'll do it publicly. They have to. If you are listening to this and I'm dead, then it's because they couldn't find this footage in the rock, and the only way to get to it was to create a fuss around my death. Somebody more intelligent found it, didn't they?'

They listened.

The story began decades ago in a lab in San Diego. Angelina had included footage which played alongside her words. People used as test animals and filmed for scientific posterity. She explained the breakthrough when the properties of glutamate, hydroxy-11 and androstene-3 had first been combined and the alarming results. Like Oppenheimer, they became death, the destroyer of worlds. Except this weapon wasn't anything like so crude as a big heavy bomb. It was insidious. Microscopic. Silent.

Angelina explained how high doses of the compound called Neurohydroxy-14 combined with regenerative biology – already in use for decades – could become a lethal weapon for any military force.

She highlighted with the aid of a neat short video how 5G radio waves and magnetism could affect the central nervous system when primed with a stimulant that also induced natural feral rage.

It had the potential to create monsters.

And that was exactly what they were doing at Hampton-Dent.

But potential wasn't the same as reality, Kelly thought.

Then things took a personal turn when Angelina was filmed in Rydal and she explained how special the place was to her. How she respected the forging of rock over millennia, its resilience and potency.

'If I'm dead and so is Jamie then congratulations, you followed my map. You broke my code which led you to the cave.'

Angelina's smile was infectious and the team at Eden House watched her in life, as she was, full of vitality, passion and grit.

She described an ex-intelligence officer, who thought he lived in the English Lake District and had a dying wife, but who was really an asset who could be awoken at any time, using nanotechnology inside his head. She said she was the natural choice to keep an eye on him from her studio in Chapel Stile. She said she was ashamed.

It was a confession.

A deathbed revelation.

The footage switched to a clip of a man throwing chairs and objects around a room. His rage almost jumped off the screen. It was like watching a wild animal at work. When he finished, he was bleeding and exhausted, and still manic. As the camera closed in on his face, they saw that it was a younger Melvin Stone they were looking at.

'Don't trust Joe Folly,' she said, and they all held their breath.

'What did she just say?' Kelly asked.

'He craves fame, not justice. Everything you need is in room 13 at the Old Man Guesthouse in Skelwith Bridge. I chose it.' She smiled. 'I hope I didn't die there but if I did, at least I'll be there forever.'

The last clip was of Jamie Robbins.

They watched in silence as the young man they'd got to know through reputation alone spoke to them from the grave.

He was charming, intelligent and engaging. He held an iPad and talked them through a demo. It involved an unnamed young man who was dressed in a hospital type gown, who appeared lucid, affable and chatty before the test. Then Jamie proceeded to tap the keys on his iPad and seemed to control him. It was the weirdest thing any of them had ever seen.

The video ended.

'What the fuck did we just watch?' Emma whispered.

'Do you think it was for real?'

'Poor wee girl,' Dan said.

'I need a smoke,' Kate said.

'How do we even begin to prosecute this?' Kelly said.

Chapter 64

'Evening, Melvin,' Kelly said.

It was late. Gone 9 p.m. by the time she went downstairs at Eden House to interview Melvin Stone.

Kevin Streeting was recovering from a gunshot wound in hospital, guarded by armed officers. His DNA was being rushed through the lab to compare to that found in room 13. Paul Burlington had been bailed because there was a question mark over whose jurisdiction Dow Bank House was. Sandy Cooper had been escorted to an undisclosed location and Del Booker told Kelly to back the hell off. She asked him where he'd left his balls, and he threatened her with early redundancy.

She was tempted to take it and fuck off into the sunset but she didn't want to leave her team. She wanted to see Emma have her baby, and Dan become a great dad. She wanted to sit in Calf Close Bay on the pebble beach, sharing a flask of coffee with a nip of Baileys in it with Kate. She wanted to listen to Fin's terrible Father Ted impressions.

In the end it was only the little people who could make a difference.

It wasn't leaders who changed the world but people who chose to follow them.

Had she heard Joe Folly say that?

The ones who gave the orders were immune from penalty; wasn't that always how it worked?

Not always, she reminded herself.

They got the unpleasantries out of the way.

Melvin was confused.

'What happened to your clothes?' he asked.

She looked at the police psychologist sitting next to him and she gave Kelly the look that suggested she was getting nothing out of this unfortunate and confused old man.

She sat back and studied him up close. He looked around the room as if he was seeing the Sistine Chapel for the first time.

It was quite a show.

He was fit to be interviewed but not to be held overnight and would be transferred to a secure ward after she'd asked him some questions.

She opened her laptop and turned it around so Melvin could see it and started the footage of him walking along the corridor behind the Heron Hall Hotel, towards the stairwell that led to Jamie's floor, at ten minutes to five o'clock on Tuesday evening. Melvin reacted vacantly.

'What's that in your hand, Melvin?'

He peered at the footage. 'That's Ursula's scarf! It was tied around Acorn's neck; where did you get it?'

It was abundantly clear that Melvin Stone was so far gone into a world they didn't understand that their only option was to hand him straight over to a public defence lawyer.

She showed him the footage they'd just watched of him in a lab, violent and aggressive, but he didn't react.

'That's you, Melvin,' she said.

He nodded and smiled.

'Did you fight with this man when you went to his room?' she asked.

She showed him a photo of Jamie Robbins.

He shook his head.

They'd taken DNA swabs and digital fingerprints from him, and they had a beautiful match with the smashed glass in Jamie's room. He still wore Paul's boots, though the mud was dry now.

It was enough to convince the CPS to charge him with Jamie's murder.

Then she showed him a photo of Ursula Brunner, a Swiss national who gained US citizenship in 1984.

'That's my wife,' Melvin said, his eyes flashing with jubilation.

They now knew that Ursula had died in 2020. She was repatriated by Hampton-Dent.

Kelly closed the laptop and sat back and closed her eyes.

'Did you write this on your computer, Melvin?' she asked him.

The fifteen-page document had been found on his MacBook inside his cottage and it seemed to be some kind of diary record of his life at Rydal with dates, names and details about his illness.

He looked blankly at her.

'It says here that Hank came to see you,' she said. 'The man in the cream suit? And Sandy, Doctor Cooper, the scientist?'

She assessed the ridiculousness of her situation. An uncommunicative murderer, another in the hospital, a chain-smoking scientist who'd been handed over to the US Embassy, and a dead CEO.

Only Hank remained standing in his cream suit (she assumed he had several clean ones) and she'd already been told by Del Booker that he was untouchable.

She thought words like that belonged in Kevin Costner movies but apparently not; they resonated around the walls of Eden House too.

Untouchable.

She couldn't imagine the level of power it took to gain such status and she shuddered to think what he might do next.

There was no diplomatic incident because firstly no one would believe her and secondly she'd lose her job if she told anyone.

Only Joe Folly could have exposed something like this and they'd found him beaten to a pulp inside a flat in Ambleside, just like Sandy said.

He was now inside one of Ted's fridges waiting to be cut open and examined, and Kelly wondered how many lies they'd find inside him.

She stood to leave, and Melvin wanted to shake her hand. He smiled up at her and she stared at him. He'd stabbed Johnny in his stomach. The blood was still on her clothes. Yet he still smiled. And it wasn't a challenging, I-told-you-so, evil grin; it was a genuine effort to make contact with another human being, because that's what Melvin Stone did. He was a respectable veteran with an impressive past who'd been decorated. But Hampton-Dent had created a monster, and she wasn't allowed to talk about it.

Kelly turned away, left the room, and went next door, where a live feed had been set up between Eden House and the Penrith and Lakes hospital.

—

Kevin Streeting was a different ball game. From the moment she'd seen Mercedes man on the first video, filmed by the hapless Instagrammer, cocking his weapon, when Jamie crashed into the atrium floor, she knew he didn't possess a gun for show. He was primed to expect something. Because Hank Hampton knew there might be trouble.

Something had gone wrong.

Melvin Stone had malfunctioned and Hank and Tilda were there to mitigate disaster, with Sandy Cooper's help.

Kelly sat next to Dan and Kate and they looked at Kevin Streeting in his hospital bed.

He was out of surgery and fed up.

Mercedes man was exactly what she expected. He'd been shot in the bushes cocking his weapon. Another second and he would have got a well-aimed round off, and not one that fired into the air. It was difficult to tell who he was aiming at, but she guessed it was her.

He stared into the camera, held by a uniform in the Penrith and Lakes. Streeting was handcuffed and physically incapacitated. Kelly could tell he was angry.

'Can you confirm your name for the record?' she began.

They confirmed nationality and DOB, as well as address and marital status.

Streeting was a British citizen and so at least she could throw the book at him.

'How long have you worked for Hank Hampton as a bodyguard?' she asked.

'Fuck off,' he said.

Kelly looked at Dan, who took over.

'That's nai way to speak to a lady, laddie,' Dan said.

'You can fuck off as well then, mate.'

'I'm not your mate.'

'Can I remind you this is an interview under caution, Kevin, which will be played in court.'

'Fuck the lot of yer,' he added for good measure.

They persevered.

'Where were you on the afternoon of Friday the 11th of July?' Kate asked.

He glared at them.

'We have you on camera arriving at the Old Man Guesthouse in Skelwith at around 8 p.m. and not leaving. Who did you go to see?'

'No comment.'

'Was it Angelina Robbins?'

'No comment.'

'Do you think the DNA we have taken from you in hospital will match the samples taken from room 13 and Angelina's body?'

'No comment.'

'Why did you rape her?' Kelly asked.

The question garnered a flicker of Kevin's left eyelid and Kelly leant into the camera.

He grinned.

Kelly wondered if Kevin Streeting had a nanochip in his skull too, because he behaved like he'd had a lobotomy. But dumb animals can be dangerous ones. Lethal ones.

'Why was it so public? Why take her to the lake and leave her to die?'

This elicited a genuine response.

He thought she was already dead.

'She drowned by the lake,' Kelly said. 'Your beating with the lampstand didn't finish her off.'

Streeting sniffed and looked away but it wasn't an emotional gesture; it was more playground bravado: the kind of tough guy snuffle that precedes a punch.

'Did she reject you? I know how this goes... She turned you down and you decided to stray from your brief. You left your DNA inside her too.'

Kate reached out her hand to place it on top of Kelly's. She squeezed it.

'Who told you to go to the address on Rydal Water? To the property of Melvin Stone?'

'Father Christmas.'

'Where were you on Saturday 12th of July?'

'In the bath.'

'We have a witness placing you in Skelwith with a dog called Potter who belongs to the post office. Did he follow you, or did you take him for a walk?'

'I wasn't there.'

'How long have you worked for Hampton-Dent?'

'Never heard of them.'

'Did you kill Joe Folly?'

'Who?'

'Is your head sore from when I twatted you in the face with a cane inside my house?'

Streeting grinned at this last question and Kelly knew it had been him. It was the jawline, the thin shoulders...

'Have you always been an arsehole?'

They ended the interview.

They had him in custody and they'd get him on forensics. But his masters would remain at large.

It seemed that some people were indeed above the law, after all.

Chapter 65

TWO MONTHS LATER

The top of Helm Crag was covered in mist. It had taken her longer than usual to climb to the top because Kelly had done the whole horseshoe of Steel Fell, Calf Crag and Gibson Knott, finishing with the Lion and Lamb. The view from there was stunning when the mist lifted, as it did for a few minutes when she most needed it to. She sat down under the Howitzer, the prominent rock tower that marked the true summit. From here, she thought the ancient boulders which looked like a lion and lamb from Grasmere in fact looked like a piano, with a maestro playing Chopin, she imagined.

Up here, there was enough noise to know she was alive, but not enough to steady the anxiety she felt when she looked to the future and didn't know what it held for her now. Some things had changed forever, and others had stayed the same. For the first time in her career, she'd accepted a half-baked resolution to a case that had taken over her life, and that of her team in such dramatic fashion. The visitors from across the pond had packed their bags and retreated in time to avoid UK law, and they'd taken Tilda's body with them, and the man responsible. Whitehall said it was out of their hands. Nobody in the office of the legal adviser to the US Department of State was willing to suggest the extradition of Hank Hampton for matters relating to fraud, conspiracy or murder. Sandy Cooper, on the other hand, as a UK national, was available to feel the full hand of the law; however, Hampton-Dent money had reached over the Atlantic and scooped her up too, as if by magic, calling her an invaluable member of the diplomatic wing of the United States overseas territorial mission on behalf of science, intelligence, technology and AI. Kelly, to this day, had no idea why they tagged on the AI, and she could only think it was to obfuscate the already lengthy and tedious extradition mechanism. Hampton-Dent's website made no mention of Neurohydroxy-14 in their tribute to Tilda Dent. A stunning portrait of her had been posted as the header of every section of the Hampton-Dent page, as well as a gushing heartfelt testimony of their loss after their CEO died in a tragic accident in the English countryside, 'doing what she loved best'.

The art world had celebrated the life of one of their best too and Kelly had read magazine spreads on what a terrible loss Angelina was to humanity. No mention had been made about her baby, and only a small nod to her brother, who'd 'been troubled by grief'.

She knew they'd never see Sandy Cooper again this side of the Atlantic.

However, they had their patsies, at least nominally. Melvin Stone had been admitted under indefinite licence to a psychiatric hospital and Kevin Streeting was being held on remand until his trial date. He'd been attacked twice inside already. His DNA matched that found on Angelina's body.

Lee Lovett had recovered from his car accident to give valuable testimony too. From the grave, Joe Folly also helped them after Ted – frustrated at being single handed for six weeks – had aided in the autopsy which discovered a USB in Joe's gut. It contained everything he had on Hampton-Dent; all that was missing was the valuable insider knowledge that fitted everything together. That's what he had missed. It's what the mother of his child would never give him. His paternity had been established and the thought of a whole family being wiped out for the sake of a secret weapon haunted her every time she closed her eyes. Together, what they'd found inside Rydal

Caves and what Joe Folly had swallowed as he was beaten to death, they had their evidence that Hampton-Dent was indeed producing a chemical primer able to awaken nanotechnology planted inside somebody's skull when programmed with 5G. But it wouldn't see the light of day.

Johnny's pal at the MOD had refused to talk again over the phone but had been happy to meet Kelly for a pint and he'd told her the Americans were now trialling the same concept using AI.

But nobody at the CPS had been interested in any of that, and counter terrorism had taken over the case, due to the sensitive nature of biohazards being involved. Kelly hadn't heard from them since. And she knew she never would. The Nirvana Project bought Heron Hall, as well as nine other Lake District hotels, all devalued in price, and she was keeping a close eye on them, from afar, and she and Ted discussed it late at night, when they talked of conspiracy theories over a new Netflix show.

She'd been denied all contact with Paul and her gut regularly turned over when she thought of him and if he made it out of witness protection alive. Johnny had called in favours with counter protection mates but nobody was talking.

She looked across the valley and towards the town of Grasmere. This morning, she'd been on the *Wendy*, Johnny's boat which was moored permanently now at Derwent Water in the marina at Portinscale.

She felt most connected to her heritage when she sat inside the tiny cabin and gazed across the water.

'You win some, you lose some,' she said.

Johnny came up behind her and put his arms around her waist.

He grinned and he kissed her neck.

'I'm sweaty,' she complained.

'And we're childless for an afternoon,' he reminded her.

'Johnny, no, not here.'

'Why?' He smiled at her, and they glanced over at the Howitzer rock. A thrill of excitement travelled up her spine and hit her stomach. He kissed her and the sun peeked from behind a cloud and remained fixed on them, as if giving them a blessing.

'You're supposed to be recuperating!' she said.

As if on cue, a black and white collie ran over to them and panted, begging for attention, and Kelly petted her. They greeted the owner, a hiker on his own, and Kelly busied herself with finding a blanket in her bag and setting out a few bites to eat that she'd brought. Johnny nuzzled in close as they sat huddled together staring over the valley.

'Close call,' he chuckled.

She grinned at him and ripped open a nut bar.

'You'll have to wait,' she said.

'Pass me a meat slice,' he said.

'Anytime, soldier.'

Acknowledgements

So many people make a finished novel a reality. Then there are all the people who buy it and support the whole series. This addition to the Kelly collection was born from reading about conspiracy theories and my fascination with questioning all narratives in the modern world. All the opinions therein are entirely fictional and attributed to nobody in particular. Neurohydroxy-14 and its components are entirely made up. As always the stunning Lake District features in all its glory and this time I chose the mysterious and captivatingly cathedral like Rydal caves for my focus, what a simply stunning place. Rydal and Grasmere are two of my favourite lakes.

A huge thank you to all the OG Kelly fans who remain so loyal and to the new ones: welcome.

To my agent, Peter Buckman, and his steadfast support of my work and all the directions I take it in. I do love a good controversy and getting my teeth into corporate corruption entertained me, at least.

To all the crew at Canelo, and DK-PRH, thank you for the hard work and the stunning cover. Louise Cullen has been with me from the beginning of my career and the books wouldn't be the same without her; Alicia and her tireless editing; Kate for the promo work and Aidan for the final edits.

To my Aussie pal, Kristy Horne, for the laughs and outtakes on our podcast *The Killer Storyteller*, what a hoot we have, far too much fun. We're available wherever you get your podcasts, as well as on YouTube. Kristy is a professional podcaster who has become a dear friend and we look for glimmers together as we navigate the dark world of crime in a unique partnership of reader and writer. Thank you also to The Fearyland Cafe on the shores of Grasmere, one of my absolute favourites, who kindly gave their permission to be featured in the book – a real place – go check it out! No surprises under the boats, honest!

Thanks as always to Adrian Priestley, who always answers my policing questions promptly and honestly. A big shout out to my personal trainer, Ryan Piggott, whose idea it was to create a sinister trial drug to control rage. His mind is as twisted as mine.

I'm eternally grateful for those who buy and review my books from all over the world and on social media. It's a great community and I love being part of it.

To my writing buddies who know who they are, our WhatsApp threads keep us all sane and supported in a crazy business. To the new friends I made at Harrogate last year, may our connections give each other space to sound off for many years to come.

Finally, to my family, Mike, Mati, Freddie and Poppy. You are my world and I love you.

Do you love crime fiction and are always on the lookout for brilliant authors?

Canelo Crime is home to some of the most exciting novels around. Thousands of readers are already enjoying our compulsive stories. Are you ready to find your new favourite writer?

Find out more and sign up to our newsletter at canelocrime.com